THE WAY OF
AN EAGLE

Ethel M. Dell

New Introduction by Rosie Thomas

Published by VIRAGO PRESS Limited 1996
20 Vauxhall Bridge Road, London SW1V 2SA

First published by T. Unwin Fisher Ltd 1912

Introduction Copyright © Rosie Thomas 1996

A CIP catalogue record for this book is available from the British Library

Typeset by Keystroke,
Jacaranda Lodge, Wolverhampton
Printed and bound in Great Britain by
Cox & Wyman Ltd, Reading, Berkshire

Introduction

The Way of an Eagle was first published in 1912, and instantly became the blockbuster of the late, ripe pre-war years. It ran through thirteen impressions in the first twelve months, and was in its twenty-third by the outbreak of the War that would change for ever the England and the English society that it depicted.

For the modern reader, coming fresh to the book, there is a feverish tension about the story that grips from the beginning and makes it a compelling read, but there is also a quaintness that makes the action and the setting feel much more remote than the British Raj of a mere eighty-odd years ago. The page-by-page reminders that it is such a period piece, a relic of a lost era as faded and fragile as a dried orchid corsage, lends it an appeal contradictory to the full-blown galloping and swooning love-story elements that would have set the contemporary readership on fire. But the appeal still remains, even though it is now some-what discordant.

Ethel M. Dell was born in 1881, the younger daughter of an insurance salesman from the Home Counties. Even as a child she loved to write and tell stories, and after the phenomenal success of *The Way of an Eagle* her path was fully mapped out. She married, at the somewhat late age of forty-one, a Lieutenant-Colonel in the Royal Army Service Corps; she was reportedly generous, modest, devoted to her dogs and to her garden. And she continued throughout her life to write novels for an adoring public.

All thirty-seven of Ethel M. Dell's subsequent books were more or less successful, but none of them quite matched the triumph of her first. This writer can't claim to have taken more than a glance at a handful of her other numerous but now hard-to-find works, but *The Way of an Eagle* appears to stand at the head of them as not only the first, but almost certainly the best, example of the writer working energetically and inventively within the dictates of her chosen genre.

The story opens in India, in a British garrison under siege, where only four white officers remain alive. The garrison commander entrusts the imperilled life of his daughter Muriel – innocent, scarcely more than a child, and weak with hunger and the strain of the siege – to one of his junior officers. The charge is not only to defend her life with his own but, if the worst happens, "to have the strength to – shoot her before your own last moment comes".

Forward steps one of the officers, Captain Nick Ratcliffe, the irrepressible joker of the garrison. He promises,

"General, if you will put your daughter in my care, I swear to you, so help me God, that no harm of any sort shall touch her."

The commander asks him if he can really be trusted with so great a responsibility. The answer is ringingly clear and confident:

"Then reckless and debonair came Nick's voice.

' . . . If I am untrustworthy, may I die tonight!' "

Here, then, is partly the quintessential hero of romance. Reckless to death itself, but ever ready to temper his heroism with a debonair shrug and a smile. Interestingly and less predictably, Nick Ratcliffe is yellow-skinned, emaciated, of smaller than average stature. More than a few of Miss Dell's heroes are painted as physically unattractive. They are often short, and ugly. But Nick's eyes glitter with an alert and fierce intelligence. In sharp contrast is his brother officer within the garrison, Captain Blake Grange. Captain Grange is a handsome giant of a man, and surely the obvious choice to be protector of the Brigadier's girl-child. But the wise Brigadier is a better judge of men, and indeed Blake Grange is not all he seems. The writer is more subtle than to make him all-out wicked: he is simply humanly flawed, and his fatal weakness is the more striking in comparison with Nick's whipcord-and-steel moral and physical strengths.

Muriel Roscoe is also both a conventional and an unconventional heroine. She is small, and lovely, and although once merry and light-hearted she is now physically and mentally weakened by her ordeal. So terrible an experience has the siege been that she has been driven to rely, for any sleep or rest, upon opium supplied by her ayah. Her dependence on the drug has passed unnoticed by her father, but all-seeing Nick spots it at once. And when Muriel fiercely refuses to abandon her father and try to save herself by escaping the besieged garrison under Nick's protection, he forcibly drugs her with her own supply and carries her away, unconscious.

The clash of wills and the outcome of the struggle for power at the very outset of their relationship is emblematic: Muriel is unhappy and courageous, but finally a victim of her womanly weakness. She is regularly described as being like a child, or possessed of a 'quivering woman's strength'. However bravely she may struggle against him she is no match for Nick, of course. She succumbs, is lifted unconscious into his arms, and is borne away from danger. But their escape only delivers them into the jaws of even more deadly peril – the hostile countryside.

It is here that – to Muriel's horror and revulsion – Nick kills a man with his bare hands. When he slaughters the black-bearded tribesman who threatens her this is how Muriel – and we, through her eyes – see it: "she saw Nick's face bent above the black-bearded face of his enemy; and remembered suddenly and horribly a picture she had once seen of *the devil in the wilderness*".

Here are an innocent virgin and a powerful man, almost strangers but now thrown together in circumstances of great hardship and mutual dependency. Together they slip through the darkness and dangers of a foreign land, longing to reach the haven of mutual safety and peace. What can the devil be, if not the old spectre of erotic attraction?

Nick and Muriel themselves are too honourable and pure for such thoughts even to enter their minds. It is also conceivable that the spicy promise of imminent but contained sexual passion was nowhere in Ethel M. Dell's consciousness either when she wrote these scenes, although this seems somewhat unlikely. It is even less likely, given the book's huge and instant popularity, that its eager public failed to be swept happily along on the steamy currents of it, with all the superficially innocent quivering and swooning and dreams of "a long breathless flight fraught with excitement and a nameless exultation that pierced [Muriel] like pain".

In fact, with its teasing foreplay drawn out by the protagonists' separation and misunderstandings, this is a book that manages to be entirely about sex or the threat of sex without ever actually mentioning it, except in the hushed whispers of Raj matrons concerning a possibly smirched reputation. Nick and Muriel are fenced off from each other by Victorian codes of decency: men must be brave and honourable, women must be utterly pure in mind, let alone action. It is left to subsidiary characters to acknowledge by their actions, the dangerous power of human sexual attraction, and even this strand of the story is partly obscured by presenting lust as a fatal weakness, or some dark blemish of the psyche that deserves to be obliterated. And yet, at a secondary level, the entire book is a dammed-up river of passion that keeps us reading and longing for release.

It is a mark of Ethel M. Dell's considerable talent that she sustains, more or less, the tension achieved in the bravura opening chapters. Back in the safety of a pine-scented Simla bungalow, Muriel tremulously consents to marry Nick. She is alone in the world, bereaved and exhausted, and even though she feels Nick holds her fast "by some magnetic force" she accepts his promise that "I only want to take care of you". With this neutered undertaking as her protection, Muriel's horror of her rescuer "sinks away like an evil dream". Or the writer manages, for the sake of delicious suspense, to consign sex to the back-burner for a few more chapters.

The scene shifts between unhappy but safe domestic England and the punishing yet liberating heat of India – atmospheric settings throughout the novel are used with great energy and effect. Distance and misunderstandings contrive to keep the couple erotically, if never quite emotionally, apart. Mortal illnesses and tragedies play their traditional, romantic fictional roles in heightening tension and underlining human fragility.

While Muriel flees to England, Nick continues his gallant soldiering in India, until at length, he is wounded and loses an *arm*. It is just possible that the author fully intended this happy symbolic substitution of one body part for another – in any event, and in spite of his loss, Nick returns finally to England to prove himself no less potently steely and no less rigidly intent on Muriel than at the moment when she was first entrusted to him by her father. Muriel has by this time managed to overcome her fear of the devil. The ultimate twist of the indefatigable plotting takes the two of them back to India. And here at last Nick gives a final demonstration of his manhood, in a piece of ingenious bravery acted out at the heart of the Raj, on the steps of the British Residency itself.

From this point, neither fate nor the author can contrive to keep the two of them apart any longer – and it is only in these concluding pages that a shadow of disappointment lurks. The stoked-up fires of passion exude little but smoke. Whilst the modern reader, used to much more explicit fare, laddishly longs for Captain Ratcliffe to get on with it and shag her senseless, there is nothing of the kind on the page. The re-engaged couple take a trip to the mountains together and here, amongst the splendour of the glittering and heavenward-straining peaks, they discuss their return. Nick whispers to her, "I shall go Home [to England] now without a pang, and so will you. We have got to feather the nest, you know. That'll be fun, eh, sweetheart?"

Fun no doubt, after all the reluctant quivering and sighing of anticipation, but we might have hoped to share a little of it. However, we leave Nick and Muriel as we find them: as recognisable and sympathetic characters who have braved dangers and emerged with their innocence threatened but never stained. Their story is told with great energy and deftness as well as with a lavish undercurrent of eroticism, and it is perhaps unfair to bring to it the expectations of modernity. The popularity of *The Way of an Eagle* in its own time, and that of its numerous successors, is sufficient indication that it delivered to its audience exactly what they wanted. In the proper, outwardly-exotic and inwardly-erotic sense of that misused term, it is a great romance.

Rosie Thomas, London 1995

There are three things which are too wonderful
for me, yea, four, which I know not –

The way of an eagle in the air;
the way of a serpent upon a rock;
the way of a ship in the midst of the sea;
and the way of a man with a maid.

Proverbs xxx. 18–19.

Contents

Part I   1

Part II   51

Part III   100

Part IV   185

Part V   256

THE WAY OF AN EAGLE

Part I

Chapter 1

The long clatter of an irregular volley of musketry rattled warningly from the naked mountain ridges; over a great grey shoulder of rock the sun sank in a splendid opal glow; from very near at hand came the clatter of tin cups and the sound of a subdued British laugh. And in the room of the Brigadier-General a man lifted his head from his hands and stared upwards with fixed, unseeing eyes.

There was an impotent, crushed look about him as of one nearing the end of his strength. The lips under the heavy grey moustache moved a little as though they formed soundless words. He drew his breath once or twice sharply through his teeth. Finally, with a curious groping movement he reached out and struck a small hand-gong on the table in front of him.

The door slid open instantly and an Indian soldier stood in the opening. The Brigadier stared full at him for several seconds as if he saw nothing, his lips still moving secretly, silently. Then suddenly, with a stiff gesture, he spoke.

'Ask the major sahib and the two captain sahibs to come to me here.'

The Indian saluted and vanished like a swift-moving shadow.

The Brigadier sank back into his chair, his head drooped forward, his hands clenched. There was tragedy, hopeless and absolute, in every line of him.

There came the careless clatter of spurred heels and loosely-slung swords in the passage outside the half-closed door, the sound of a stumble, a short ejaculation, and again a smothered laugh.

'Confound you, Grange! Why can't you keep your feet to yourself, you ungainly Triton, and give us poor minnows a chance?'

The Brigadier sat upright with a jerk. It was growing rapidly dark.

'Come in, all of you,' he said. 'I have something to say. As well to shut the door, Ratcliffe, though it is not a council of war.'

'There being nothing left to discuss, sir,' returned the voice that had laughed. 'It is just a simple case of sitting tight now till Bassett comes round the corner.'

The Brigadier glanced up at the speaker and caught the last glow of the fading sunset reflected on his face. It was a clean-shaven face that should have possessed a fair skin, but by reason of unfavourable circumstances it was burnt to a deep yellow-brown. The features were pinched and wrinkled – they might have belonged to a very old man; but the eyes that smiled down into the Brigadier's were shrewd, bright, monkey-like. They expressed a cheeriness almost grotesque. The two men whom he had followed into the room stood silent among the shadows. The gloom was such as could be felt.

Suddenly, in short, painful tones the Brigadier began to speak.

'Sit down,' he said. 'I have sent for you to ask one among you to undertake for me a certain service which must be accomplished, but which I – ' he paused and again audibly caught his breath between his teeth – 'which I – am unable to execute for myself.'

An instant's silence followed the halting speech. Then the young officer who stood against the door stepped briskly forward.

'What's the job, sir? I'll wager my evening skilly I carry it through.'

One of the men in the shadows moved, and spoke in a repressive tone. 'Shut up, Nick! This is no mess-room joke.'

Nick made a sharp, half-contemptuous gesture.

'A joke only ceases to be a joke when there is no one left to laugh, sir,' he said. 'We haven't come to that at present.'

He stood in front of the Brigadier for a moment – an insignificant figure but for the perpetual suggestion of simmering activity that pervaded him; then stepped behind the commanding officer's chair, and there took up his stand without further words.

The Brigadier paid no attention to him. His mind was fixed upon one subject only. Moreover, no one ever took Nick Ratcliffe seriously. It seemed a moral impossibility.

'It is quite plain to me,' he said heavily at length, 'that the time has come to face the situation. I do not speak for the discouragement of you brave fellows. I know that I can rely upon each one of you to do your duty to the utmost. But we are bound to look at things as they are, and so prepare for the inevitable. I for one am firmly convinced that General Bassett cannot possibly reach us in time.'

He paused, but no one spoke. The man behind him was leaning forward, listening intently.

He went on with an effort. 'We are a mere handful. We have dwindled to four white men among a host of dark. Relief is not even within a remote distance of us, and we are already bordering upon starvation. We may hold out for three days more. And then' – his breath came suddenly short, but he forced himself to continue – 'I have to think of my child. She will be in your hands. I know you will all defend her to the last ounce of your strength; but which of you' – a terrible gasping checked his utterance for many labouring seconds;

he put his hand over his eyes – 'which of you,' he whispered at last, his words barely audible, 'will have the strength to – shoot her before your own last moment comes?'

The question quivered through the quiet room as if wrung from the twitching lips by sheer torture. It went out in silence – a dreadful, lasting silence in which the souls of men, stripped naked of human convention, stood confronting the first primæval instinct of human chivalry.

It continued through many terrible seconds – that silence, and through it no one moved, no one seemed to breathe. It was as if a spell had been cast upon the handful of Englishmen gathered there in the deepening darkness.

The Brigadier sat bowed and motionless at the table, his head sunk in his hands.

Suddenly there was a quiet movement behind him and the spell was broken. Ratcliffe stepped deliberately forward and spoke.

'General,' he said quietly, 'if you will put your daughter in my care, I swear to you, so help me God, that no harm of any sort shall touch her.'

There was no hint of emotion in his voice, albeit the words were strong; but it had a curious effect upon those who heard it. The Brigadier raised his head sharply, and peered at him; and the other two officers started as men suddenly stumbling at an unexpected obstacle in a familiar road.

One of them, Major Marshall, spoke, briefly, and irritably, with a touch of contempt. His nerves were on edge in that atmosphere of despair.

'You, Nick!' he said. 'You are about the least reliable man in the garrison. You can't be trusted to take even reasonable care of yourself. Heaven only knows how it is you weren't killed long ago. It was thanks to no discretion on your part. You don't know the meaning of the word.'

Nick did not answer, did not so much as seem to hear. He was standing before the Brigadier. His eyes gleamed in his alert face – two weird pin-points of light.

'She will be safe with me,' he said, in a tone that held not the smallest shade of uncertainty.

But the Brigadier did not speak. He still searched young Ratcliffe's face as a man who views through field-glasses a region distant and unexplored.

After a moment the officer who had remained silent throughout came forward a step and spoke. He was a magnificent man with the physique of a Hercules. He had remained on his feet, impassive but observant, from the moment of his entrance. His voice had that soft quality peculiar to some big men.

'I am ready to sell my life for Miss Roscoe's safety, sir,' he said.

Nick Ratcliffe jerked his shoulders expressively, but said nothing. He was waiting for the General to speak. As the latter rose slowly, with evident effort, from his chair, he thrust out a hand, as if almost instinctively offering help to one in sore need.

General Roscoe grasped it and spoke at last. He had regained his self-command. 'Let me understand you, Ratcliffe,' he said. 'You suggest that I should place my daughter in your charge. But I must know first how far you are prepared to go to ensure her safety.'

He was answered instantly, with an unflinching promptitude he had scarcely expected.

'I am prepared to go to the uttermost limit, sir,' said Nicholas Ratcliffe, his fingers closing like springs upon the hand that gripped his, 'if there is a limit. That is to say, I am ready to go through hell for her. I am a straight shot, a cool shot, a dead shot. Will you trust me?'

His voice throbbed with sudden feeling. General Roscoe was watching him closely. 'Can I trust you, Nick?' he said.

There was an instant's silence, and the two men in the background were aware that something passed between them – a look or a rapid sign – which they did not witness. Then reckless and debonair came Nick's voice.

'I don't know, sir. But if I am untrustworthy, may I die to-night!'

General Roscoe laid his free hand upon the young man's shoulder.

'Is it so, Nick?' he said, and uttered a heavy sigh. 'Well – so be it then. I trust you.'

'That settles it, sir,' said Nick cheerily. 'The job is mine.'

He turned round with a certain arrogance of bearing, and walked to the door. But here he stopped, looking back through the darkness at the dim figures he had left.

'Perhaps you will tell Miss Roscoe that you have appointed me deputy-governor,' he said. 'And tell her not to be frightened, sir. Say I'm not such a bogey as I look, and that she will be perfectly safe with me.' His tone was half-serious, half-jocular. He wrenched open the door, not waiting for a reply.

'I must go back to the guns,' he said, and the next moment was gone, striding carelessly down the passage, and whistling a music-hall ballad as he went.

Chapter 2

In the centre of the little Frontier fort there was a room which one and all of its defenders regarded as sacred. It was an insignificant chamber, narrow as a prison cell and almost as bare; but it was the safest place in the fort. In it General Roscoe's daughter – the only white woman in the garrison – had dwelt safely since the beginning of that dreadful siege.

Strictly forbidden by her father to stir from her refuge without his express permission, she had dragged out the long days in close captivity, living in the midst of nerve-shattering tumult but taking no part therein. She was little more than a child, and accustomed to render implicit obedience to the father she idolized, or she had scarcely been persuaded to submit to this rigorous seclusion. It would perhaps have been better for her physically and even mentally to have gone out and seen the horrors which were being daily enacted all around her. She had at first pleaded for at least a limited freedom, urging that she might take her part in caring for the wounded. But her father had refused this request with such decision that she had never repeated it. And so she had seen nothing while hearing much, lying through many sleepless nights with nerves strung to a pitch of torture far more terrible than any bodily exhaustion, and vivid imagination ever at work upon pictures more ghastly than even the ghastly reality which she was not allowed to see.

The strain was such as no human frame could have endured for long. Her strength was beginning to break down under it. The long sleepless nights were more than she could bear. And there came a time when Muriel Roscoe, driven to extremity, sought relief in a remedy from which in her normal senses she would have turned in disgust.

It helped her, but it left its mark upon her – a mark which her father must have noted, had he not been almost wholly occupied with the burden that weighed him down. Morning and evening he visited her, yet failed to read that in her haunted eyes which could not have escaped a clearer vision.

Entering her room two hours after his interview with his officers regarding her, he looked at her searchingly indeed, but without understanding. She lay among cushions on a *charpoy* of bamboo in the light of a shaded lamp. Young and slight and angular, with a pale little face of utter weariness, with great dark eyes that gazed heavily out of the black shadows that ringed them round, such was Muriel Roscoe. Her black hair was simply plaited and gathered up at the neck. It lay in cloudy masses about her temples – wonderful hair, quite lustreless, so abundant that it seemed almost too much for the little head that bore it. She did not rise at her father's entrance. She scarcely raised her eyes.

'So glad you've come, Daddy,' she said, in a soft low voice. 'I've been wanting you. It's nearly bedtime, isn't it?'

He went to her, treading lightly. His thoughts had been all

of her for the past few hours and in consequence he looked at her more critically than usual. For the first time he was struck by her pallor, her look of deathly weariness. On the table near her lay a plate of boiled rice piled high in a snowy pyramid. He saw that it had not been touched.

'Why, child,' he said, a sudden new anxiety at his heart, 'you have had nothing to eat. You're not ill?'

She roused herself a little, and a very faint colour crept into her white cheeks. 'No, dear, only tired – too tired to be hungry,' she told him. 'That rice is for you.'

He sat down beside her with a sound that was almost a groan. 'You must eat something, child,' he said. 'Being penned up here takes away your appetite. But all the same you must eat.'

She sat up slowly, and pushed back the heavy hair from her forehead with a sigh.

'Very well, Daddy,' she said submissively. 'But you must have some too, dear. I couldn't possibly eat it all.'

Something in his attitude or expression seemed to strike her at this point, and she made a determined effort to shake off her lethargy. A spoon and fork lay by the plate. She handed him the former and kept the latter for herself.

'We'll have a picnic, Daddy,' she said, with a wistful little smile. 'I told *ayah* always to bring two plates, but she has forgotten. We don't mind though, do we?'

It was childishly spoken, but the pathos of it went straight to the man's heart. He tasted the rice under her watching eyes and pronounced it very good; then waited for her to follow his example which she did with a slight shudder.

'Delicious, Daddy, isn't it?' she said. And even he did not guess what courage underlay the words.

They kept up the farce till the pyramid was somewhat reduced then by mutual consent they suffered their ardour to flag. There was a faint colour in the girl's thin face as she leaned back again. Her eyes were brighter, the lids drooped less.

'I had a dream last night, Daddy,' she said, 'such a curious dream, and so vivid. I thought I was out on the mountains with someone. I don't know who it was, but it was someone very nice. It seemed to be very near the sunrise, for it was quite bright up above, though it was almost dark where we stood. And, do you know – don't laugh, Daddy, I know it was only a silly dream – when I looked up, I saw that everywhere the mountains were full of horses and chariots of fire. I felt so safe, Daddy, and so happy. I could have cried when I woke up.'

She paused. It was rather difficult for her to make conversation for the silent man who sat beside her so gloomy and preoccupied. Save that she loved her father as she loved no one else on earth, she might have felt awed in his presence.

As it was, receiving no response, she turned to look, and the next instant was on her knees beside him, her thin young arms clinging to his neck.

'Daddy, darling, darling!' she whispered, and hid her face against him in sudden, nameless terror.

He clasped her to him, holding her close, that she might not again see his face and the look it wore. She began to tremble, and he tried to soothe her with his hand, but for many seconds he could find no words.

'What is it, Daddy?' she whispered at last, unable to endure the silence longer. 'Won't you tell me? I can be very brave. You said so yourself.'

'Yes,' he said. 'You will be a brave girl, I know.' His voice quivered and he paused to steady it. 'Muriel,' he said then, 'I don't know if you have ever thought of the end of all this. There will be an end, you know. I have had to face it to-night.'

She looked up at him quickly, but he was ready for her. He had banished from his face the awful despair that he carried in his soul.

'When Sir Reginald Bassett comes – ' she began uncertainly.

He put his hand on her shoulder. 'You will try not to be

afraid,' he said. 'I am going to treat you, as I have treated my officers, with absolute candour. We shall not hold out more than three days more. Sir Reginald Bassett will not be here in time.'

He stopped. Muriel uttered not a word. Her face was still upturned, and her eyes had grown suddenly intensely bright, but he read no shrinking in them.

With an effort he forced himself to go on. 'I may not be able to protect you when the end comes. I may not even be with you. But – there is one man upon whom you can safely rely whatever happens, who will give himself up to securing your safety alone. He has sworn to me that you shall not be taken, and I know that he will keep his word. You will be safe with him, Muriel. You may trust him as long as you live. He will not fail you. Perhaps you can guess his name?'

He asked the question with a touch of curiosity in the midst of his tragedy. That upturned, listening face had in it so little of a woman's understanding, so much of the deep wonder of a child.

Her answer was prompt and confident, and albeit her very lips were white, there was a faint hint of satisfaction in her voice as she made it.

'Captain Grange, of course, Daddy.'

He started and looked at her narrowly. 'No, no!' he said. 'Not Grange! What should make you think of him?'

He saw a look of swift disappointment, almost of consternation, darken her eyes. For the first time her lips quivered uncertainly.

'Who then, Daddy? Not – not Mr. Ratcliffe?'

He bent his head. 'Yes, Nick Ratcliffe. I have placed you in his charge. He will take care of you.'

'Young Nick Ratcliffe!' she said slowly. 'Why, Daddy, he can't even take care of himself yet. Every one says so. Besides' – a curiously womanly touch crept into her speech – 'I don't like him. Only the other day I heard him laugh at something that was terrible – something it makes me sick to think of. Indeed, Daddy, I would far rather have Captain Grange to take care of me. Don't you think he would if you asked him? He is so much bigger and stronger, and – and kinder.'

'Ah! I know,' her father said. 'He seems so to you. But it is nerve that your protector will need, child; and Ratcliffe possesses more nerve than all the rest of the garrison put together. No, it must be Ratcliffe, Muriel. And remember to give him all your trust, all your confidence. For whatever he does will be with my authority – with my – full – approval.'

His voice failed suddenly and he rose, turning sharply away from the light. She clung to his arm silently, in a passion of tenderness, though she was far from understanding the suffering those last words revealed. She had never seen him this moved before.

After a few seconds he turned back to her, and bending kissed her piteous face. She clung closely to him with an agonized longing to keep him with her; but he put her gently from him at last.

'Lie down again, dear,' he said, 'and get what rest you can. Try not to be frightened at the noise. There is sure to be an assault, but the fort will hold to-night.'

He stood a moment, looking down at her. Then again he stooped and kissed her 'Good-bye, my darling,' he said huskily, 'till we meet again?'

And so hurriedly, as if not trusting himself to remain longer, he left her.

Chapter 3

There came again the running rattle of rifle-firing from the valley below the fort, and Muriel Roscoe, lying on her couch, pressed both hands to her eyes and shivered. It seemed impossible that the end could be so near. She felt as if she had existed for years in this living nightmare of many horrors, had lain down and had slept with that dreadful sound in her ears from the very beginning of things. The life she had led before these ghastly happenings had become so vague a memory that it almost seemed to belong to a previous existence, to an earlier and a happier era. As in a dream she now recalled the vision of her English school-life. It lay not a year behind her, but she felt herself to have changed so fundamentally since those sunny, peaceful days that she seemed to be a different person altogether. The Muriel Roscoe of those days had been a merry, light-hearted personality. She had revelled in games and all outdoor amusements. Moreover, she had been quick to learn, and her lessons had never caused her any trouble. A daring sprite she had been, with a most fertile imagination and a longing for adventure that had never been fully satisfied, possessing withal so tender and loving a heart that the very bees in the garden had been among her cherished friends. She remembered all the sunny ideals of that golden time and marvelled at herself, forgetting utterly the eager, even passionate, craving that had then been hers for the wider life, the broader knowledge, that lay beyond her reach, forgetting the feverish impatience with which she had longed for the day of her emancipation when she might join her father in the wonderful, glowing East which she often pictured in her dreams. Of her mother she had no memory. She had died at her birth. Her father was all the world to her; and when at last he had travelled home on a brief leave and taken her from her quiet English life to the strange, swift existence of the land of his exile, her soul had overflowed with happiness.

Nevertheless she had not been carried away by the gaieties of this new world. The fascinations of dance and gymkhana had not caught her. The joy of being with her father was too sacred and too precious to be foregone for these lesser pleasures, and she very speedily decided to sacrifice all social entertainments to which he could not accompany her. She rode with him, camped with him, and became his inseparable companion. Undeveloped in many ways, shy in the presence of strangers, she soon forgot her earlier ambition to see the world and all that it contained. Her father's society was to her all-sufficing, and it was no sacrifice to her to withdraw herself from the gay crowd and dwell apart with him.

He had no wish to monopolize her, but it was a relief to him that the constant whirl of pleasure about her attracted her so little. He liked to have her with him, and it soon became a matter of course that she should accompany him on all his expeditions. She revelled in his tours of inspection. They were so many picnics to her, and she enjoyed them with the zest of a child.

And so it came to pass that she was with him among the Hills of the Frontier when, like a pent flood suddenly escaping, the storm of rebellion broke and seethed about them, threatening them with total annihilation.

No serious trouble had been anticipated. A certain tract of country had been reported unquiet, and General Roscoe had been ordered to proceed thither on a tour of inspection and also, to a very mild degree, of intimidation. Marching through the district from fort to fort, he had encountered no shadow of opposition. All had gone well. And then, his work over, and all he set out to do satisfactorily accomplished, his face towards India and his back to the mountains, the unexpected had come upon him like a thunderbolt.

Hordes of tribesmen, gathered Heaven knew how or whence, had suddenly burst upon him from the south, had cut off his advance by sheer immensity of numbers, and, hemming him in, had forced him gradually back into the mountain fastnesses through which he had just passed unmolested.

It was a stroke so wholly new, so subtly executed that it had won success almost before the General had realized the weight of the disaster that had come upon him. He had believed himself at first to be involved in a mere fray with border thieves. But before he reached the fort upon which he found himself obliged to fall back, he knew that he had to cope with a general rising of the tribes, and that the means at his disposal were as inadequate to stem the rising flood of rebellion as a pebble thrown into a mountain stream to check its flow.

The men under his Command, with the exception of a few officers, were all native soldiers, and he soon began to have a strong suspicion that among these he numbered traitors. Nevertheless, he established himself at the fort, determined there to make his stand till relief should arrive.

The telegraph wires were cut, and for a time it seemed that all communication with the outside world was an impossibility. Several runners were sent out, but failed to break through the besieging forces. But at last after many desperate days there came a message from without – a scrap of paper attached to a stone and flung over the wall of the fort at night. News of the disaster had reached Peshawur, and Sir Reginald Bassett, with a hastily collected force, was moving to their assistance.

The news put heart into the garrison, and for a time it seemed that the worst could be averted. But it became gradually evident to General Roscoe that the relieving force could not reach them in time. The water supply had run very low, and the men were already subsisting upon rations that were scarcely sufficient for the maintenance of life. There was sickness among them, and there were also many wounded. The white men were reduced to four, including himself, the native soldiers had begun to desert, and he had been forced at last to face the fact that the end was very near.

All this had Muriel Roscoe come through, physically scatheless, mentally torn and battered, and she could not bring herself to realize that the long-drawn-out misery of the siege could ever be over.

Lying there, tense and motionless, she listened to the shots and yells in the distance with a shuddering sense that it was all a part of her life, of her very being even. The torture and the misery had so eaten into her soul. Now and then she heard the quick thunder of one of the small guns that armed the fort, and at the sound her pulses leaped and quivered. She knew that the ammunition was running very low. These guns did not often speak now.

Then, during a lull, there came to her the careless humming of a British voice, the free, confident tread of British feet, approaching her door.

She caught her breath as a hand rapped smartly upon the panel. She knew who the visitor was, but she could not bring herself to bid him enter. A sudden awful fear was upon her. She could neither speak nor move. She lay, listening intently, hoping against hope that he would believe her to be sleeping and go away.

The knock was not repeated. Dead silence reigned. And then quickly and decidedly the door opened, and Nick Ratcliffe stood upon the threshold. The light struck full upon his face as he halted – a clever, whimsical face that might mask almost any quality good or bad.

'May I come in, Miss Roscoe?' he asked.

For she had not moved at his appearance. She lay as one dead. But as he spoke she uncovered her face, and terror incarnate stared wildly at him from her starting eyes. He entered without further ceremony and closed the door behind him. In the shaded lamplight his features seemed to twitch as if he wanted to smile. So at least it seemed to her wrought-up fancy.

He gazed greedily at the plate of rice on the table as he came forward. 'Great Jupiter?' he said 'What a sumptuous repast?'

The total freedom from all anxiety or restraint with which he made this simple observation served to restore to some degree the girl's tottering self-control. She sat up, sufficiently recovered to remember that she did not like this man.

'Pray have some if you want it,' she said coldly.

He turned his back on it promptly. 'No, don't tempt me,' he said. 'It's a fast day with me. I'm acquiring virtue, being conspicuously destitute of all other forms of comfort. Why don't you eat it yourself ? Are you acquiring virtue too?'

He stood looking down at her quizzically, under rapidly flickering eyelids. She sat silent, wishing with all her heart that he would go away.

Nothing, however, was apparently further from his thoughts. After a moment he sat down in the chair that her father had occupied an hour before. It was very close to her, and she drew herself away slightly with a small, instinctive movement of repugnance. But Nick was sublimely impervious to hints.

'I say, you know,' he said abruptly, 'you shouldn't take opium. Your donkey of an *ayah* ought to know better than to let you have it.'

Muriel gave a great start. 'I don't – ' she faltered. 'I – I – '

He shook his head at her, as though reproving a child.

'Pussy's out,' he observed. 'It is no good giving chase. But really, you know, you mustn't do it. You used to be a brave girl once, and now your nerves are all to pieces.'

There was a species of paternal reproach in his tone. Looking at him, she marvelled that she had ever thought him young and headlong. Almost in spite of herself she began to murmur excuses.

'I can't help it. I must have something. I don't sleep. I lie for hours, listening to the fighting. It – it's more than I can bear.' Her voice quivered, and she turned her face aside, unable to hide her emotion, but furious with herself for displaying it.

Nick said nothing at all to comfort her, and she bitterly resented his silence. After a pause he spoke again, as if he had banished the matter entirely from his mind.

'Look here,' he said. 'I want you to tell me something. I don't know what sort of a fellow you think I am, though I fancy you don't like me much. But you're not afraid of me, are you ? You know I'm to be trusted?'

It was her single chance of revenge, and she took it.

'I have my father's word for it,' she said.

He nodded thoughtfully as if unaware of the thrust. 'Yes, your father knows me. And so' – he smiled at her suddenly – 'you are ready to trust me on his recommendation? You are ready to follow me blindfold through danger if I give you my hand to hold?

She felt a sharp chill strike her heart. What was it he was asking of her? What did those words of his portend?

'I don't know,' she said. 'I don't see that it makes much difference how I feel.'

'Well, it does,' he assured her. 'And that is exactly what I have come to talk about. Miss Roscoe, will you leave the fort with me, and escape in disguise? I have thought it all out, and it can be done without much difficulty. I do not need to tell you that the idea has your father's full approval.'

They were her father's own words, but at sound of them she thrank and shivered, in sheer horror at the coolness with which they were uttered. He might have been asking her to stroll with him in the leafy quiet of some English lane.

Could it be, she asked herself incredulously, could it be that her father had ever sanctioned and approved so ghastly a risk for her? She put her hand to her temples. Her brain was reeling. How could she do this thing? How could she have permitted it to be even suggested to her? And then, swift through her tortured mind flashed his words: 'There will be an end. I have had to face it to-night.' Was it this that he had meant? Was it for this that he had been preparing her?

With a muffled exclamation she rose, trembling in every limb. 'I can't!' she cried piteously. 'Oh, I can't! Please go away!'

It might have been the frightened prayer of a child, so beseeching was it, so full of weakness. But Nick Ratcliffe heard it unmoved. He waited a few seconds till she came to a stand by the table, her back towards him. Then with a quiet movement he rose and followed her.

'I beg your pardon,' he said. 'But you can't afford to shirk things at this stage. I am offering you deliverance, though you don't realize it.'

He spoke with force, and if his aim had been to rouse her to a more practical activity, he gained his end. She turned upon him in swift and desperate indignation. Her voice rang almost harsh.

'How can you call it deliverance? It is at best a choice of two horrible evils. You know perfectly well that we could never get through. You must be mad to suggest such a thing. We should be made prisoners and massacred under the very guns of the fort.'

'I beg your pardon,' he said again, and his eyelids quivered a little as if under the pressure of some controlled emotion. 'We shall not be made prisoners. I know what I am saying. It is deliverance that I am offering you. Of course you can refuse, and I shall still do my utmost to save you. But the chances are not equal. I hope you will not refuse.'

The moderation of this speech calmed her somewhat. In her first wild panic she had almost imagined that he could take her against her will. She saw that she had been unreasonable, but she was too shaken to tell him so. Moreover there was still that about him, notwithstanding his words, that made her afraid to yield a single inch of ground lest by some hidden means he should sweep her altogether from her precarious foothold. Even in the silence, she felt that he was doing battle with her, and she did not dare to face him.

With a childish gesture of abandonment she dropped into a chair and laid her head upon her arms.

'Oh, please go away!' she besought him weakly. 'I am so tired – so tired.'

But Ratcliffe did not move. He stood looking down at her, at the black hair that clustered about her neck, at the bowed, despairing figure, the piteous, clenched hands.

A little clock in the room began to strike in silvery tones, and he glanced up. The next instant he bent and laid a bony hand upon her two clasped ones.

'Can't you decide?' he said. 'Will you let me decide for you? Don't let yourself get scared. You have kept so strong till now.' Firmly as he spoke, there was somehow a note of soothing in his voice, and almost insensibly the girl was moved by it. She remained silent and motionless, but the strong grip of his fingers comforted her subtly notwithstanding.

'Come,' he said, 'listen a moment and let me tell you my plan of campaign. It is very simple, and for that reason it is going to succeed. You are listening now?'

His tone was vigorous and insistent. Muriel sat slowly up in response to it. She looked down at the thin hand that grasped hers, and wondered at its strength; but she lacked the spirit at that moment to resent its touch.

He leaned down upon the table, his face close to hers, and began to unfold his plan.

'We shall leave the fort directly the moon is down. I have a disguise for you that will conceal your face and hair. And I shall fake as a tribesman, so that my dearest friend would never recognize me. They will be collecting the wounded in the dark, and I will carry you through on my shoulder as if I had got a dead relation. You won't object to playing a dead relation of mine?'

He broke into a sudden laugh, but sobered instantly when he saw her shrink at the sound.

'That's about all the plan,' he resumed. 'There is nothing very alarming about it for they will never spot us in the dark. I'm as yellow as a Chinaman already. We shall be miles away by morning. And I know how to find my way afterwards.'

He paused, but Muriel made no comment. She was staring straight before her.

'Can you suggest any amendments?' he asked.

She turned her head and looked at him with newly-roused aversion in her eyes. She had summoned all her strength to the combat, realizing that now was the moment for resistance if she meant to resist.

'No, Mr. Ratcliffe,' she said, with a species of desperate firmness very different from his own. 'I have nothing to suggest. If you wish to escape, you must go alone. It is quite useless to try to persuade me any further. Nothing – nothing will induce me to leave my father.'

Whether or not he had expected this opposition was not apparent on Nick's face. It betrayed neither impatience nor disappointment.

'There would be some reason in that,' he gravely rejoined, 'if you could do any good to your father by remaining. Of course I see your point, but it seems to me that it would be harder for him to see you starve with the rest of the garrison than to know that you had escaped with me. A woman in your position is bound to be a continual burden and anxiety to those who protect her. The dearer she is to them, so much the heavier is the burden. Miss Roscoe, you must see this. You are not an utter child. You must realize that to leave your father is about the greatest sacrifice you can make for him at the present moment. He is worn out with anxiety on your behalf, literally bowed down by it. For his sake, you are going to do this thing, it being the only thing left that you can do for him.'

There was more than persuasion in his voice. It held authority. But Muriel heard it without awe. She had passed that stage. The matter was too momentous to allow of weakness. She had strung herself to the highest pitch of resistance as a hunted creature at bay. She threw back her head, a look of obstinacy about her lips, her slight figure straightened to the rigidity of defiance.

'I will not be forced,' she said, in sharp, uneven tones. 'Mr. Ratcliffe, you may go on persuading and arguing till doomsday. I will not leave my father.'

Ratcliffe stood up abruptly. A curious glitter shone in his eyes, and the light eyebrows twitched a little. She felt that he had suddenly ceased to do battle with her, yet that the victory was not hers. And for a second she was horribly frightened, as though an iron trap had closed upon her and held her at his mercy.

He walked to the door without speaking and opened it. She expected him to go, sat waiting breathlessly for his departure, but instead he stood motionless, looking into the dark passage.

She wondered with nerves on edge what he was waiting for. Suddenly she heard a step without, a few murmured words, and Nick stood on one side. Her father's Sikh orderly passed him, carrying a tray on which was a glass full of some dark liquid. He set it down on the table before her with a deep salaam.

'The General Sahib wishes Missy Sahib to have a good night,' he said. 'He cannot come to her himself, but he sends her this by his servant, and he bids her drink it and sleep.'

Muriel looked up at the man in surprise. Her father had never done such a thing before, and the message astonished her not a little. Then, remembering that he had shown some anxiety regarding her appearance that evening, she fancied she began to understand. Yet it was strange, it was utterly unlike him, to desire her to take an opiate. She looked at the glass with hesitation.

'Give him my love, Purdu,' she said finally to the waiting orderly. 'Tell him I will take it if I cannot sleep without.'

The man bowed himself again and withdrew. To her disgust, however, Nick remained. He was looking at her oddly.

'Miss Roscoe,' he said abruptly, 'I beg you, don't drink that stuff. Your father must be mad to offer it to you. Let me take the beastliness away.'

She faced him indignantly. 'My father knows what is good for me better than you do,' she said.

He shrugged his shoulders. 'I don't profess to be a sage. But anyone will tell you that it is madness to take opium in this reckless fashion. For Heaven's sake be reasonable. Don't take it.'

He came back to the table, but at his approach she laid her hand upon the glass. She was quivering with angry excitement.

'I will not endure your interference any longer,' she declared, goaded to headlong, nervous fury by his persistence. 'My father's wishes are enough for me. He desires me to take it, and so I will.'

She took up the glass in a sudden frenzy of defiance. He had frightened her – yes, he had frightened her – but he should see how little he had gained by that. She took a taste of the liquid, then paused, again assailed by a curious hesitancy. Had her father really meant her to take it all?

Nick had stopped short at her first movement, but as she began to lower the glass in response to that disquieting doubt, he swooped suddenly forward like a man possessed.

For a fleeting instant she thought he was going to wrest it from her, but in the next she understood – understood the man's deep treachery, and with what devilish ingenuity he had worked upon her. Holding her with an arm that felt like iron, he forced the glass back between her teeth, and tilted the contents down her throat. She strove to resist him, strove wildly, frantically, not to swallow the draught. But he held her pitilessly. He compelled her, gripping her right hand with the glass, and pinning the other to her side.

When it was over, when he had worked his will and the hateful draught was swallowed, he set her free and turned himself sharply from her.

She sprang up trembling and hysterical. She could have slain him in that instant had she possessed the means to her hand. But her strength was more nearly exhausted than she knew. Her limbs doubled up under her weight, and as she tottered, seeking for support, she realized that she was vanquished utterly at last.

She saw him wheel quickly and start to support her, sought to evade him, failed – and as she felt his arm lift her, she cried aloud in anguished helplessness.

What followed dwelt ever after in her memory as a hideous dream, vivid yet not wholly tangible. He laid her down upon the couch and bent over her, his hands upon her, holding her still; for every muscle, every nerve twitched spasmodically, convulsively, in the instinctive effort of the powerless body to be free. She had a confused impression also that he spoke to her, but what he said she was never able to recall. In the end, her horror faded, and she saw him as through a mist bending above her, grim and tense and silent, controlling her as it were from an immense distance. And even while she yet dimly wondered, he passed like a shadow from her sight, and wonder itself ceased. . . .

Half an hour later Nicholas Ratcliffe, the wit and clown of his regiment, regarded by many as harebrained or wantonly reckless, carried away from the beleaguered fort among the hostile mountains the slight, impassive figure of an English girl.

The night was dark, populated by terrors alive and ghastly. But he went through it as one unaware of its many dangers. Light-footed and fearless, he passed through the midst of his enemies, marching with the sublime audacity of the dominant race, despising caution – yea, grinning triumphant in the very face of Death.

Chapter 4

Out of a deep abyss of darkness in which she seemed to have wandered ceaselessly and comfortlessly for many days, Muriel Roscoe came haltingly back to the surface of things. She was very weak, so weak that to open her eyes was an exertion requiring all her resolution, and to keep them open during those first hours of returning life a physical impossibility. She knew that she was not alone, for gentle hands ministered to her, and she was constantly aware of someone who watched her tirelessly, with never-failing attention. But she felt not the smallest interest regarding this faithful companion, being too weary to care whether she lived or fell away for ever down those unending steeps up which some unseen influence seemed magnetically to draw her.

It was a stage of returning consciousness that seemed to last even longer than the period of her wandering, but this also began to pass at length. The light grew stronger all about her, the mists rolled slowly away from her clogged brain, leaving only a drowsing languor that was infinitely restful to her tired senses.

And then while she lay half-dreaming and wholly content, a remorseless hand began to bathe her face and head with ice-cold water. She awoke reluctantly, even resentfully.

'Don't!' she entreated like a child. 'I am so tired. Let me sleep.'

'My poor dear, I know all about it,' a motherly voice made answer. 'But it's time for you to wake.'

She did not grasp the words – only, very vaguely their meaning; and this she made a determined, but quite fruitless effort to defy. In the end, being roused in spite of herself, she opened her eyes and gazed upwards.

And all his life long Nick Ratcliffe remembered the reproach that those eyes held for him. It was as if he had laid violent hands upon a spirit that yearned towards freedom, and had dragged it back into the sordid captivity from which it had so nearly escaped.

But it was only for a moment that she looked at him so. The reproach faded swiftly from the dark eyes and he saw a startled horror dawn behind it.

Suddenly she raised herself with a faint cry. 'Where am I?' she gasped. 'What – what have you done with me?'

She stared around her wildly, with unreasoning nightmare terror. She was lying on a bed of fern in a narrow, dark ravine. The place was full of shadow though far overhead she saw the light of day. At one end, only a few yards from her, a stream rushed and gurgled among great boulders, and its insistent murmur filled the air. Behind her rose a great wall of grey rock, clothed here and there with some dark growth. Its rugged face was dented with hollows that looked like the homes of wild animals. There was a constant trickle of water on all sides, an eerie whispering, remote but incessant. As she sat there in growing panic, a great bat-like creature, immense and shadowy, swooped soundlessly by her. She shrank back with another cry, and found Nick Ratcliffe's arm thrust protectingly about her.

'It's all right,' he said, in a matter-of-fact tone. 'You're not frightened at flying-foxes, are you?'

Recalled to the fact of his presence, she turned sharply, and flung his arm away, as though it had been a snake.

'Don't touch me!' she gasped, passionate loathing in voice and gesture.

'Sorry,' said Nick imperturbably. 'I meant well.'

He began to busy himself with a small bundle that lay upon the ground, whistling softly between his teeth, and for a few seconds Muriel sat and watched him. He was dressed in a flowing native garment, that covered him from head to feet. Out of the heavy enveloping folds his smooth, yellow face looked forth, sinister and terrible to her fevered vision. He looked like some evil bird, she thought to herself.

Glancing down, she saw that she was likewise attired, save that her head was bare. The hair hung wet on her forehead, and the water dripped down her face. She put up her hand half-mechanically to wipe the drops away. Her fear was mounting rapidly higher.

She knew now what had happened. He had drugged her forcibly – she shivered at the remembrance – and had borne her away to this dreadful place during her unconsciousness. Her father was left behind in the fort. He had sanctioned her removal. He had given her, a helpless captive, into this man's keeping.

But no! Her whole soul rose up in sudden fierce denial of this. He had never done this thing. He had never given his consent to an act so cowardly and so brutal. He was incapable of parting with her thus. He could never have permitted so base a trick, so cruel, so outrageous, a deed of treachery.

Strength came suddenly to her – the strength of frenzy. She leaped to her feet. She would escape She would go back to him through all the hordes of the enemy. She would face anything – anything in the world – rather than remain at the mercy of this man.

But – he had not been looking at her, and he did not look at her – his arm shot out as she moved, and his hand fastened claw-like upon her dress.

'Sorry,' he said again, in the same practical tone. 'But you'll have something to eat before you go.'

She stooped and strove wildly, frantically, to shake off the detaining hand. But it held her like a vice, with awful skeleton fingers that she could not, dared not, touch.

'Let me go!' she cried impotently. 'How dare you! How dare you!'

Still he did not raise his head. He was on his knees and he would not even trouble himself to rise.

'I can't help myself,' he told her coolly. 'It's not my fault. It's yours.'

She made a final, violent effort to wrest herself free. And then – it was as if all powers were suddenly taken from her – her strained nerves gave way completely and she dropped down upon the ground again in a quivering agony of helplessness.

Nick's hand fell away from her. 'You shouldn't,' he said gently. 'It's no good, you know.'

He returned to his former occupation while she sat with her face hidden, in a stupor of fear, afraid to move lest he should touch her again.

'Now,' said Nick, after a brief pause, 'let me have the pleasure of seeing you break your fast. There is some of that excellent boiled rice of yours here. You will feel better when you have had some.'

She trembled at the sound of his voice. Could he make her eat also against her will, she wondered?

'Come!' said Nick again, in a tone of soft wheedling that he might have employed to a fractious child. 'It'll do you good, you know, Muriel. Won't you try? Just a mouthful – to please me?'

Reluctantly she uncovered her face, and looked at him. He was kneeling in front of her, the *chuddah* pushed back from his face, humbly offering her an oatmeal biscuit with a small heap of rice piled upon it.

She drew back shuddering. 'I couldn't eat anything – possibly,' she said, and even her voice seemed to shrink. 'You can. You take it. I would rather die.'

Nick did not withdraw his hand. 'Take it, Muriel,' he said quietly. 'It is going to do you good.'

She flashed him a desperate glance in which anger, fear, abhorrence, were strongly mingled. He advanced the biscuit a little nearer. There was a queer look on his yellow face, almost a bullying look.

'Take it,' he said again.

And against her will, almost without conscious movement, she obeyed him. The untempting morsel passed from his hand to hers, and under the compulsion of his insistence she began to eat.

She felt as if every mouthful would choke her, but she persevered, urged by the dread certainty that he would somehow have his way.

Not until the last fragment was gone did she feel his vigilance relax, but he ate nothing himself though there remained several biscuits and a very little of the rice.

'You are feeling better?' he asked her then.

A curious suspicion that he was waiting to tell her something made her answer almost feverishly in the affirmative. It amounted to a premonition of evil tidings, and instinctively her thoughts flew to her father.

'What is it?' she questioned nervously. 'You have something to say.'

Nick's face was turned from her. He seemed to be gazing across the ravine.

'Yes,' he said, after a moment.

'Oh, what?' she broke in. 'Tell me quickly – quickly! It is my father, I know, I know. He has been hurt – wounded – '

She stopped. Nick had lifted one hand as if to silence her. 'My dear,' he said, his voice very low, 'your father died last night – before we left the fort.'

At her cry of agony he started up, and in a second he was on his knees by her side and had gathered her to him as though she had been a little child in need of comfort. She did not shrink from him in her extremity. The blow had been too sudden, too overwhelming. It blotted out all lesser sensibilities. In those first terrible moments she did not think of Nick at all, was scarcely conscious of his presence, though she vaguely felt the comfort of his arms.

And he, holding her fast against his breast, found no consolation, no word of any sort wherewith to soothe her. He only rocked her gently, pressing her head to his shoulder, while his face, bent above her, quivered all over as the face of a man in torture.

Muriel spoke at last, breaking her stricken silence with a strangely effortless composure. 'Tell me more,' she said.

She stirred in his arms as if to free herself from some oppression, and finally drew herself away from him though not as if she wished to escape his touch. She still seemed to be hardly aware of him. He was the medium of her information, that was all. Nick dropped back into his former attitude, his hands clasped firmly round his knees, his eyes, keen as a bird's and extremely bright, gazing across the ravine. His lips still quivered a little, but his voice was perfectly even and quiet.

'It happened very soon after the firing began. It must have been directly after he left you. He was hit in the breast, just over the heart. We couldn't do anything for him. He knew himself that it was mortal. In fact, I think he had almost expected it. We took him into the guard-room and made him as easy as possible. He lost consciousness before he died. He was lying unconscious when I came to you.'

Muriel made a sharp movement. 'And you never told me,' she said, in a dry whisper.

'I thought it best,' he answered with great gentleness. 'You could not have gone to him. He didn't wish it.'

'Why not?' she demanded, and suddenly her voice rang harsh again. 'Why could I not have gone to him? Why didn't he wish it?'

Nick hesitated for a single instant. Then, 'It was for your own sake,' he said, not looking at her.

'You mean he suffered?'

'While he remained conscious – yes.' Nick spoke reluctantly. 'It didn't last long,' he said.

She scarcely seemed to hear him. 'And so you tricked me,' she said, 'you tricked me while my father was lying dying. I was not to see him – either then or after – for my own sake! And do you think' – her voice rising – 'do you think that you were in any way justified in treating me so? Do you think it was merciful to blind me and to take from me all I should ever have of comfort to look back upon? Do you think I couldn't have borne it all ten thousand times easier if I could have seen and known the very worst? It was my right – it was my right! How dared you take it from me? I will never forgive you – never!'

She was on her feet as the passionate protest burst from her, but she swayed as she stood and flung out her arms with a groping gesture.

'I could have borne it,' she cried again wildly, piteously. 'I could have borne anything – anything – if I had only known!'

She broke into a sudden terrible sobbing, and threw herself down headlong upon the earth, clutching at the moss with shaking, convulsive fingers, and crying between her sobs for 'Daddy! Daddy!' as though her agony could pierce the dividing barrier and bring him back to her. Nick made no further attempt to help her. He sat gazing stonily out before him in a sphinx-like stillness that never varied while the storm of her anguish spent itself at his side.

Even after her sobs had ceased from sheer exhaustion he made no movement, no sign that he was so much a thinking of her.

Only when at last she raised herself with difficulty and put the heavy hair back from her disfigured face, did he turn slightly and hold out to her a small tin cup.

'It's only water,' he said gently. 'Have some.'

She took it almost mechanically and drank, then lay back with closed eyes and burning head, sick and blinded by her paroxysm of weeping.

A little later she felt his hands moving about her again, but she was too spent to open her eyes. He bathed her face with a care equal to any woman's, smoothed back her hair, and improvised a pillow for her head.

And afterwards she knew that he sat down by her, out of sight but close at hand, a silent presence watching over her, till at last, worn out with grief and the bitter strain of the past weeks, she sank into natural, dreamless slumber, and slept for hours.

Chapter 5

It was dark when Muriel awoke – so dark that she lay for awhile dreamily fancying herself in bed. But this illusion passed very quickly as her brain, refreshed and active, resumed its work. The cry of a jackal at no great distance roused her to full consciousness, and she started up in the chill darkness, trembling and afraid.

Instantly a warm hand grasped hers, and a low voice spoke. 'It's all right!' said Nick. 'I'm here.'

'Oh, isn't it dark?' she said. 'Isn't it dark?'

'Don't be frightened,' he answered gently. 'Come close to me. You are cold.'

She crept to him shivering, thankful for the shielding arm he threw around her.

'The sunrise can't be far off,' he said. 'I expect you are hungry, aren't you?'

She was very hungry, and he put a biscuit into her hand. The very fact of eating there in the darkness in some measure reassured her. She ate several biscuits, and began to feel much better.

'Getting warmer?' questioned Nick. 'Let me feel your hands.' They were still cold, and he took them and thrust them down against his breast. She shrank a little at the touch of his warm flesh.

'It will make you so cold,' she murmured.

But he only laughed at her softly, and pressed them closer. 'I am not easily chilled,' he said. 'Besides, it's sleeping that makes you cold. And I haven't slept.'

Muriel heard the news with astonishment. She was no longer angry with Nick, and her fears of him were dormant. Though she would never forget and might never forgive his treachery, he was her sole protector in that wilderness of many terrors, and she lacked the resolution to keep him at arm's length. There was, moreover, something comforting in his presence, something that vastly reassured her, making her lean upon him almost in spite of herself.

'Haven't you slept at all?' she asked him in wonder. 'How in the world did you keep awake?'

He did not answer her, only laughed again as though at some secret joke. He seemed to be in rather good spirits, she noticed, and she marvelled at him with a heavy pain at her heart that was utterly beyond expression or relief.

She sat silent for a little, then at length withdrew her hands, assuring him that they were quite warm.

'And I want to talk to you,' she added, in a more practical tone than she had previously managed to assume. 'Mr. Ratcliffe, you may be in command of this expedition, but I think you ought to tell me your plans.'

'Call me Nick, won't you?' he said. 'It'll make things easier. You are quite welcome to know my plans, such as they are. I haven't managed to develop anything very ingenious during all these hours. You see, we are to a certain extent, at the mercy of circumstances. This place isn't more than a dozen miles from the fort, and the hills all round are infested with tribesmen. I hoped at first that we should get clear in the night, but you were asleep, and on the whole it seemed best to lie up for another day. We might make a bolt for it to-morrow night if all goes well. I have a sort of instinct for these mountains. There is always plenty of cover for those who know how to find it. It will be slow progress of course, but we will keep moving south, and, given luck, we may fall in with Bassett's relief column before many days.'

So with much serenity he disclosed his plans, and Muriel marvelled afresh at the confidence that buoyed him up. Was he really as sublimely free from anxiety as he wished her to believe, she wondered? It was difficult to think otherwise, even though he had admitted that they were governed by circumstance. She began to think that there was magic in him, some hidden reserve force upon which he could always draw when all other resources failed.

Another matter had also caught her attention, and this she presently decided to investigate. She had never thought of Nick Ratcliffe as in any sense a remarkable person before.

'Did you actually carry me ten miles?' she asked.

'Something very near it,' said Nick.

'How in the world did you do it?' Her interest was quickened. Undoubtedly there was something uncanny in this man's strength.

'You're not very heavy, you know,' he said.

His arm was still around her, and she suffered it; for the darkness still frightened her when she allowed herself to think. 'Have you had anything to eat?' she asked him next.

'Not quite lately,' said Nick. 'I've been smoking. I wonder you didn't notice it.'

His tone was somehow repressive, but she ignored it

with a growing temerity. After all, he did not seem such an alarming person on a nearer acquaintance.

'Does smoking do as well as eating?' she asked.

'Much better,' said Nick promptly. 'Care to try?'

She shook her head in the darkness. 'I don't think you are telling the truth,' she said.

'What?' said Nick.

He spoke carelessly, but she did not repeat her assertion. A sudden shyness descended upon her, and she became silent. Nick was quiet too, and she wondered what was passing in his mind. But for the tenseness of the arm that encircled her, she could have believed him to be dozing. The silence was becoming oppressive when abruptly he broke it.

'See?' he said. 'Here comes the dawn!'

She started and stared in front of her, seeing nothing.

'Over to your left,' said Nick. And turning she beheld a lightening of the darkness high above them.

She breathed a sigh of thankfulness, and watched it grow. It spread rapidly. The walls of the ravine showed ghastly grey, then faintly pink. Through the dimness the boulders scattered about the stream stood up like mediæval monsters, and for a few panic-stricken seconds Muriel took the twining roots of a rhododendron close at hand for the coils of a gigantic snake. Then as the ordinary light of day filtered down into the gloomy place she sighed again with relief, and looked at her companion.

He was sitting with his chin on his hand, gazing across the ravine. He did not stir or glance in her direction. His yellow face was seamed in a thousand wrinkles.

A vague misgiving assailed her as she looked at him. There was something unnatural in his stillness.

'Nick?' she said at length with hesitation.

He turned sharply, and in an instant the ready grin leaped out upon his face. 'Good-morning,' he said lightly. 'I was just thinking how nice it would be to go down there and have a

wash. We've got to pass the time somehow, you know. Will
you go first?'

His gaiety baffled her, but she did not feel wholly reassured.
She got up slowly, and as she did so, her attention was caught
by something that sent a thrill of dismay through her.

'Don't look at my feet, please,' said Nick. 'They won't bear
inspection at present.'

She turned horrified eyes to his face, as he thrust them down
into a bunch of fern. 'How dreadful!' she exclaimed. 'They are
all cut and gashed. I didn't know you were bare-footed.'

'I wasn't,' said Nick. 'I've got some sandals here. Don't
look like that! You make me want to cry. I assure you it
doesn't hurt in the least.'

He grinned again as he uttered this cheerful lie, but Muriel
was not deceived.

'You must let me bind them up,' she said.

'Not for the world,' laughed Nick. 'I couldn't walk with my
feet in poultice-bags, and we shall have some more rough
marching to do to-night. Now don't you worry. Run along
like a good girl. I'm going to say my prayers.'

It was flippantly spoken, but Muriel realized that it would
be better to obey. She turned about slowly, and began to
make her way down to the stream.

The sunlight was beginning to slant through the ravine,
and here and there the racing water gleamed silvery. It was
intensely refreshing to kneel and bathe face and hands in its
icy coldness. She lingered long over it. Its sparkling purity
seemed to reach and still the throbbing misery at her heart.
In some fashion it brought her peace.

She would have prayed, but she felt she had no prayer to
offer. She had no favour to ask for herself, and her world
was quite empty now. She had no one in her heart for whom
to pray.

Yet for awhile she knelt dumb among the lifeless stones,
her face hidden, her thoughts with the father whose loss
she had scarcely begun to realize. It might be that God

would understand and pity her silence, she thought drearily to herself.

The rush of the water drowned all sound but its own, and the memory of Nick, waiting above, faded from her consciousness like a dream. Her brain felt numb and heavy still. She did not want to think. She leaned her head against a rock, closing her eyes. The continuous babble of the stream was like a lullaby.

Under its soothing influence she might have slept, a blessed drowsiness was stealing over her, when suddenly there flashed through her being a swift warning of approaching danger. Whence it came she knew not, but its urgency was such that instinctively she started up and looked about her.

The next instant, with a sound half-gasp, half-cry, she was on her feet, and shrinking back against her sheltering boulder in the paralysis of a great horror. There, within a few yards of her and drawing nearer, ever nearer, with a beast-like stealth, was a tall, blackbearded tribesman. Transfixed by terror, she stood and gazed at him, waiting, waiting dumbly, cold from head to foot, feeling as though her very heart had turned to stone.

Nearer he came, and yet nearer, soundlessly over the stones. His eyes, gleaming, devilish, were to her as the eyes of a devouring monster. In her agony she tried to shriek aloud, but her voice was gone, her throat seemed locked. She was powerless.

Close to her, for a single instant he paused; then, as in a lightning flash, she saw the narrow, sinewy hand and snake-like arm dart forward to seize her, felt every muscle in her body stiffen to rigidity in anticipation of its touch, and shrank – shrank in every nerve though she made no outward sign of shrinking.

But on the instant, with a panther-like spring, sure, noise-less, deadly, another figure leapt suddenly across her vision. There followed a violent struggle in front of her, a confused swaying to and fro, a cry choked instantly and terribly, the tinkling sound of steel falling upon stone. And then both figures were on the ground almost at her feet, locked together in mortal combat, fighting, fighting like demons in a silence that throbbed with the tumult of unrestrained savagery.

Later she never could remember how long it took her to realize that the second apparition was Nick, or if she had known it from the first. She felt herself hovering upon the brink of a great emptiness, a void immense, and yet all her senses were alive and tingling with horror. With agonized perception of what was passing, she yet felt numbed; as though her body were dead, but still contained a vital, tortured soul.

And it was thus that she presently saw Nick's face bent above the black-bearded face of his enemy; and remembered suddenly and horribly a picture she had once seen of the devil in the wilderness.

With his knees he was gripping the writhing body of his fallen foe. With his hands – it came upon her as she watched with a shock of anguished comprehension – he was deliberately and with deadly intention choking out the man's life.

'Curse you! Die!' she heard him say, and his voice sounded like the snarl of a wild beast. His upper lip was drawn back, the lower one was between his teeth, and from it the blood dripped continuously upon his hands and upon the dark throat he gripped.

'Give me that knife?' he suddenly said, with an upward jerk of the head.

A dagger was lying almost within his reach, close to her foot. She could have kicked it towards him had not her body been fast bound in that deathly inertia. But her whole soul rose up in wild revolt at the order. She tried to cry out, to implore him to have mercy, but she could not make a sound. She could only stand in frozen horror, and witness this awful thing.

She saw Nick shift his grip to one hand and reach out with the other for the weapon. He grasped it and recovered himself. A great darkness was descending upon her, but it did not come at once. It hovered before her eyes, and seemed to pass, and again she saw the horror at her feet – saw Nick bent to destroy like an eagle above his prey, merciless, full of strength, terrible – saw the man beneath him, writhing, convulsed, tortured – saw his upturned face, and starting eyes – saw the sudden downward swoop of Nick's right hand – the flash of the descending steel . . .

In her agony she burst the spell that bound her, and shrieking turned to flee from that awful sight.

But even as she moved, the darkness came suddenly back upon her, enveloping her, overwhelming her – a darkness that could be felt. For a little she fought against it frantically, impotently. Then her feet seemed to totter over the edge of a dreadful, formless silence. She knew that she fell. . . .

Chapter 6

'Wake up?' said Nick softly. 'Wake up! Don't be afraid.'

But Muriel turned her face from the light with a moan. Memory winged with horror was sweeping back upon her, and she wanted never to wake again.

'Wake up!' Nick said again, and this time there was insistence in his voice. 'Open your eyes, Muriel. There is nothing to frighten you.'

Shuddering, she obeyed him. She was lying once more upon her couch of ferns, and he was stooping over her looking closely into her face. His eyes were extraordinarily bright, like the eyes of an eagle, but the lids flickered so rapidly that he seemed to be looking through her rather than at her. There was a wound upon his lower lip, and at the sight she shuddered again, closing her eyes. She remembered that the last time she had looked upon that face, it had been the face of a devil.

'Oh, go away! Go away!' she wailed. 'Let me die!'

'I will go away,' he answered swiftly, 'if you will promise to drink what is in this cup.'

He pressed it against her hand, and she took it almost mechanically. 'It is only brandy and water,' he said. 'You will drink it?'

'If I must,' she answered weakly.

'You must,' he rejoined, and she heard him rise and move away. She strained her ears to listen, but she very soon ceased to hear him; and then raising herself cautiously, she drank. A warm thrill of life ran through her veins with the draught, steadying her, refreshing her. But it was long before she could bring herself to look round.

The miniature roar of the stream was the only sound to be heard, and when at length she glanced downwards there was no sign anywhere of the ghastly spectacle she had just witnessed. She saw the rock behind which she had knelt, and again a violent fit of shuddering assailed her. What did that rock conceal?

Nevertheless she presently took courage to rise, looking about her furtively, half afraid that Nick might pop up at any moment to detain her. For she felt that she could not stay longer in that place, whatever he might say or do. The one idea that possessed her was to get away from him, to escape from his horrible presence, whither she neither knew nor cared. If he appeared to stop her then, she thought that she would go raving mad.

But she saw nothing of him as she stood there, and with deep relief she began to creep away. Half a dozen yards she covered, and then stood suddenly still with her heart in her throat. There, immediately in front of her, flung prone upon the ground with his face on his arms, was Nick. He did not move at her coming, did not seem to hear. And the thought came to her to avoid him by a circuit, and yet escape. But something – a queer, indefinable something – made her pause. Why was he lying there? Had he been hurt in that awful struggle? Was he – was he unconscious? Was he – dead?

She fought back the impulse to fly, not for its unworthiness, but because she felt that she must know.

Trembling, she moved a little nearer to the prostrate, motionless figure.

'Nick?' she whispered under her breath.

He made no sign.

Her doubt turned to sudden, overmastering fear that pricked her forward in spite of herself.

'Nick!' she said again, and finding herself close to him she bent and very slightly touched his shoulder.

He moved then, and she almost gasped with relief. He turned his head sharply without raising himself, and she saw the grim lines of his lean cheek and jaw.

'That you, Muriel?' he said, speaking haltingly, spasmodically. 'I'm awfully sorry. Fact is – I'm not well. I shall be – better – directly. Go back, won't you?'

He broke off, and lay silent, his hands clenched as if he were in pain.

Muriel stood looking down at him in consternation. It was her chance to escape – a chance that might never occur again – but she had no further thought of taking it.

'What is it?' she asked him timidly. 'Can I – do anything?'

And then she suddenly saw what was the matter. It burst upon her – a startling revelation. Possibly the sight of those skeleton fists helped her to enlightenment She turned swiftly and sped back to their camping ground.

In thirty seconds or less, she was back again and stooping over him with a piece of brown bread in her hand.

'Eat this,' she ordered, in a tone of authority.

Nick's face was hidden again. He seemed to be fighting with himself. His voice came at length muffled and indistinct.

'No, no! Take it away! I'll have a drain of brandy. And I've got some tobacco left.'

Muriel stooped lower. She caught the words though they were scarcely audible. She laid her hand upon his arm, stronger in the moment's emergency than she had been since leaving the fort.

'You are to eat it,' she said very decidedly. 'You shall eat it. Do you hear, Nick? I know what is the matter with you. You are starving. I ought to have seen it before.'

Nick uttered a shaky laugh, and dragged himself up on to his elbows. 'I'm not starving,' he declared. 'Take it away, Muriel. Do you think I'm going to eat your luncheon, tea, and dinner, and to-morrow's breakfast as well?'

'You are going to eat this,' she answered.

He flashed her a glance of keen curiosity. 'Am I?' he said.

'You must,' she said, speaking with an odd vehemence which later surprised herself. 'Why should you go out of your way to tell me a lie ? Do you think I can't see?'

Nick raised himself slowly. Something in the situation seemed to have deprived him of his usual readiness. But he would not take the bread, would not even look at it.

'I'm better now,' he said. 'We'll go back.'

Muriel stood for a second irresolute, then sharply turned her back. Nick sat and watched her in silence. Suddenly she wheeled. 'There?' she said. 'I've divided it. You will eat this at least. It's absurd of you to starve yourself. You might as well have stayed in the fort to do that.'

This was unanswerable. Nick took the bread without further protest. He began to eat, marvelling at his own docility; and abruptly he knew that he was ravenous.

There was very little left when at length he looked up.

'Show me what you have saved for yourself,' he said.

But Muriel backed away with a short, hysterical laugh.

He started to his feet and took her rudely by the shoulder. 'Do you mean to say – ' he began, almost with violence; and then checked himself, peering at her with fierce, uncertain eyes.

She drew away from him, all her fears returning upon her in a flood; but at her movement he set her free and turned his back.

'Heaven knows what you did it for,' he said, seeming to control his voice with some difficulty. 'It wasn't for your own sake, and I won't presume to think it was for mine. But when the time comes for handing round rewards, may it be remembered that your offering was something more substantial than a cup of cold water.'

He broke off with a queer sound in the throat, and began to move away.

But Muriel followed him, an unaccountable sense of responsibility overcoming her reluctance.

'Nick?' she said.

He stood still without turning. She had a feeling that he was putting strong restraint upon himself. With an effort she forced herself to continue.

'You want sleep, I know. Will you – will you lie down while I watch?'

He shook his head without looking at her.

'But I wish it,' she persisted. 'I can wake you if – anything happens.'

'You wouldn't dare,' said Nick.

'I suppose that means you are afraid to trust me,' she said.

He turned at that. 'It means nothing of the sort. But you've had one scare, and you may have another. I think myself that that fellow was a scout on the look out for Bassett's advance guard. But Heaven only knows what brought him to this place, and there may be others. That's why I didn't dare to shoot.'

He paused, his light eyebrows raised, surveying her questioningly; for Muriel had suddenly covered her face with both hands. But in another moment she looked up again, and spoke with an effort.

'Your being awake couldn't lessen the danger. Won't you – please – be reasonable about it? I am doing my best.'

There was a deep note of appeal in her voice, and abruptly Nick gave in.

He moved back to their resting-place without another

word, and flung himself face downwards beside the nest of fern that he had made for her, lying stretched at full length like a log.

She had not expected so sudden and complete a surrender. It took her unawares, and she stood looking down at him, uncertain how to proceed.

But after a few seconds he turned his head towards her and spoke.

'You'll stay by me, Muriel?'

'Of course,' she answered, that unwonted sense of responsibility still strongly urging her.

He murmured something unintelligible, and stirred uneasily. She knew in a flash what he wanted, but a sick sense of dread held her back. She felt during the silence that followed as though he were pleading with her, urging her, even entreating her. Yet still she resisted, standing near him indeed, but with a desperate reluctance at her heart, a shrinking unutterable from the bare thought of any closer proximity to him that was as the instinctive recoil of purity from a thing unclean.

The horror of his deed had returned upon her overwhelmingly with his brief reference to it. His lack of emotion seemed to her a hideous callousness, more horrible than the deed itself. His physical exhaustion had called her out of herself, but the reaction was doubly terrible.

Nick said no more. He lay quite motionless, hardly seeming to breathe, and she realized that there was no repose in his attitude. He was not even trying to rest.

She wrung her hands together. It could not go on, this tension. Either she must yield to his unspoken desire, or he would sit up and cry off the bargain. And she knew that sleep was a necessity to him. Common-sense told her that he was totally unfit for further hardship without it.

She closed her eyes a moment, summoning all her strength for the greatest sacrifice she had ever made. And then in silence she sat down beside him, within reach of his hand.

He uttered a great sigh, and suffered his whole body to relax. And she knew by the action, though he did not speak a word, that she had set his mind at rest.

Scarcely a minute later, his quiet breathing told her that he slept, but she sat on by his side without moving during the long empty hours of her vigil. He had trusted her without a question, and, as her father's daughter, she would at whatever cost prove herself worthy of his trust.

Chapter 7

Through a great part of the night that followed they tramped steadily southward. The stars were Nick's guide, though as time passed he began to make his way with the confidence of one well acquainted with his surroundings. The instinct of locality was a sixth sense with him. Hand in hand, over rocky ground, through deep ravines, by steep and difficult tracks, they made their desperate way. Sometimes in the distance dim figures moved mysteriously, revealed by starlight, but none questioned or molested them. They passed from rock to rock through the heart of the enemy's country, unrecognized, unobserved. There were times when Nick grasped his revolver under his disguise, ready, ready at a moment's notice, to keep his word to the girl's father, should detection be their portion; but each time as the danger passed them by he tightened his hold upon her, drawing her forward with greater assurance.

They scarcely spoke throughout the long, long march. Muriel had moved at first with a certain elasticity, thankful to escape at last from the horrors of their resting-place. But very soon a great weariness came upon her. She was physically unfit for any prolonged exertion. The long strain of the siege had weakened her more than she knew.

Nevertheless she kept on bravely, uttering no complaint, urged to utmost effort by the instinctive desire to escape. It was this one idea that occupied all her thoughts during that night. She shrank with a vivid horror from looking back. And she could not see into the dim blank future. It was mercifully screened from her sight.

At her third heavy stumble, Nick stopped, and made her swallow some raw brandy from his flask. This buoyed her up for a while, but it was evident to them both that her strength was fast failing. And presently, he stopped again, and without a word lifted her in his arms. She gasped a protest to which he made no response. His arms compassed her like steel, making her feel helpless as an infant. He was limping himself, she noticed; yet he bore her strongly, without faltering, sure-footed as a mountain goat over the broken ground, till he found at length what he deemed a safe halting-place in a clump of stunted trees.

The sunrise revealed a native village standing among rice and cotton fields in the valley below them.

'I shall have to go foraging,' Nick said.

But Muriel's nerves that had been tottering on the verge of collapse for some time here broke down completely. She clung to him hysterically and entreated him not to leave her.

'I can't bear it! I can't bear it!' she kept reiterating. 'If you go, I must go to. I can't – I can't stay here alone.'

He gave way instantly, seeing that she was in a state of mind that bordered upon distraction, and that he could not safely leave her. He sat down beside her therefore, making her as comfortable as he could; and she presently slept with her head upon his shoulder. It was but a broken slumber however, and she awoke from it crying wildly that a man was being murdered – murdered – murdered – and imploring him with agonized tears to intervene.

He quieted her with a steady insistence that gained its end, though she crouched against him sobbing for some time after. As the sun rose higher her fever increased, but she remained conscious and suffering intensely all through the heat of the day. Then, as the evening drew on, she slipped into a heavy stupor.

It was the opportunity Nick had awaited for hours, and he seized it. Laying her back in the deep shadow of a boulder, he went swiftly down into the valley. The last light was passing as he strode through the village, a gaunt, silent figure in a hillman's dress, a native dagger in his girdle. Save that he had pulled the *chuddah* well over his face, he attempted no concealment.

He glided by a ring of old men seated about a fire, moving like a shadow through the glare. They turned to view him, but he had already passed with the tread of a wolf, and the mud wall of one of the cottages hid him from sight.

Into this hut he dived as though some instinct guided him. He paid no heed to a woman on a string-bedstead with a baby at her breast, who chattered shrilly at his entrance. Preparations for a meal were in progress, and he scarcely paused before he lighted upon what he sought. A small earthen pitcher stood on the mud floor. He swooped upon it, caught it up, splashing milk in all directions, clapped his hand yellow and claw-like upon the mouth, and was gone.

There arose a certain hue and cry behind him, but he was swiftly beyond detection, a fleeing shadow up the hill-side. And the baffled villagers returning found comfort in the reflection that he was doubtless a holy man and that his brief visit would surely entail a blessing.

By the time they arrived at this conclusion, Nick was kneeling by the girl's side, supporting her while she drank. The nourishment revived her. She came to herself, and thanked him.

'You will have some too,' said she anxiously.

And Nick drank also with a laugh and a joke to cloak his eagerness. That draught of milk was more to him at that moment than the choicest wine of the gods.

He sat down beside her again when he had thus refreshed himself. He thought that she was drowsy and was surprised when presently she laid a trembling hand upon his arm.

He bent over her quickly. 'What is it? Anything I can do?'

She did not shrink from him any longer. He could but dimly see her face in the strong shadow cast by the moonlight behind the trees.

'I want just to tell you, Nick,' she said faintly, 'that you will have to go on without me when the moon sets. You needn't mind about leaving me any more. I shall be dead before the morning comes. I'm not afraid. I think I'm rather glad. I am so very, very tired.'

Her weak voice failed.

Nick was stooping low over her. He did not speak at once. He only took the nerveless hand that lay upon his arm and carried it to his lips, breathing for many seconds upon the cold fingers.

When at length he spoke, his tone was infinitely gentle, but it possessed notwithstanding a certain quality of arresting force.

'My dear,' he said, 'you belong to me now, you know. You have been given into my charge, and I am not going to part with you.'

She did not resist him or attempt to withdraw her hand, but her silence was scarcely the silence of acquiescence. When she spoke again after a long pause, there was a piteous break in her voice.

'Why don't you let me die? I want to die. Why do you hold me back?'

'Why?' said Nick swiftly. 'Do you really want me to tell you why?'

But there he checked himself with a sharp, indrawn breath. The next instant he laid her hand gently down.

'You will know some day, Muriel,' he said. 'But for the present you will have to take my reason on trust. I assure you it is a very good one.'

The restraint of his words was marked by a curious vehemence, but this she was too ill at the time to heed. She turned her face away almost fretfully.

'Why should I live?' she moaned. 'There is no one wants me now.'

'That will never be true while I live,' Nick answered steadily, and his tone was the tone of a man who registers a vow.

But again she did not heed him. She had suffered too acutely and too recently to be comforted by promises. Moreover, she did not want consolation. She wanted only to shut her eyes and die. In her weakness she had not fancied that he could deny her this.

And so when presently he roused her by lifting her to resume the journey, she shed piteous tears upon his shoulder, imploring him to leave her where she was. He would not listen to her. He knew that it was highly dangerous to rest so close to habitation, and he would not risk another day in such precarious shelter.

So for hours he carried her with a strength almost super-human, forcing his physical powers into subjection to his will. Though limping badly, he covered several miles of wild and broken country, deserted for the most part, almost incredibly lonely, till towards sunrise he found a resting-place in a hollow high up the side of a mountain, overlooking a winding, desolate pass.

Muriel was either sleeping or sunk in the stupor of exhaustion. There was some brandy left in his flask, and he made her take a little. But it scarcely roused her, and she was too weak to notice that he did not touch any himself.

All through the scorching day that followed, she dozed and woke in feverish unrest, sometimes rambling incoherently till he brought her gravely back, sometimes crying weakly, sometimes making feeble efforts to pray.

All through the long, burning hours he never stirred away from her. He sat close to her, often holding her in his arms, for she seemed less restless so; and perpetually he gazed out with terrible, bloodshot eyes over the savage mountains, through the long, irregular line of pass, watching eagle-like, tireless and intent, for the deliverance which, if it came at all, must come that way. His face was yellow and sunken, lined in a thousand wrinkles like the face of a monkey; but his eyes remained marvellously bright. They looked as if they had not slept for years, as if they would never sleep again. He was at the end of his resources and he knew it, yet he would watch to the very end. He would die watching.

As the sun sank in a splendour that transfigured the eternally white mountain-crest to a mighty shimmer of rose and gold he turned at last and looked down at the white face pillowed upon his arm. The eyes were closed. The ineffable peace of Death seemed to dwell upon the quiet features. She had lain so for a long time, and he had fancied her sleeping.

He caught his breath, feeling for his flask, and for the first time his hands shook uncontrollably. But as the raw spirit touched her lips, he saw her eyelids quiver, and a great gasp of relief went through him. As she opened her eyes he stayed his hand. It seemed cruel to bring her back. But the suffering and the half-instinctive look of horror passed from them like a shadow as they rested upon him. There was even the very faint flicker of a smile about them.

She turned her face slightly towards him with the gesture of a child nestling against his breast. Yet though she lay thus in his arms, he felt keenly, bitterly, that she was very far away from him.

He hung over her, still holding himself in with desperate strength, not daring to speak lest he should disturb the holy peace that seemed to be drawing all about her.

The sunset glory deepened. For a few seconds the crags above them glittered golden as the peaks of Paradise. And in the wonderful silence Muriel spoke.

'Do you see them?' she said.

He saw that her eyes were turned upon the shining mountains. There was a strange light on her face.

'See what, darling' he asked her softly.

Her eyes came back to him for a moment. They had a thoughtful, wondering look.

'How strange!' she said slowly. 'I thought it was – an eagle.'

The detachment of her tone cut him to the heart. And suddenly the pain of it was more than he could bear.

'It is I – Nick,' he told her, with urgent emphasis. 'Surely you know me!'

But her eyes had passed beyond him again. 'Nick?' she questioned to herself. 'Nick? But this – this was an eagle.'

She was drawing away from him, and he could not hold her, could not even hope to follow her whither she went. A great sob broke from him, and in a moment, like the rush of an overwhelming flood from behind gates long closed, the anguish of the man burst its bonds.

'Muriel!' he cried passionately. 'Muriel! Stay with me, look at me, love me! There is nothing in the mountains to draw you. It is here – here beside you, touching you, holding you. O God,' he prayed, brokenly, 'she doesn't understand me. Let her understand – open her eyes – make her see!'

His agony reached her, touched her, for a moment held her. She turned her eyes back to his tortured face.

'But, Nick,' she said softly, 'I can see.'

He bent lower. 'Yes?' he said, in a choked voice. 'Yes?'

She regarded him with a faint wonder. Her eyes were growing heavy, as the eyes of a tired child. She raised one hand and pointed vaguely.

'Over there,' she said wearily. 'Can't you see them? Then perhaps it was a dream, or even – perhaps – a vision. Don't you remember how it went? "And behold – the mountain – was full – of horses – and chariots – of – fire!" God sent them, you know.'

The tired voice ceased. Her head sank lower upon Nick's breast. She gave a little quivering sigh, and seemed to sleep.

And Nick turned his tortured eyes upon the pass below him, and stared downwards spellbound.

Was he dreaming also? Or was it perchance a vision – the trick of his fevered fancy? There, at his feet, not fifty yards from where he sat, he beheld men, horses, guns, winding along in a narrow, unbroken line as far as he could see.

A great surging filled his ears, and through it he heard himself shout, once, twice, and yet a third time to the phantom army below.

The surging swelled in his brain to a terrific tumult – a confusion indescribable. And then something seemed to crack inside his head. The dark peaks swayed giddily against the darkening sky, and toppled inwards without sound.

The last thing he knew was the call of a bugle tense and shrill as the buzz of a mosquito close to his ear. And he laughed aloud to think how so small a thing had managed to deceive him.

Part II

Chapter 8

The jingling notes of a piano playing an air from a comic opera floated cheerily forth into the magic silence of the Simla pines, and abruptly, almost spasmodically, a cracked voice began to sing. It was a sentimental ditty treated jocosely, and its frivolity rippled out into the midday silence with something of the effect of a monkey's chatter. The *khitmutgar* on the verandah would have looked scandalized or at best contemptuous had it not been his role to express nothing but the dignified humility of the native servant. He was waiting for his mistress to come out of the nursery where her voice could be heard talking imperiously to her baby's *ayah*. He had already waited some minutes, and he would probably have waited much longer, for his patience was inexhaustible, had it not been for that sudden irresponsible and wholly tuneless burst of song. But the second line was scarcely ended before she came hurriedly forth, nearly running into his stately person in her haste.

'Oh, dear, Sammy!' she exclaimed with some annoyance. 'Why didn't you tell me Captain Ratcliffe was here?'

She hastened past him along the verandah with the words, not troubling about his explanation, and entered the room whence the music proceeded at a run.

'My dear Nick,' she cried impulsively, 'I had no idea!'

The music ceased in a jangle of wrong notes, and Nick sprang to his feet, his yellow face wearing a grin of irrepressible gaiety.

'So I gathered, O elect lady,' he rejoined, seizing her outstretched hand and kissing first one and then the other. 'And I took the first method that presented itself of making myself known. So they beguiled you to Simla after all?'

'Yes, I had to come for my baby's sake. They thought at first it would have to be Home and no compromise. I'm longing to show him to you, Nick. Only six months and such a pet already! But tell me about yourself. I am sure you have come off the sick list too soon. You look as if you had come straight from a lengthy stay with the *bandar-log*.'

'*Tu quoque!*' laughed Nick. 'And with far less excuse. Only you manage to look charming notwithstanding, which is beyond me. Do you know, Mrs. Musgrave, you don't do justice to the compromise? I should be furious with you if I were Will.'

Mrs. Musgrave frowned at him. She was a very pretty woman, possessing a dainty and not wholly unconscious charm. 'Tell me about yourself, Nick,' she commanded. 'And don't be ridiculous. You can't possibly judge impartially on that head, as you haven't the smallest idea as to how ill I have been. I am having a rest cure now, you must know, and I don't go anywhere; or I should have come to see you in hospital.'

'Good thing you didn't take the trouble,' said Nick. 'I've been sleeping for the last three weeks, and I am only just awake.'

Mrs. Musgrave looked at him with a very friendly smile. 'Poor Nick!' she said. 'And Wara was relieved after all.'

He jerked up his shoulders. 'After a fashion. Grange was the only white man left, and he hadn't touched food for three days. If Muriel Roscoe had stayed, she would have been dead before Bassett got anywhere near them. There are times when the very act of suffering actively keeps people alive. It was that with her.'

He spoke briefly, almost harshly, and immediately turned from the subject. 'I suppose you were very anxious about your cousin?'

'Poor Blake Grange? Of course I was. But I was anxious – horribly anxious – about you all.' There was a quiver of deep feeling in Mrs. Musgrave's voice.

'Thank you,' said Nick. He reached out a skeleton finger and laid it on her arm. 'I thought you would be feeling soft-hearted, so I have come to ask you a favour. Not that I shouldn't have come in any case, but it seemed a suitable moment to choose.'

Mrs. Musgrave laughed a little. 'Have you ever found me anything but kind?' she questioned.

'Never,' said Nick. 'You're the best pal I ever had, which is the exact reason for my coming here today. Mrs. Musgrave, I want you to be awfully good to Muriel Roscoe. She needs someone to help her along just now.'

Mrs. Musgrave opened her eyes wide, but she said nothing at once, for Nick had sprung to his feet and was restlessly pacing the room.

'Come back, Nick,' she said at last. 'Tell me a little about her. We have never met, you know. And why do you ask this of me when she is in Lady Bassett's care?'

'Lady Bassett!' said Nick. He made a hideous grimace, and said no more.

Mrs. Musgrave laughed. 'How eloquent! Do you hate her too, then? I thought all men worshipped at that shrine.'

Nick came back and sat down. 'I nearly killed her once,' he said.

'What a pity you didn't quite!' ejaculated Mrs. Musgrave.

Nick grinned. 'Sits the wind in that quarter? I wonder why.'

'Oh, I hate her by instinct,' declared Mrs. Musgrave recklessly, 'though her scented notes to me always begin, "Dearest Daisy"! She always disapproved of me openly till baby came. But she has found another niche for me now. I am not supposed to be so fascinating as I was. She prefers unattractive women.'

'Gracious heaven!' interjected Nick.

'Yes, you may laugh. I do myself.' Daisy Musgrave spoke almost fiercely notwithstanding. 'She's years older than I am anyhow, and I shall score some day if I don't now. Have you ever watched her dance? There's a sort of snaky, coiling movement runs up her whole body. Goodness!' breaking off abruptly. 'I'm getting venomous myself. I had better stop before I frighten you away.'

'Oh, don't mind me!' laughed Nick. 'No one knows better than I that she is made to twist all ways. She hates me as a cobra hates a mongoose.'

'Really?' Daisy Musgrave was keenly interested. 'But why?'

He shook his head. 'You had better ask Lady Bassett. It may be because I had the misfortune to set fire to her once. It is true I extinguished her afterwards, but I don't think she enjoyed it. It was a humiliating process. Besides, it spoilt her dress.'

'But she is always so gracious to you,' protested Daisy.

'Honey-sweet. That's exactly how I know her cobra feelings. And that brings me round to Muriel Roscoe again, and the favour I have to ask.'

Daisy shot him a sudden shrewd glance. 'Do you want to marry her?' she asked him point blank.

Nick's colourless eyebrows went up till they nearly met his colourless hair. 'Dearest Daisy,' he said, 'you are a genius. I mean to do that very thing.'

Daisy got up and softly closed the window. 'Surely she is very young,' she said. 'Is she in love with you?'

She did not turn at the sound of his laugh. She had almost expected it. For she knew Nick Ratcliffe as very few knew him. The bond of sympathy between them was very strong.

'Can you imagine any girl falling in love with me?' he asked.

'Of course I can. You are not so unique as that. There isn't a man in the universe that some woman couldn't be fool enough to love.'

'Many thanks!' said Nick. 'Then – I may count upon your support, may I? I know Lady Bassett will put a spoke in my wheel if she can. But I have Sir Reginald's consent. He is Muriel's guardian, you know. Also, I had her father's approval in the first place. It has got to be soon, you see, Daisy. The present state of affairs is unbearable. She will be miserable with Lady Bassett.'

Daisy still stood with her back to him. She was fidgeting with the blind-cord. her pretty face very serious.

'I am not sure,' she said slowly, 'that it lies in my power to help you. O course I am willing to do my best, because, as you say, we are pals. But, Nick, she is very young. And if – if she really doesn't love you, you mustn't ask me to persuade her.'

Nick sprang up impulsively. 'Oh, but you don't understand,' he said quickly. 'She would be happy enough with me. I would see to that. I – I would be awfully good to her, Daisy.'

She turned swiftly at the unwonted quiver in his voice. 'My dear Nick,' she said earnestly, 'I am sure of it. You could make any woman who loved you happy. But no one – no one – knows the misery that may result from a marriage without love on both sides – except those who have made one.'

There was something almost passionate in her utterance. But she turned it off quickly with a smile and a friendly hand upon his arm.

'Come,' she said lightly. 'I want to show you my boy. I left him almost in tears. But he always smiles when he sees his mother.'

'Who doesn't?' said Nick gallantly, following her lead.

Chapter 9

The aromatic scent of the Simla pines literally encircled and
pervaded the Bassetts' bungalow, penetrating to every corner.
Lady Bassett was wont to pronounce it 'distractingly sweet,'
when her visitors drew her attention to the fact. Hers was
among the daintiest as well as the best situated bungalows in
Simla, and she was pleasantly aware of a certain envy on the
part of her many acquaintances which added a decided relish
to the flavour of her own appreciation. But notwithstanding
this, she was hardly ever to be found at home except by
appointment. Her social engagements were so numerous that,
as she often pathetically remarked, she scarcely ever enjoyed
the luxury of solitude. As a hostess she was indefatigable, and
being an excellent bridge player as well as a superb dancer,
it was not surprising that she occupied a fairly prominent
position in her own select circle. In appearance she was
a woman of about five-and-thirty, though the malicious
added a full dozen years more to her credit, with fair hair, a
peculiarly soft voice, and a smile that was slightly twisted. She
was always exquisitely dressed, always cool, always gentle,
never hasty in word or deed. If she ever had reason to rebuke
or snub, it was invariably done with the utmost composure,
but with deadly effect upon the offender. Lady Bassett was
generally acknowledged to be unanswerable at such times by
all but the very few who did not fear her.

There were not many who really felt at ease with her, and
Muriel Roscoe was emphatically not one of the number. Her
father had nominated Sir Reginald her guardian, and Sir
Reginald, aware of this fact, had sent her at once to his wife
at Simla. The girl had been too ill at the time to take any
interest in her destination or ultimate disposal. It was true
that she had never liked Lady Bassett, that she had ever felt
shy and constrained in her presence, and that, had she been
consulted, she would probably have asked to be sent to
England. But Sir Reginald had been too absorbed in the task

before him to spend much thought upon his dead comrade's child at that juncture, and he had followed the simplest course that presented itself, allowing Nick Ratcliffe to retain the privilege which General Roscoe himself had bestowed. Thus Muriel had come at last into Lady Bassett's care, and she was only just awaking to the fact that it was by no means the guardianship she would have chosen for herself had she been in a position to choose. As the elasticity of her youth gradually asserted itself, and the life began to flow again in her veins, the power to suffer returned to her, and in the anguish of her awakening faculties she knew how utterly she was alone. It was in one sense a relief that Lady Bassett, being caught in the full swing of the Simla season, was unable to spare much of her society for the suddenly bereaved girl who had been thrust upon her. But there were times during that period of dragging convalescence when any presence would have been welcome.

She was no longer acutely ill, but a low fever hung about her, a species of physical inertia against which she had no strength to struggle. And often she wondered to herself with a dreary amazement, why she still lived, why she had survived the horrors of that flight through the mountains, why she had been thus, as it were, cast up upon a desert rock when all that had made life good in her eyes had been ruthlessly swept away. At such times there would come upon her a loneliness almost unthinkable, a shrinking more terrible than the fear of death, and the future would loom before her black as night, a blank and awful desert which she felt she could never dare to travel.

Sometimes in her dreams there would come to her other visions – visions of the gay world that throbbed so close to her, the world she had entered with her father so short a time before. She would hear again the hubbub of laughing voices, the music, the tramp of dancing feet. And she would start from her sleep to find only a great emptiness, a listening silence, an unspeakable desolation.

If she ever thought of Nick in those days, it was as a phantom that belonged to the nightmare that lay behind her. He had no part in her present, and the future she could not bring herself to contemplate. No one even mentioned his name to her till one day Lady Bassett entered her room before starting for a garden-party at Vice-Regal Lodge, a faint flush on her cheeks and her blue eyes rather brighter than usual.

'I have just received a note from Captain Ratcliffe, dear Muriel,' she said. 'I have already mentioned to him that you are too unwell to think of receiving anyone at present, but he announces his intention of paying you a visit notwithstanding. Perhaps you would like to write him a note yourself, and corroborate what I have said.'

'Captain Ratcliffe!' Muriel echoed blankly, as though the name conveyed nothing to her; and then with a great start as the blood rushed to her white cheeks, 'Oh, you mean Nick. I – I had almost forgotten his other name. Does he want to see me? Is he in Simla still?'

She turned her hot face away with a touch of petulance from the peculiar look with which Lady Bassett was regarding her. What did she mean by looking at her so, she wondered irritably?

There followed a pause, and Lady Bassett began to fasten her many-buttoned gloves.

'Of course, dear,' she said gently at length, 'there is not the smallest necessity for you to see him. Indeed if my advice were asked, I should recommend you not to do so; for after such a terrible experience as yours, one cannot be too circumspect. It is so perilously easy for rumours to get about. I will readily transmit a message for you if you desire it, though I think on the whole it would be more satisfactory if you were to write him a line yourself to say that you cannot receive him.'

'Why?' demanded Muriel, with sudden unexpected energy. She turned back again, and looked at Lady Bassett with a quick gleam that was almost a challenge in her eyes. 'Why should I not see him? After all, I suppose I ought to thank him. Besides – besides – Why should I not?'

She could not have said what moved her to this unwonted self-assertion. Had Lady Bassett required her to see Nick she would probably have refused to do so, and listlessly dismissed the matter from her mind. But there was that in Lady Bassett's manner which aroused her antagonism almost instinctively. But vaguely understanding, she yet resented the soft-spoken words. Moreover, a certain perversity, born of her weakness, urged her. What right had Lady Bassett to deny her to anyone?

'When is he coming?' she asked. 'I will see him when he comes.'

Lady Bassett yielded the point at once with the faintest possible shrug. 'As you wish, dear child, of course; but I do beg of you to be prudent. He speaks of coming this afternoon. But would you not like him to postpone his visit till I can be with you?'

'No, I don't think so,' Muriel said, with absolute simplicity.

'Ah, well!' Lady Bassett spoke in the tone of one repudiating all responsibility. She bent over the girl with a slightly wry smile, and kissed her forehead. 'Good-bye, dearest! I shouldn't encourage him to stay long if I were you. And I think you would be wise to call him Captain Ratcliffe now that you are living a civilized life once more.'

Muriel turned her face aside with a species of bored patience that could scarcely be termed tolerance. She did not understand these veiled warnings, and she cared too little for Lady Bassett and her opinions to trouble herself about them. She had never liked her, though she knew that her father had conscientiously tried to do so for the sake of his friend, Sir Reginald.

As Lady Bassett went away she rubbed the place on her forehead which her cold lips had touched. 'If she only knew how I hate being kissed!' she murmured to herself.

And then with an effort she rose and moved wearily across the room to ring the bell. Since by some unaccountable impulse she had decided to see Nick, it might be advisable, she reflected, to give her own orders regarding his visit.

Having done so, she lay down again. But she did not sleep. Sleep was an elusive spirit in those days. It sometimes seemed to her that she was too worn out mentally and physically ever to rest naturally again.

Nearly an hour passed away while she lay almost unconsciously listening. And then suddenly, with a sense of having experienced it all long before, there came to her the sound of careless footsteps and of a voice that hummed.

It went through her heart like a sword-thrust as she called to mind that last night at Fort Wara when she had clung to her father for the last time, and had heard him bid her good-bye – until they should meet again.

With a choked sensation she rose, and stood steadying herself by the back of the sofa. Could she go through this interview? Could she bear it? Her heart was beating in heavy, sickening throbs. For an instant she almost thought of escaping and sending word that she was not equal to seeing anyone, as Lady Bassett had already intimated. But even as the impulse flashed through her brain, she realized that it was too late. The shadow of the native servant had already darkened the window, and she knew that Nick was just behind him on the verandah. With a great, sobbing gasp, she turned herself to meet him.

Chapter 10

He came in as lightly and unceremoniously as though they had parted but the day before, a smile of greeting upon his humorous, yellow face, words of careless good-fellowship upon his lips.

He took her hand for an instant, and she felt rather than

saw that he gave her a single, scrutinizing glance from under eyelids that flickered incessantly.

'I see you are better,' he said, 'so I won't put you to the trouble of saying so. I suppose dear Lady Bassett has gone to the Vice-Regal garden-party. But it's all right. I told her I was coming. Did you have to persuade her very hard to let you see me?'

Muriel stiffened a little at this inquiry. Her agitation was rapidly subsiding. It left her vaguely chilled, even disappointed. She had forgotten how cheerily inconsequent Nick could be.

'I didn't persuade her at all,' she said coldly. 'I simply told her that I should see you in order – '

'Yes?' queried Nick, looking delighted. 'In order – '

To her annoyance she felt herself flushing. With a gesture of weariness she dismissed the sentence and sat down. She had meant to make him a brief and gracious speech of gratitude for his past care of her, but somehow it stuck in her throat. Besides, it was quite obvious that he did not expect it.

He came and sat down beside her on the sofa. 'Let's talk things over,' he said. 'You are out of the doctor's hands, I'm told.'

Muriel was leaning back against the cushions. She did not raise her heavy eyes to answer. 'Oh, yes, ever so long ago. I'm quite well, only rather tired still.'

She frowned slightly as she gave this explanation. Though his face was not turned in her direction, she had a feeling that he was still closely observant of her.

He nodded to himself twice while he listened, and then suddenly he reached out and laid his hand upon both of hers as they rested in her lap. 'I'm awfully pleased to hear you are quite well,' he said, in a voice that seemed to crack on a note of laughter. 'It makes my business all the easier. I've come to ask you, dear, how soon you can possibly make it convenient to marry me. To-day? To-morrow? Next week?

I don't of course want to hurry you unduly, but there doesn't seem to be anything to wait for. And – personally – I abhor waiting. Don't you?'

He turned towards her with the last words. He had spoken very gently, but there seemed to be an element of humour in all that he said.

Muriel's eyes were wide open by the time he ended. She was staring at him in blank astonishment. The flush on her face had deepened to crimson.

'Marry you?' she gasped at length, stammering in her confusion. 'I? Why – why – whatever made you dream of such a thing?'

'I'll tell you,' said Nick instantly, and quite undismayed. 'I dreamed that a certain friend of mine was lonely and heart-sick and sad. And she wanted – horribly – someone to come and take care of her, to cheer her up, to lift her over the bad places, to give her things which, if they couldn't compensate for all she had lost, would be anyhow a bit of a comfort to her. And then I remembered how she belonged to me, how she had been given to me by her own father to cherish and care for. And so I plucked up courage to intrude upon her while she was still wallowing in her Slough of Despair. And I didn't pester her with preliminaries. We're past that stage, you and I, Muriel. I simply came to her because it seemed absurd to wait any longer. And I just asked her humble-like to fix a day when we would get up very early, and bribe the padre and sweet Lady Bassett to do likewise, and have a short – very short service all to ourselves at church, and when it was over we would just say good-bye to all kind friends and depart. Won't you give the matter your serious consideration? Believe me, it is worth it.'

He still held her hand closely in his while he poured out his rapid explanation, and his eyebrows worked up and down so swiftly that Muriel was fascinated by them. His eyes baffled her completely. They were like a glancing flame. She listened to his proposal with more of bewilderment than consternation.

It took her breath away without exactly frightening her. The steady grasp of his hand and the exceedingly practical tones of his voice kept her from unreasoning panic; but she was too greatly astounded to respond very promptly.

'Tell me what you think about it,' he said gently.

But she was utterly at a loss to describe her feelings. She shook her head and was silent.

After a little he went on, still quickly but with less impetuosity. 'It isn't just a sudden fancy of mine – this. Don't think it. There's nothing capricious about me. Your father knew about it. And because he knew, he put you in my care. It was his sole reason for trusting you to me. I had his full approval.'

He paused, for her fingers had closed suddenly within his own. She was looking at him no longer. Her memory had flashed back to that last terrible night of her father's life. Again she heard him telling her of the one man to whom he had entrusted her, who would make it his sole business to save her, who would protect her life with his own, heard his speculative question as to whether she knew whom he meant, recalled her own quick reply, and his answer – and his answer.

With a sudden sense of suffocation, she freed her hand and rose. Once more her old aversion to this man swept over her in a nauseating wave. Once more there rose before her eyes the dread vision which for many, many nights had haunted her persistently, depriving her of all rest, all peace of mind – the vision of a man in his death-struggle, fighting, agonizing, under those merciless fingers.

It was more than she could bear. She covered her eyes, striving to shut out the sight that tortured her weary brain. 'Oh, I don't know if I can!' she almost wailed. 'I don't know if I can!'

Nick did not move. And yet it seemed to her in those moments of reawakened horror as if by some magnetic force he still held her fast. She strove against it with all her frenzied strength, but it eluded her, baffled her – conquered her.

When he spoke at length, she turned and listened, lacking the motive-power to resist.

'There is nothing to frighten you, anyhow,' he said, and the tone in which he said it was infinitely comforting, infinitely reassuring. 'I only want to take care of you; for you're a lonely little soul, not old enough or wise enough to look after yourself. And I'll be awfully good to you, Muriel, if you'll have me.'

Something in those last words – a hint of pleading, of coaxing even – found its way to her heart as it were against her will. Moreover, what he said was true. She was lonely; miserably, unspeakably lonely. All her world was in ashes around her, and there were times when its desolation positively appalled her.

But still she stood irresolute. Could she, dared she, take this step? What if that phantom of horror pursued her relentlessly to the day of her death? Would she not come in time to shrink with positive loathing from this man whose offer of help she now felt so strangely tempted in her utter friendlessness to accept?

It was impossible to answer these tormenting questions satisfactorily. But there was nothing – so she told herself – to be gained by waiting. She had no one to advise her, no one really to mind what happened to her, with the single exception of this friend of hers who only wanted to take care of her. And after all, since misery was to be her portion, what did it matter? Why should she refuse to listen to him? Had he not shown her already that he could be kind?

A sudden warmth of gratitude towards him stirred in her heart – a tiny flame springing up among the ashes of her youth. Her horror sank away like an evil dream.

She turned round with a certain deliberation that had grown upon her of late and went back to Nick still seated on the sofa.

'I don't care much what I do now,' she said wearily. 'I will marry you, if you wish it, if – if you are quite sure you will never wish you hadn't.'

'Well done!' said Nick, with instant approval. 'That's settled then, for I was quite sure of that ages ago.'

He smiled at her quizzically, his face a mask of banter. Of what his actual feelings were at that moment she had not the faintest idea.

With a piteous little smile in answer she laid her hand upon his knee. 'You will have to be very patient with me,' she said tremulously. 'For remember – I have come to the end of everything, and you are the only friend I have left.'

He took her hand into his own again, with a grasp that was warm and comforting. 'My dear,' he said very kindly, 'I shall always remember that you once told me so.'

Chapter 11

Muriel lay awake for hours that night, going over and over that interview with Nick till her tired brain reeled. She was not exactly frightened by this new element that had come into her life. The very fact of having something definite to look forward to was a relief after dwelling for so long in the sunless void of non-expectancy. But she was by no means sure that she welcomed so violent a disturbance at the actual heart of her darkened existence. She could not, moreover, wholly forget her fear of the man who had saved her by main force from the fate she would fain have shared with her father. His patience – his almost womanly gentleness – notwithstanding, she could not forget the demon of violence and bloodshed that she knew to be hidden away somewhere behind that smiling, yellow mask.

She marvelled at herself for her tame surrender, but she felt it to be irrevocable nevertheless. So broken was she by adversity, that she lacked the energy to resist him or even to desire to do so. She tried to comfort herself with the thought that she was carrying out her father's wishes for her; but this did not take her very far. She could not help the doubt arising as to whether he had ever really gauged Nick's exceedingly elusive character.

Tired out at last she slept, and dreamed that an eagle had caught her and was bearing her swiftly, swiftly, through wide spaces to his eyrie in the mountains.

It was a long, breathless flight fraught with excitement and a nameless exultation that pierced her like pain. She awoke from it with a cry that was more of disappointment than relief, and started up gasping to hear horses' hoofs dancing in the compound below her window to the sound of a cracked, hilarious voice.

She almost laughed as she realized what it was, and in a moment all her misgivings of the night vanished like wraiths of the darkness. He had extracted a promise from her to ride with him at dawn, and he meant to keep her to it. She got up and pulled aside the blind.

A wild view-halloa greeted her, and she dropped it again sharply; but not before she had seen Nick prancing about the drive on a giddy, long-limbed Waler, and making frantic signs to her to join him. Another horse with a side-saddle was waiting, held by a grinning little *saîce*. The sun was already rising rapidly behind the mountains. She began to race through her toilet at a speed that showed her to have caught some of the fever of her cavalier's impatience.

She wondered what Lady Bassett thought of the disturbance (Lady Bassett never rose early), and nearly laughed aloud.

Hastening out at length she found Nick dismounted and waiting for her by the verandah-steps. He sprang up to meet her with an eager whoop of greeting.

'Hope you enjoyed my serenade. Come along! There's no time to waste. Jakko turned red some minutes ago. Were you asleep?'

Muriel admitted the fact.

'And dreaming of me,' he rattled on, 'as was sweet and proper?'

She did not answer, and he laughed like a boy, rudely but not insolently.

'Didn't I know it? Jump up! We're going to have a glorious gallop. I've brought some slabs of chocolate to keep you from starvation. Ready? Heave ho! My dear girl, you're disgracefully light still. Why don't you eat more?'

'You're as thin as a herring yourself,' Muriel retorted, with a most unwonted flash of spirit.

He lifted his grinning face to her as she settled herself in the saddle, and then uncovering swiftly he bent and kissed the black cloth of her habit, humbly, reverently, as became a slave.

It sent a queer thrill through her, that kiss of his. She felt that it was in some fashion a revelation; but she was still too blinded by groping in dark places to understand its message. As they trotted side by side out of the compound, she knew her face was burning, and turned it aside that he might not see.

It was a wonderful morning. There was intoxication in the scent of the pines. The whole atmosphere seemed bewitched. They gave their horses the rein and raced with the wind through an enchanted world. It was the wildest, most alluring ride that she had ever known, and when Nick called a halt at last she protested with a flushed face and sparkling eyes.

Nevertheless it was good to sit and watch the rapid transformation that the sun-god was weaving all about them. She saw the spurs of Jakko fade from pink to purest amber, and then in the passage of a few seconds gleam silver in the flood of glory that topped the highest crests. And her heart fluttered oddly at the sight while again she thought of the eagle of her dream, cleaving the wide spaces, and bearing her also.

She glanced round for Nick, but he had wheeled his horse and was staring out towards the Plains. She wondered what was passing in his mind, for he sat like a statue, his face turned from her. And suddenly the dread loneliness of the mountains gripped her as with a chilly hand. It seemed as if they two were alone together in all the world.

She walked over to him. 'I'm cold, Nick,' she said, breaking in upon his silence almost apologetically. 'Shall we go?'

He stretched out a hand to her without turning his head, without speaking. But she would not put her own within it, for she was afraid.

After a long pause he gave a sudden sharp sigh, and pulled his horse round. 'Eh? Cold? We'll fly down to Annandale. There's plenty of time before us. By the way, I want to introduce you to a friend of mine, —Daisy Musgrave. Ever heard of her? She and Blake Grange are first cousins. You'll like Daisy. We are great chums, she and I.'

Muriel had heard of her from Captain Grange. She had also once upon a time met Daisy's husband.

'I liked him rather,' she said. 'But I thought he must be very young.'

'So he is,' said Nick. 'A mere infant. He's in the Civil Service, and works like an ox. Mrs. Musgrave is very delicate. She and the baby were packed off up here in a hurry. I believe she has a weak heart. She may have to go Home to recruit even now. She doesn't go out at all herself, but she hopes I will take you to see her. Will you come?'

Muriel hesitated for a moment. 'Nick,' she said, 'are you telling everybody – of our – engagement?'

'Of course,' said Nick instantly. 'Why not?'

She could not tell him, only she was vaguely dismayed.

'I told Lady Bassett yesterday evening,' he went on. 'Didn't she say anything to you?'

'Oh, yes. She kissed me and said she was very pleased.' Muriel's cheeks burned at the recollection.

'How nice of her!' commented Nick. He shot her a side-long glance. 'Dear Lady Bassett always says and does the right thing at the right moment. It's her speciality. That's why we are all so fond of her.'

Muriel made no response, though keenly aware of the subtlety of this speech. So Nick disliked her hostess also. She wondered why.

'You see,' he proceeded presently, 'it is as well to be quite open about it as we are going to be married so soon. Of course everyone realizes that it is to be a strictly private affair. You needn't be afraid of any demonstration.'

It was not that that had induced her feeling of dismay, but she could not tell him so.

'And Mrs. Musgrave knows?' she questioned.

'I told her first,' said Nick. 'But you mustn't mind her. She won't commit the fashionable blunder of congratulating you.'

Muriel laughed nervously. She longed to say something careless and change the subject, but she was feeling stiff and unnatural, and words failed her.

Nick brought his horse up close to hers.

'There's one thing I want to say to you, Muriel, before we go down,' he said.

'Oh, what?' She turned a scared face towards him.

'Nothing to alarm you,' said Nick, frowning at her quizzically. 'I wanted to say it some minutes ago, only I was shy. Look here, dear.' He held out to her a twist of tissue-paper on the palm of his hand. 'It's a ring I want you to wear for me. There's a message inside it. Read it when you are alone.'

Muriel looked at the tiny packet without taking it. She had turned very white. 'Oh, Nick,' she faltered at last, 'are you – are you – quite sure?'

'Quite sure of what?' questioned Nick. 'Your mind? Or my own?'

'Don't!' she begged tremulously. 'I can't laugh over this.'

'Laugh!' said Nick sharply. And then swiftly his whole manner changed. 'Yes, it's all right, dear,' he said, smiling at her. 'Take it, won't you? I am – quite – sure.'

She took it obediently, but her reluctance was still very manifest. Nick, however, did not appear to notice this.

'Don't look at it now,' he said. 'Wait till I'm not there. Put it away somewhere for the present, and let's have another gallop.'

She glanced at him as she slipped his gift into her pocket. 'Won't you let me thank you, Nick?' she asked shyly.

'Wait till you've seen it,' he returned. 'You may not think it worth it. Ready? One! Two! Three!'

In the scamper that followed, the blood surged back to her face, and her spirits rose again; but in her secret heart there yet remained a nameless dread that she was as powerless to define as to expel.

Chapter 12

Lady Bassett was still invisible when Muriel returned to the bungalow though breakfast was waiting for them on the verandah. She passed quickly through to her room and commenced hasty preparations for a bath. It had been a good ride, and she realized that though tired, she was also very hungry.

She slipped Nick's gift out of the pocket of her riding-habit, but she would not stop to open it then. That should come presently, when she had the whole garden to herself, and all the leisure of the long summer morning before her. She felt that in a sense she owed him that.

But a note that caught her eye lying on her table, she paused to open and hastily peruse. The writing was unfamiliar to her – a dashing, impetuous scrawl that excited her curiosity.

'DEAR MISS ROSCOE,' it ran,— 'Don't think me an unmitigated bore if you can help it. I am wondering if you would have the real kindness to waive ceremony and pay me a visit this afternoon. I shall be quite alone, unless my baby can be considered in the light of a social inducement. I know that Nick contemplates bringing you to see me, and so he shall, if you prefer it. But personally I consider that he would be decidedly *de trop*. I feel that we shall soon know each other so well, that a normal introduction seems superfluous. Let me know your opinion by word of mouth, or if not, I shall understand. Nick, being of the inferior species, could hardly be expected to do so, though I admit that he is more generously equipped in the matter of intellect than most. – Your friend to be,

'DAISY MUSGRAVE.'

Muriel laid down the letter with a little smile. Its spontaneous friendliness was like a warm hand clasping hers. Yes, she would go, she decided, as she splashed refreshingly in her bath, and that not for Nick's sake. She knew instinctively that she was going to discover a close sympathy with this woman, who, though an utter stranger to her, yet knew how to draw her as a sister. And Muriel's longing for such human fellowship had already driven her to extremes.

She had the note in her hand when she finally joined Lady Bassett upon the verandah.

Lady Bassett, though ever gracious, was seldom at her best in the morning. She greeted the girl with a faint, wry smile and proffered her nearest cheek to be kissed.

'Quite an early bird, dear child!' was her comment. 'I should imagine Captain Ratcliffe's visitation awakened the whole neighbourhood. I think you must not go out again with him before sunrise. I should not have advised it this morning if you had consulted me.'

Muriel flushed at the softly-conveyed reproof. 'It is not the first time,' she said, in her deep voice that was always deepest when indignation moved her. 'We have seen the sun rise together and the moon rise too, before to-day.'

Lady Bassett sighed gently. 'I am sure, dearest,' she said, 'that you do not mean to be uncouth or unmannerly, far less – that most odious of all propensities in a young girl – forward. But though my authority over you were to be regarded as so slight as to be quite negligible, I should still feel it my duty to remonstrate when I saw you committing a breach of the conventions which might be grievously misconstrued. I trust, dear Muriel, that you will bear my protest in mind and regulate your actions by it in the future. Will you take coffee?'

Muriel had seated herself at the other side of the table, and was regarding her with wide, dark eyes that were neither angry nor ashamed, only quite involuntarily disdainful.

After a distinct pause she decided to let the matter drop, reflecting that Lady Bassett's subtleties were never worth pursuing.

'I am going to see a friend of Nick's this afternoon,' she said presently. 'I expect you know her – Mrs. Musgrave.'

Lady Bassett's forehead puckered a little. It could hardly be called a frown. 'Have you ever met Mrs. Musgrave?' she asked.

'No, never. But she is Nick's friend, and of course I know her cousin, Captain Grange, quite well.'

Lady Bassett made no comment upon this. 'Of course, dear,' she said, 'you are old enough to please yourself, but it is not usual, you know, to plunge into social pleasures after so recent a bereavement as yours.'

The sudden silence that followed this gentle reminder had in it something that was passionate. Muriel's face turned vividly crimson, and then gradually whitened to a startling pallor.

'It is the last thing I should wish to do,' she said, in a stifled voice.

Lady Bassett continued, softly suggestive. 'I say nothing of your marriage, dear child. For that, I am aware, is practically a matter of necessity. But I do think that under the circumstances you can scarcely be too careful in what you do. Society is not charitably inclined towards those who even involuntarily transgress its rules. And you most emphatically are not in a position to do so wilfully.'

She paused, for Muriel had risen unexpectedly to her feet. Her eyes were blazing in her white face.

'Why should you call my marriage a matter of necessity?'

she demanded. 'Sir Reginald told me that my father had provided for me.'

'Of course, of course, dear.' Lady Bassett uttered a faint, artificial laugh. 'It is not a question of means at all. But there, since you are so childishly unsophisticated, I need not open your eyes. It is enough for you to know that there is a sufficiently urgent reason for your marriage, and the sooner it can take place, the better. But in the meantime let me counsel you to be as prudent as possible in all that you do. I assure you, dear, it is very necessary.'

Muriel received this little homily in silence. She did not in the least understand to what these veiled allusions referred, and she decided impatiently that they were unworthy of her serious consideration. It was ridiculous to let herself be angry with Lady Bassett. As if it mattered in the least what she said or thought! She determined to pay her projected visit notwithstanding, and quietly said so, as she turned at length from the table.

Lady Bassett raised no further remonstrance beyond a faint, eloquent lift of the shoulders. And Muriel went away into the shady compound, her step firmer and her dark head decidedly higher than usual. She felt for Nick's gift as she went with a little secret sensation of pleasure. After all, why had she been afraid? All girls wore rings when they became engaged to be married.

Reaching her favourite corner, she drew it forth from its hiding-place, a quiver of excitement running through her.

She was sitting in the hammock under the pines as she unwrapped it. The hot sunshine, glinting through the dark boughs overhead, flashed upon precious stones and dazzled her as the wisp of tissue-paper fell from her hand.

And in a moment she was looking at an old marquise ring of rubies in a setting of finely-wrought gold. Her heart gave a throb of sheer delight at the beauty of the thing. She slipped it impetuously on to her finger, and held it up to the sunlight.

The rubies shone with a deep lustre – red, red as heart's blood, ardent as flame. She gazed and gazed with sparkling, fascinated eyes.

Suddenly his words flashed into her mind. A message inside it! She had been so caught by the splendour of the stones that she had not looked inside. She drew the ring from her finger, and examined it closely, with burning cheeks.

Yes, there was the message – three words engraved in minute, old-fashioned characters inside the gold band. They were so tiny that it took her a long time to puzzle them out. With difficulty at length she deciphered the quaint letters, but even then it was some time before she grasped the meaning that they spelt.

It flashed upon her finally, as though a voice had spoken into her ear. The words were: OMNIA VINCIT AMOR. And the ring in her hand was no longer the outward visible sign of her compact. It was a love-token, given to her by a man who had spoken no word of love.

Chapter 13

'So you didn't bring Nick after all. That was nice of you,' said Daisy Musgrave, with a little, whimsical smile. 'I wanted to have you all to myself. The nicest of men can be horribly in the way sometimes.'

She smiled upon her visitor whom she had placed in the easiest chair and in the pleasantest corner of her drawing-room. Her pretty face was aglow with friendliness. No words of welcome were needed.

Muriel was already feeling happier than she had felt for many, many weary weeks. It had been an effort to come, but she was glad that she had made it.

'It was kind of you to ask me,' she said, 'though of course I know that you did it for Nick's sake.'

'You are quite wrong,' Daisy answered instantly. 'He told me about you, I admit. But after that, I wanted you for your own. And now I have got you, Muriel, I am not going to stand on ceremony the least bit in the world. And you mustn't either; but I can see you won't. Your eyes are telling me things already. I don't get on with stiff people somehow. Lady Bassett calls me effusive. And I think myself there must have been something meteoric about my birth star. Doubtless that is why I agree so well with Nick. He's meteoric too.' She slipped cosily down upon a stool by Muriel's side. 'He's a nice boy, isn't he?' she said sympathetically. 'And is that his ring? Ah, let me look at it! I think I have seen it before. No, don't take it off! That's unlucky.'

But Muriel had already drawn it from her finger.

'It's beautiful,' she said warmly. 'Do you know anything about it? It looks as if it had a history.'

'It has,' said Daisy. 'I remember now. He showed it to me once when I was staying at his brother's house in England. I know the Ratcliffes well. My husband used to live with them as a boy. It came from the old maiden aunt who left him all his money. She gave it to him before she died, I believe, and told him to keep it for the woman he was sure to love some day. Nick was an immense favourite of hers.'

'But the ring?' urged Muriel.

Daisy was frowning over the inscription within it, but she was fully aware of the soft colour that had flooded the girl's face at her words.

'OMNIA VINCIT AMOR,' she read slowly. That is it, isn't it? Ah, yes, and the history of it. It's rather sad. Do you mind?'

'I am used to sad things,' Muriel reminded her, with her face turned away toward the mountains.

Daisy pressed her hand gently. 'It is a French ring,' she said. 'It belonged to an aristocrat who was murdered in the Reign of Terror. He sent it by the servant to the girl he loved from the steps of the guillotine. I don't know their names. Nick didn't tell me that. But she was English.'

Muriel had turned quickly back. Her interest was aroused. 'Yes,' she said eagerly, as Daisy paused. 'And she?'

'She!' Daisy's voice had a sudden hard ring in it. 'She remained faithful to him for just six months. And then she married an Englishman. It was said that she did it against her will. Still she did it. Luckily for her perhaps she died within the year – when her child was born.'

Daisy rose abruptly and moved across the room. 'That was more than a hundred years ago,' she said, 'and women are as great fools still. If they can't marry the man they love – they'll marry – anything.'

Muriel was silent. She felt as if she had caught sight of something that she had not been intended to see.

But in a moment Daisy came back, and, kneeling beside her, slipped the ring on to her finger again. 'Yet Love conquers all the same, dear,' she said, passing her arm about the girl. 'And yours is going to be a happy love story. The ring came finally into the possession of the lady's grandson, and it was he who gave it to Nick's aunt – the maiden aunt. It was her engagement ring. She never wore any other, and she only gave it to Nick when her fingers were too rheumatic to wear it any longer. Her lover, poor boy, was killed in the Crimea. There! Forgive me if I have made you sad. Death is not really sad, you know, where there is love. People talk of it as if it conquered love, whereas it is in fact all the other way round. Love conquers death.'

Muriel hid her face suddenly on Daisy's shoulder. 'Oh, are you quite sure?' she whispered.

'I am quite sure, darling.' The reply was instant and full of conviction. 'It doesn't need a good woman to be quite sure of that. Over and over again it has been the only solid thing I have had to hold by. I've clung to it blindly in outer darkness, God only knows how often.'

Her arms tightened about Muriel, and she fell silent. For minutes the room was absolutely quiet. Then Muriel raised her head.

'Thank you,' she whispered. 'Thank you so much.'

Her eyes were full of tears as her lips met Daisy's, but she brushed them swiftly away before they fell.

Daisy was smiling at her. 'Come,' she said, 'I want to show you my baby. He is just the wee-est bit fractious, as he is cutting a tooth. The doctor says he will be all right, but he still threatens to send us both to England.'

'And you don't want to go?' questioned Muriel.

Daisy shook her head. 'I want to see my cousin Blake,' she said lightly, 'when he comes marching home again. Did you hear the rumour that he is to have the V.C.? They ought to give it to Nick too if he does.

'Oh, I shouldn't think so. Nick didn't do anything. At least,' Muriel stumbled a little, 'nothing to be proud of.'

Daisy laughed and caught her face between her hands. 'Except save his girl from destruction,' she said. 'Doesn't that count? Oh, Muriel, I know exactly what made him want you. No, you needn't be afraid. I'm not going to tell you. Wild horses shan't drag it from me. But he's the luckiest man in India, and I think he knows it. What lovely hair you have! I'll come round early on your wedding-day and do it for you. And what will you wear? It mustn't be a black wedding whatever etiquette may decree. You look too pathetic in black, and it's a barbarous custom anyway. I have warned my husband fairly that if he goes into mourning for me, I'll never speak to him hereafter again. He is coming up to see us next week, and to discuss our fate with the doctor. Have you ever met Will?'

'Once,' said Muriel. 'It was at a dance at Poonah early last summer.'

'Ah! When I was at Mahableshwar. He is a good dancer, isn't he? He does most things well, I think.'

Daisy smiled tolerantly as she indicated the photograph of a boy upon the mantelpiece. 'He isn't sixteen,' she said. 'He is nearly twenty-eight. Now come and see his son and the light of my eyes.' She linked her arm in Muriel's and, still smiling, led her from the room.

Chapter 14

The week that followed that first visit of hers was a gradual renewal of life to Muriel. She had come through the darkest part of her trouble, and, thick though the shadows might still lie about her, she had at last begun to see light ahead. She went again and yet again to see Daisy, and each visit added to her tranquillity of mind. Daisy was wonderfully brisk for an invalid, and her baby was an endless source of interest. Even Lady Bassett could not cavil when her charge spoke of going to nursery tea at Mrs. Musgrave's. She made no attempt to check the ripening friendship, though Muriel was subtly aware that she did not approve of it.

She also went every morning for a headlong gallop with Nick who, in fact, would take no refusal in the matter. He came not at all to the house except for these early visits, and she had a good many hours to herself. But her health was steadily improving, and her loneliness oppressed her less than formerly. She spent long mornings lying in the hammock under the pines with only an occasional monkey far above her to keep her company. It was her favourite haunt, and she grew to look upon it as exclusively her own. There was a tiny rustic summer-house near it, which no one ever occupied, so far as she knew. Moreover, the hammock had been decorously slung behind it, so that even though a visitor might conceivably penetrate far as the arbour, it was extremely unlikely that the hammock would come into the range of discovery.

Even Lady Bassett had never sought her here, her time being generally quite fully occupied with her countless social engagements. Muriel often wondered that that garden on the mountain-side in which she revelled, seemed to hold so slight an attraction for its owner. But then of course Lady Bassett was so much in demand that she had little leisure to admire the beauties that surrounded her.

Growing daily stronger, Muriel's half-childish panic

regarding her approaching marriage as steadily diminished. She enjoyed her rides with Nick, becoming daily more and more at her ease with him. They seldom touched upon intimate matters. She wore his ring, and once she shyly thanked him for it. But he made no further reference to the words engraved within it, and she was relieved by his forbearance.

Nick on his part was visiting Daisy Musgrave every day, and sedulously imbibing her woman's wisdom. He had immense faith in her insight and her intuition, and when she entreated him to move slowly and without impatience he took a sterner grip of himself and resolutely set himself to cultivate the virtue she urged upon him.

'You mustn't do anything in a hurry,' Daisy assured him, 'either before your marriage or after. She has had a very bad shock, and she is only just getting over it. You will throw everything back if you try to precipitate matters. She is asleep, you know, Nick, and it is for you to waken her, but gradually – oh, very gradually – or she will start up in the old nightmare terror again. If she doesn't love you yet, she is very near it. But you will only win her by waiting for her. Never do anything sudden. Always remember what a child she is, though she has outgrown her years. And children, you know, though they will trust those they love to the uttermost, are easily frightened.'

Nick knew that she was right. He knew also that he was steadily gaining ground, and that knowledge helped him more than all Daisy's counsels. He was within sight, so he felt, of the great consummation of all his desires, and he was drawing daily nearer.

Their wedding-day was little more than a week away. He had already made full preparation for it. It was to be as quiet a ceremony as it was possible to arrange. Daisy Musgrave had promised to be there, and he expected her husband also. Lady Bassett, whose presence he realized with a grimace to be indispensable, would complete the wedding-party.

He had arranged to leave Simla directly the service was

over, and to go into Nepal. It would not be his first visit to
that most wonderful country, and it held many things that he
desired to show her. He expected much from that wedding
journey, from the close companionship, the intimacy that
must result. He would teach her first beyond all doubting
that she had nothing to fear, and then – then at last, as the
reward of infinite patience, he would win her love. His blood
quickened whenever be thought of it. Alone with her once
more among the mountains, in perfect security, surrounded
by the glory of the eternal snows, so he would win her. They
would come back closely united, equipped to face the whole
world hand-in-hand, so joined together that no shadow of
evil could ever come between them any more. For they
would be irrevocably made one. Thus ran the current of
his splendid dream, and for this he curbed himself, mastered
his eagerness, controlled his passion.

On the day that Daisy's husband arrived, he considerately
absented himself from their bungalow, knowing how the boy
loved to have his wife to himself. He had in consequence
the whole afternoon at his disposal and he contemplated
paying a surprise visit to his betrothed. He had ridden with
her that morning, and he did not doubt that she was to be
found somewhere in Lady Bassett's compound. So in fact she
was, and had he carried out his first intention, he would have
explored behind the summer-house and found her in her
retreat.

But he did not after all pay his projected visit. A very small
matter frustrated his plans – a matter of no earthly importance, but which he always looked upon afterwards as a
piece of the devil's own handiwork. He remembered some
neglected correspondence, and decided to clear it off. She
would not be expecting him, possibly she might not welcome
his intrusion. And so in consequence of that rigid self-restraint
that he was practising he suffered this latter reflection to
sway him in the direction of his unanswered letters, and sat
down to his writing-table with a strong sense of virtue, utterly

unsuspicious of the evil which even at that moment was drawing near imperceptibly but surely to the girl he loved.

She was lying in her hammock with an unread book on her knees. It was a slumberous afternoon, making for drowsiness. The mountains were wrapped in a vague haze, and the whole world was very still. Very far overhead, the pines occasionally whispered to one another, but below there was no movement, save when a lizard scuttled swiftly over the pine-needles, and once when an enquiring monkey-face peered at her round the red bole of a pine.

It was all very restful, and Muriel was undeniably sleepy. She had ridden farther than usual with Nick that morning, and it did not take much to tire her still. Lady Bassett had gone to a polo-match, she knew, and she luxuriated in undisturbed solitude. It lay all about her like a spell of enchantment. With her cheek pillowed on her hand she presently floated into serene slumber. It was like drifting down a tidal river into a summer sea. . . .

Her awakening was abrupt, almost startling. She felt as if someone had touched her, though she realized in a moment that this was impossible. For she was still alone. No one was in sight. Only from the arbour a few feet away there came the sound of voices, and the tinkle of tea-cups.

Visitors evidently! Lady Bassett had returned and brought back a couple of guests with her. She frowned impatiently over the discovery, realizing that she was a prisoner unless she elected to show herself. For her corner behind the summer-house was bounded by the wall of the compound, and there was no retreat save by the path that led to the bungalow and this wound in front of the arbour itself.

It was very annoying, but there was no help for it. She knew very few people in Simla, and neither of the voices that mingled with Lady Bassett's was familiar to her. It did not take her long to decide that she had no desire for a closer acquaintance with their owners. One was a man's voice, sonorous and weighty, that sounded as if it were accustomed to propound mighty problems from the pulpit. The other was a woman's, high-pitched as the wail of a cat on a windy night, that caused the listening girl to nestle back on her pillow with the instant resolution to remain where she was until the intruders saw fit to depart, even if by so doing she had to forgo her tea.

She opened her book with an unwarrantable feeling of resentment. Of course Lady Bassett could not know she was there, and of course she was at liberty to go whither she would in her own garden. But no one likes to have their cherished privacy invaded even in ignorance. And Lady Bassett might surely have concluded that she would be out somewhere under the pines.

Well, they probably would not stay for long, and she was in no hurry. With a faint sigh of lingering annoyance she began to read.

But the piercing, feline voice soon pounded flail-like into her consciousness, scattering her thoughts with ruthless insistence.

'Of course,' it asserted, 'it was the only thing he could possibly do. No man with any decent feeling could have done otherwise. But it was a little hard on him. Surely you agree with me there?'

Lady Bassett's voice, soft and precise, made answer. 'Indeed I think he has behaved most generously in the matter. As you say, it would have been but a gentleman's duty to make an offer of marriage considering all the circumstances. But he went further than that. He actually insisted upon the arrangement. I suppose he felt bound to do so as the poor child's father had placed her in his charge. She is quite unformed still, and is very far from realizing her grave position. Indeed I scarcely expected her to accept him without the urgent reason for the match being explained to her. For it is quite obvious that she does not care for him in that way. Poor child, she is scarcely old enough to know the true meaning of love. It is very sad for them both.'

A gentle sigh closed the sentence. Muriel's book had slid down upon a cushion of pine-needles. She had raised herself in the hammock, and was staring at the rustic woodwork of the summer-house as though she saw a serpent twining there.

There followed a brief silence. Then came the man's voice, deliberate and resounding.

'I am sure it must have caused you much anxiety, dear Lady Bassett. With my knowledge of Nicholas Ratcliffe I confess that I should have felt very grave misgivings as to whether he were endowed with the chivalry to fulfil the obligation he had incurred. My esteem for him has increased fourfold since I heard of his intention to shoulder his responsibilities this courageously. I had not deemed him capable of such a sacrifice. I sincerely trust that he will be given strength to carry it through worthily.'

'I shall not feel really easy till they are married,' confessed Lady Bassett.

'Ah!' The sonorous voice broke in again with friendly reproof. 'But – pardon me – does not that indicate a certain lack of faith, Lady Bassett? Since the young man has been led to see that the poor girl has been so sadly compromised, surely we may trust that he will be enabled to carry out his engagement. I consider it doubly praiseworthy that he has taken this action on his own initiative. I may tell you in confidence that I was seriously debating with myself as to whether it were not my duty to approach him on the subject. But the news of his engagement relieved me of all responsibility. It is no doubt something of a sacrifice to a man of his stamp. We can only trust that he will be duly rewarded.'

Here the shrill feline voice suddenly made itself heard, tripping in upon the deeper tones without ceremony.

'Oh, but poor Nick! I can't picture him married and done for. He has always been so gay. Why, look at him with Daisy Musgrave! I know for a fact that he goes there every day at least, and she refusing to receive anyone else. I call it quite scandalous.'

'My dear! My dear!' It was Lady Bassett's turn to reprove. 'Not quite every day surely!'

I do assure you that isn't the smallest exaggeration,' protested her informant. 'I had it from Mrs. Gybbon-Smythe who never misstates anything. It was she who first told me of this engagement, and she considered that Nick was positively throwing himself away. A mere chivalrous fad she called it, and declared that it would simply ruin his prospects. For it is well known that married officers are almost invariably passed over by the powers that be. And he is regarded as so promising too. Really I am almost inclined to agree with her. Just a little more tea, dear, if I may. Your tea is always so delicious, and doubly so out here under the pines.'

The soft jingling of tea-cups ensued, and through it presently came Lady Bassett's gentle tones. They sounded as if she were smiling.

'Well, all I can say is, I was unspeakably relieved when I heard that Captain Ratcliffe had decided to treat the matter as a point of honour and marry dear Muriel. She is a sweet girl and I am devoted to her, which made it doubly hard for me. For I should scarcely have dared to venture, after what has happened, to ask any of my friends to receive her. Naturally, she shrinks from speaking of that terrible time, but I understand that she spent no less than three nights alone in the mountains with him. And that fact in itself would be more than sufficient to blight any girl's career from a social standpoint. I often think that the rules of our modern etiquette are very rigid, though I know well that we cannot afford to disregard them.' Again came that soft, regretful sigh; and then in an apologetic tone, '*You* will say, I know, that for the good of the community this must be so, but you are great enough to make allowances for a woman's weakness. And I must confess that I cannot but feel the pity of it in such a case as this.'

'Indeed, Lady Bassett, I think your feminine weakness does

you credit,' was the kind response this elicited. 'We must all of us sympathize most deeply with the poor little wanderer who, I am well assured, could not be in better hands than she is at the present moment. Your protecting care must, I am convinced, atone to her in a very great measure for all that she has been called upon to undergo.'

'So sweet of you to say so!' murmured Lady Bassett. 'Words cannot express my reluctance to explain to her the actual state of affairs, or my relief that I have been able to avoid doing so with a clear conscience. Ah! Your cup is empty! Will you let me refil it? No? But you are not thinking of leaving me yet surely?'

'Ah, but indeed we must. We are dining with the Boltons to-night, and going afterwards to the Parkers' dance. You will be there of course? How delightful? Then we shall soon meet again.'

The penetrating voice was accompanied by the sounds of a general move, and there ensued the usual interchange of compliments at departure, Lady Bassett protesting that it had been so sweet of her friends to visit her, and the friends assuring her of the immense pleasure it had given them to do so. All the things that are never said by people who are truly intimate with each other were said several times over as the little party moved away. Their voices receded into the distance, though they continued for a while to prick through the silence that fell like a velvet curtain behind them.

Finally they ceased altogether. The summer-house was empty, and an enterprising monkey slipped down the trunk of a tree and peered in. But he was a nervous beast, and he had a feeling that the place was not so wholly devoid of human presence as it seemed. He approached cautiously, gibbering a little to himself. It looked safe enough, and there was some dainty confectionery within. But, uneasy instinct still urging him, he deemed it advisable to peer round the corner of the summer-house before he yielded to the promptings of a rapacious appetite.

The next instant his worst fears were realised, and he was scudding up the nearest tree in a panic.

There, on the ground, face downwards on the pine-needles, lay a human form. True, it was only a woman lying there. But her silence and her stillness were eloquent of tragedy even to his monkey-intelligence. From a safe height he sat and reviled her till he was tired for having spoilt his sport. Finally, as she made no movement, he forgot his grievance, and tripped airily away in quest of more thrilling adventures.

But the woman remained prone upon the ground for a long, long time.

Chapter 15

Nick's fit of virtue evaporated with his third letter, and he got up, feeling that he had spent an unprofitable afternoon. He also discovered that he was thirsty, and while quenching his thirst he debated with himself whether he would after all stroll round to the Musgraves. He and Will were old school-fellows, and the friendship between them was of the sort that wears for ever. He was moreover dissatisfied with regard to Daisy's appearance, and he wanted to know the doctor's verdict.

He had just decided to chance his welcome and go, when a note was brought to him which proved to be from Will himself.

'DEAR OLD NICK,' it ran— 'I have been wanting to shake your hand ever since I heard of your gallant return from the jaws of death. Well done, old chap if it isn't a stale sentiment!

'Will you come and dine with us? Do thy diligence, for though we are neither of us the best of company, we both want you. The doctor has ordered Daisy and the youngster

Home. They are to leave before the *chota-bursat*. Damn the *chota-bursat*, and the whole beastly show! —Yours ever,

'WILL.'

Nick considered this outburst with a sympathetic frown, and at once despatched an answer in the affirmative. He had almost expected the news. It had been quite plain to him that Daisy was not making any progress towards the recovery of her strength. Her quick temperament would not allow her to be listless but he had not been deceived. And he was glad that Will had come up at length to see for himself.

It was horribly unlucky for them both, he reflected, for he knew that Will could not accompany his wife to England. And the thought presently flashed across him. How would it go with him if he ever had to part with Muriel in that way? Having once possessed her, would he ever bear to let her go again? Would he not rather relinquish his profession for her sake, dear though it was to him? He had made her his own by sheer dogged effort. He had planned for her, fought for her, suffered for her – almost he had died for her. Now that she was his at last, he knew that he could never let her go.

He turned impetuously to a calendar on his writing-table, and ticked off another day. There were only six left before his wedding-day. He counted them with almost savage exultation. Finally he tossed down the pencil with a sudden, quivering laugh, and stood up with wide-flung arms. She was his – his – his! No power or force of circumstance could ever come between them now. He would trample every obstacle underfoot.

But there were no obstacles left. He had overcome them all. He had won her fairly; and the reward of patience was very near.

For the first time he slackened the bonds of his self-restraint; and instantly the fire of his passion leapt up, free and fierce, overflowing its confines in a widespread, molten stream that carried all before it.

When later he departed to keep his engagement, he was as a man treading upon air. Not a dozen yards from the gate one of Lady Bassett's servants met him and presented a note. He guessed it was from Muriel, and the blood rose in a hot wave to his head and pounded at his temples as he opened it. It was the first she had ever written to him.

'I must see you at once.– M.'

That was all. He dismissed the waiting native, and returned to his room. There he wrote a note to Will Musgrave warning him that he had been delayed.

Then he suddenly straightened himself and stood tense. Something had happened. He was sure of it. That urgent summons rang in his brain like a cry for help. Some demand was about to be made upon him, a demand which he might find himself ill-equipped to meet. He was not lacking in courage. He could meet adversity without a quiver. But for once he was not sure of himself. He was not prepared to resist any sudden strain that night.

Several minutes passed before he moved. Then, glancing down, he saw her message fast gripped in his hand. With a swift, passionate movement he carried the paper to his lips. And he remembered suddenly how he had once held her hand there and breathed upon the little cold fingers to give them life. He had commanded himself then. Was he any the less his own master now? And was he fool enough to destroy all in a moment that trust of hers which he had built up so laboriously? He felt as if a fiend had ensnared him, and with a fierce effort he broke free. Surely he was torturing himself in vain. She had only sent for him to explain that she could not ride with him in the morning, or some other matter equally trifling. He would go to her at once since she had desired it, and set her mind at rest on whatever subject happened to be troubling it.

And so with steady tread, he left the house once more. She had called him for the first time. He would not keep her waiting.

Chapter 16

The drawing-room was empty when he entered it, the windows standing flung wide to the night. Strains of dance music were wafted in from somewhere lower down the hill, and he guessed that Lady Bassett would be from home. The pine-trees of the compound stood black and silent. There seemed to be a hush of expectancy in the air.

He stood with his back to the room and his face to the mountains. The moon was still below the horizon, but stars blazed everywhere with a marvellous brightness. It was a night for dreams, and he thought with a quickening heart of the nights that were coming when they two would be alone once more among the Hills, no longer starved and fleeing for their lives, but wandering happily together in an enchanted world where the past was all forgotten, and the future gleamed like the peaks of Paradise.

At sound of a quiet footfall, he turned back into the room. Muriel had entered and was closing the door behind her. At first sight he fancied that she was ill, so terribly did her deep mourning and heavy hair emphasize her pallor. But as she moved forward he reassured himself. It was growing late. Doubtless she was tired.

He went impetuously to meet her, and in a moment he had her hands in his; but they lay in his grasp cold and limp, with no responding pressure. Her great eyes, as they looked at him, were emotionless and distant, remote as the lights of a village seen at night across a far-reaching plain. She gave him no word or smile of welcome.

A sudden dark suspicion flashed through his brain, and he drew her swiftly to the light, looking at her closely, searchingly.

'What have you been doing?' he said.

She fathomed his suspicion, and faintly smiled.

'Nothing – nothing whatever. I have never touched opium since the night you – '

He cut in sharply, as if the reminiscence hurt him.

'I beg your pardon. Well, what is it then? There's something wrong.'

She did not contradict him. Merely with a slight gesture of weariness, she freed herself and sat down.

Nick remained on his feet, looking down at her, waiting grimly for enlightenment.

It did not come very readily. Seconds had passed into minutes before she spoke, and then her words did not bear directly upon the matter in hand.

'I hope it was quite convenient to you to come to-night. I was a little afraid you would have an engagement.'

He remembered the urgency of her summons and decided that she spoke thus conventionally to gain time. On another occasion he might have humoured such a whim, but to-night it goaded him almost beyond endurance. Surely they had passed that stage, he and she.

With an effort he controlled himself, but it sounded in his voice as he made reply.

'My engagement to you stands before any other. What is it you want to say to me?'

Her expression changed slightly at his words, and a shade of apprehension flitted across her face. She threw him a swift upward glance half-scared, half-questioning. Unconsciously her hands locked themselves together.

'I want you not to be vexed, Nick,' she said, in a low voice.

He made an abrupt movement. 'My dear girl, don't be silly. What's the trouble? Let me hear it and have done.'

His tone was reassuring. She looked up at him with more confidence.

'Yes, I am silly,' she acknowledged. 'I'm perfectly idiotic to fancy for a moment that it can make any difference to you. Nick, I have been thinking things over seriously, and – and – I find that I can't marry you after all. I hope you won't mind, though of course – ' she uttered a little laugh that was piteously insincere – 'I know you will feel bound to say you

do. But – anyhow – you needn't say it to me, because I understand. I thought it was only fair to let you know at once.'

'Thank you,' said Nick, and there was that in his voice
which was like the sudden snapping of a tense spring.

She saw his hands clench with the words, and an overwhelming sense of danger swept over her. Instinctively she
started to her feet. If a tiger had leapt in upon her through
the window she could not have been more terrified.

Nick took a single stride towards her, and she stopped as
if struck powerless. His face was the face she had once seen
bent over a man in his death-agony, convulsed with passion,
savage, merciless – the face of a devil.

She shrank away from him in nameless terror gasping and
panic-stricken. 'Nick,' she whispered, 'are you – mad?'

He answered her jerkily in a strangled voice that was like
the snarl of a beast? 'Yes – I am mad. If you try to run away
from me now – I won't answer for myself.'

She gazed at him with widening eyes. 'But, but – ' she
faltered – 'I don't understand. Oh, Nick, you frighten me?'

It was the cry of a child, lost, bewildered, piteous. Had she
withstood him, had she sought to escape, the demon in
him would have burst the last restraining bond, and have
shattered in one moment of unshackled violence all the
chivalrous patience which during the last few weeks he had
spent his whole strength to achieve.

But that cry of desolation pierced straight through his
madness, cutting deeper than reproach or protest, wounding
him to the heart.

With a sound that was half-sob, half-groan, he turned his
back upon her and covered his face.

For a space of seconds he stood so, not moving, seeming
not even to breathe. And Muriel, steadying herself by the
mantelpiece, watched him with a panting heart.

Then abruptly, moving with a quick, light tread that made
no sound, he crossed the room to one of the wide-flung
windows, and stopped there.

From across the quiet garden there came the strains of 'The Blue Danube,' fitful, alluring, plaintive – that waltz to which countless lovers have danced and wooed and whispered through the years. Muriel longed intensely to shut it out, to stop her ears, to make some noise to drown it. Her nerves were all on edge, and she felt as if its persistent sweetness would drive her mad.

Surely Nick felt the same; but if he did, he made no sign. He stood without movement with his face to the night, gripping the woodwork of the window with both hands, every bone of them standing out in sharp, skeleton lines.

She watched him, fascinated, for a long time, but he did not stir from his tense position. He seemed to have utterly forgotten her presence in the room behind him. And still that maddening waltz kept on and on and on till she felt sick and dazed with listening to it. It seemed as if for the rest of her life she would never again be free from those haunting strains.

The soft shutting of the window made her start and quiver. Nick had moved at last, and her heart began to throb quick and fast as he turned. She tried to read his face, but she could not even see it. There was a swimming mist before her eyes, and her limbs felt powerless, heavy as lead.

In every nerve, she felt him drawing near, and in an agony of helplessness she awaited him, all the surging horror of that night when he had drugged her rushing back upon her with tenfold force. Again she saw him as she had seen him then, monstrous, silent, terrible, a man of super-human strength, whose mastery appalled her. Again in desperate fear she shrank from him, seeking wildly, fruitlessly, for a way of escape.

And then came the consciousness of his arm about her supporting her, and the voice that had quieted her wildest delirium was speaking in her ear.

'The goblins are all gone, dear,' she heard him say. 'Don't be frightened.'

He led her gently to a sofa and made her sit down bending over her and softly rubbing her cold cheek.

'Tell me when you're better,' he said, 'and we'll talk this thing out. But don't be frightened anyway. It's all right.'

The tenderness of voice and touch, the sudden cessation of all tension, the swift putting to flight of her fear, all combined to produce in her a sense of relief so immense that the last shred of her self-control went from her utterly. She laid her head down upon the cushions and burst into a storm of tears.

Nick's hand continued to stroke and soothe, but he said no more while her paroxysm of weeping lasted. He who was usually so ready of speech, so quick to console, found no voice for once wherewith to comfort her.

Only when her distress had somewhat spent itself he bent a little lower and dried her tears with his own handkerchief, his lips twitching as he did it, his eyes flickering so rapidly that it was impossible to read their expression.

'There!' he said at last. 'There's nothing to cry about. Finish what you were saying when I interrupted you. I think you were in the middle of throwing me over, weren't you? At least, you had got through that part of it, and were just going to tell me why.'

His tone was reassuringly flippant.

Looking up at him, she saw the old kindly, quizzical look on his face. He met her eyes, nodding shrewdly.

'Let's have it,' he said, 'straight from the shoulder. You're tired of me, eh?'

She drew back from him, but with no gesture of shrinking. 'I'm tired of everything – everything,' she said, a little passionate quiver in her voice. 'I wish – I wish with all my heart, you had left me to die.'

'Is that the grievance?' said Nick. He sat down on the head of the sofa, and drove his fist into the cushion. 'If I could explain things to you, I would. But you're such a chicken, aren't you, dear, and about as easily scared? Since when have you harboured this grudge against me?'

The gentle banter of his tone did not deceive her into imagining that she could trifle with him, nor was she addicted to trifling. She made answer with a certain warmth of indignation that seemed to have kindled on its own initiative and wholly without her volition.

'I haven't, I don't. I'm not so absurd. It isn't that at all.'

'You're not tired of me?' queried Nick.

'No.'

'If I were to die to-morrow for instance – and there's no telling, you know, Muriel – you'd be a little sorry?'

Again though scarcely aware of it, she resented the question. 'Why do you ask me that? Of course I should be sorry.'

'Of course,' acquiesced Nick. 'But all the king's horses and all the king's men wouldn't bring me back again. That's the worst of being mortal. You can't dance at your own funeral.'

'What do you mean?' There was a note of exasperation in Muriel's voice. She saw that he had an object in view but his method of attaining it was too tortuous for her straightforward understanding.

He explained himself with much patience. His mood had so completely changed that she could barely recall to mind the vision that had so appalled her but a few minutes before.

'What I mean is that it's infernal to think that someone may be shedding precious tears on your grave and you not there to see. I've often wondered if one could get a ticket of leave for such an occasion.' He smiled down at her with baffling directness. 'I should value those tears unspeakably,' he said,

Muriel made a slight movement of impatience. The discussion seemed to her inconsequent and unprofitable.

Nick began to enumerate his points. 'You're not tired of me – though I see I'm boring you hideously; put up with it a little longer, I've nearly finished – and you'd shed quite a respectable number of tears if I were to die young. Yes, I am young though as ugly as Satan. I believe you think I'm some sort of connection, don't you? Is that why you don't want to marry me?'

He put the question with startling suddenness, and Muriel glanced up quickly, but was instantly reassured. He was no more formidable at that moment than a grinning school-boy. She still not did feel wholly at her ease with him. She had a curious suspicion that he was in some fashion testing her.

'No,' she answered, after a moment. 'It is nothing of that sort.'

'Quite sure there is a reason?' he asked quizzically.

Her white cheeks flushed. 'Yes, of course. But – I would rather not tell you what it is.'

'Quite so,' said Nick. 'I suppose that also is "only fair"?'

Her colour deepened. He made her feel unaccountably ashamed. 'I will tell you if you wish to know,' she said reluctantly. 'But I would rather not.'

Nick made an airy gesture. 'Not for the world! My intelligence department is specially fitted for this sort of thing. Besides, I know exactly what happened. It was something like this.' He passed his hand over his face, then turned to her with a faint, wry smile so irresistibly reminiscent of Lady Bassett that Muriel gasped with a sudden hysterical desire to laugh.

He silenced her by beginning to speak in soft, purring accents. 'You know, darling Muriel, I have never looked upon Nicholas Ratcliffe as a marrying man. He is such a gay butterfly.' (This with an indulgent shake of the head.) 'Indeed, I have heard dear Mrs Gybbon-Smythe describe him as a shocking little flirt. And they say he is fond of his glass too, but let us hope this is an exaggeration. I know for a fact that he has a very violent temper, and this may have given rise to the rumour. I assure you, dearest, he is quite formidable, notwithstanding his size. But there if I tell you any more you will think I am prejudiced against him, whereas we are really the greatest friends – the greatest possible friends. I only thought it kind to warn you not to expect too much. It is a mistake so many young girls make, and I want you to be as happy as you can, poor child.'

Muriel was laughing helplessly when he stopped. The mimicry of voice and action was so perfect, so free from exaggeration, so sublimely spontaneous.

Nick did not laugh with her. Behind his mask of banter he was watching, watching closely. He had clad himself in jester's garb to feel for the truth. Perhaps she realized something of this as she recovered herself, for again that glance half-questioning, half-frightened, flashed up at him as she made reply.

'No, Nick. She never said that indeed. I wouldn't have cared if she had. It was only – only – '

'I know,' he broke in abruptly. 'If it wasn't that, there is only one thing left that it could have been. I don't want you to tell me. It's as plain as daylight. Let me tell you instead. It's all for the sake of your poor little personal pride. I know – yes, I know. They've been throwing mud at you, and it's stuck. You'd sooner die than marry me, wouldn't you? But what will you do if I refuse to set you free?'

She turned suddenly crimson. 'You – you wouldn't Nick! You couldn't! You haven't – the right.'

'Haven't I?' said Nick, with an odd smile. 'I thought I had.'

He looked down at her, and a queer little flame leaped up like an evil spirit in his eyes, flickered an instant, and was gone. 'I thought I had,' he said again, in a different tone. 'But we won't quarrel about that. Tell me what you want to do.'

Her answer came with a vehemence that perhaps he had hardly expected. 'Oh, I want to get away – right away. I want to go Home. I – I hate this place.'

'And everyone in it?' suggested Nick.

'Almost,' Muriel spoke recklessly, even defiantly. She was fighting for her freedom, and the battle was infinitely harder than she had anticipated.

He nodded. 'The sole exception being Mrs. Musgrave. Do you know Mrs. Musgrave is going Home? You would like to go with her.'

Muriel looked at him with sudden hope. 'Alone with her?' she said.

'Oh, I'm not going,' declared Nick. 'I'm going to Khatmandu for my honeymoon.'

The hope died out of Muriel's eyes. 'Don't – jeer at me, Nick,' she said, in a choked voice. 'I can't bear it.'

'Jeer!' said Nick. 'I!' He reached down suddenly and took her hand. The light sparkled on the ring he had given her, and he moved it slowly to and fro watching it.

'I am going to ask you to take it back,' she said.

He did not raise his eyes. 'And I am going to refuse,' he answered promptly. 'I don't say you must wear it, but you are to keep it – not as a bond, merely in remembrance of a promise which you will make to me.'

'A promise' – she faltered.

Still he did not look up. He was watching the stones with eyes half-shut.

'Yes,' he said, after a moment. 'I will let you go on the sole condition that you give me this promise.'

She began to tremble a little. 'What is it?' she whispered.

He glanced at her momentarily, but his expression was enigmatical. She felt as if his look lighted and dwelt upon something beyond her.

'Simply this,' he said. 'You'll laugh, I daresay; but if you are able to laugh it won't hurt you to promise. I want your word of honour that if you ever change your mind about marrying me, you will come to me like a brave woman and tell me so.'

Thus, quite calmly, he made known to her his condition, and in the amazed silence with which she received it he continued to flash hither and thither the wonderful rays that shone from the gems upon her hand. He did not appear to be greatly concerned as to what her answer would be. Simply with an inscrutable countenance he waited for it.

'Is it a bargain?' he asked at last.

She started with an involuntary gesture of shrinking.

'Oh no, Nick! How could I promise you that? You know I shall never change my mind.'

He raised his eyebrows ever so slightly. 'That isn't the point under discussion. If it's an impossible contingency, it costs you the less to promise.'

He kept her hand in his as he said it though she fidgeted to be free. 'Please, Nick,' she said earnestly, 'I would so much rather not.'

'You prefer to marry me at once?' he asked, and suddenly it seemed to her that this was the alternative to which he meant to drive her.

She rose in a panic, and he rose also, still keeping her hand. His face looked like a block of yellow granite.

'Must it – must it – be one or the other?' she panted.

He looked at her under flickering eyelids. 'I have said it,' he remarked.

Her resistance flagged, sank, rose again, and finally died away. After all, why should she hesitate? What was there in such an undertaking as this to send the blood so wildly to her heart?

'Very well,' she said faintly at last. 'I promise. But – but – I never shall change my mind, Nick – never – never.'

He was still looking at her with veiled, impenetrable eyes. He paid no attention to her protest. It was as if he had not so much as heard it.

'You've done your part,' he said. 'Now hear me do mine. I swear to you – before God – that I will never marry you unless you ask me to.'

He bent with the words, and solemnly, reverently, he pressed his lips upon the hand he held.

Muriel waited half-frightened still and wholly awe-struck. She did not know Nick in this mood.

But when he straightened himself again, the old whimsical smile was on his face, and she breathed a sigh of relief. With a quick, caressing movement he took her by the shoulders.

'That's over then,' he said lightly. 'Turn over and start another page. Go back to England, go back to school; and let them teach you to be young again.'

They were his last words to her. Yet an instant longer he waited, and very deep down in her heart something that was hidden there stirred and quivered as a blind creature moves at the touch of the sun. It awoke a vague pain within her, that was all.

The next moment Nick had turned upon his heel and was departing.

She heard him humming a waltz tune under his breath as he went away with his free British swagger. And she knew with no sense of elation that she had gained her point.

For good or ill he had left her, and he would not return.

Part III

Chapter 17

'There!' said Daisy, standing back from the table to review her handiwork with her head on one side. 'I may be outrageously childish, but if Blake fails to appreciate this masterpiece of mine, I shall feel inclined to turn him out-of-doors, and leave him to spend the night on the step.'

Muriel, curled up in the old-fashioned window-seat, looked round with her low laugh. 'It's snowing hard,' she remarked.

Daisy did not heed her. 'Come and look at it,' she said.

The masterpiece in question consisted of an enormous red scroll bearing in white letters the words: 'Welcome to the Brave.'

'It never occurred to me that Blake was brave before,' observed Daisy. 'He is so shy and soft and retiring. I can't somehow feel as if I am going to entertain a lion. He ought to be here by this time. Let's go and hang my work of art in the hall.'

She slipped her hand through Muriel's arm, and glanced at her sharply when she felt it tremble.

'It will be good to see him again, won't it?' she said.

'Yes,' Muriel agreed, but there was a little tremor in her voice as well.

Very vividly were the circumstances under which she had last seen this man in her mind that night. Eight months that were like as many years stretched between that tragic time and the present, but the old wild horror had still the power to make her blood turn cold, the old wound had not lost its ache. Those things had made a woman of her before her time, but yet she was not as other women. It seemed that she was destined all her life to live apart, and only to look on at the joys of others. They did not attract her, and she had no heart or gaiety. Yet she was not cold, or Daisy had not found her so congenial a companion. But even Daisy seldom penetrated behind the deep reserve that had grown over the girl's sad young heart. They were close friends, but their friendship lay mainly in what they left unsaid. For all her quick warmth, Daisy too had her inner shrine – a place so secret that she herself never entered it save as it were by stealth.

But something of Muriel's mood she understood on that bitter night in January on which they awaited the coming of Blake Grange, and her close hand pressure conveyed as much as they passed out together into the little hall that glowed so snugly in the firelight.

'He is sure to be frozen, poor boy,' she said. 'I hope Jim Ratcliffe won't forget to send the motor to the station as he promised.'

'I am quite sure he never forgets anything,' Muriel declared, with reassuring confidence.

Daisy laughed lightly. 'Yes, he's very dependable, deliciously solid, isn't he? A trifle domineering perhaps, but all doctors are. They rule us weak women with a rod of iron I am a little afraid of Dr. Jim myself, and most unfortunately he knows it.'

Muriel's silence expressed a certain scepticism that provoked another laugh from Daisy. She was almost frivolously lighthearted that night.

'It's a fact, I assure you. Have you never noticed how docile

I am in his presence? I always feel as if I want to confess all my sins to him. I should like intensely to have his opinion upon some of them. I think it would do me good.'

'Then why not ask for it?' suggested Muriel.

'For the reason afore-mentioned – a slavish timidity.' Daisy broke off to carol a few bars of a song. 'I've known the Ratcliffe family ever since I became engaged to Will,' she said presently. 'Jim Ratcliffe, you know, was left his guardian, and he was always very good to him. Will made his home with them, and he and Nick are great pals, just like brothers. I should think Dr. Jim had his hands full with the two of them.' Again Daisy stopped to sing. Muriel was stooping over the fire. It was seldom that Nick's name was mentioned between them, though the fact that Daisy had placed herself and her baby in the hands of his half-brother formed a connecting link which could not always be ignored. She always dropped into silence when any reference was made to him. Not in the most casual conversation had Daisy ever heard her utter his name.

Having successfully fixed her message of welcome in a prominent position, she joined the girl in front of the fire. Her face was flushed and her eyes were sparkling, Muriel thought that she had never seen her look so well or so happy.

'You're quite excited,' she said.

Daisy put up a hand to her hot cheek. 'Yes, isn't it absurd? I hope Dr. Jim won't come with him, or he will be cross. But I can't help it. Blake and I have been chums all our lives, and of course I am glad to see him after all this while. So nice too not to have Lady Bassett looking on.'

There was a spice of venom in this, over which Muriel smiled in her sad way.

'Does she disapprove?' she asked.

Daisy nodded impatiently. 'She chose altogether to overlook the fact that we are first cousins. It was intolerable. But – ' again came her light laugh – 'everything is intolerable till you learn to shrug you shoulders and laugh. Hark! Surely I heard something!'

Both listened intently. Footsteps were approaching the door. Daisy sprang to open it.

But it was only the evening post, and she came back holding a letter with a very unwonted expression of disappointment.

'From Will,' she said. 'I forgot it was mail night. I don't suppose there is anything very exciting in it.'

She pushed the flimsy envelope into the front of her dress and fell again to listening.

'Can he have missed the train? Surely it's getting very late. 'A fog on the line perhaps. No! What's that? Ah! It really is this time! That's the horn, and, yes, Jim Ratcliffe's voice.'

In a moment she had the door open again, and was out upon the step crying welcome to her guest.

Muriel crouched a little lower over the fire. Her hands were fast gripped together. It was more of an ordeal than she had thought it possibly could be.

An icy blast blew in through the open door, and she heard Dr. Ratcliffe's voice, sharp and curt, ordering Daisy back into the house. Then came another voice slow and soft as a woman's, and for an instant Muriel covered her face, overwhelmed by bitter memory.

When she looked up they were entering the hall together, Daisy, radiant, eager, full of breathless questioning; Blake, upright, soldierly, magnificent, wearing the shy, pleased smile that she so well remembered.

He did not at once see her, and she stood hesitating, till Daisy, who was clinging to her cousin's arm, turned swiftly round and called her. 'Muriel dear, where are you? Why are you hiding yourself? See, Blake! Here is Muriel Roscoe! You knew we were living together?'

He saw her then, and came across to her, with both hands outstretched.

'Forgive me, Miss Roscoe,' he said, with his pleasant smile. 'You know how glad I am to meet you again.'

He looked down at her with eyes full of frank and friendly sympathy, and the grasp of his hands was such that she felt it for long after. It warmed her through and through, but she could not speak just then, and with ready understanding he turned back to Daisy.

'Dr. Ratcliffe told me you had sent him to fetch me from the station,' he said. 'I am immensely grateful to you and to him.'

Daisy was greeting the doctor with much animation and a hint of mischief.

'I knew you would come,' she laughed. 'You never trust me to take care of myself, do you?'

He brushed some flakes of snow from her dress.

'Events prove me to be justified,' he remarked dryly.

'Since Will has put you in my care, I labour under a two-fold responsibility. What possessed you to go out in that murderous north-easter?'

He frowned at her heavily, his black brows meeting, but notwithstanding her avowal of a few minutes before, Daisy only grimaced in return. He was generally regarded as somewhat formidable, this gruff, square-shouldered doctor, with his iron-grey hair and black moustache, and keenly critical eyes. There was no varnish in his curt speech, no dissimulation in any of his dealings. It was said of him that he never sugared his pills. But his popularity was wide-spread nevertheless. His help was sought in a thousand ways outside his profession. To see his strong face melt into a smile was like sunshine on a gloomy day, the village mothers declared.

But Daisy's gay effrontery did not manage to provoke it at that moment.

'You have no business to take risks,' he said. 'How's the boy?'

Daisy sobered instantly. 'His teeth have been worrying him rather to-day. *Ayah* is with him. I left her crooning him to sleep. Will you go up?'

Jim Ratcliffe nodded and turned aside to the stairs. But he had not reached the top when Muriel overtook him, moving more quickly than was her wont.

'Let me come with you, doctor,' she said.

He put his hand on her arm unceremoniously. 'Miss Roscoe,' he said, 'I have a message for you – from my scapegrace Olga. She wants to know if you will play hockey in her team next Saturday. I have promised to exert my influence – if I have any – on her behalf.'

Muriel looked at him in semi-tragic dismay. 'Oh, I can't indeed. Why, I haven't played for ages – not since I was at school. Besides – '

'How old are you?' he cut in.

'Nearly twenty,' she told him.' But – '

He brought his hand down sharply on her shoulder. 'I shall never call you Miss Roscoe again. You obtained my veneration on false pretences, and you have lost it for ever. Now look here, Muriel!' Arrived at the top of the stairs, he stood still and confronted her with that smile of his that so marvellously softened his rugged face. 'I am thirty years older than you are, and I haven't lived for any part of them with my eyes shut. I've been wanting to give you some advice – medical advice – for a long time. But you wouldn't have it. And now I'm not going to offer it to you. You shall take the advice of a friend instead. You join Olga's hockey team, and go paper-chasing with her too. The monkey is a rare sportswoman. She'll give you a good run for your money. Besides, she has set her heart on having you, and she is a young woman that likes her own way, though, to be sure, she doesn't always get it. Come, you can't refuse when a friend asks you.'

It was difficult certainly, but Muriel plainly desired to do so. She had escaped from the whirling vortex of Life with strenuous effort, and dragged herself bruised and aching to the bank. She did not want to step down again into even the minutest eddy of that ruthless flood. Moreover in addition to this morbid reluctance she lacked the physical energy that such a step demanded of her.

'It's very kind of your little daughter to think of asking me,' she said. 'But really, I shouldn't be any good. I get tired so quickly. No, there's nothing the matter with me,' seeing his intent look. 'I'm not ill. I never have been actually ill. Only – ' her voice quivered a little – 'I think I always shall be tired for the rest of my life.'

'Skittles!' he returned bluntly. 'That isn't what's the matter with you. Go out into the open air. Go out into the north-east wind and sweep the snow away. Shall I tell you what is wrong with you? You're stiff from inaction. It's a species of cramp, my dear, and there's only one remedy for it. Are you going to take it of your own accord, or must I come round with physic spoon and make you?'

She laughed a little, though the deep pathos of her shadowed eyes never varied. Daisy's merry voice rose from the lower regions gaily chaffing her cousin.

'Goodness, Blake! I shouldn't have known you. You're as gaunt as a camel. Haven't you got over your picnic at Fort Wara yet? You're almost as scanty a bag of bones as Nick was six months ago.'

Blake's answer was inaudible. Dr. Ratcliffe did not listen for it. He had seen the swift look of horror that the brief allusion had sent into the girl's sad face, and he understood it though he made no sign.

'Very well,' he said, turning towards the nursery. 'Then I take you in hand from this day forward. And if I don't find you in the hockey-field on Saturday, I shall come myself and fetch you.'

There was nothing even vaguely suggestive of Nick about him, but Muriel knew as surely as if Nick had said it that he would keep his word.

Chapter 18

'Now,' said Daisy briskly, 'you two will just have to entertain each other for a little while, for I am going up to sit with my son while *ayah* is off duty.'

'Mayn't we come too?' suggested her cousin, as he rose to open the door.

She stood a moment and contemplated him with shining eyes. 'You are too magnificent altogether for this doll's house of ours,' she declared. 'I am sure this humble roof has never before sheltered such a lion as Captain Blake Grange, V.C.'

'Only an ass in a lion's skin, my dear Daisy,' said Grange modestly.

She laughed. 'An excellent simile, my worthy cousin. I wish I had thought of it myself.'

She went lightly away with this thrust, and Grange, after a brief pause, turned slowly back into the room.

Muriel was seated in a low chair before the fire. She was working at some tiny woollen socks, knitting swiftly in dead silence.

He moved to the hearthrug, and stood there, obviously ill at ease. A certain shyness was in his nature, and Muriel's nervousness reacted upon him. He did not know how to break the silence.

At length, with an effort, he spoke. 'You heard about Nick Ratcliffe's wound, I expect, Miss Roscoe?'

Muriel's hands leapt suddenly and fell into her lap. 'Nick Ratcliffe! When was he wounded? No, I have heard nothing.'

He looked down at her with an uneasy suspicion that he had lighted upon an unfortunate subject.

'I thought you would have heard,' he said. 'Didn't Daisy know? He came back to us from Simla – got himself attached to the punitive expedition. I was on the sick list myself, so did not see him; but they say he fought like a dancing dervish, and did a lot of damage too. Everyone thought he would have the V.C., but there was a rumour that he refused it.'

'And – he was wounded, you say?' Muriel's voice sounded curiously strained. Her knitting lay jumbled together on her lap. Her dark face was lifted, and it seemed to Grange, unskilled observer though he was, that he had never seen deeper tragedy in any woman's eyes.

Somewhat reluctantly he made reply. 'He had his arm injured by a sword-thrust at the very end of the campaign. He made light of it for ever so long till things began to look serious. Then he had to give in, and had a pretty sharp time of it, I believe. He's better again now though, so his brother told me this evening. I never heard any details. I daresay he's all right again.' He stooped to pick up a completed sock that had fallen. 'He's the sort of chap who always comes out on top,' he ended consolingly.

Muriel stiffened a little as she sat. She had a curious longing to hear more, and an equally curious reluctance to ask for it.

'I never heard anything about it – naturally,' she remarked.

Grange, having fitted the sock on to two fingers, was examining it with a contemplative air. It struck her abruptly that he was trying to say something. She waited silently, not without apprehension. She had no idea as to how much he knew of what had passed between herself and Nick.

'I say, Miss Roscoe,' he blurted out suddenly, 'do you hate talking about these things – very badly, I mean?'

She looked up at him, and was surprised to see emotion on his face. It had an odd effect upon her, placing her unaccountably at her ease with him, banishing all her stiffness in a moment. She remembered with a quick warmth at her heart how she had always liked this man in those far-off days of her father's protection, how she had always found something reassuring in his gentle courtesy.

'No,' she said, after a moment, speaking with absolute sincerity. 'I can't bear to with – most people, but I don't think I mind with you.'

She saw his pleasant smile for an instant. He laid the sock

down upon her knee, and in doing so touched and lightly pressed her hand.

'Thank you,' he said simply. 'I know I'm not good at expressing myself, but please believe that I wouldn't hurt you for the world. Miss Roscoe, I have brought some things with me, I think you will like to have – things that belonged to your father. Sir Reginald Bassett entrusted them to me – left them in fact in my charge, as he found them. I was coming Home, and I asked leave to bring them to you. Perhaps you would like me to fetch them?'

She was on her feet as he asked the question, on her face such a look of eagerness as it had not worn for many weary months.

'Oh, please – if you would!' she said, her words falling fast and breathless. 'It has been – such a grief to me – that I had nothing of his to – to treasure.'

He turned at once to the door. The desolation that those words of hers revealed to him went straight to his man's heart. Poor little girl! Had the parting been so infernally hard as even now to bring that look to her eyes? Was her father's memory the only interest she had left in her sad young life? And all the evening, save for that first brief moment of their meeting, he had been thinking her cold, impassive, even cynical.

With a deep pity in his soul he departed on his errand.

Returning with the soft tread which was his peculiarity, he surprised her with her face in her hands in an attitude of such abandonment that he drew back hesitating. But suddenly aware of him, she sprang up swiftly, with no sign of tears upon her face.

'Oh, come in, come in!' she said impatiently. 'Why do you stand there?'

She ran forward to meet him with hands hungrily out-stretched, and he put into them those trifles which were to her so infinitely precious – a cigarette-case, a silver match-box, a pen-knife, a little old prayer-book very worn at the edges,

with all the gilt faded from its leaves. She gathered them to
her breast closely, passionately. All but the prayer-book had
been her gifts to the father she had worshipped. With a wrung
heart she called to mind the occasion upon which each had
been offered, his smile of kindly appreciation, the old-world
courtliness of his thanks. With loving hands she laid them
down one by one, lingering over each, seeing them through
a blur of tears. She was no longer conscious of Grange, as
reverently, even diffidently, she opened last of all the little
shabby prayer-book that her father had been wont to take
with him on all his marches. She knew that he had cherished
it as her mother's gift.

It opened upon a scrap of white heather which marked
the Service for the Burial of the Dead. Her tears fell upon the
faded sprig, and she brushed her hand swiftly across her
eyes, looking more closely as certain words underlined
caught her attention. Other words had been written by her
father's hand very minutely in the margin.

The passage underlined was . . . 'not to be sorry, as men
without hope, for them that sleep . . . ' and in a moment she
guessed that her father had made that mark on the day
of her mother's death. It was like a message to her, the echo
of a cry.

The words in the margin were so small that she had to carry
them to the light to read them. And then they flashed out at
her as if sprung suddenly to light on the white paper. There,
in the beloved handwriting, sure and indelible, she read it, and
across the desert of her heart, voiceless but insistent, there
swept the hunger-cry of a man's soul: OMNIA VINCIT AMOR.

It pulsed through her like an electric current, seeming to
overwhelm every other sensation, shutting her off as it were
from the home-world to which she had fled, how fruitlessly,
for healing. Once more skeleton fingers held hers, shifting to
and fro, to and fro, slowly, ceaselessly, flashing the deep rays
that shone from ruby hearts hither and thither. Once more –
But she would not bear it! She was free! She was free! She

flung out the hand that once had worn those rubies, and, resisting wildly, broke away from the spell that the words her father had written had woven afresh for her.

It might be true that Love conquered all things – he had believed it – but ah, what had this uncanny force to do with Love? Love was a pure, a holy thing, the bond imperishable – the Eternal Flame at which all the little torches of the world are lighted.

Moreover, there was no fear in Love, and she – she was sick with fear whenever she encountered that haunting phantom of memory.

With a start she awoke to the fact that she was not alone. Blake Grange had taken her out-flung hand, and was speaking to her softly, soothingly.

'Don't grieve so awfully, Miss Roscoe,' he urged, a slight break in his own voice. 'You're not left friendless. I know how it is. I've felt like it myself. But it gets better afterwards.'

Muriel suffered him with a dawning sense of comfort. It surprised her to see tears in his eyes. She wondered vaguely if they were for her.

'Yes,' she said, after a pause. 'It does get better, I know, in a way. Or at least one gets used to an empty heart. One gets to leave off listening for what one will never, never hear any more.'

'Never is a dreary word,' said Grange.

She bent her head silently, and again his heart overflowed with pity for her. He looked down at the hand that lay so passively in his.

'I hope you will always think of me as a friend,' he said.

She looked up at him, a quick gleam of gratitude in her eyes. 'Thank you,' she said. 'Yes, always.'

He still held her hand. 'You know,' he said, blundering awkwardly. 'I always blamed myself that – that I wasn't the one to be with you when you escaped from Wara. I might have been. But I – I wasn't prepared to pay the possible price.'

She was still looking at him with those aloof, tragic eyes of hers. 'I don't understand,' she said, 'I never did understand – exactly – why Nick was chosen to protect me. I always wished it had been you.'

'It ought to have been,' Grange said, with feeling. 'It should have been. I blame myself. But Nick is a better fighter than I. He keeps his head. Moreover, he's a savage in some respects. I wasn't savage enough.'

He smiled with a hint of apology.

Muriel repressed a shudder at his words. 'I don't understand,' she said again.

He hesitated. 'It's a difficult thing to explain to you,' he said reluctantly. 'You see, the fellow who took charge of you had to be prepared for – well – anything. You know what devils those tribesmen are. There was to be no chance of your falling into their hands. It didn't mean just fighting for you, you understand. We would all have done that to the last drop of our blood. But – your father – was forced to ask of us – something more. And only Ratcliffe would undertake it. He's a queer chap. I used to think him a rotter till I saw him fight, and then I had to change my mind. That was, I believe, the main reason why General Roscoe selected him as your protector. He knew he could trust the fellow's nerve. The rest of us were like women compared to Nick.'

He paused. Muriel's eyes had not flinched from his. She heard his explanation as one not vitally concerned.

'Have I not made myself intelligible?' he asked, as she did not speak.

'Do you mean I was to be shot if things went wrong?' she returned, in her deep, quiet voice.

He nodded. 'It must have been that. Your father saw it in that light, and so did we. Of course you are bound to see it too. But we stuck at it – Marshall and I. There was only Nick left, and he volunteered.'

'Only Nick left!' she repeated slowly. 'Nick would stick at nothing, Captain Grange.'

'I honestly don't think he would,' said Grange. 'Still, you know, he's awfully plucky. He would have gone any length to save you first.'

She drew back with a sudden shrinking of her whole body. 'Oh, I know, I know!' she said. 'I sometimes think there is a devil in Nick.'

She turned aside, bending once more over her father's things, putting them together with unsteady fingers. So this was the answer to the riddle – the secret of his choice for her? She understood it all now.

After a short pause, she spoke again more calmly. 'Did Nick ever speak to you about me?'

'Never,' said Grange.

'Then please, Captain Grange' – she stood up again and faced him – 'never speak to me again about him. I – want to forget him.'

Very young and slight she looked standing there, and again he felt his heart stir within him with an urgent pity. Vague rumours he had heard of those few weeks at Simla during which her name and Nick Ratcliffe's had been coupled together, but he had never definitely known what had taken place. Had Nick been good to her, he wondered for the first time? How was it that the bare mention of him was unendurable to her? What had he done that she should shudder with horror when she remembered him, and should seek thus with loathing to thrust him out of her life?

Involuntarily the man's hands clenched and his blood quickened. Had the General's trust been misplaced? Was Nick a blackguard?

Finding her eyes still upon him, he made her a slight bow that was wholly free from gallantry.

'I will remember your wish, Miss Roscoe,' he said. 'I am sorry I mentioned a painful subject though I am glad for you to know the truth. You are not vexed with me, I hope?'

Her eyes shone with sincere friendliness. 'I am not vexed,' she answered. 'Only – let me forget – that's all.'

And in those few words she voiced the prayer of her soul. It was her one longing, her one prayer – to forget. And it was the one thing of all others denied to her.

In the silence that followed, she was conscious of his warm and kindly sympathy, and she was grateful for it, though something restrained her from telling him so.

Daisy, coming lightly in upon them, put an end to their *tête-à-tête*. She entered softly, her face alight and tender, and laid her two hands upon Grange's great shoulders as he sat before the fire.

'Come upstairs, Blake,' she whispered, 'and see my baby boy. He's sleeping so sweetly. I want you to see him first while he's good.'

He raised his face to her smiling, his hands on hers. 'I am sure to admire anything that belongs to you, Daisy,' he said.

'You're a dear old pal,' responded Daisy lightly, 'Come along.'

When they were gone Muriel spied Will Musgrave's letter lying on the ground by Grange's chair as it had evidently fallen from Daisy's dress. She went over and picked it up. It was still unopened.

With an odd little frown she set it up prominently on the mantelpiece.

'Does Love conquer after all?' she murmured to herself, and there was a faint twist of cynicism about her lips as she asked the question. There seemed to be so many forms of Love.

Chapter 19

'Well played! Oh, well played! Miss Roscoe, you're a brick.'

The merry voice of the doctor's little daughter Olga aged fourteen, shrilled across the hockey-ground, keen with enthusiasm. She was speeding across the field like a hare to congratulate her latest recruit.

'I'm so pleased!' she cried, bursting through the miscellaneous crowd of boys and girls that surrounded Muriel. 'I wanted you to shoot that goal.'

She herself had been acting as goal-keeper at her own end of the field, a position of limited opportunities which she had firmly refused to assign to the newcomer. A child of unusual character was Olga Ratcliffe, impulsive but shrewd, with quick, pale eyes which never seemed to take more than a brief glance at anything, yet which very little ever escaped. At first sight Muriel had experienced a certain feeling of aversion to her, so marked was the likeness this child bore to the man whom she desired so passionately to shut out of her very memory. But a nearer intimacy had weakened her antipathy till very soon it had altogether disappeared. Olga had a swift and fascinating fashion of endearing herself to all who caught her fancy and, somewhat curiously, Muriel was one of the favoured number. What there was to attract a child of her quick temperament in the grave, silent girl in mourning who held aloof so coldly from the rest of the world was never apparent. But that a strong attraction existed for her was speedily evident, and Muriel, who was quite destitute of any near relations of her own, soon found that a free admittance to the doctor's home circle was accorded her on all sides, whenever she chose to avail herself of it.

But though Daisy was an immense favourite and often ran into the Ratcliffes' house, which was not more than a few hundred yards away from her own little abode, Muriel went but seldom. The doctor's wife, though always kind, was too busy to seek her out. And so it had been left to the doctor himself to drag her at length from her seclusion, and he had done it with a determination that would take no refusal. She did not know him very intimately, had never asked his advice, or held any confidential talk with him. At the outset she had been horribly afraid lest he should have heard of her engagement to Nick, but, since he never referred to her life in India or to Nick as in any fashion connected with herself, this fear had gradually subsided. She was able to tell herself thankfully that Nick was dropping away from her into

the past, and to hope with some conviction that the great
gulf that separated them would never be bridged.

Yet, notwithstanding this, she had a fugitive wish to know
how her late comrade in adversity was faring. Captain
Grange's news regarding him had aroused in her a vague
uneasiness, which would not be quieted.

She wondered if by any means she could extract any
information from Olga, and this she presently assayed to do,
when play was over for the day and Olga had taken her
upstairs to prepare for tea.

Olga was the easiest person in the world to deal with upon
such a subject. She expanded at the very mention of Nick's
name.

'Oh, do you know him? Isn't he a darling? I have a photograph of him somewhere. I must try and find it. He is in
fancy dress and standing on his head – such a beauty.
Weren't you awfully fond of him? He has been ill, you know.
Dad was very waxy because be wouldn't come home. He
might have had sick leave, but he wouldn't take it. However,
he may have to come yet, Dad says, if something happens.
He didn't say what. It was something to do with his wound.
Dad wants him to leave the Army and settle down on his
estate. He owns a big place about twelve miles away that an
old great-aunt of his left him. Dad thinks a landowner ought
to live at home if he can afford to. And of course Nick might
go into Parliament, too. He's so clever, and rich as well. But
he won't do it. So it's no good talking.'

Olga jumped off the dressing-table, and wound her
arm impulsively through Muriel's. 'Miss Roscoe,' she said
coaxingly, 'I do like you most awfully. May I call you by
your Christian name?'

'Why, do!' Muriel said. 'I should like it best.'

'Oh, that's all right.' said Olga, well pleased. 'I knew you
weren't stuck-up really. I hate stuck-up people, don't you?
I'm awfully pleased that you like Nick. I simply love him –
better almost than anyone else. He writes to me sometimes,

pages and pages. I never show them to anyone, and he doesn't show mine either. You see, we're pals. But I can show you his photograph – the one I told you about. It's just like him – his grin and all. Come up after tea, and I'll find it.'

And with her arm entwined in Muriel's she drew her still talking eagerly from the room.

Chapter 20

'I have been wondering,' Grange said in his shy rather diffident way, 'if you would care to do any riding while I am here.'

'I?' Muriel looked up in some surprise.

They were walking back from church together by a muddy field-path, and since neither had much to say at any time, they had accomplished more than half the distance in silence.

'I know you do ride,' Grange explained, ' and it's just the sort of country for a good gallop now and then. Daisy isn't allowed to, but I thought perhaps you – '

'Oh, I should like to of course,' Muriel said. 'I haven't done any riding since I left Simla. I didn't care to be alone.'

'Ah! Lady Bassett rides, doesn't she? She is an accomplished horsewoman, I believe?'

'I don't know,' Muriel's reply was noticeably curt. I never rode with her.'

Grange at once dropped the subject, and they became silent again. Muriel walked with her eyes fixed straight before her. But she did not see the brown earth underfoot or the bare trees that swayed overhead in the racing winter wind. She was back again in the heart of the Simla pines, hearing horses' feet that stamped below her window in the dawning, and a gay, cracked voice that sang.

Her companion's voice recalled her. 'I suppose Daisy will stay here for the summer.'

'I suppose so,' she answered.

Grange went on with some hesitation. 'The little chap doesn't look as if he would ever stand the Indian climate. What will happen? Will she ever consent to leave him with the Ratcliffes?'

'I am quite certain she won't,' Muriel answered, with unfaltering conviction. 'She simply lives for him.'

'I thought so,' Grange said rather sadly. 'It would go hard with her if – if – '

Muriel's dark eyes flashed swift entreaty. 'Oh, don't say it! Don't think it! I believe it would kill her.'

'She is stronger though?' he questioned almost sharply.

'Yes, yes, much stronger. Only – not strong enough for that Captain Grange, it simply couldn't happen.'

They had reached a gate at the end of the field. Grange stopped before it, and spoke with sudden, deep feeling.

'If it does happen, Muriel,' he said, using her Christian name quite unconsciously, 'we shall have to stand by her, you and I. You won't leave her, will you? You would be of more use to her than I. Oh, it's – it's damnable to see a woman in trouble, and not to be able to comfort her.'

He brought his ungloved hand down upon the gatepost with a violence that drew blood; then, seeing her face of amazement, thrust it hastily behind him.

'I'm a fool,' he said, with his shy, semi-apologetic smile. 'Don't mind me, Miss Roscoe. You know, I – I'm awfully fond of Daisy, always was. My people were her people, and when they died we were the only two left, as it were. Of course she was married by that time, and there are some other relations somewhere. But we've always hung together, she and I. You can understand it, can't you? '

Muriel fancied she could, but his vehemence startled her none the less. She had not deemed him capable of such intensity.

'I suppose you feel almost as if she were your sister,' she remarked, groping half-unconsciously for an explanation.

Grange was holding the gate open for her. He did not instantly reply.

Then, 'I don't know exactly what that feels like,' he said, with an odd shame-facedness. 'But in so far as that we have been playfellows and chums all our lives, I suppose you might describe it in that way.'

And Muriel, though she wondered a little at the laborious honesty of his reply, was satisfied that she understood.

She was drifting into a very pleasant friendship with Blake Grange. He seemed to rely upon her in an indefinable fashion that made their intercourse of necessity one of intimacy. Moreover, Daisy's habits were still more or less those of an invalid, and this fact helped very materially to throw them together.

To Muriel, emerging slowly from the long winter of her sorrow, the growing friendship with this man whom she both liked and admired was as a shaft of sunshine breaking across the grey landscape. Insensibly it was doing her good. The deep shadow of a horror that once had overwhelmed her was lifting gradually away from her life. In her happier moments it almost seemed that she was beginning to forget.

Grange's suggestion that they should ride together awoke in her a keener sense of pleasure than she had known since the tragedy of Wara had darkened her young life, and for the rest of the day she looked forward eagerly to the resumption of this her favourite exercise.

Daisy was delighted with the idea, and when on the following morning Grange ransacked the town for suitable mounts and returned triumphant, she declared gaily that she should take no further trouble for her guest's entertainment. The responsibility from that day forth rested with Muriel.

Muriel was by no means loth to assume it. They got on excellently together, and their almost daily rides became a source of keen pleasure to her. Winter was fast merging into spring, and the magic of the coming season was working in her blood. There were times when a sense of spontaneous happiness would come over her, she knew not wherefor. Jim Ratcliffe no longer looked at her with stern-browed disapproval.

She and Grange both became regular members of Olga's hockey team. They shared most of their pursuits. Among other things she was learning the accompaniments of his songs. Grange had a well-cultivated tenor voice, to which Daisy the restless would listen for any length of time.

Altogether they were a very peaceful trio, and as the weeks slipped on it almost seemed as if the quiet home life they lived were destined to endure indefinitely. Grange spoke occasionally of leaving, but Daisy would never entertain the idea for an instant, and he certainly did not press it very strongly. He was not returning to India before September, and the long summer months that intervened made the date of his departure so remote as to be outside discussion. No one ever thought of it.

But the long, quiet interval in the sleepy little country town, interminable as it might feel, was not destined to last for ever. On a certain afternoon in March, Grange and Muriel, riding home together after a windy gallop across open country, were waylaid outside the doctor's gate by one of the Ratcliffe boys.

The urchin was cheering at the top of his voice and dancing ecstatically in the mud. Olga, equally dishevelled but somewhat more coherent, was seated on the gate-post, her long legs dangling.

'Have you seen Dad? Have you heard?' was her cry. 'Jimmy, come out of the road. You'll be kicked.'

Both riders pulled up to hear the news, Jimmy squirming away from the horses' legs after a fashion that provoked even the mild-tempered Grange to a sharp reproof.

'You haven't heard?' pursued Olga, ignoring her small brother's escapade as too trifling to notice at such a supreme moment. 'But you haven't of course, if you haven't seen Dad. The letter only came an hour ago. It's Nick, dear old Nick!

He's coming home at last!' In her delight over imparting the information Olga nearly toppled over backwards, only saving herself by a violent effort. 'Aren't you glad, Muriel? Aren't you glad?' she cried. 'I was never so pleased in my life?'

But Muriel had no reply ready. For some reason her animal had become suddenly restive, and occupied the whole of her attention.

It was Grange who after a second's hesitation asked for further particulars. 'What is he coming for? Is it sick leave?'

Olga nodded. 'He isn't to stay out there for the hot weather. It's something to do with his wound. He doesn't want to come a bit. But he is to start almost at once. He may be starting now.'

'Not likely,' put in Jimmy. 'The end of March was what he said. Dad said he couldn't be here before the third week in April.'

'Oh, well, that isn't long, is it?' said Olga eagerly. 'Not when you come to remember that it's three years since he went away. I do think they might have given him the V.C., don't you? Captain Grange why hasn't he got the V.C.?'

Grange couldn't say really. He advised her to ask the man himself. He was observing Muriel with some uneasiness, and when she at length abruptly waved her whip and rode sharply on as though her horse were beyond her control, he struck spurs into his own and started in pursuit.

Muriel passed her own gate at a canter, but hearing Grange behind her she soon reined in, and they trotted some distance side by side in silence.

But Grange was still uneasy. The girl's rigid profile had that stony, aloof look that he had noted upon his arrival weeks before, and that he had come to associate with her escape from Wara.

Nevertheless when she presently addressed him, it was in her ordinary tone and upon a subject indifferent to them both. She had received a shock, he knew, but she plainly did not wish him to remark it.

They rode quite soberly back again, and separated at the door.

Chapter 21

To Daisy the news that Grange imparted was more pleasing than startling. 'I knew he would come before long if he were a wise man,' she said.

But when her cousin wanted to know what she meant, she would not tell him.

'No, I can't, Blake,' was her answer. 'I once promised Muriel never to speak of it. She is very sensitive on the subject.'

Grange did not press for an explanation. It was not his way. He left her moodily, a frown of deep dissatisfaction upon his handsome face. Daisy did not spend much thought upon him. Her interests at that time were almost wholly centred upon her boy, who was so backward and delicate that she was continually anxious about him. She was in fact so preoccupied that she hardly noticed at dinner that Muriel scarcely spoke and ate next to nothing.

Grange remarked both facts, and his moodiness increased. When Daisy went up to the nursery, he at once followed Muriel into the drawing-room. She was standing by the window when he entered, a slim, straight figure in unrelieved black; but though she must have heard him, she neither spoke nor turned her head.

Grange closed the door and came softly forward. There was an unwonted air of resolution about him that made him look almost grim. He reached her side and stood there silently. The wind had fallen, and the sky was starry.

After a brief silence Muriel dropped the blind and looked at him. There was something of interrogation in her glance.

'Shall we go into the garden?' she suggested.

He fell in at once with the proposal, 'You will want a cloak,' he said. 'Can I fetch you one?'

'Oh, thanks! Anything will do. I believe there's one of Daisy's in the hall.'

She moved across the room quickly, as one impatient to escape from a confined space. Grange followed her. He was not smoking as usual. They went out together into the warm darkness, and passed side by side down the narrow path that wound between the bare flowerbeds. It was a wonderful night. Once as they walked, there drifted across them a sudden fragrance of violets.

They reached at length a rustic gate that led into the doctor's meadow, and here with one consent they stopped. Very far away a faint wind was stirring, but close at hand there was no sound. Again, from the wet earth by the gate, there rose the magic scent of violets.

Muriel rested her clasped hands upon the gate, and spoke in a voice unconsciously hushed.

'I never realized how much I liked this place before,' she said. 'Isn't it odd? I have been actually happy here and I didn't know it.'

'You are not happy to-night,' said Grange.

She did not attempt to contradict him. 'I think I am rather tired,' she said.

'I don't think that is quite all,' he returned, with quiet conviction.

She moved, turning slightly towards him; but she said nothing, though he obviously waited for some response.

For awhile he was discouraged, and silence fell again upon them. Then at length he braced himself for an effort. For all his shyness he was not without a certain strength.

'Miss Roscoe,' he said, 'do you remember how you once promised that you would always regard me as a friend?'

She turned fully towards him then, and he saw her face dimly in the starlight. He thought she looked very pale.

'I do,' she said simply.

In a second his diffidence fell away from him. He realized that the ground on which he stood was firm. He bent towards her.

'I want you to keep that promise of yours in its fullest sense to-night, Muriel,' he said, and his soft voice had in it almost a caressing note. 'I want you – if you will – to tell me what is the matter.'

Muriel stood before him with her face upturned. He could not read her expression, but he knew by her attitude that she had no thought of repelling him.

'What is it?' he urged gently. 'Won't you tell me?'

'Don't you know?' she asked him slowly.

'I only know that what we heard this afternoon upset you,' he answered. 'And I don't understand it. I am asking you to explain.'

'You will only think me very foolish and absurd.'

There was a deep quiver in the words, and he knew that she was trembling. Very kindly he laid his hand upon her shoulder.

'Can't you trust me better than that?' he asked.

She did not answer him. Her breathing became suddenly sharp and irregular, and he realized that she was battling for self-control.

'I don't know if I can make you understand,' she said at last. 'But I will try.'

'Yes, try!' he said gently. 'You won't find it so very difficult.'

She turned back to the gate, and leaned wearily upon it.

'You are very kind. You always have been. I couldn't tell anyone else – not even Daisy. You see, she is – his friend. But you are different. I don't think you like him, do you?'

Grange hesitated a little. 'I won't go so far as to say that,' he said finally. 'We get on all right. I was never very intimate with the fellow. I think he is a bit callous.'

'Callous!' Muriel gave a sudden hard shudder. 'He is much worse than callous. He is hideously, almost devilishly cruel. But – but – he isn't only that Blake, do you think he is quite human? He is so horribly, so unnaturally strong.'

Grange heard the scared note in her voice, and drew very close to her. 'I think,' he said quietly, 'that – without knowing it – you exaggerate both his cruelty and his strength. I know he is a queer chap. I once heard it said of him that he has the eyes of a snake-charmer, and I believe it more or less. But I assure you he is human – quite human. And – ' he spoke with unwonted emphasis – 'he has no more power over you – not an inch – than you choose to give him.'

Muriel uttered a faint sigh. 'I knew I should never make you understand.'

Grange was silent. He might have retorted that she had given him very little information to go upon, but he forebore. There was an almost colossal patience about this man. His silence had in it nothing of resentment.

After a few seconds Muriel went on, her voice very low. 'I would give anything – all I have – not to meet him when he comes back. But I don't know how to get away from him. He is sure to seek me out. And I – I am only a girl. I can't prevent it.'

Again there sounded that piteous quiver in her words. It was like the cry of a lost child. Grange heard it, and clenched his hands, but he did not speak. He was gazing straight ahead, stern-eyed and still.

Muriel scarcely noticed his attitude. Having at length broken through her barrier of reserve, she found a certain relief in speech.

'I might go away, of course,' she said. 'I expect I shall do that, for I don't think I could endure it here. But I haven't many friends. My year in India seemed to cut me off from everyone. It's a little difficult to know where to go. And then too there is Daisy.'

She paused, and suddenly Grange spoke, with more abruptness than was his wont.

'Why do you think he is sure to seek you out? Did he ever say so?'

She shivered. 'No, he never said so. But – but – in a way I feel it. He is so merciless. He always makes me think of an eagle swooping down on its prey. No doubt you think me very fanciful and ridiculous. Perhaps I am. But once – in the mountains – he told me that I belonged to him – that he would not let me go, and – and – I have never been able to forget it.'

Her voice sank, and it seemed to Grange that she was crying in the darkness. Her utter forlornness pierced him to the heart. He leaned towards her, trying ineffectually to see her face.

'My dear little girl,' he said gently, 'don't be so distressed. He deserves to be kicked for frightening you like this.'

'It's my own fault,' she whispered back. 'If I were stronger, or if Daddy were with me – it would be different. But I am all alone. There is no one to help me. I used to think it didn't matter what happened to me, but I am beginning to feel it does.'

'Of course it does,' Grange said. His hand felt along the rail for hers, and, finding them, held them closely. Her weakness gave him confidence. 'Poor child!' he murmured softly. 'Poor little girl! You do want someone to take care of you.'

Muriel mastered herself with an effort. It was not often now that she gave way so completely.

'It's only now and then,' she said. 'It's better than it used to be. Only somehow I got frightened when I heard that Nick was coming. I daresay – when I begin to get used to the idea – I shan't mind it quite so much. Never mind about my silly worries any more. No doubt I shall get wiser as I grow older.'

She tried to laugh with the words, but somehow no laugh came. Grange's great hand closed very tightly upon hers, and she looked up in surprise.

Almost instantly he began to speak, very humbly, but also very resolutely. 'Muriel,' he said, 'I'm an unutterable fool at expressing things. I can only say them straight out and hope for the best. You want a protector, don't you? And I – should like to be the one to protect you if – if it were ever possible for you to think of me in that light.'

He spoke with immense effort. He was afraid of scaring

her, afraid of hurting her desolate young heart, afraid almost of the very impulse that moved him to speak.

Absolute silence reigned when he ended.

Muriel had become suddenly rigid, and so still that she did not seem to breathe. For several seconds he waited, but still she made no sign. He had not the remotest clue to guide him. He began to feel as if a door had unexpectedly closed against him, not violently, but steadily, soundlessly, barring him out.

It was but a fleeting impression. In a few moments more it was gone. She drew a long quivering breath, and turned slightly towards him.

'I would rather trust myself to you,' she said, 'than to anyone else in the world.'

She spoke in her deep, sincere voice which gave him no doubt that she meant what she said, and at once his own trepidation departed. He put his arm around her, and pressed her close to him.

'Come to me then,' he said very tenderly. 'And I will take such care of you, Muriel, that no one shall ever frighten you again.'

She yielded to his touch as simply as a child, leaning her head against him with a little, weary gesture of complete confidence. She was desperately tired of standing alone.

'I know I shall be safe with you,' she whispered.

'Quite safe, dear,' he answered gravely.

He paused a moment as though irresolute; then, still holding her closely, he bent and kissed her forehead.

He did it very quietly and reverently, but at the action she started, almost shrank. One of those swift flashes of memory came suddenly upon her, and as in a vision she beheld another face bending over her – a yellow, wrinkled face of terrible emaciation, with eyes of flickering fire – eyes that never slept – and heard a voice, curiously broken and incoherent, that seemed to pray. She could not catch the words it uttered.

The old wild panic rushed over her, the old frenzied longing to escape. With a sobbing gasp she turned in Grange's arms, and clung to him.

'Oh, Captain Grange,' she panted piteously, 'promise – promise you will never let me go!'

Her agitation surprised him, but it awaked in him a responsive tenderness that compassed her with a strength bred rather of emergency than habit.

'My little girl, I swear I will never let you go,' he said, with grave reassurance. 'You are quite safe now. No one shall ever take you from me.'

And it was to Muriel as if, after long and futile battling in the open sea, she had drifted at last into the calm haven which surely had always been the goal of her desires.

Chapter 22

Jim Ratcliffe was in the drawing-room with Daisy when they returned. He scrutinized them both somewhat sharply as they came in, but he made no comment upon their preference for the garden. Very soon he rose to take his leave.

Grange accompanied him to the door, and Muriel, suddenly possessed by an overwhelming sense of shyness, bent over Daisy and murmured a hasty goodnight.

Daisy looked at her for a moment. 'Tired, dear?'

'A little,' Muriel admitted.

'I hope you haven't been catching cold – you and Blake,' Daisy said, as she kissed her.

Muriel assured her to the contrary, and hastened to make her escape. In the hall she came face to face with Blake. He met her with a smile.

'What! Going up already?'

She nodded. Her face was burning. For an instant her hand lay in his.

'You tell Daisy,' she whispered, and fled upstairs like a scared bird.

Grange stood till she was out of sight; then turned aside to the drawing-room, the smile wholly gone from his face.

Daisy, from her seat before the fire, looked up with her gay laugh. 'I'm sure there is a secret brewing between you two,' she declared. 'I can feel it in my bones.'

Grange closed the door carefully. There was a queer look on his face, almost an apprehensive look. He took up his stand on the hearth-rug before he spoke.

'You are not far wrong, Daisy,' he said then.

She answered him lightly as ever. 'I never am, my dear Blake. Surely you must have noticed it. Well, am I to be let into the plot, or not?'

He looked at her for a moment uneasily. 'Of course we shall tell you,' he said. 'It – it's not a thing we could very well keep to ourselves for any length of time.'

A sudden gleam of understanding flashed into Daisy's upturned face, and instantly her expression changed. With a swift, vehement movement she sprang up and stood before him.

'Blake!' she exclaimed, and in her voice astonishment, dismay, and even reproach, were mingled.

He averted his eyes from hers. 'Won't you congratulate me, Daisy?' he said, speaking almost under his breath.

Daisy had turned very white. She put out both hands, and leaned upon the mantelpiece.

'But my dear Blake,' she said, after a moment, 'she is not for you.'

'What do you mean?' Grange's jaw suddenly set itself. He squared his great shoulders as if instinctively bracing himself to meet opposition.

'I mean' – Daisy spoke very quietly and emphatically – 'I mean, Blake, that she is Nick's property. She belonged to Nick before ever you thought of wanting her. I never dreamed that you would do anything so shabby as to step in at the last moment, just when Nick is coming home, and cut him out. How could you do such a thing, Blake? But surely it isn't irrevocable? You can't have said anything definite?'

Grange's face had become very stern. He no longer avoided her eyes. For once he was really angry, and showed it.

'You make a mistake,' he told her curtly. 'I have done nothing whatever of which I am ashamed, or of which any man could be ashamed. Certainly I have taken a definite step. I have proposed to her and she has accepted me. With regard to Nick Ratcliffe, I believe myself that the fellow is something of a blackguard, but in any case she both fears and hates him. He can have no shadow of a right over her.'

'You forget that he saved her life,' said Daisy.

'Is she to hold herself at his disposal on that account? I must say I fail to see the obligation.'

There was even a hint of scorn in Grange's tone. At sound of it, Daisy turned round, and laid her hand winningly upon his arm.

'Dear old boy,' she said gently, 'don't be angry. I'm not against you.'

He softened instantly. It was not in him to harbour resentment against a woman. He took her hand, and heaved a deep sigh.

'No, Daisy,' he said half sadly, 'you mustn't be against me. I always count on you.'

Daisy laughed a little wistfully. 'Always did, dear, didn't you? Well, tell me some more. What made you propose all of a sudden like this? Are you – very much in love?'

He looked at her. 'Perhaps not quite as we used to understand the term,' he said, seeming to speak half-reluctantly.

'Oh, we were very extravagant and foolish,'' rejoined Daisy lightly. 'I didn't mean quite in that way, Blake. You at least are past the age for such feathery nonsense, or should be. I was – æons and æons ago.'

'Were you?' he said, and still he looked at her half in wonder, it seemed, and half in regret.

Daisy nodded at him briskly. The colour had come back to her face. 'Yes, I have arrived at years of discretion,' she assured him. 'And I quite agree with Solomon that childhood and youth are vanity. But now let us talk about this. Is she in love with you, I wonder? I must be remarkably blind not to have seen it. How in the world I shall ever face Nick again I can't imagine.'

Grange frowned. 'I'm getting a bit tired of Nick,' he said moodily. 'He crops up everywhere.'

Daisy's face flushed. 'Don't you ever again say a word against him in my hearing,' she said. 'For I won't bear it. He may not be handsome like you. But for all that, he's about the finest man I know.'

'Good heavens!' said Blake. 'As much as that!'

She nodded vehemently 'Yes, quite as much. And he loves her too, loves her with his whole soul. Perhaps you never knew that they would have been married long ago in Simla if Muriel hadn't overheard some malicious gossip and thrown him over. How in the world she made him let her go I never knew, but she did it though I believe it nearly broke his heart. He came to me afterwards and begged me to keep her with me as long as I could, and take care of her.'

'All this,' broke in Grange, 'is what you promised never to speak of.'

'Yes,' she admitted recklessly. 'But it is what you ought to know – what you must know – before you go any further.'

'It will make no difference to me,' he observed. 'It is quite obvious that she never cared for him in the smallest degree. Why, my dear girl, she hates the man!'

Daisy gave vent to a sigh of exasperation. 'When you come to talk about women's feelings, Blake, you make me tired. You will never be anything but a great big booby in that respect as long as you live.'

Grange became silent. He never argued with Daisy. She had always had the upper hand. He watched her as she sat down again, her pretty face in the glow of the fire; but though fully aware of the fact she would not look at him.

'She is a dear girl, and you are not half good enough for her,' she said, stooping a little to the blaze.

'I know that,' he answered bluntly. 'I wasn't good enough for you either, but you would have had me – once.'

She made a dainty gesture with one shoulder. 'That also was æons ago. Why disturb that poor old skeleton?'

He did not answer, but he continued to watch her steadily with eyes that held an expression of dumb faithfulness – like the eyes of a dog.

Daisy was softly and meditatively poking the fire, 'If you marry her, Blake,' she said, 'you will have to be enormously good to her. She isn't the sort of girl to be satisfied with anything but the best.'

'I should do my utmost to make her happy,' he answered.

She glanced up momentarily. 'I wonder if you would succeed,' she murmured.

For a single instant their eyes met. Daisy's fell away at once, and the firelight showed a swift deepening of colour on her face.

As for Blake, he stood quite stiff for a few seconds, then with an abruptness of movement unusual with him, he knelt suddenly down beside her.

'Daisy,' he said, and his voice sounded strained, almost hoarse, 'you're not vexed about it? You don't mind my marrying? It isn't – you know – it isn't – as if – '

He broke off, for Daisy had jerked upright as if at the piercing of a nerve. She looked at him fully, with blazing eyes. 'How can you be so ridiculous, Blake?' she exclaimed, with sharp impatience. 'That was all over and done with long, long ago, and you know it. Besides, even if it hadn't been, I'm not a dog in the manger. Surely you know that too. Oh, go away, and don't be absurd!'

She put her hand against his shoulder, and gave him a small but vehement push.

He stood up again immediately, but he did not look hurt, and the expression of loyalty in his eyes never wavered.

There was a short pause before Daisy spoke again.

'Well,' she said, with a brief sigh, 'I suppose it's no good crying over spilt milk, but I wish you'd chosen any girl in the world but Muriel, Blake; I do indeed. You will have to write to Sir Reginald Bassett. He is her guardian, subject to his wife's management. Perhaps she will approve of you. She hated Nick for some reason.'

'I don't see how they can object,' Grange said, in the moody tone he always used when perplexed.

'No,' said Daisy. 'Nor did Nick. But Lady Bassett managed to put a spoke in his wheel notwithstanding. Still if Muriel wants to marry you – or thinks she does – she will probably take her own way. And possibly regret it afterwards.'

'You think I shall not make her happy?' said Grange.

Daisy hesitated a little. 'I think,' she said slowly, 'that you are not the man for her. However,' – she rose with another shrug – 'I may be wrong. In any case you have gone too far for me to meddle. I can't help either of you now. You must just do what you think best.' She held out her hand. 'I must go up now. Baby is restless to-night, and may want me. Good-night.'

Blake stooped and, carried her hand softly and suddenly to his lips. He seemed for an instant on the verge of saying something, but no words came. There was a faint half-mocking smile on Daisy's face as she turned away. But she was silent also. It seemed that they understood each other.

Chapter 23

It was an unspeakable relief to Muriel that, in congratulating her upon her engagement, Daisy made no reference to Nick. She did not know that this forbearance had been dictated long before by Nick himself.

The days that followed her engagement had in them a sort of rapture that she had never known before. She felt as a young wild creature suddenly escaped from the iron jaws of a trap in which it had long languished, and she rioted in the sense of liberty that was hers. Her youth was coming back to her in leaps and bounds with the advancing spring.

She missed nothing in Blake's courtship. His gentleness had always attracted her, and the intimacy that had been growing up between them made their intercourse always easy and pleasant. They never spoke of Nick. But ever in Muriel's heart there lay the soothing knowledge that she had nothing more to fear. Her terrible, single-handed contests against overwhelming odds were over, and she was safe. She was convinced that, whatever happened, Blake would take care of her. Was he not the protector she would have chosen from the beginning, could she but have had her way?

So placidly and happily, the days drifted by, till March was nearly gone; and then, sudden and staggering as a shell from a masked battery, there fell the blow that was destined to end that peaceful time.

Very late one night there came a nervous knocking at Muriel's door, and springing up from her bed she came face to face with Daisy's *ayah*. The woman was grey with fright, and babbling incoherently. Something about 'baba' and the 'mem-sahib' Muriel caught, and instantly guessed that the baby had been taken ill. She flung a wrap round her, and hastened to the nursery.

It was a small room opening out of Daisy's bedroom. The light was turned on full, and here Daisy herself was walking up and down with the baby in her arms.

Before Muriel was well in the room, she stopped and spoke. Her face was ghastly pale, and she could not raise her voice above a whisper though she made repeated efforts. 'Go to Blake!' she panted. 'Go quickly! Tell him to fetch Jim Ratcliffe. Quick! Quick!'

Muriel flew to do her bidding. In her anxiety she scarcely

waited to knock at Blake's door, but burst in upon him head-long. The room was in total darkness but he awoke instantly.

'Hullo! What is it? That you, Muriel?'

'Oh, Blake!' she gasped. 'The child's ill. We want the doctor.'

He was up in a moment. She heard him groping for matches, but he only succeeded in knocking something over.

'Can't you find them?' she asked. 'Wait! I'll get you a light.'

She ran back to her own room and fetched a candle. Her hands were shaking so that she could scarcely light it. Returning, she found Grange putting on his clothes in the darkness. He was fully as flurried as she.

As she set down the candle there arose a sudden awful sound in Daisy's room.

Muriel stood still. 'Oh what is that?'

Grange paused in the act of dragging on his coat. 'It's that damned *ayah*,' he said savagely.

And in a second Muriel understood. Daisy's *ayah* was wailing for the dead.

She put her hands over her ears. The dreadful cry seemed to pierce right through to her very soul. Then she remembered Daisy, and turned to go to her.

Out in the passage she met the white-faced English servants huddling together and whispering. One of them was sobbing hysterically. She passed them swiftly by.

Back in Daisy's room she found the *ayah*, crouched on the floor and rocking herself to and fro while she beat her breast and wailed. The door that led into the nursery was closed.

Muriel advanced fiercely upon the woman. She almost felt as if she could have choked her. She seized her by the shoulders without ceremony. The *ayah* ceased her wailing for a moment, then recommenced in a lower key. Muriel pulled her to her feet, half-dragged, half-led her to her own room, thrust her within, and locked the door upon her. Then she returned to Daisy.

She found her sunk in a rocking-chair before the waning

fire, softly swaying to and fro with the baby on her breast. She looked at Muriel entering, with a set, still face.

'Has Blake gone?' she asked, still in that dry, powerless whisper.

Muriel moved to her side, and knelt down. 'He is just going,' she began to say, but the words froze on her lips.

She remained motionless for a long second, gazing at the tiny, waxen face on Daisy's breast. And for that second her heart stood still. For she knew that the baby was dead.

From the closed room across the passage came the muffled sound of the *ayah*'s wailing. Daisy made a slight impatient movement.

'Stir the fire,' she whispered. 'He feels so cold.'

But Muriel did not move to obey. Instead, she held out her arms.

'Let me take him, dear,' she begged tremulously.

Daisy shook her head with a jealous tightening of her clasp. 'He has been so ill, poor wee darling,' she whispered. It came on suddenly. There was no time to do anything. But he is easier now. I think he is asleep. We won't disturb him.'

Muriel said no more. She rose and blindly poked the fire. Then – for the sight of Daisy rocking her dead child with that set, ashen face was more than she could bear – she turned and stole away, softly closing the door behind her.

Again meeting the English servants hovering outside, she sent them downstairs to light the kitchen fire, going herself to the dining-room window to watch for the doctor. Her feet were bare and freezing, but she would not return to her room for slippers. She felt she could not endure that awful wailing at close quarters again. Even as it was, she heard it fitfully; but from the nursery there came no sound.

She wondered if Blake had gone across the meadow to the doctor's house – it was undoubtedly the shortest cut – and tried to calculate how long it would take him.

The waiting was intolerable. She bore it with a desperate endurance. She could not rid herself of the feeling that somehow Nick was near her. She almost expected to see him come lightly in and stand beside her. Once or twice she turned shivering to assure herself that she was really alone.

There came at last the click of the garden-gate. They had come across the drenched meadows. In a transient gleam of moonlight she saw the two figures striding towards her. Grange stopped a moment to fasten the gate. The doctor came straight on.

She ran to the front door and threw it open. The wind blew swirling all about her, but she never felt it though her very lips were numb and cold.

'It's too late!' she gasped, as he entered. 'It's too late!'

Jim Ratcliffe took her by the shoulders and forced her away from the open door.

'Go and put something on,' he ordered, 'instantly!'

There was no resisting the mastery of his tone. She responded to it instinctively, hardly knowing what she did.

The *ayah*'s paroxysm of grief had sunk to a low moaning when she re-entered her room. It sounded like a dumb creature in pain. Hastily she dressed, and twisted up her hair with fingers that she strove in vain to steady.

Then noiselessly she crept back to the nursery.

Daisy was still rocking softly to and fro before the fire, her piteous burden yet clasped against her heart. The doctor was stooping over her, and Muriel saw the half-eager, half-suspicious look in Daisy's eyes as she watched him. She was telling him in rapid whispers what had happened.

He listened to her very quietly, his keen eyes fixed unblinking upon the baby's face. When she ended, he stooped a little lower, his hand upon her arm.

'Let me take him,' he said.

Muriel trembled for the answer, remembering the instant refusal with which her own offer had been met. But Daisy made no sort of protest. She seemed to yield mechanically.

Only, as he lifted the tiny body from her breast, a startled, almost a bereft look crossed her face, and she whispered quickly, 'You won't let him cry?'

Jim Ratcliffe was silent a moment while he gazed intently at the little lifeless form he held. Then very gently, very pitifully, but withal very steadily, his verdict fell through the silent room.

'He will never cry any more.'

Daisy was on her feet in a moment, the agony in her eyes terrible to see, 'Jim! Jim!' she gasped, in a strangled voice. 'He isn't dead! My little darling, – my baby – the light of my eyes; tell me – he isn't – dead!'

She bent hungrily over the burden he held, and then gazed wildly up into his face. She was shaking as one in an ague.

Quietly he drew the head-covering over the baby's face. 'My dear,' he said, 'there is no death.'

The words were few, spoken almost in an undertone but they sent a curious, tingling thrill through Muriel – a thrill that seemed to reach her heart. For the first time, unaccountably, wholly intangibly she was aware of a strong resemblance between this man whom she honoured and the man she feared. She almost felt as if Nick himself had uttered the words.

Standing dumbly by the door, she saw the doctor stoop to lay the poor little body down in the cot, saw Daisy's face of anguish, and the sudden, wide-flung spread of her empty arms.

The next moment, her woman's instinct prompting her, she sprang forward; and it was she who caught the stricken mother as she fell.

Chapter 24

It was growing very hot in the Plains. A faint breeze born at sunset had died away long ago, leaving a wonderful, breathless stillness behind. The man who sat at work on his

verandah with his shirt-sleeves turned up above his elbows
sighed heavily from time to time as if he felt some oppression
in the atmosphere. He was quite a young man, fair-skinned
and clean-shaven, with an almost pathetically boyish look
about him, a wistful expression as of one whose youth
still endured though the zest thereof was denied to him. His
eyes were weary and bloodshot, but he worked on steadily,
indefatigably, never raising them from the paper under his
hand.

Even when a step sounded in the room behind him, he
scarcely looked up. 'One moment, old chap!' He was still
working rapidly as he spoke. 'I've a toughish bit to get
through. I'll talk to you in a minute.'

There was no immediate reply. A man's figure, dressed in
white linen, with one arm quite invisible under the coat,
stood halting for a moment in the doorway, then moved out
and slowly approached the table at which the other sat.

The lamplight, gleaming upwards, revealed a yellow face
of many wrinkles, and curious, glancing eyes that shone like
fireflies in the gloom.

He stopped beside the man who worked. 'All right,' he
said. 'Finish what you are doing.'

In the silence that followed he seemed to watch the hand
that moved over the paper with an absorbing interest. The
instant it rested he spoke.

'Done?'

The man in the chair stretched out his arms with a long
gesture of weariness; then abruptly leapt to his feet.

'What am I thinking of, keeping you standing here? Sit
down, Nick! Yes, I've done for the present. What a restless
beggar you are! Why couldn't you lie still for a spell?'

Nick grimaced. 'It's an accomplishment I have never been
able to acquire. Besides, there's no occasion for it now. If
I were going to die, it would be a different thing, and even
then I think I'd rather die standing. How are you getting on,
my son? What mean these hieroglyphics?'

He dropped into the empty chair and pored over the paper.

'Oh, you wouldn't understand if I told you,' the other answered. 'You're not an engineer.'

'Not even a greaser of wheels,' admitted Nick modestly. 'But you needn't throw it in my teeth. I suppose you are going to make your fortune soon and retire – you and Daisy and the imp – to a respectable suburb. You're a very lucky chap, Will.'

'Think so?' said Will.

He was bending a little over his work. His tone sounded either absent or dubious.

Nick glanced at him, and suddenly swept his free right hand across the table. 'Put it away!' he said. 'You're over-doing it. Get the wretched stuff out of your head for a bit, and let's have a smoke before dinner. I'll bring her out to you next winter. See if I don't!'

Will turned towards him impulsively. 'Oh, man, if you only could!'

'Only could!' echoed Nick. 'I tell you I will. Ten quid on it if you like. Is it done?'

But Will shook his head with a queer, unsteady smile. 'No, it isn't. But come along and smoke, or you will be having that infernal neuralgia again. It was confoundedly good of you to look me up like this when you weren't fit for it.'

Nick laughed aloud. 'Man alive! You don't suppose I did it for your sake, do you? Don't you know I wanted to break the journey to the coast?'

'Odd place to choose!' commented Will.

Nick arose in his own peculiarly abrupt fashion, and thrust his hand through his friend's arm.

'Perhaps I thought a couple of days of your society would cheer me up,' he observed lightly. 'I daresay that seems odd too.'

Will laughed in spite of himself. 'Well, you've seen me with my nose to the grindstone anyhow. You can tell Daisy I'm working like a troop-horse for her and the boy. Jove!

What a knowing little beggar that youngster used to be! He isn't very strong though, Daisy writes.'

'How often do you hear?' asked Nick.

'Oh, the last letter came three weeks ago. They were all well then, but she didn't stop to say much because Grange was there. He is staying with them, you know.'

'You haven't heard since then?' There was just a hint of indignation in Nick's query.

Will shook his head. 'No. She's a bad correspondent, always was. I write by every mail, and of course, if there were anything I ought to know, she would write too. But they are leading a fairly humdrum existence just now. She can't have much to tell me.'

Nick changed the subject. 'How long has Grange been there?'

'I don't know. Some time, I think. But I really don't know. They are very old pals, you know, he and Daisy. There was a bit of a romance between them, I believe, years ago, when she was in her teens. Their people wouldn't hear of it because they were first cousins, so it fizzled out. But they are still great friends. A good sort of fellow, I always thought.'

'To soft for me,' said Nick. 'He's like a well-built ship adrift without a rudder. He's all manners and no grit – the sort of chap who wants to be pushed behind before he can do anything. I often ached to kick him when we were boxed up at Wara.'

Will smiled. 'The only drawback to indulging in that kind of game is that you may get kicked back, and a kick from a giant like Grange would be no joke.'

Nick looked supremely contemptuous. 'Fellows like Grange don't kick. They don't know how. That's why I had to leave him alone.'

He turned into Will's sitting-room, and stretched himself out upon an ancient *charpoy* furnished with many ancient cushions that stood by the window.

Will gave him a cigarette, and lighted it. 'I wonder how

many nights I have spent on that old shake-down,' he remarked as he did it.

Nick glanced upwards. 'Last year?'

Will nodded. 'It was like hell,' he said, with terrible simplicity. 'I came straight back here, you know, after Daisy left Simla. I suppose the contrast made it worse. Then too the sub was ill, and it meant double work. Well,' with another great sigh, 'we pulled through somehow, and I suppose we shall again. But, Nick, Daisy couldn't possibly stand this place more than four months out of the twelve. And as for the kiddie – '

Nick removed his cigarette to yawn.

'You won't be here all your life, my son,' he said. 'You're a rising man, remember. There's no sense in grizzling anyhow, and you're getting round-shouldered. Why don't you have some gymnastics? You've got a swimming-bath. Go and do a quarter of a mile breast-stroke every day. Jupiter! What wouldn't I give to – ' He broke off abruptly. 'Well I'm not going to cry for the moon either. There's the *khit* on the verandah. What does he want?'

Will went out to see. Nick, idly watching, saw the native hand him something on a salver which Will took to the lamp by which he had been working. Dead silence ensued. From far away there came the haunting cry of a jackal, but near at hand there was no sound. A great stillness hung upon all things.

To Nick, lying at full length upon the cushions, there presently came the faint sound of paper crackling, and a moment later his friend's voice, pitched very low, spoke to the waiting servant. He heard the man softly retire, and again an intense stillness reigned.

He could not see Will from where he lay, and he smoked on placidly for nearly five minutes in the belief that he was either answering some communication or looking over his work. Then at last, growing impatient of the prolonged silence, he lifted his voice without moving.

'What in the world are you doing, you unsociable beggar? Can't you tear yourself away from that beastly work for one night even? Come in here and entertain me. You won't have the chance to-morrow.'

There was no reply. Only from far away there came again the weird yell of a jackal. For a few seconds more Nick lay frowning. Then swiftly and quietly he arose, and stepped to the window.

There he stopped dead as if in sudden irresolution. For Will was sunk upon his knees by the table with his head upon his work and his arms flung out with clenched hands in an attitude of the most utter, the most anguished despair. He made no sound of any sort; only, as Nick watched, his bowed shoulders heaved once convulsively.

It was only for a moment that Nick stood hesitating. The next, obeying an impulse that he never stopped to question, he moved straight forward to Will's side. And then he saw – what he had not seen at first – a piece of paper crumpled and gripped in one of his hands.

He bent over him and spoke rapidly, but without agitation. 'Hullo, old boy! What is it! Bad news, eh?'

Will started and groaned, then sharply turned his face upwards. It was haggard and drawn and ghastly but even then its boyishness remained.

He spoke at once, replying to Nick in short, staccato tones. 'I've had a message – just come through. It's the kiddie – our little chap – he died – last night.'

Nick heard the news in silence. After a moment he stooped forward and took the paper out of Will's hand, thrusting it away without a glance into his own pocket. Then he took him by the arm and hoisted him up. 'Come inside!' he said briefly.

Will went with him blindly, too stricken to direct his own movements.

And so he presently found himself crouching forward in a chair staring at Nick's steady hand mixing whisky and water in a glass at his elbow. As Nick held it towards him he burst into sudden, wild speech.

'I've lost her!' he exclaimed harshly. 'I've lost her! It was only the kiddie that bound us together. She never cared a halfpenny about me. I always knew I should never hold her unless we had a child. And now – and now – '

'Easy!' said Nick. 'Easy! Just drink this like a good chap. There's no sense in letting yourself go.'

Will drank submissively, and covered his face. 'Oh, man,' he whispered brokenly, 'you don't know what it is to be despised by the one being in the world you worship.'

Nick said nothing. His lips twitched a little, that was all.

But when several miserable seconds had dragged away and Will had not moved, he bent suddenly down and put his arm round the huddled shoulders. 'Keep a stiff upper lip, old chap,' he urged gently. 'Don't knock under. She'll be coming to you for comfort presently.'

'Not she!' groaned Will. 'I shall never get near her again. She'll never come back to me. I know. I know.'

'Don't be a fool!' said Nick still gently. 'You don't know. Of course she will come back to you. If you stick to her, she'll stick to you.'

Will made a choked sound of dissent. Nevertheless after a moment he raised his quivering face, and gripped hard the hand that pressed his shoulder. 'Thanks, dear fellow! You're awfully good. Forgive me for making an ass of myself. I – I was awfully fond of the little nipper too. Poor Daisy! She'll be frightfully cut up.' He broke off, biting his lips.

'Do you know,' he said presently in a strained whisper. 'I've wanted her sometimes – so horribly that – that I've been even fool enough to pray about it.'

He glanced up as he made this confidence, half expecting to read ridicule on the alert face above him, but the expression it wore surprised him. It was almost a fighting look, and wholly free from contempt.

Nick seated himself on the edge of the table, and smote

him on the shoulder. 'My dear chap,' he said, with a sudden burst of energy, 'you're only at the beginning of things. It isn't just praying now and then that does it. You've got to keep up the steam, never slack for an instant, whatever happens. The harder going it is, the more likely you are to win through if you stick to it. But directly you slack, you lose ground. If you've only got the grit to go on praying, praying hard, even against your own convictions, you'll get it sooner or later. You are bound to get it. They say God doesn't always grant prayer because the thing you want may not do you any good. That's gammon – futile gammon. If you want it hard enough, and keep on clamouring for it, it becomes the very thing of all others you need – the great essential. And you'll get it for that very reason. It's sheer pluck that counts, nothing else – the pluck to go on fighting when you know perfectly well you're beaten, the pluck to hang on and worry, worry, worry, till you get your heart's desire.'

He sprang up with a wide-flung gesture. 'I'm doing it myself,' he said, and his voice rang with a certain grim elation. 'I'm doing it myself. And God knows I shan't give Him any peace till I'm satisfied. I may be small, but if I were no bigger than a mosquito I'd keep on buzzing.'

He walked to the end of the room, stood for a second, and came slowly back.

Will was looking at him oddly, almost as if he had never seen him before.

'Do you know,' he said, smiling faintly, 'I always thought you were a rotter.'

'Most people do,' said Nick. 'I believe it's my physiognomy that's at fault. What can anyone expect from a fellow with a face like an Egyptian mummy? Why, I've been mistaken for the devil himself before now.' He spoke with a semi-whimsical ruefulness, and, having spoken, he went to the window and stood there with his face to the darkness.

'Hear that jackal, Will?' he suddenly said. 'The brute is hungry. You bet, he won't go empty away.'

'Jackals never do,' said Will, with his weary sigh.

Nick turned round. 'It shows what faithless fools we are,' he said.

In the silence that followed, there came again to them, clear through the stillness, and haunting in its persistence, the crying of the beast that sought its meat from God.

Chapter 25

There is no exhaustion more complete or more compelling than the exhaustion of grief, and it is the most restless temperaments that usually suffer from it the most keenly. It is those who have watched constantly, tirelessly, selflessly, for weeks or even months, for whom the final breakdown is the most utter and the most heartrending.

To Daisy, lying silent in her darkened room, the sudden ending of the prolonged strain, the cessation of the anxiety that had become a part of her very being, was more intolerable than the sense of desolation itself. It lay upon her like a physical, crushing weight, this absence of care, numbing all her faculties. She felt that the worst had happened to her, the ultimate blow had fallen, and she cared for nought besides.

In those first days of her grief she saw none but Muriel and the doctor. Jim Ratcliffe was more uneasy about her than he would admit. He knew as no one else knew what the strain had been upon the over-sensitive nerves, and how terribly the shock had wrenched them. He also knew that her heart was still in a very unsatisfactory state, and for many hours he dreaded collapse.

He was inclined to be uneasy upon Muriel's account as well at first, but she took him completely by surprise. Without a question, without a word, simply as a matter of course, she assumed the position of nurse and constant companion to her friend. Her resolution and steady self-control astonished him, but he soon saw that these were qualities upon which he could firmly rely. She had put her own weakness behind her, and in the face of Daisy's utter need she had found strength.

He suffered her to have her way, seeing how close was the bond of sympathy between them, and realizing that the very act of supporting Daisy would be her own support.

'You are as steady-going as a professional,' he told her once.

To which she answered with her sad smile, 'I served my probation in the school of sorrow last year. I am only able to help her because I know what it is to sit in ashes.'

He patted her shoulder and called her a good girl. He was growing very fond of her, and in his blunt, unflattering way he let her know it.

Certain it was that in those terrible days following her bereavement, Daisy clung to her as she had never before clung to anyone, scarcely speaking to her, but mutely leaning upon her steadfast strength.

Muriel saw but little of Blake though he was never far away. He wandered miserably about the house and garden, smoking endless cigarettes, and invariably asking her with a piteous, dog-like wistfulness whenever they met if there were nothing that he could do. There never was anything, but she had not the heart to tell him so, and she used to invent errands for him to make him happier. She herself did not go beyond the garden for many days.

One evening, about three weeks after her baby's death, Daisy heard his step on the gravel below her window and roused herself a little.

'Who is taking care of Blake?' she asked.

Muriel glanced down from where she sat at the great, listless figure nearing the house. 'I think he is taking care of himself,' she said.

'All alone?' said Daisy.

'Yes, dear.'

Daisy uttered a sudden hard sigh. 'You mustn't spend all your time with me any longer,' she said. 'I have been very selfish. I forgot. Go down to him, Muriel.'

Muriel looked up, struck by something incomprehensible in her tone. 'You know I like to be with you,' she said. 'And of course he understands.'

But Daisy would not be satisfied. 'That may be. But – but – I want you to go to him. He is lonely, poor boy. I can hear it in his step. I always know.'

Wondering at her persistence, and somewhat reluctant, Muriel rose to comply. As she was about to pass her, with a swift movement Daisy caught her hand and drew her down.

'I want you – so – to be happy, dearest,' she whispered, a quick note of passion in her voice. 'It's better for you – it's better for you – to be together. I'm not going to monopolize you any longer. I will try and come down to-morrow, if Jim will let me. It's hockey day, isn't it? You must go and play as usual, you and he.'

She was quivering with agitation as she pressed her lips to the girl's cheek. Muriel would have embraced her, but she pushed her softly away. 'Go – go dear,' she insisted. 'I wish it.'

And Muriel went, seeing that she would not otherwise be pacified.

She found Blake depressed indeed, but genuinely pleased to see her, and she walked in the garden with him in the soft spring twilight till the dinner hour.

Just as they were about to go in, the postman appeared with foreign letters for them both, which proved to be from Sir Reginald and Lady Bassett.

The former had written briefly but very kindly to Grange, signifying his consent to his engagement to his ward, and congratulating him upon having won her. To Muriel he sent a fatherly message, telling her of his pleasure at hearing of her happiness, and adding that he hoped she would return to them in the following autumn to enable him to give her away.

Grange put his arm round his young *fiancée* as he read this passage aloud, but she only stood motionless within it, not yielding to his touch. It even seemed to him that she stiffened slightly. He looked at her questioningly, and saw that she was very pale.

'What is it?' he asked gently. 'Will that be too soon for you?'

She met his eyes frankly, but with unmistakable distress. 'I – I didn't think it would be quite so soon Blake,' she faltered. 'I don't want to be married at present. Can't we go on as we are for a little? Shall you mind?'

Blake's face wore a puzzled look, but it was wholly free from resentment. He answered her immediately and reassuringly.

'Of course not, dear. It shall be just when you like. Why should you be hurried?'

She gave him a smile of relief and gratitude, and he stooped and kissed her forehead with a soothing tenderness that he might have bestowed upon a child.

It was with some reluctance that she opened Lady Bassett's letter in his presence, but she felt that she owed him this small mark of confidence.

There was a strong aroma of attar of roses as she drew it from the envelope, and she glanced at Grange with an expression of disgust.

'What is the matter?' he asked. 'Nothing wrong, I hope?'

'It's only the scent,' she explained, concealing a faint sense of irritation.

He smiled. 'Don't you like it? I thought all women did.'

'My dear Blake!' she said, and shuddered.

The next minute she threw a sharp look over her shoulder, suddenly assailed by an uncanny feeling that Nick was standing grimacing at her elbow. She saw his features so clearly for the moment with his own peculiarly hideous grimace upon them that she scarcely persuaded herself that her fancy had tricked her. But there was nothing but the twilight of the garden all around her, and Blake's huge bulk by her side, and she promptly dismissed the illusion, not without a sense of shame.

With a gesture of impatience she unfolded Lady Bassett's letter. It commenced 'Dearest Muriel,' and proceeded at once in terms of flowing elegance to felicitate her upon her engagement to Blake Grange.

'In according our consent,' wrote Lady Bassett, 'Sir Reginald and I have not the smallest scruple or hesitation. Only, dearest, for Blake Grange's sake as well as for your own, make quite sure this time that your mind is fully made up, and your choice final.'

When Muriel read this passage a deep note of resentment crept into her voice, and she lifted a flushed face.

'It may be very wicked,' she said deliberately, 'but I hate Lady Bassett.'

Grange looked astonished, even mildly shocked. But Muriel returned to the letter before he could reply.

It went on to express regret that the writer could not herself return to England for the summer to assist her in the purchase of her trousseau and to chaperon her back to India in the autumn; but her sister, Mrs. Langdale, who lived in London, would, she was sure, be delighted to undertake the part of adviser in the first case, and in the second she would doubtless be able to find among her many friends who would be travelling East for the winter, one who would take charge of her. No reference was made to Daisy till the end of the letter, when the formal hope was expressed that Mrs. Musgrave's health had benefited by the change.

'She dares to disapprove of Daisy for some reason,' Muriel said, closing the letter with the rapidity of exasperation.

Grange did not ask why. He was engrossed in brushing a speck of mud from his sleeve, and she was not sure that he even heard her remark.

'You – I suppose you are not going to bother about a trousseau yet then?' he asked rather awkwardly.

She shook her head with vehemence. 'No, no, of course not. Why should I hurry? Besides, I am in mourning.'

'Exactly as you like,' said Grange gently. 'My leave will be up in September as you know, but I am not bound to stay in the Army. I will send in my papers if you wish it.'

Muriel looked at him in amazement. 'Send in your papers! Why no, Blake! I wouldn't have you do it for the world. I never dreamed of such a thing.'

He smiled good-humouredly. 'Well, of course, I should be sorry to give up polo, but there are plenty of other things I could take to. Personally, I like a quiet existence.'

Was there just a shade of scorn in Muriel's glance as it fell away from him? It would have been impossible for any bystander to say with certainty, but there was without doubt a touch of constraint in her voice as she made reply.

'Yes. You are quite the most placid person I know. But please don't think of leaving the Army for my sake. I am a soldier's daughter, remember. And – I like soldiers.'

Her lip quivered as she turned to enter the house. Her heart at that moment was mourning over a soldier's unknown grave. But Grange did not know it, did not even see that she was moved.

His eyes were raised to an upper window at which a dim figure stood looking out into the shadows. And he was thinking of other things.

Chapter 26

Daisy maintained her resolution on the following day, and though she did not speak again of going downstairs, she insisted that Muriel should return to the hockey-field and resume her place in Olga's team. It was the last match of the season, and she would not hear of her missing it.

'You and Blake are both to go,' she said. 'I won't have either of you staying at home for me.'

But Blake, when Muriel conveyed this message to him,

moodily shook his head. 'I'm not going. I don't want to. You must of course. It will do you good. But I couldn't play if I went. I've strained my wrist.'

'Oh, have you?' Muriel said, with concern. 'What a nuisance! How did you manage it?'

He reddened, and looked slightly ashamed. 'I vaulted the gate into the meadow this morning. Idiotic thing to do. But I shall be all right. Never mind about me. I shall smoke in the garden. I may go for a walk.'

Thus pressed on all sides, though decidedly against her own inclination, Muriel went. The day was showery with brilliant intervals. Grange saw her off at the field-gate.

'Plenty of mud,' he remarked.

'Yes, I shall be a spectacle when I come back. Goodbye! Take care of yourself.' Muriel's hand rested for an instant on his arm, and then she was gone – a slim, short-skirted figure walking swiftly over the grass.

He stood leaning on the gate watching her till a clump of trees intervened between them, then lazily he straightened himself and began to stroll back up the garden. He was not smoking. His face wore a heavy, almost a sullen, look. He scarcely raised his eyes from the ground as he walked.

Nearing the house the sudden sound of a window being raised made him look up, and in an instant, swift as a passing cloud-shadow, his moodiness was gone. Daisy was leaning on her window-sill, looking down upon him.

Though she had not spoken to him for weeks, she gave him no greeting. Her voice even sounded a trifle sharp.

'What are you loafing there for?' she demanded. 'Why didn't you go with Muriel to the hockey?'

He hesitated for a single instant. Then – for he never lied to Daisy – quite honestly he made reply.

'I didn't want to.'

Her pale face frowned down at him, though the eyes had a soft light that was like a mother's indulgence for her wayward child.

'How absurd you are! How can you be so lazy? I won't have it, Blake. Do you hear?'

He moved forward a few steps till he was immediately below her, and there stood with uplifted face. 'What do you want me to do?'

'Do!' echoed Daisy. 'Why, anything – anything rather than nothing. There's the garden-roller over there by the tool-shed. Go and get it, and roll the lawn.'

He went off obediently without another word, and presently the clatter of the roller testified to his submissive fulfilment of her command. He did not look up again. Simply, with his coat off and shirt-sleeves turned above his elbows, he tackled his arduous task, labouring up and down in the soft spring rain, patient and tireless as an ox.

He had accomplished about half the job when again Daisy's voice broke imperiously in upon him.

'Blake! Blake! Come in! You'll get wet to the skin.'

He stopped at once, straightening his great frame with a sigh of relief. Daisy was standing at the drawing-room window.

He pulled on his coat and went to join her.

She came to meet him with a sharp reproach. 'Why are you so foolish? I believe you would have gone on rolling if there had been an earthquake. You must be wet through and through.'

She ran her little thin hand over him. 'Yes, I knew you were. You must go and change.'

But Grange's fingers closed with quiet intention upon her wrist. He was looking down at her with the faithful adoration of a dumb animal.

'Not yet,' he said gently. 'Let me see you while I can.'

She made a quick movement as if his grasp hurt her, and in an instant she was free.

'Yes, but let us be sensible,' she said. 'Don't let us talk about hard things. I'm very tired, you know, Blake. You must make it easy for me.'

There was a piteous note of appeal in her voice. She sat down with her back to the light. He could see that her hands were trembling, but because of her appeal he would not seem to see it.

'Don't you think a change would be good for you?' he suggested.

'I don't know,' she answered. 'Jim says so. He wants me to go to Brethaven. It's only ten miles away, and he would motor over and look after me. But I don't think it much matters. I'm not particularly fond of the sea. And Muriel assures me she doesn't mind.'

'Isn't it at Brethaven that Nick Ratcliffe owns a place?' asked Grange.

'Yes. Redlands is the name. I went there once with Will. It's a beautiful place on the cliff – quite thrown away on Nick though, unless he marries, which he never will now.'

Grange looked uncomfortable. 'It's not my fault,' he remarked bluntly.

'No, I know,' said Daisy, with a faint echo of her old light laugh. 'Nothing ever was, or could be, your fault, dear old Blake. You're just unlucky sometimes, aren't you? That's all.'

Blake frowned a little. 'I play a straight game – generally,' he said.

'Yes, dear, but you always drive almost into a bunker,' Daisy insisted. 'It's not your fault, as we said before. It's just your misfortune.'

She never flattered Blake. It was perhaps the secret of her charm for him. To other women he was something of a paladin; to Daisy he was no more than a man – a man moreover of many weaknesses, each one of which she knew, each one of which was in a fashion dear to her.

'We will have some tea, shall we?' she said, as he sat silently digesting her criticism. 'I must try and write to Will presently. I haven' t written to him since – since – ' She broke off short and began again, 'I got Muriel to write for me once. But he keeps writing by every mail. I wish he wouldn't.'

Grange got up and walked softly to the window. 'When do you think of going back?' he asked.

'I don't know.' There was a keen note of irritation in the reply. Daisy leaned suddenly forward, her fingers locked together. 'You might as well ask me when I think of dying,' she said, with abrupt and startling bitterness.

Grange remained stationary, not looking at her. 'Is it as indefinite as that?' he asked presently.

'Yes, quite.' She spoke recklessly, even defiantly. 'Where would be the use of my going to a place I couldn't possibly live in for more than four months in the year? Besides – besides – ' But again, as if checked by some potent inner influence, she broke off short. Her white face quivered suddenly, and she turned it aside. Her hands were convulsively clenched upon each other.

Her cousin did not move. He seemed to be unaware of her agitation. Simply with much patience he waited for the end of her sentence.

It came at last in a voice half-strangled. She was making almost frantic efforts to control herself. 'Besides, I couldn't stand it – yet. I am not strong enough. And he – he wouldn't understand, poor boy. I think – I honestly think – I am better away from him for the present.'

Blake made no further enquiries. From Daisy's point of view he seemed to be standing motionless, but in reality he was quite unconsciously, though very deliberately, pulling the tassel of the blind-cord to shreds.

The clouds had passed, and the sun blazed down full upon him, throwing his splendid outline into high relief. Every detail of his massive frame was strongly revealed. There was about him a species of careless magnificence, wholly apart from arrogance, unfettered, superb.

To Daisy, familiar as she was with every line of him, the sudden revelation of the sunlight acted like a charm. She had been hiding her eyes for many days from all light, veiling them in the darkness of her grief, and the splendour of the man fairly dazzled her. It rushed upon her, swift, overmastering as a tidal wave, and before it even the memory of her sorrow grew dim.

Blake, turning at last, met her eyes fixed full upon him with that in their expression which no man could ignore. She had not expected him to turn. The movement disconcerted her. With a sharp jerk she averted her face, seeking to cover that momentary slip, to persuade him even then, if it were possible, into the belief that he had not seen aright.

But it was too late. That unguarded look of hers had betrayed her, rending asunder in an instant the veil with which for years she had successfully baffled him.

In a second he was on his knees beside her, his arms about her, holding her with a close and passionate insistence.

'Daisy!' he whispered huskily. And again, 'Daisy!'

And Daisy turned with a sudden deep sob, and hid her face upon his breast.

Chapter 27

In spite of Olga's ecstatic welcome, Muriel took her place in the hockey-field that afternoon with a heavy heart. Her long attendance upon Daisy had depressed her. But gradually, as the play proceeded, she began to forget herself and her troubles. The spring air exhilarated her, and when they returned to the field after a sharp shower her spirits had risen. She became even childishly gay in the course of a hotly-contested battle, and the sadness gradually died out of her eyes. She had grown less shy, less restrained, than of old. Youth and health, and a dawning, unconscious beauty had sprung to life upon her face. She was no longer the frightened, bereft child of Simla days. She no longer hid a monstrous fear in her heart. She had put it all away from her wisely, resolutely, as a tale that is told.

The wild wind had blown the hair all loose about her face

by the time the last goal was won. Hatless, flushed, and laughing, she drew back from the fray, Olga, elated by victory, clinging to her arm. It was a moment of keen triumph, for the fight had been hard, and she enjoyed it to the full as she stood there with her face to the sudden, scudding rain. The glow of exercise had braced every muscle. Every pulse was beating with warm, vigorous life.

She laughed aloud in sheer exultation, a low, merry laugh, and turned with Olga to march in triumphant procession from the field.

In that instant from a gate a few yards away that led into the road there sounded the short, imperious note of a motor-horn, repeated many times in a succession of sharp blasts. Everyone stood to view the intruder with startled curiosity for perhaps five seconds. Then there came a sudden squeal of rapture from Olga, and in a moment she had torn her arm free and was gone, darting like a swallow over the turf.

Muriel stood looking after her, but she was as one turned to stone. She was no longer aware of the children grouped around her. She no longer saw the fleeting sunshine, or felt the drift of rain in her face. Something immense and suffocating had closed about her heart. Her racing pulses had ceased to beat.

A figure familiar to her – a man's figure, unimposing in height, unremarkable in build, but straight, straight as his own sword-blade – had bounded from the car and scaled the intervening gate with monkey-like agility.

He met the child's wild rush with one arm extended; the other – Muriel frowned sharply, peering with eye half closed, then uttered a queer, choked sound that had the semblance of a laugh – in place of the other arm there was an empty sleeve.

Through the rush of the wind she heard his voice.

'Hullo, kiddie, hullo! Hope I don't intrude. I've come over on purpose to pay my respects.'

Olga's answer did not reach her. She was hanging round

her hero's neck, and her head was down upon Nick's shoulder. It seemed to Muriel that she was crying, but if so, she received scant sympathy from the object of her solicitude. His cracked, gay laugh rang out across the field.

'What? Why, yesterday, to be sure. Spent the night in town. No, I know I didn't. Never meant to. Wanted to steal a march on you all. Why not? say, is that – Muriel?'

For the first time he seemed to perceive her, and instantly with a dexterous movement he had disengaged himself from Olga's clinging arms and was briskly approaching her. Two of the doctor's boys sprang to greet him, but he waved them airily aside.

'All right, you chaps, in a minute! Where's Dr. Jim? Go and tell him I'm here.'

And then in a couple of seconds more they were face to face.

Muriel stared at him speechlessly. She felt cold from head to foot. She had known that he was coming. She had been steeling herself for weeks to meet him in an armour of conventional reserve. But all her efforts had come to this. Swift, swift as the wind over wheat, his coming swept across her new-born confidence. It wavered and bent its head.

'Does your Excellency deign to remember the least and humblest of her servants?' queried Nick, with a deep salaam.

The laugh in his tone brought her sharply back to the demand of circumstance. Before the watching crowd of children, she forced her white lips to smile in answer, and in a moment she had recovered her self-possession. She remembered with a quick sense of relief that this man's power over her belonged to the past alone – to the tale that was told.

The hand she held out to him was almost steady. 'Yes, I remember you, Nick,' she said, with chilly courtesy. 'I am sorry you have been ill. Are you better?'

He made a queer grimace at her words, and for the second that her hand lay in his, she knew that he looked at her closely, piercingly.

'Thanks – awfully,' he said. 'As you may have noticed, there is a little less of me than there used to be. I hope you think it's an improvement.'

She felt as if he had flung back her conventional sympathy in her face, and she stiffened instinctively. 'I am sorry to see it,' she returned icily.

Nick laughed enigmatically. 'I thought you would be. Well, Olga, my child, what do you mean by growing up like this in my absence? You used to be just the right size for a kid, and now you are taller than I am.'

'I'm not, Nick,' the child declared with warmth. 'And I never will be, there!'

She slid her arm again round his neck. Her eyes were full of tears.

Nick turned swiftly and bestowed a kiss upon the face which, though the face of a child, was so remarkably like his own.

'Aren't you going to introduce me to your friends?' he said.

'There's no need,' said Olga, hugging him closer. 'They all know Captain Ratcliffe of Wara. Why haven't you got the V.C., Nick, like Captain Grange?'

'Didn't qualify for it,' returned Nick. 'You see I only distinguished myself by running away. Hullo! It's raining. Just run and tell the chauffeur to drive round to the house. You can go with him. And take your friends too. It'll carry you all. I'm going the garden way with Muriel.'

Muriel realized the impossibility of frustrating this plan, though the last thing in the world that she desired was to be alone with him. But the distance to the house was not great. As the children scampered away to the waiting motor car she moved briskly to leave the field.

Nick walked beside her with his free, elastic swagger. In a few moments he reached out and took her hockey-stick from her.

'Jove!' he said. 'It did me good to see you shoot that goal.'

'I had no idea you were watching,' she returned stiffly.

He grinned. 'No, I saw that. Fun, wasn't it? Like to know what I said to myself?'

She made no answer, and his grin became a laugh. 'I'm sure you would, so I'll tell you. I said, "Prayer Number One is granted," and I ticked it off the list, and duly acknowledged the same.'

Muriel was plainly mystified. He was in the mood that most baffled her. 'I don't know what you mean,' she said at last.

Nick swung the hockey-stick idly. His yellow face, for all its wrinkles, looked peculiarly complacent.

'Let me explain,' he said coolly; 'I wanted to see you young again, and – my want has been satisfied, that's all.'

Muriel looked sharply away from him, the vivid colour rushing all over her face. She remembered – and the memory seemed to stab her – a day long, long ago when she had lain in this man's arms in the extremity of helpless suffering, and had heard him praying above her head, brokenly, passionately, for something far different – something from which she had come to shrink with a nameless, overmastering dread.

She quickened her pace in the silence that followed. The rain was coming down sharply. Reaching the door that led into the doctor's walled garden, she stretched out her hand with impetuous haste to push it open.

Instantly, with disconcerting suddenness, Nick dropped the hockey-stick and swooped upon it like a bird of prey.

'Who gave you that?' he demanded.

He had spied a hoop of diamonds upon her third finger. She could not see his eyes under the flickering lids, but he held her wrist forcibly, and it seemed to her that there was a note of savagery in his voice.

Her heart beat fast for a few seconds, so fast that she could not find her voice. Then, almost under her breath, 'Blake gave it to me,' she said. 'Blake Grange.'

'Yes?' said Nick. 'Yes?'

Suddenly he looked straight at her, and his eyes were alight, fierce, glowing. But she felt a curious sense of scared relief, as if he were behind bars – an eagle caged, of which she need have no fear.

'We are engaged to be married,' she said quietly.

There fell a momentary silence, and a voice cried out in her soul that she had stabbed him through the bars.

Then in a second Nick dropped her hand and stooped to pick up the hockey-stick. His face as he stood up again flashed back to its old, baffling gaiety.

'What ho!' he said lightly. 'Then I'm in time to dance at the wedding. Pray accept my heartiest congratulations!'

Muriel murmured her thanks with her face averted. She was no longer afraid merely, but strangely, inexplicably ashamed.

Chapter 28

The news of Nick's return spread like wildfire through the doctor's house, and the whole establishment assembled to greet him. Jim himself came striding out into the rain to shake his hand and escort him in.

His 'Hullo, you scapegrace!' had in it little of sentiment, but there was nothing wanting in his welcome in the opinion of the recipient thereof.

Nick's rejoinder of 'Hullo, you old buffer!' was equally free from any gloss of eloquence, but he hooked his hand in the doctor's arm as he made it, and kept it there.

Jim gave him one straight, keen look that took in every detail, but he made no verbal comment of any sort. His heavy brows drew together for an instant, that was all.

It was an exceedingly clamorous home-coming. The children, having arrived in the motor, swarmed all about the returned hero, who was more than equal to the occasion, and obviously enjoyed his boisterous reception to the uttermost. There never had been any shyness about Nick.

Muriel, standing watching in the background with a queer, unaccountable pain at her heart, assured herself that the news of her engagement had meant nothing to him whatever. He had managed to deceive her as usual. She realized it with burning cheeks, and ardently wished that she had borne herself more proudly. Well, she was not wanted here. Even Olga, her faithful and loving admirer, had eyes only for Nick just then. As for Dr. Jim, he had not even noticed her.

Quietly she stole away from the merry, chattering group. The hall-door stood open, and she saw that it was raining heavily; but she did not hesitate. With a haste that was urged from within by something that was passionate, she ran out hatless into the storm.

The cracked, careless laugh she knew so well pursued her as she went, and once she fancied that someone called her by name. But she did not slacken speed to listen. She only dashed on a little faster than before.

Drenched and breathless, she reached home at length, to be met upon the threshold by Blake. In her exhaustion she almost fell into his arms.

'Hullo!' he said, steadying her. 'You shouldn't run like that. I never dreamed you would come back in this, or I would have come across with an umbrella to fetch you.'

She sank into a chair in the hall, speechless and gasping, her hair hanging about her neck in wildest disorder.

Blake stood beside her. He was wearing his worried, moody look.

'You shouldn't,' he said again. 'It's horribly bad for you.'

'Ah, I'm better,' she gasped back. 'I had to run – all the way – because of the rain.'

'But why didn't you wait?' said Blake. 'What were they thinking of to let you come in this downpour?'

'They couldn't help it.' Muriel raised herself with a great sobbing sigh. 'It was nobody's fault but my own. I wanted to get away. Oh, Blake, do you know – Nick is here?'

Blake started. 'What? Already? Do you mean he is actually in the place?'

She nodded. 'He came up in a motor while we were playing. I suppose he is staying at Redlands, but I don't know. And – and – Blake, he has lost his left arm. It makes him look so queer.' She gave a sudden, uncontrollable shudder. The old dumb horror looked out of her eyes. 'I thought I shouldn't mind,' she said, under her breath. 'Perhaps – if you had been there – it would have been different. As it was – as it was – ' She broke off, rising impetuously to her feet, and laying trembling hands upon his arms. 'Oh, Blake,' she whispered, like a scared child. 'I feel so helpless. But you promised – you promised – you would never let me go.'

Yes, he had promised her that. He had sworn it, and, sick at heart, he remembered that in her eyes at least he was a man of honour. It had been in his mind to tell her the simple truth, just so far as he himself was concerned, and thereafter to place himself at her disposal to act exactly as she should desire. But suddenly this was an impossibility to him. He realized it with desperate self-loathing. She trusted him. She looked to him for protection. She leaned upon his strength. She needed him. He could not – it almost seemed as if in common chivalry he could not – reveal to her the contemptible weakness which lay like a withering blight upon his whole nature. To own himself the slave of a married woman, and that her closest friend, would be to throw her utterly upon her own resources at a time when she most needed the support and guidance of a helping hand. Moreover, the episode was over; so at least both he and Daisy resolutely persuaded themselves. There had been a lapse – a vain and futile lapse – into the long-cherished idyll of their romance. It must never recur. It never should recur. It must be covered over and forgotten as speedily as might be. They had come to their senses again. They were ready, not only to thrust away the evil that had dominated them, but to ignore it utterly as though it had never been.

So, rapidly, the man reasoned with himself with the girl's hands clasping his arm in earnest entreaty, and her eyes of innocence raised to his.

His answer when it came was low and soft and womanly, but, in her ears at least, there was nothing wanting in it. She never dreamed that he was reviling himself for a blackguard even as he uttered it.

'My dear little girl, there is nothing whatever for you to be afraid of. You're a bit overstrung, aren't you? The man isn't living who could take you from me.'

He patted her shoulder very kindly, soothing her with a patient, almost fatherly tenderness, and gradually her panic of fear passed. She leaned against him with a comforting sense of security.

'I can't think how it is I'm so foolish,' she told him, 'You are good to me, Blake. I feel so safe when I am with you.'

His heart smote him, yet he bent and kissed her. 'You're not quite strong yet, dear,' he said. 'It takes a long time to get over all that you had to bear last year.'

'Yes,' she agreed with a sigh. 'And do you know I thought I was so much stronger than I am? I actually thought that I shouldn't mind – much – when he came. And yet I did mind – horribly. I – I – told him about our engagement, Blake.'

'Yes, dear,' said Blake.

'Yes, I told him. And he laughed and offered his congratulations. I don't think he cared,' said Muriel, again with that curious, inexplicable sensation of pain at her heart.

'Why should he?' said Blake.

She looked at him with momentary irresolution. 'You know, Blake, I never told you. But I was – I was engaged to him for about a fortnight that dreadful time at Simla.'

To her relief she marked no change in Blake's courteously attentive face.

'You need not have told me that, dear,' he said quietly.

'No, I know,' she answered, pressing his arm. 'It wouldn't make any difference to you. You are too great. And it was always a little bit against my will. But the breaking with him was terrible – terrible. He was so angry. I almost thought he would have killed me.'

'My dear,' Blake said, 'you shouldn't dwell on these things. They are best forgotten.'

'I know, I know,' she answered. 'But they are just the very hardest of all things to forget. You must help me, Blake. Will you?'

'I will help you,' he answered steadily.

And the resolution with which he spoke was an unspeakable comfort to her. Once more there darted across her mind the wonder at her father's choice for her. How was it – how was it – that he had passed over this man and chosen Nick?

Blake's own explanation of the mystery seemed to her suddenly weak and inadequate. She simply could not bring herself to believe that in a supreme moment he could be found wanting. It was unthinkable that the giant frame and mighty sinews could belong to a personality that was lacking in a corresponding greatness.

So she clung to her illusion, finding comfort therein, wholly blind to those failings in her protector which to the woman who had loved him from her earliest girlhood were as obvious and well-nigh as precious as his virtues.

Chapter 29

'I must be getting back,' said Nick.

He was sprawling at ease on the sofa in Jim's study, blinking comfortably at the ceiling, as he made this remark.

Jim himself had just entered the room. He drew up a chair to Nick's side.

'You will be doing nothing of the sort to-night,' he returned, with a certain grimness. 'The motor has gone back to Redlands for your things. I saw to that an hour ago.'

'The deuce you did!' said Nick. He turned slightly to send

a shifting glance over his brother. 'That was very officious of you, Jimmy,' he remarked.

'Very likely,' conceded the doctor. 'I have to be officious occasionally. And if you think that I mean to let you out of my sight in your present state of health, you make a big mistake. No, lie still, I tell you! You're like a monkey on wires. Lie still! Do you hear me, Nick?'

Nick's feet were already on the ground, but he did not rise. He sat motionless, as if weighing some matter in his mind.

'I can't stay with you, Jimmy,' he said at last. 'I'll spend to-night of course with all the pleasure in the world. But I'm going back to Redlands to-morrow. I have a fancy for sleeping in my own crib just now. Come over and see me as often as you feel inclined, the oftener the better. And if you care to bring your science to bear upon all that is left of this infernally troublesome member of mine, I shall be charmed to let you. You may vivisect me to your heart's content. But don't ask me to be an in-patient, for it can't be done. There are reasons.'

Jim frowned at him. 'Do you know what will happen if you don't take care of yourself?' he said brusquely. 'You'll die.'

Nick burst into a laugh, and lay back on the cushions. 'I was driven out of India by that threat,' he said. 'It's getting a bit stale. You needn't be afraid. I'm not going to die at present. I'll take reasonable precautions to prevent it. But I won't stay here, that's flat. I tell you, man, I can't.'

He glanced again at Jim, and, finding the latter closely watching him, abruptly shut his eyes.

'I'm going to open Redlands,' he said. 'And I will have Olga to come and keep house for me. It'll be good practice for her. I'll take her back with me tomorrow, if you have no objection.'

'Fine mischief you'll get up to, the pair of you,' grumbled Jim.

'Very likely,' said Nick cheerily. 'But we shan't come to any harm, either of us. To begin with, I shall make her wait on me, hand and foot. She'll like that, and so shall I.'

'Yes, you'll spoil her thoroughly,' said Jim. 'And I shall have the pleasure of breaking her in afterwards.'

Nick laughed again. 'What an old tyrant you are! But you needn't be afraid of that. I'll make her do as she's told. I'm particularly good at that. Ask Muriel Roscoe.'

Jim's frown deepened. 'You know of that girl's engagement to Grange, I suppose?'

Nick did not trouble to open his eyes. 'Oh, rather. She took care that I should. I gave her my blessing.'

'Well, I don't like it,' said Jim plainly.

'What's the matter with him?' questioned Nick.

'Nothing that I know of. But she isn't in love with him.'

Nick's eyelids parted a little, showing a glint between.

'You funny old ass!' he murmured affectionately.

Jim leaned forward and looked at him hard.

'Quite so,' said Nick in answer, closing his eyes again. 'But you don't by any chance imagine she's in love with me, do you? You know how a woman looks at a worm she has chopped in half by mistake? That's how Muriel Roscoe looked at me to-day when she expressed her regret for my mishap.'

'She wouldn't do that for nothing,' observed Jim, with a hint of sternness.

'She wouldn't,' Nick conceded placidly.

'Then why the devil did you ever give her reason?' Jim spoke with unusual warmth. Muriel was a favourite of his.

But he obtained scant satisfaction notwithstanding.

'Ask the devil,' said Nick flippantly. 'I never was good at definitions.'

It was a tacit refusal to discuss the matter, and as such Jim accepted it.

He turned from the subject with a grunt of discontent. 'Well if I am to undertake your case, you had better let me look at you. But we'll have a clear understanding first, mind, that you obey my orders. I won't be responsible otherwise.'

Nick opened his eyes with a chuckle. 'I'll do anything under the sun to please you, Jimmy,' he said generously. 'When did you ever find me hard to manage?'

'You've given me plenty of trouble at one time and another,' Jim said bluntly.

'And shall again before I die,' laughed Nick, as he submitted to his brother's professional handling. 'There's plenty of kick left in me. By the way, tell me what you think about Daisy. I must call on her to-morrow before I leave.'

This intention however was not fulfilled, for Daisy herself came early to the doctor's house to visit him. Far from well though she was, she made the effort as a matter of course. Nick was too near a friend to neglect. Blake did not accompany her. He was riding with Muriel.

She found Nick stretched out in luxurious idleness on a couch in the sunshine. He made a movement to spring to meet her, but checked himself with a laugh.

'This is awfully good of you, Daisy. I was coming to see you later, but I'm nailed to this confounded sofa for the next two hours, having solemnly sworn to Jim that nothing short of battle, murder, or sudden death should induce me to move. I'm afraid I can't reasonably describe your coming as any of these, so I must remain a fixture. It's Jimmy's rest cure.'

He reached out his hand to Daisy, who took it in both her own. 'My poor dear Nick!' she said, and stooping impulsively kissed him on the forehead.

'Bless you!' said Nick. 'I'm ten times better for that. Sit down here, won't you? Pull up close. I've got a lot to say.'

Of sympathy for her recent bereavement, however, he said no word whatever. He only held her hand.

'There's poor old Will,' he said; 'I spent the night with him on my way down. He's beastly homesick – sent all sorts of messages to you. You'll be going out in the winter?'

'It depends,' said Daisy.

'He's breaking his heart for you, like a silly ass,' said Nick. 'How long has Muriel been engaged to Grange?'

Daisy started at the sudden question.

'It's all right,' Nick assured her. 'I'm not a bit savage. It'll be a little experience for her. When did it begin?'

Daisy hesitated. 'Some weeks ago now.'

Nick nodded. 'Exactly. As soon as she heard I was coming. Funny of her. And what of Grange? Is he smitten?'

Daisy flushed painfully, and tried to laugh. 'Don't be so cold-blooded, Nick. Of course he – he's fond of her.'

'Oh, he – he's fond of her, is he?' said Nick. He looked at her suddenly, and laughed with clenched teeth. 'I'm infernally rude, I know. But why put it in that way? Should you say I was "fond" of her?'

Daisy met his darting, elusive glance with a distinct effort. 'I shouldn't say you were fond of anyone, Nick. The term doesn't apply where you are concerned. There never were two men more totally different than you and Blake. But he isn't despicable for all that. He's a child compared to you, but he's a good child. He would never do wrong unless someone tempted him.'

'That's so with a good many of us,' remarked Nick, sneering faintly. 'Let us hope that when the account comes to be totted up, allowance will be made.'

Daisy's hand upon his banished the sneer. 'Be fair, Nick,' she urged. 'We are not all made with wills of iron. I know you are bitter because you think he isn't good enough for her. But would you think any man good enough? Don't think I wanted this. I was on your side. But I – I was busy at the time with – other things. And I didn't see it coming.'

Nick's face softened. He said nothing.

She bent towards him. 'I would have given anything to have stopped it when I knew. But it was too late. Will you forgive me, Nick?'

He patted her hand lightly. 'Of course, of course. Don't fret on my account.'

'But I do,' she whispered vehemently. 'I do. I know – how horribly – it hurts.'

Nick's fingers closed suddenly upon hers. His eyes went beyond her.

'Mrs. Musgrave,' he said, 'I am gifted with a superhuman intelligence, remember. I know some cards by their backs.'

Daisy withdrew her hand swiftly. His tone had been one of warning. She threw him a look of sharp uneasiness. She did not ask him what he meant.

'Tell me some more about Will,' she said. 'I was thinking of writing to him to-day.'

And Nick forthwith plunged into a graphic account of the man who was slaving night and day in the burning Plains of the East for the woman of his heart.

Chapter 30

It was with unspeakable relief that Muriel learned of Nick's departure. That he had elected to take Olga with him surprised her considerably and caused her some regret. Grange had discovered some urgent business that demanded his presence in town, and she missed the child in consequence more than she would otherwise have done.

Daisy was growing stronger, and was beginning to contemplate a change, moved at last by Jim Ratcliffe's persistent urging. There was a cottage at Brethaven which, he declared, would suit her exactly. Muriel raised no objection to the plan. She knew it would be for Daisy's benefit, but her heart sank whenever she thought of it. She was glad when early in June Blake came back to them for a few days before starting on a round of visits.

He approved of the Brethaven plan warmly, and he and Muriel rode over one morning to the little seaside village to make arrangements. Muriel said no more to him upon the subject of Nick. On this one point she had come to know that it was vain to look for sympathy. He had promised to help her indeed, but he simply did not understand her nervous shrinking from the man. Moreover, Nick had made it so abundantly evident that he had no intention of thrusting himself upon her. There could be no ground for fear on that score. Besides, was not her engagement her safeguard?

As for Blake, her silence upon the matter made him hope that she was getting over her almost childish panic. With all the goodwill in the world, he could not see that his presence as a watch-dog was required.

Yet, as they turned from the cottage on the shore with their errand accomplished, he did say after some hesitation, 'Of course, if for any reason you should want me when I am away, you must let me know. I would come at once.'

She thanked him with a heightened colour, and he had a feeling that his allusion had been unwelcome. They rode up from the beach in silence.

Turning a sharp corner towards the village where they proposed to lunch, they came suddenly upon a motor stationary by the roadside. A whoop of cheery recognition greeted them before either of them realized that it was occupied, and they discovered Nick seated on the step, working with his one hand at the foot-brake. Olga was with him, endeavouring to assist.

Nick's face grinned welcome impartially to the new-comers. 'Hullo! This is luck. Delighted to see you, Grange, my boy, here's a little job exactly suited to your Herculean strength. Climb down like a good fellow, and lend a hand.'

Grange glanced at Muriel, and with a slight shrug handed her his bridle. 'I'm not much good at this sort of thing,' he remarked, as he dismounted.

'Never thought you were for a moment,' responded Nick. 'But I suppose you can do as you're told at a pinch. This filthy thing has got jammed. It's too tough a job for a single-handed pigmy like me.' He glanced quizzically up at Muriel with the last remark, but she quickly averted her eyes, bending to speak to Olga at the same instant.

Olga was living in the seventh heaven just then, and her radiant face proclaimed it. 'I'm learning to drive,' she told Muriel. 'It's the greatest fun. You would just love it. I know you would.' She stood fondling the horses and chattering while the two men wrestled with the motor's internal arrangements, and Muriel longed desperately to give her animal the rein and flee away from the mocking sprite that gibed at her from Nick's eyes. Whence came it, this feeling of insecurity, this perpetual sense of fighting against the inevitable? She had fancied that Blake's presence would be her safeguard, but now she bitterly realized that it made no difference to her. He stood as it were outside the ropes, and was powerless to intervene.

Suddenly she saw them stand up. The business was done. They stood for a second side by side – Blake gigantic, well-proportioned, splendidly strong; Nick, meagre, maimed, almost shrunken, it seemed. But in that second she knew with unerring conviction that the greater fighter of the two was the man against whom she had pitted her quivering woman's strength. She knew at a single glance that for all his bodily weakness Nick possessed the power to dominate even so mighty a giant as Blake. What she had said to herself many a time before, she said again. He was abnormal, superhuman even; more – where he chose to exert himself, he was irresistible.

The realization went through her, sharp and piercing, horribly distinct. She had sought shelter like a frightened rabbit in the densest cover she could find, but, crouching low, she heard the rush of the remorseless wings above her. She knew that at any moment he could rend her refuge to pieces and hold her at his mercy.

Abruptly he left Blake and came to her side. 'I want you and Grange to come to Redlands for luncheon,' he said. 'Olga is hostess there. Don't refuse.'

'Oh, do come!' urged Olga, dancing eagerly upon one leg. 'You've never been to Redlands, have you? It's such a lovely place. Say you'll come, Muriel.'

Muriel scarcely heard her. She was looking down into Nick's face, seeking, seeking for the hundredth time, to read that baffling mask.

'Don't refuse,' he said again. 'You'll get nothing but underdone chops at the inn here, and I can't imagine that to be a weakness of yours.'

She gave up her fruitless search. 'I will come,' she said.

'It's exactly as you like, you know, Muriel,' Grange put in awkwardly.

She understood the precise meaning of Nick's laugh. She even for a moment wanted to laugh herself. 'Thank you. I should like to,' she said.

Nick nodded and turned aside. 'Olga, stop capering,' he ordered, 'and drive me home.'

Olga obeyed him promptly, with the gaiety of a squirrel. As Nick seated himself by her side, Muriel saw her turn impulsively and rub her cheek against his shoulder. It gave her a queer little tingling shock to see the child's perfect confidence in him. But then – but then – Olga had never looked on horror, had never seen the devil leap out in naked fury upon her hero's face.

They waited to let the car go first, Olga proudly grasping the wheel; then, trotting briskly, followed in its wake.

Muriel had an uneasy feeling that Blake wanted to apologize, and she determined that he should not have the opportunity. Each time that he gave any sign of wishing to draw nearer to her, she touched her horse's flank. Something in the nature of a revelation had come to her during that brief halt by the roadside. For the first time she had caught a glimpse, plain and unvarnished, of the actual man that inhabited the giant's frame, and it had given her an odd, disturbing suspicion that the strength upon which she leaned was in simple fact scarcely equal to her own.

The way to Redlands lay through leafy woodlands through which here and there the summer sea gleamed blue. Turning in at the open gates, Muriel uttered an exclamation of delight.

She seemed to have suddenly entered fairyland. The house, long, low, rambling, roofed with thatch, stood at the end of a winding drive that was bordered on both sides by a blaze of rhododendron flowers. Down below her on the left was a miniature glen from which arose the tinkle of running water. On her right the trees grew thickly, completely shutting out the road.

'Oh, Blake!' she exclaimed. 'What a perfect paradise!'

'Like it?' said Nick; and with a start she saw him coolly step out from a shadowy path behind them and close the great iron gate.

Impulsively she pulled up and slipped to the ground. 'Take my horse, Blake,' she said. 'I must run down to that stream.'

He obeyed her, not very willingly, and Nick with a chuckle turned and plunged after her down the narrow path. 'Go straight ahead!' he called back. 'Olga is waiting for you at the house.'

He came up with Muriel on the edge of the fairy stream. Her face was flushed and her eyes nervous, but she met him bravely. She had known in her heart that be would follow. As he stopped beside her, she turned with a little desperate laugh and held out her hand.

'Is it peace?' she said rather breathlessly.

She felt his fingers, tense as wire, close about her own. 'Seems like it,' he said. 'What are you afraid of? Me?'

She could not meet his look. But the necessity for some species of understanding pressed upon her. She wanted unspeakably to conciliate him.

'I want to be friends with you, Nick,' she said, 'if you will let me.'

'What for?' asked Nick sharply.

She was silent. She could not tell him that her sure defence had crumbled at a touch. Somehow she was convinced that he knew it already.

'You never wanted such a thing before,' he said. 'You certainly weren't hankering after it the last time we met.'

Her cheeks burned at the memory. Again she felt ashamed. With a great effort she forced herself to speak with a certain frankness.

'I am afraid,' she said – 'I have thought since – that I was rather heartless that day. The fact was, I was taken by surprise. But I am sorry now, Nick. I am very sorry.'

Her tone was unconsciously piteous. Surely he must see that if they were to meet often, as inevitably they must, some sort of agreement between them was imperative. She must feel stable ground beneath her feet. Their intercourse could not be one perpetual passage of arms. Flesh and blood could never endure it.

But Nick did not apparently view the matter in the same light. 'Pray don't be sorry,' he airily begged her. 'I quite understand. I never take offence where none is intended, and not always where it is. So dismiss the matter from your mind with all speed. There is not the smallest occasion for regret.'

He meant to elude her, she saw, and she turned from him without another word. There was to be no understanding then, no friendly feeling, no peace of mind. She had not trusted to his generosity, and it was quite clear that he had no intention of being generous.

As they walked by a mossy pathway towards the house, they talked upon indifferent things. But the girl's heart was very bitter within her. She would have given almost anything to have flung back his hospitality in his grinning, triumphant face, and have departed with her outraged pride to the farthest corner of the earth.

Chapter 31

Luncheon in the low, old-fashioned dining-room at Redlands with its windows facing the open sea, with Olga beaming at the head of the table, should have been a peaceful and pleasant meal, had Muriel's state of mind allowed her to enjoy it. But Nick's treatment of her overture had completely banished all enjoyment for her. She forced herself to eat and to appear unconcerned, but she was quivering inwardly with a burning sense of resentment. She was firmly determined that she would never be alone with him again. He had managed by those few scoffing words of his to arouse in her all the bitterness of which she was capable. If she had feared him before, she hated him now with the whole force of her nature.

He seemed to be blissfully unconscious of her hostility and played the part of host with complete ease of manner. Long before the meal was over, Grange had put aside his sullenness, and they were conversing together as comrades.

Nick had plenty to say. He spoke quite openly of his illness, and declared himself to have completely recovered from it. 'Even Jim has ceased his gruesome threats,' he said cheerily. 'There will be no more lopping of branches this season. Just as well, for I chance to have developed an affection for what is left.'

'You're going back to the Regiment, I suppose?' Blake questioned.

'No, he isn't,' thrust in Olga, and was instantly frowned upon by Nick.

'Speak when you're spoken to, little girl! That's a question you are not qualified to answer. I'm on half-pay at present, and I haven't made up my mind.'

'I should quit in your place,' Grange remarked, with his eyes on the dazzling sea.

'No doubt you would,' Nick responded dryly. 'And what should you advise, Muriel?'

The question was unexpected, but she had herself in hand, and answered it instantly. 'I shouldn't certainly advise you to quit.'

He raised his eyebrows. 'Might one ask why?'

She was quite ready for him, inspired by an over-mastering longing to hurt him if that were possible. 'Because if you gave up your profession, you would be nothing but a vacuum.

If the chance to destroy life were put out of your reach, you would simply cease to exist.'

She spoke rapidly, her voice pitched very low. She was trembling all over, and her hands were clenched under the table to hide it.

The laugh with which Nick received her words jarred intolerably upon her. She heard nothing in it but deliberate cruelty.

'Great Lucifer!' he said. 'You have got me under the microscope with a vengeance. But you can't see through me, you know. I have a reverse side. Hadn't you better turn me over and look at that? There may be sorcery and witchcraft there as well.' There might be. She could well have imagined it. But these were lesser things in which she had no concern. She turned his thrust aside with disdain.

'I am not sufficiently interested,' she said. 'The little I know is enough.'

'Well hit!' chuckled Nick. 'I retire from the fray, discomfited. Olga *mia*, I wish you would find the cigars. You know where they are.'

Olga sprang to do his bidding. Having handed the box to Grange, she came to Nick and stood beside him while she cut and lighted a cigar for him.

He put his arm round her for a moment, and she stooped a flushed face and kissed the top of his head.

'Run along,' said Nick. 'Take Muriel into the garden. She hasn't seen it all.'

Muriel rose. 'We mustn't be late in starting back,' she remarked to Blake.

But Olga lingered to whisper vehemently in Nick's ear.

He laughed and shook his head. 'Go, child, go! You don't know anything about it. And Muriel is waiting. You should never keep a guest waiting.'

Olga went reluctantly. They passed out into the clear June sunshine together and down towards the shady shrubberies beyond the lawns.

'Can Nick play tennis?' Muriel asked, as they crossed a marked-out court.

'Yes, he can do anything,' the child said proudly. 'He was on horseback this morning, and he managed splendidly. We generally play tennis in the evening. He almost always wins. His services are terrific. I can't think how he does it. He calls it juggling. I try to manage with only one hand sometimes – just to keep him company – but I always make a mess of things. There's no one in the world as clever as Nick.'

Muriel felt inclined to agree with her, though in her opinion this distinguishing quality was not an altogether admirable one. She infinitely preferred people with fewer brains. She would not, however, say this to Olga, and they paced on together under the trees in silence. Suddenly a warm hand slid within her arm, and Olga's grey eyes, very loving and wistful, looked up into hers.

'Muriel, darling,' she whispered softly, 'don't you – don't you – like Nick after all?'

The colour rushed over Muriel's face in a vivid flood. 'Like him! Like him!' she stammered. 'Why do you ask?'

'Because, dear – don't be vexed, I love you frightfully – you did hurt him so at lunch,' explained Olga, pressing very close to her.

'Hurt him! Hurt him!' Again Muriel repeated her words, then, recovering sharply, broke into a sudden laugh. 'My dear child, I couldn't possibly do such a thing if I tried.'

'But you did, you did!' persisted Olga, a faint note of indignation in her voice. 'You don't know Nick. He feels – tremendously. Of course you might not see it, for it doesn't often show. But I know – I always know – when he is hurt, by the way he laughs. And he was hurt to-day.'

She stuck firmly to her point notwithstanding Muriel's equally persistent attitude of incredulity, till even Muriel was conscious at last in her inner soul of a faint wonder, a dim and wholly negligible sense of regret. Not that she would under any circumstances have recalled that thrust of hers.

She felt it had been dealt in fair fight; but even in fair fight there come sometimes moments of regret, when one feels that the enemy's hand has been intentionally slack. She knew well that had he chosen, Nick might have thrust back, instantly and disconcertingly, as his manner was. But he had refrained, merely covering up his wound – if wound there had been – with the laugh that had so wrung Olga's loving heart. His ways were strange. She would never understand him. But she would like to have known how deep that thrust had gone.

Could she have overheard the conversation between Nick and his remaining guest that followed her departure, she might have received enlightenment on this point, but Nick took very good care to ensure that that conversation should be overheard by none.

As soon as Grange had finished his coffee, he proposed a move to the library, and led the way thither, leaving his own drink untouched behind him.

The library was a large and comfortable apartment completely shut away from the rest of the house, and singularly ill-adapted for eavesdroppers. The windows looked upon a wide stretch of lawn upon which even a bird could scarcely have lingered unnoticed. The light that filtered in through green sun-blinds was cool and restful. An untidy writing-table and a sofa strewn with cushions in disorderly attitudes testified to the fact that Nick had appropriated this room for his own particular den. There was also a sun-bonnet tossed upon a chair which seemed to indicate that Olga at least did not regard his privacy as inviolable. The ancient brown volumes stacked upon shelves that ranged almost from floor to ceiling were comfortably undisturbed. It was plainly a sanctum in which ease and not learning ruled supreme.

Nick established his visitor in an easy-chair and hunted for an ash-tray. Grange watched him uncomfortably.

'I'm awfully sorry about your arm, Ratcliffe,' he said at length. 'A filthy bit of bad luck that.'

'Damnable,' said Nick.

'I've been meaning to look you up for a long time,' Grange proceeded, 'but somehow it hasn't come off.'

Nick laughed rather dryly. He was perfectly well aware that Grange had been steadily avoiding him ever since his return. 'Very good of you,' he said, subsiding upon the sofa and pulling the cushions about him. 'I've been saving up my congratulations for you all these weeks. I might have written of course, but I had a notion that the spoken word would be more forcible.'

Grange stirred uneasily, neither understanding nor greatly relishing Nick's tone. He wished vehemently that he would leave the subject alone.

Nick however had no such intention. A faint, fiendish smile was twitching the corners of his lips. He did not even glance in Blake's direction. There was no need.

'Well, I wish you joy,' he said lightly.

'Thank you,' returned Grange, without elation and very little gratitude. In some occult fashion, Nick was making it horribly awkward for him. He longed to change the subject, but could find nothing to say – possibly because Nick quite obviously had not yet done with it.

'Going to get married before you sail?' he asked abruptly.

'I don't think so.' Very reluctantly Grange made reply.

'Why not?' said Nick.

'Muriel doesn't want to be married till she is out of mourning,' Grange explained.

'Why doesn't she go out of mourning then?'

Grange didn't know, hadn't even thought of it.

'Perhaps she will elect to wear mourning all her life,' suggested Nick. 'Have you thought of that?'

There was a distinct gibe in this, and Grange at once retreated to a less exposed position. 'I am quite willing to wait for her,' he said. 'And she knows it.'

'You're deuced easily pleased then,' rejoined Nick. 'And let me tell you – for I'm sure you don't know – there's not a single woman under the sun who appreciates that sort of patience.'

Grange ignored the information with a decidedly sullen air. He did not regard Nick as particularly well qualified to give him advice upon such a subject.

After a moment Nick saw his attitude, and laughed aloud. 'Yes, say it, man! It's quite true in a sense, and I shouldn't contradict you if it weren't. But has it never occurred to you that I was under a terrific disadvantage from the very beginning? Do you remember that I undertook the job that you shirked? Or do you possibly present the matter to yourself – and others – in some more attractive form?'

He turned upon his elbow with the question and regarded Grange with an odd expectancy. But Grange smoked in silence, not raising his eyes.

Suddenly Nick spoke in a different tone, a tone that was tense without vibrating. 'It doesn't matter how you put it. The truth remains. You didn't love her then. If you had loved her, you must have been ready – as I was ready – to make the final sacrifice. But you were not ready. You hung back. You let me take the place which only a man who cared enough to protect her to the uttermost could have taken. You let me do this thing, and I did it. I brought her through untouched. I kept her – night and day I kept her – from harm of any sort. And she has been my first care ever since. You won't believe this, I daresay, but it's true. And – mark this well – I will only let her go to the man who will make her happy. Once I meant to be that man. You don't suppose, do you, that I brought her safe through hell just for the pleasure of seeing her marry another fellow? But it's all the same now what I did it for. I've been knocked out of the running.' His eyelids suddenly quivered as if at a blow. 'It doesn't matter to you how. It wasn't because she fancied anyone else. She hadn't begun to think of you in those days. I let her go, never mind why. I let her go, but she is still in my keeping, and will be till she is the actual property of another man –

yes, and after that too. I saved her, remember. I won the right of guardianship over her. So be careful what you do. Marry her if you love her. But if you don't, leave her alone. She shall be no man's second best. That I swear.'

He ceased abruptly. His yellow face was full of passion. His hand was clenched upon the sofa-cushion. The whole body of the man seemed to thrill and quiver with electric force.

And then in a moment it all passed. As at the touching of a spring his muscles relaxed. The naked passion was veiled again – the old mask of banter replaced.

He stretched out his hand to the man who had sat in silence and listened to that one fierce outburst of a force which till then had contained itself.

'I speak as a fool,' he said lightly. 'Nothing new for me, you'll say. But just for my satisfaction – because she hates me so – put your hand in mine and swear you will seek her happiness before everything else in the world. I shall never trouble you again after this fashion. I have spoken.'

Blake sat for several seconds without speaking. Then, as if impelled thereto, he leaned slowly forward and laid his hand in Nick's. He seemed to have something to say, but it did not come.

Nick waited.

'I swear,' Blake said at length.

His voice was low, and he did not attempt to look Nick in the face, but he obviously meant what he said.

And Nick seemed to be satisfied. In less than five seconds, he had tossed the matter carelessly aside as one having no further concern in it. But the memory of that interview was as a searing flame to Blake's soul for long after.

For he knew that the man from whom Muriel had sought his protection was more worthy of her than he, and his heart cried bitter shame upon him for that knowledge.

It was with considerable difficulty that he responded to Nick's airy nothings during the half-hour that followed, and the unusual alacrity with which he seized upon his host's suggestion that he might care to see the garden, testified to his relief at being released from the obligation of doing so.

They went out together on to the wide lawn, and sauntered down to a summer-house on the edge of the cliff, over-looking the whole mighty expanse of sea. It lay dreaming in the sunlight, with hardly a ripple upon the long white beach below. And here they came upon Muriel and Olga, sitting side by side on the grass.

Olga had just finished pulling a daisy to pieces. She tossed it away at Nick's approach, and sprang to meet him.

'It's very disappointing,' she declared. 'It's the fourth time I've done it, and it always comes the same. I've been making the daisies tell Muriel's fortune, and it always comes to "He would if he could, but he can't." You try this time, Nick.'

'All right. You hold the daisy,' said Nick.

Muriel looked up with a slightly heightened colour. 'I think we ought to be going,' she remarked.

'We have just ordered the horses for four o'clock,' Grange said apologetically.

She glanced at the watch on her wrist – half-past three. Nick, seated cross-legged on the grass in front of her, had already with Olga's able assistance, begun his game.

Swiftly the tiny petals fell from his fingers. He was very intent, and in spite of herself Muriel became intent too, held by a most unaccountable fascination. So handicapped was he that he could not even pull a flower to pieces without assistance. And yet –

Suddenly he looked across at her. 'He loves her!' he announced.

'Oh, Nick!' exclaimed Olga reproachfully. 'You cheated! You pulled off two!'

'He usually does cheat,' Muriel observed, plucking a flower of grass and regarding it with absorption.

'So do you,' retorted Nick unexpectedly.

'I!' She looked at him in amazement. 'What do you mean?'

'I shan't tell you,' he returned, 'because you know, or you would know if you took the trouble to find out. Grange, I wish you would give me a light. Hullo, Olga, there's a hawk! See him? Straight above that cedar!'

All turned to look at the dark shape of the bird hovering in mid-air. Seconds passed. Suddenly there was a flashing, downward swoop, and the sky was empty.

Olga exclaimed, and Nick sent up a wild whoop of applause. Muriel gave a great start and glanced at him. For a single instant his look met hers, then with a sick shudder, she turned aside.

'You are cold,' said Grange.

Yes, she was cold. It was as if an icy hand had closed upon her heart. As from an immense distance, she heard Olga's voice of protest.

'Oh, Nick, how can you cheer?'

And his careless reply. 'My good child, don't grudge the poor creature his dinner. Even a bird of prey must live. Come along! We'll go in to tea. Muriel is cold.'

They went in, and again his easy hospitality overcame all difficulties.

When at length the visitors rode away, they left him grinning a cheery farewell from his doorstep. He seemed to be in the highest spirits.

They were more than half-way home when Muriel turned impetuously to her companion, breaking a long silence.

'Blake,' she said, 'I am ready to marry you as soon as you like.'

Part IV

Chapter 32

Muriel saw very little of her *fiancé* during the weeks that followed their visit to Redlands. There was not indeed room for him at the cottage at Brethaven which she and Daisy had taken for the summer months. He had moreover several visits to pay, and his leave would be up in September.

Muriel herself, having once made her decision, had plenty to occupy her. They had agreed to adhere to Sir Reginald Bassett's plan for them, and to be married in India some time before Christmas. But she did not want to go to Lady Bassett's sister before she left England, and she was glad when Daisy declared that she herself would go to town with her in the autumn.

A change had come over Daisy of late, a change which Muriel keenly felt, but which she was powerless to define. It seemed to date from the arrival of Nick though she did not definitely connect it with him. There was nothing palpable in it, nothing even remotely suggestive of a breach between them; only, subconsciously as it were, Muriel had become aware that their silence which till then had been the silence of sympathy had subtly changed till it had become the silence of a deep though unacknowledged reserve. It was wholly intangible, this change. No outsider would have guessed of its existence. But to the younger girl it was always vaguely present. She knew that somewhere between herself and her friend there was a locked door. Her own reserve never permitted her to attempt to open it. With a species of pride that was largely composed of shyness, she held aloof. But she was never quite unconscious of the opposing barrier. She felt that the old sweet intimacy that had so lightened the burden of her solitude, was gone.

Meanwhile, Daisy was growing stronger, and day by day more active. She never referred to her baby, and very seldom to her husband. When his letters arrived she invariably put them away with scarcely a glance. Muriel sometimes wondered if she even read them. It was pitifully plain to her that Will Musgrave's place in his wife's heart was very, very narrow. It had dwindled perceptibly since the baby's death.

On the subject of Will's letters, Nick could have enlightened her, for he always appeared at the cottage on mail-day for news. But Muriel, having discovered this habit, as regularly absented herself, with the result that they seldom met. He never made any effort to see her. On one occasion when she came unexpectedly upon him and Olga, shrimping along the shore, she was surprised that he did not second the child's eager proposal that she should join them. He actually seemed too keen upon the job in hand to pay her much attention.

And gradually she began to perceive that this was the attitude towards her that he had decided to assume. What it veiled she knew not, nor did she inquire. It was enough for her that hostilities had ceased. Nick apparently was bestowing his energies elsewhere.

Midsummer passed, and a July of unusual heat drew on. Dr. Jim and his wife and boys had departed to Switzerland. Nick and Olga had elected to remain at Redlands. They were out all day long in the motor or dogcart, on horseback or on foot. Life was one perpetual picnic to Olga just then, and she was not looking forward to the close of the summer holidays when, so her father had decreed, she was to return to her

home and the ordinary routine. Nick's plans were still unsettled though he spoke now and then of a prospective
return to India. He must in any case return thither, so he
once told her, whether he decided to remain or not. It was
not a pleasant topic to Olga, and she always sought to avoid
any allusion to it. After the fashion of children, she lived in
the present, and enjoyed it to the full; bathing with Muriel
every morning and spending the remainder of the day in
Nick's society. The friendship between these two was based
upon complete understanding. They had been comrades
as long as Olga could remember. Given Nick, it was very
seldom that she desired anyone besides.

Muriel had ceased to marvel over this strange fact. She had
come to realize that Nick was, and always must be, an enigma
to her. In the middle of July, when the heat was so intense as
to be almost intolerable, Daisy received a pressing invitation
to visit an old friend, and to go yachting on the Broads. She
refused it at first point-blank, but Muriel, hearing of the
matter before the letter was sent, interfered, and practically
insisted upon a change of decision.

'It is the very thing for you,' she declared. 'Brethaven has
done its best for you. But you want a dose of more bracing
air to make you quite strong again. It's absurd of you to
dream of throwing away such an opportunity. I simply won't
let you do it.'

'But how can I possibly leave you all alone?' Daisy
protested. 'If the Ratcliffes were at home, I might think of it,
but – '

'That settles it,' Muriel announced with determination.
'I never heard such nonsense in my life. What do you think
could possibly happen to me here? You know perfectly well
that a couple of weeks of my own society would do me no
harm whatever.'

So insistent was she, that finally she gained her point, and
Daisy, albeit somewhat reluctantly, departed for Norfolk,
leaving her to her own devices.

The heat was so great in those first days of solitude, that Muriel was not particularly energetic. Apart from her early swim with Olga, and an undeniably languid stroll in the evening, she scarcely left the precincts of the cottage. No visitors came to her. There were none but fisher-folk in the little village. And so her sole company consisted of Daisy's *ayah* and the elderly English cook.

But she did not suffer from loneliness. She had books and work in plenty, and it was even something of a relief, though she never owned it, to be apart from Daisy for a little. They never disagreed, but always at the back of her mind there lay the consciousness of a gulf between them.

She was at first somewhat anxious lest Nick should feel called upon to entertain her, and should invite her to accompany him and Olga upon some of their expeditions. But he did not apparently think of it, and she was always very emphatic in assuring Olga that she was enjoying her quiet time.

She and Nick had not met for some weeks, and she began to think it more than probable that they would not do so during Daisy's absence. Under ordinary circumstances this expectation of hers would doubtless have been realized, for Nick had plainly every intention of keeping out of her way; but the day of emergency usually dawns upon a world of sleepers.

The brooding heat culminated at last in an evening of furious storm, and Muriel speedily left the dinner-table to watch the magnificent spectacle of vivid and almost continuous lightning over the sea. It was a wonder that always drew her. She did not feel the nervous oppression that torments so many women, or if she felt it she rose above it. The splendour of the rising storm lifted her out of herself. She had no thought for anything else.

For more than half an hour she stood by the little sitting-room window, gazing out upon the storm-tossed water. It had not begun to rain, but the sound of it was in the air. And the earth was waiting expectantly. There seemed to be a feeling of expectation everywhere. She was vaguely restless under it, curiously impatient for the climax.

It came at last, so suddenly, so blindingly, that she reeled back against the curtain in sheer, physical recoil. The whole sky seemed to burst into flame, and the crash of thunder was so instantaneous that she felt as if a shell had exploded at her feet. Trembling, she hid her face. The world seemed to rock all around her. For the first time she was conscious of fear.

Then as the thunder died into a distant roar, the heavens opened as if at a word of command, and in one marvellous, glittering sheet the rain burst forth.

She lifted her head to gaze upon this new wonder that the incessant lightning revealed. The noise was like the sharp rattle of musketry, and it almost drowned the heavier artillery overhead. The window was blurred and streaming, but the brilliance outside was such that every detail in the little garden was clear to her notwithstanding. And though she still trembled, she nerved herself to look forth.

An instant later she sprang backwards with a wild cry of terror. A face – a wrinkled face that she knew – was there close against the window-pane, and had looked into her own.

Chapter 33

Out of a curious numbness that had almost been a swoon there came to her the consciousness of a hand that rapped and rapped and rapped upon the pane. She had fled away to the farther end of the room in her panic. She had turned the lamp low at the beginning of the storm, and now it burned so dimly that it scarcely gave out any light at all. Beyond the window, the lightning flashed with an awful luridness upon the rushing hail. Beyond the window, looking in upon her, and knocking, knocking, knocking, stood the figure of her dread.

She came to herself slowly, with a quaking heart. It was

more horrible to her than anything she had known since the days of her flight from the beleaguered fort; but she knew that she must fight down the horror, she knew as certainly as if a physical force compelled her that she would have to go to the window, would have to open to the man who waited there.

Slowly she brought her quivering body into subjection, while every nerve twitched and clamoured to escape. Slowly she dragged herself back to the vision that had struck her with that paralysis of terror. Resisting feebly, invisibly compelled, she went.

He ceased to knock, and his face against the pane, he spoke imperatively. What he said, she could not hear in that tumult of mighty sound. Only she felt his insistence, answered to it, was mastered by it.

White-faced, with horror clutching at her heart, she undid the catch. His one hand, strong, instinct with energy, helped her to raise the sash. In a moment he was in the room, bare-headed, drenched from head to foot.

She fell back before him, but he scarcely looked at her. He shut the window sharply, then strode to the lamp, and turned it up. Then abruptly he wheeled and spoke in a voice half-kindly, half-contemptuous.

'Muriel, you're a little idiot!'

There was little in the words to comfort her, yet she was instantly and vastly reassured. She was also for the moment overwhelmingly ashamed, but he did not give her time to think of that.

'I couldn't get in any other way,' he said. 'I tried the doors first, hammered at them, but no one came. Look here! Olga is ill, very ill, and she wants you badly. Are you brave enough to come?'

'Oh!' Muriel said, with a gasp. 'Now, do you mean? With – with you?'

He threw her an odd look under his flickering eyelids, and she noted with a scared minuteness of attention the gleam of the lamplight on their pale lashes. She had always hated pale eyelashes. They seemed to her untrustworthy.

'Yes,' he told her grimly. 'All alone – with me – in the storm. Shall you be afraid – if I give you my hand to hold? You've done it before.'

Was he mocking her weakness? She could not say. She only knew that he watched her with the intensity of an eagle that marks its quarry. He did not mean her to refuse.

'What is the matter with Olga?' she asked.

'I don't know. I believe it is sunstroke. We were motoring in the midday heat. She didn't seem to feel it at the time, but her head ached when we got in. She is in a high fever now. I've sent my man off in the motor to fetch Jim's locum from Weir. I should have brought the dogcart myself to fetch you, but I couldn't trust the horse in this.'

'You left her alone to come here?' Muriel questioned.

He nodded. 'I had no choice. She wished it. Besides, there were none but women-folk left. She's got one of them with her, the least imbecile of the lot, which isn't saying much. They're all terrified of course at the storm – all except Olga. She is never afraid of anything.'

A frightful crash of thunder carried away his words. Before it had rolled away, Muriel was at the door. She made a rapid sign to him, and was gone.

Nick chafed up and down the room, waiting for her. The storm continued with unabated violence, but he did not give it a thought. He was counting the moments with feverish impatience.

Muriel's absence scarcely lasted for five minutes, but when she came back all trace of fear had left her. Her face showed quiet and matter-of-fact above the long waterproof in which she had wrapped herself. Over her arm she carried a waterproof cloak.

She held it out to him. 'It's one of Daisy's, but you are to wear it. I think you must be mad to have come out without anything.'

She put it round his shoulders; and he thanked her with a smothered laugh.

A terrific blast of wind and rain met them as they emerged from the cottage, nearly whirling Muriel off her feet. She made an instinctive clutch at her companion and instantly her hand was caught fast in his. He drew her arm close under his own, and she did not resist him. There was something reassuring in his touch.

Later she wondered if they spoke at all during that terrible walk. She could never recall a word on either side. And yet, though in a measure frightened, she was not panic-stricken.

The storm was beginning to subside a little before they reached Redlands, though the rain still fell heavily. In the intervals between the lightning it was pitch dark. They had no lantern, but Nick was undismayed. He walked as lightly and surely as a cat, and Muriel had no choice but to trust herself unreservedly to his guidance. She marvelled afterwards at the complete trust with which that night he had managed to inspire her, but at the time she never questioned it.

Yet when the lights of Redlands shone at last through the gloom, she breathed a sigh of relief. Instantly Nick spoke.

'Well done!' he said briefly. 'You are your father's daughter still.'

She knew that she flushed in the darkness, and was glad that he could not see her face.

'You must go and get dry, first of all,' he went on. 'I told them to light a fire somewhere. And you are to have some coffee too. Mind, I say it.'

To this she responded with some spirit. 'I will if you will.'

'I must go straight to Olga,' he said. "I promised I would.'

'Not in your wet things!' 'Muriel exclaimed. 'No, Nick! Listen! I am not wet, not as you are. Let me go to Olga first. You can send me some coffee in her room if you like. But you must go at once and change. Promise you will, Nick!'

She spoke urgently. For some reason the occasion seemed to demand it.

Nick was silent for a little, as if considering. Then as they finally reached the porch he spoke in a tone she did not altogether fathom.

'I say, you are not going to shut me out, you know.'

She looked up in astonishment. 'Of course not. I never dreamt of such a thing.'

'All right,' he said, and this time she knew he spoke with relief. 'I will do as you like then.'

A moment more, and he opened the door, standing aside for her to pass. She entered quickly, glad to be in shelter, and paused to slip off her streaming waterproof. He took it from her, passing his hand over her sleeve.

'You are sure you are not wet through?'

'Quite sure,' she told him. 'Take me straight up, won't you?'

'Yes. Come this way.'

He preceded her up the wide stairs where he might have walked beside her, not pausing for an instant till he stood at Olga's door.

'Go straight in,' he said then. 'She is expecting you. Tell her, if she wants to know, that I am coming directly.'

He passed on swiftly with the words, and disappeared into a room close by.

Very softly Muriel turned the door-handle and entered. Olga's voice greeted her before she was well in the room. It sounded husky and strained.

'Muriel! Dear Muriel! I'm so glad you've come. I've wanted you so – you can't think. Where's Nick?'

'He is coming, dearest.' Muriel went forward to the bed, and took the two hands eagerly extended in hers.

The child was lying in an uneasy position, her hair streaming in a disordered tangle about her flushed face. She was shivering violently though the hands Muriel held were burning. 'You came all through this awful storm,' she whispered. 'It was lovely of you, dear. I hope you weren't frightened.'

Muriel sat down beside her. 'And you have been left all alone,' she said.

'I didn't mind,' gasped Olga. 'Mrs. Ellis – that's the cook – was here at first. But she was such an ass about the thunder that I sent her away. I expect she's in the coal cellar.'

A gleam of fun shone for an instant in her eyes, and was gone. The fevered hands closed tightly in Muriel's hold. 'I feel so ill,' she murmured, 'so ill.'

'Where is it, darling?' Muriel asked her tenderly.

'It's – it's all over me,' moaned Olga. 'My head worst, and my throat. My throat is dreadful. It makes me want to cry.'

There was little that Muriel could do to ease her. She tied back the tossing hair, and rearranged the bedclothes; then sat down by her side, hoping she might get some sleep.

Not long after, Nick crept in on slippered feet, but Olga heard him instantly, and started up with outflung arms. 'Nick, darling, I want you! I want you! Come quite close! I think I'm going to die. Don't let me, Nick!'

Muriel rose to make room for him, but he motioned her back sharply; then knelt down himself by the child's pillow and took her head upon his arm.

'Stick to it, sweetheart!' he murmured softly. 'There's a medicine man coming, and you'll be better presently.'

Olga cuddled against him with a sigh, and comforted by the close holding of his arm dropped presently into an uneasy doze.

Nick never stirred from his position, and mutely Muriel sat and watched him. There was a wonderful tenderness about him just then, a softness with which she was strangely familiar, but which almost she had forgotten. If she had never seen him before that moment, she knew that she would have liked him.

He seemed to have wholly forgotten her presence. His entire attention was concentrated upon the child. His lips twitched from time to time, and she knew that he was very anxious, intensely impatient under his stillness for the doctor's coming. She remembered that old trick of his. She had never before associated it with any emotion.

Suddenly he turned his head as if he had felt her scrutiny, and looked straight into her eyes. It was only for a moment. His glance flickered beyond her with scarcely a pause. Yet it was to her as if by that swift look he had spoken, had for the first time made deep and passionate protest against her bitter judgment of him, had as it were shown her in a single flash the human heart beneath the jester's garb.

And again very deep down in her soul there stirred that blind, unconscious entity, of the existence of which she herself had so vague a knowledge, feeling upwards, groping outwards, to the light.

There came upon her a sudden curious sense of consternation – a feeling as of mental earthquake when the very foundations of the soul are shaken. Had she conceivably been mistaken in him? With all her knowledge of him, had she by some strange mischance – some maddening, some inexplicable misapprehension – failed utterly and miserably to see this man as he really was?

For the first time the question sprang up within her. And she found no answer to it – only that breathless, blank dismay.

Softly Nick's voice broke in upon her seething doubt. He had laid Olga back upon the pillow.

'The doctor is here. Do you mind staying with her while I go?'

'You'll come back, Nick?' the child urged, in her painful whisper.

'Yes, I'll come back,' he promised. 'Honest Injun!'

He touched her cheek lightly at parting, and Olga caught the caressing hand and pressed it against her burning lips. Muriel saw his face as he turned from the bed. It was all softened and quivering with emotion.

Chapter 34

In the morning they knew the worst. Olga had scarlet fever.

The doctor imparted the news to Nick and Muriel standing outside the door of the sick-room. Nick's reception of it was by no means characteristic. For the first time in her life Muriel saw consternation undisguised upon the yellow face.

'Great Jupiter!' he said. 'What a criminal ass I am!'

At another moment she could have laughed at the tragic force of his self-arraignment. Even as it was, she barely repressed a smile as she set his mind at rest. She needed no explanation. It was easy enough to follow the trend of his thoughts just then.

'If you are thinking of me,' she said, 'I have had it.'

She saw his instant relief, though he merely acknowledged the statement by a nod.

'We must have a nurse,' he said briefly. 'We shall manage all right then. I'll do my turn. Oh, stuff!' at a look from the doctor. 'I shan't hurt. I'm much too tough a morsel for microbes to feed on.'

Possibly the doctor shared this opinion, for he made no verbal protest. It fell to Muriel to do this later in the day when the nurse was installed, and she was at liberty to leave Olga's room. Nick had just returned from the post-office whence he had been sending a message to the child's father. She came upon him stealing up to take a look at her. Seeing Muriel he stopped. 'How is she?'

Muriel moved away to an open window at the end of the passage before she made reply. He followed her and they stood together, looking out upon the sunset.

'The fever is very high,' she said. 'And she is suffering a good deal of pain. She is not quite herself at times.'

'You mean she is worse?' He looked at her keenly.

It was exactly what she did mean. Olga had been growing steadily worse all day. Yet when abruptly he turned to leave her, Muriel laid a hasty hand upon his arm.

'Nick,' she said, and he voice was almost imploring, 'don't go in! Please don't go in!'

He stopped short. 'Why not?'

She removed her hand quickly. 'It's so dangerous – besides being unnecessary. Won't you be sensible about it?'

He gave his head a queer upward jerk, and stood as one listening, not looking at her. 'What for?'

She could not think of any very convincing reason for the moment. Yet it was imperative that he should see the matter as she saw it.

'Suppose I had not had it,' she ventured, 'what would you have done?'

'Packed you off to the cottage again double quick,' said Nick promptly.

It was the answer she had angled for. She seized upon it. 'Well, tell me why.'

He spun round on his heels and faced her. He was blinking very rapidly. 'You asked me that question once before,' he said. 'And out of a sentimental consideration for your feelings – I didn't answer it. Do you really want an answer this time, or shall I go on being sentimentally considerate?'

She heard the old subtle jeering note in his voice but its effect upon her was oddly different from what it had ever been before. It did not anger her, nor did it wholly frighten her. It dawned upon her suddenly that though possibly it lay in his power to hurt her, he would not do so.

She answered him with composure. 'I don't want you to be anything but sensible, Nick. And it isn't sensible to expose yourself to unnecessary risk. It's wrong.'

'That's my lookout,' said Nick.

It was indubitably, but she wanted very much to gain her point.

'Won't you at least keep away unless she asks for you?' she urged.

'You seem mighty anxious to get rid of me,' said Nick.

'I am not,' she returned quickly. 'I am not. You know it isn't that.'

'Do I?' he said quizzically. 'It's one of the few things I shouldn't have known without being told. Well, I'm sorry I can't consent to be sensible as you call it. I am quite sure personally that there isn't the slightest danger. It isn't so infectious at this stage, you know. Perhaps by-and-by, when she is through the worst, I will think about it.'

He spoke lightly, but she was aware of the anxiety that underlay the words. She said no more, reminding herself that argument with Nick was always futile, sometimes worse. Nevertheless she found some comfort in the smile with which he left her. He had refused to treat with her, but his enmity – if enmity it could be called – was no longer active. He had proclaimed a truce which she knew he would not break.

Olga was delirious that night, and privately Muriel was glad that she had not been able to exclude him. For his control over the child was wonderful. As once with a tenderness maternal he had soothed her, so now he soothed Olga, patiently, steadfastly, even with a certain cheeriness. It all came back to her as she watched him, the strength of the man, his selfless devotion.

She could see that both doctor and nurse thought very seriously of the child. The former paid a late visit, but said very little beyond advising her to rest if she could in an adjacent room. Both Nick and the nurse seconded this, and, seeing there was nothing that she could do, she gave way in the matter, lying down as she was with but small expectation of sleep. But she was wearier than she knew, and the slumber into which she fell was deep, and would have lasted for some hours undisturbed.

It was Nick who roused her, and starting up at his touch, she knew instantly that what they had all mutely feared had drawn very near. His face told her at a glance, for he made no effort to dissemble.

'The nurse thinks you had better come,' was all he said.

She pushed the hair from her forehead, and turned without a word to obey the summons. But at the door something checked her, something cried aloud within her, bidding her pause. She stopped. Nick was close behind her. Swiftly, obedient to the voice that cried, she stretched out her hand to him. He gripped it fast and she was conscious for an instant of a curious gladness, a willingness to leave it in his hold, that she had never experienced before. But at the door of Olga's room, he softly relinquished it, and drew back.

Olga was lying propped on pillows, and breathing quickly. The nurse was bending over her with a glass, but Olga's face was turned away. She was watching the door.

As Muriel came to her, the light eyes brightened to quick intelligence, and the parted lips tried to speak. But no sound came forth, and a frown of pain succeeded the effort.

Muriel stooped swiftly and grasped the slender hand that lay clenched upon the sheet.

'There, darling! Don't try to talk. It hurts you so. We are both here, Nick and I, and we understand all about it.'

It was the first time she had ever voluntarily coupled herself with him. It came to her instinctively to do it in that moment.

But Olga had something to say, something apparently that must be said. With infinite difficulty she forced a husky whisper. Muriel stooped lower to catch it, so low that her face was almost touching the face upon the pillow.

'Muriel,' came haltingly from the parched lips, 'there's something – I want – to say to you – about Nick.'

Muriel felt the blood surging at her temples as the faint words reached her. She would have given anything to know that he was out of earshot.

'Won't you say it in the morning darling?' she said, almost with pleading in her voice. 'It's so late now.'

It was not late. It was very early – the solemn hour when countless weary ones fall into their long sleep. And the moment she had spoken, her heart smote her. Was she for her own peace of mind trying to silence the child's last words on earth?

'No, never mind, dear,' she amended tenderly. 'I'm listening to you. Tell me now.'

'Yes,' panted Olga. 'I must. I must. You remember – that day – with the daisies – the day we saw – the hawk?'

Yes, well Muriel remembered it. The thought of it went through her like a stab.

'Yes, dear. What of it?' she heard herself say.

'Well you know – I've thought since – that the daisies meant Nick, not – not – I can't remember his name, Muriel.'

'Do you mean Captain Grange, dear?'

'Yes, yes of course. He was there too, wasn't he? I'm sure now – quite sure – they didn't mean him.'

'Very likely not, dear.'

'And Muriel – do you know – Nick was just miserable – after you went. I sort of felt he was. And late – late that night I woke up, and I crept down to him – in the library. And he had his head down on the table – as if – as if – he was crying. Oh, Muriel!'

A sharp sob interrupted the piteous whisper. Muriel folded her arms about the child, pillowing the tired head on her breast. All the fair hair had been cut off earlier in the day. Its absence gave Olga a very babyish appearance.

Brokenly with many gasping pauses, the pathetic little story came to an end. 'I went to him – and I asked him what it was. And he – he looked up with that funny face he makes – you know – and he just said, "Oh, it's all right. I've been feeding on dust and ashes all day long, that's all. And it's dry fare for a thirsty man!" He thought I wouldn't know what he meant. But I did, Muriel. And I always wanted to tell you. But – somehow – you wouldn't let me. He meant you. He was hurt – so hurt – because you weren't kind to him. Oh, Muriel, won't you – won't you – try to be kind to him now? Please, dear, please!'

Muriel's eyes sought Nick, and instantly a thrill of surprise and relief shot through her. He had not heard that request of Olga's. She doubted if he'd heard anything. He was sunk in a chair well in the background with his head on his hand, and looking at him she saw his shoulders shake with a soundless sob.

She looked away again with a sense of trespass. This – this was the man who had fought and cursed and lain under her eyes – the man from whose violence she had shrunk appalled, whose strength had made her shudder many a time. She had never imagined that he could grieve thus – even for his little pal Olga.

Tenderly she turned back to the child. That single glimpse of the man in pain had made it suddenly easy to grant her earnest prayer.

'I won't be unkind to him again, darling,' she promised softly.

'Never any more?' insisted Olga.

'Never any more, my darling.'

Olga made a little nestling movement against her. It was all she wanted, and now that the effort of asking was over she was very tired.

The nurse drew softly back into the shadow, and a deep silence fell in the room. Through it in a long, monotonous roar there came the sound of the sea breaking, eternally breaking, along the beach.

No one moved. Olga's breathing was growing slower, so much slower that there were times when Muriel, listening intently, fancied that it had wholly ceased. She held the little slim body close in her arms, jealously close, as though she were defying Death itself. And ever through the stillness she could hear her own heart beating like the hoofs of a galloping horse.

Slowly the night began to pass. The outline of the window-frame became visible against a faint grey glimmer. The window was open, and a breath of the coming dawn wandered in with the fragrance of drenched roses. A soft rain was falling. The patter of it could be heard upon the leaves.

Again Muriel listened for the failing breath, listened closely, tensely, her face bent low to the fair head that lay so still upon her breast.

But she heard nothing – nothing but her own heart quickening, quickening, from fear to suspense, from suspense to the anguish of conviction.

She lifted her face at last, and in the same instant there arose a sudden flood of song from the sleeping garden, as the first lark soared to meet the dawn.

Half-dazed, she listened to that marvellous outpouring of gladness, so wildly rapturous, so weirdly holy. On, ever on, pealed the bird-voice; on to the very Gates of Heaven, and it seemed to the girl who listened as though she heard a child's spirit singing up the steeps of Paradise. With her heart she followed it, till suddenly she heard it no more. The voice ceased as it had begun, ceased as a burst of music when an open door is closed – and there fell in its stead a silence that could be felt.

Chapter 35

She could not have said for how long she sat motionless, the slight, inert body clasped against her breast. Vaguely she knew that the night passed, and with it the wondrous silence that had lain like a benediction upon the dawn. A thousand living things awoke to rejoice in the crystal splendour of the morning; but within the quiet room the spell remained unlifted, the silence lay untouched. It was as though the presence of Death had turned it into a peaceful sanctuary that no mere earthly tumult could disturb.

She sat in a species of waking stupor for a long, long time, not daring to move lest the peace that enfold her should be shattered. Higher and higher the sun climbed up the sky till at last it topped the cedar-trees and shone in upon her, throwing a single ray of purest gold across the foot of the bed. Fascinated, she watched it travel slowly upwards, till a silent, one-armed figure arose and softly drew the curtain.

The room grew dim again. The world was shut out. She was not conscious of physical fatigue, only of a certain weariness of waiting, waiting for she knew not what. It seemed interminable, but she would not seek to end it. She was as a soldier waiting for the order to quit his post.

There came a slight movement at last. Someone touched her, whispered to her. She looked up blankly and saw the nurse. But understanding seemed to have gone from her during those long hours. She could not take in a word. There arose a great surging in her brain, and the woman's face faded into an indistinct blur. She sat rigid, afraid to move lest she should fall.

She heard vague whisperings over her head, and an arm that was like a steel spring encircled her. Someone lifted her burden gently from her, and a faint murmur reached her, such as a child makes in its sleep.

Then the arm that supported her gradually raised her up till she was on her feet. Mechanically she tried to walk, but was instantly overcome by a sick sense of powerlessness.

'I can't!' she gasped. 'I can't!'

Nick's voice answered her in a quick, confident whisper. 'Yes, you can, dear. It's all right. Hang on to me. I won't let you go.'

She obeyed him blindly. There was nothing else to do. And so, half-led, half-carried, she tottered from the room.

A glare of sunlight smote upon her from a passage-window with a brilliance that almost hurt her. She stood still, clinging to Nick's shoulder.

'Oh, Nick,' she faltered weakly, 'why don't they – pull down the blinds?'

Nick turned aside, still closely holding her, into the room in which she had rested for the earlier part of the night.

'Because, thank God,' he said, 'there is no need. Olga is going to live.'

He helped her down into an easy-chair, and would have left her; but she clung to him still, weakly but persistently.

'Oh, Nick, don't laugh! Tell me the truth for once! Please, Nick, please!'

He yielded to her so abruptly that she was half-startled, dropping suddenly down upon his knees beside her, the morning light full upon his face.

'I am telling you the truth,' he said. 'I believe you have saved her life. She has been sleeping ever since sunrise.'

Muriel gazed at him speechlessly; but she no longer suspected him of trying to deceive her. If he had never told her the truth before that moment, he was telling it to her then.

She gave a little gasping cry of relief unspeakable and hid her face. The next moment Nick was on his feet. She heard his quick, light step as he crossed the threshold, and realized thankfully that he had left her alone.

A little later, a servant brought her a breakfast-tray with a message from the master of the house to the effect that he hoped she would go to bed and take a long rest.

It was excellent advice, and she acted upon it; for since the worst strain was over, sleep had become an urgent necessity to her. She wondered as she lay down if Nick were following the same course. She hoped he was, for she had a curiously vivid memory of the lines that sleeplessness had drawn about his eyes.

It was late afternoon when she awoke, and sat swiftly up with a confused sense of being watched.

'Don't jump like that!' a gruff voice said. 'Lie down again at once. You are not to get up till to-morrow morning.'

She turned with a shaky laugh of welcome to find Dr. Jim seated frowning by her side. He laid a compelling hand upon her shoulder.

'Lie down again, do you hear? There's nothing for you to do. Olga is much better, and doesn't want you.'

'And Nick?' said Muriel.

They were the first words that occurred to her. She said them hurriedly, with heightened colour.

Jim Ratcliffe frowned more than ever. He was feeling her pulse. 'A nice couple of idiots you are!' he grimly remarked. 'You needn't worry about Nick. He has gone for a ride. As soon as he comes back, he will dine and go to bed.'

'Can't I get up to dinner?' Muriel suggested.

She could scarcely have said why she made the proposal, and she was certainly surprised when Jim Ratcliffe fell in with it. He looked at his watch. 'Well, you may if you like. You will probably sleep the better for it. But I'll have no nonsense, mind, Muriel. You're to do as you're told.'

Muriel smiled acquiescence. She felt that everything was right now that Dr. Jim had returned to take the direction of affairs into his own hands. He had come back alone, and he intended to finish his holiday under Nick's roof. So much he told her before with an abrupt smile he thanked her for her care of his little girl and took himself off.

She almost regretted her decision when she came to get up, for the strain was telling upon her more than she had realized. Not since Simla days had she felt so utterly worn out. She was glad of the cup of tea which Dr. Jim sent in to her before she left her room.

Sitting on the cushioned window-seat to drink it, she heard the tread of a horse's feet along the drive, and with a start she saw Nick come into view round a bend.

Her first impulse was to draw back out of sight, but the next moment she changed her mind and remained motionless. Her heart was suddenly beating very fast.

He was riding very carelessly, the bridle lying on the horse's neck. The evening sun was shining full in his face, but he did not seem to mind. His head was thrown back. He rode like a returning conqueror, wearied it might be, but triumphant.

Passing into the shadow of the house, he saw her instantly,

and the smile that flashed into his face was one of sheer exultation. He dropped the bridle altogether to wave to her.

'Up already? Have you seen old Jim?'

She nodded. It was impossible at the moment not to reflect his smile. 'I am coming down soon,' she told him.

'Come now,' said Nick persuasively.

She hesitated. He was slipping from his horse. A groom came up and took the animal from him.

Nick paused below her window, and once more lifted his grinning, confident face.

'I say, Muriel!'

She leaned down a little. 'Well?'

'Don't come if you don't want to, you know.'

She laughed half-reluctantly, conscious of a queer desire to please him. Olga's words were running in her brain. He had fed on dust and ashes.

Yet still she hesitated. 'Will you wait for me?'

'Till doomsday,' said Nick obligingly.

And drawn by a power that would not be withstood, she went down, still smiling, and joined him in the garden.

Chapter 36

Olga's recovery when the crisis of the disease was past was more rapid than even her father had anticipated; and this fact, combined with a spell of glorious summer weather, made the period of her quarantine very tedious, particularly as Nick was rigidly excluded from the sick-room.

At Olga's earnest request Muriel consented to remain at Redlands. Daisy had written to postpone her own return to the cottage, having received two or three invitations which she wished to accept if Muriel could still spare her.

Blake was in Scotland. His letters were not very frequent, and though his leave was nearly up, he did not speak of returning.

Muriel was thus thrown upon Jim Ratcliffe's care – a state of affairs which seemed to please him mightily. It was in fact his presence that made life easy for her just then. She saw considerably more of him than of Nick, the latter having completely relegated the duties of host to his brother. Though they met every day, they were seldom alone together, and she began to have a feeling that Nick's attitude towards her had undergone a change. His manner was now always friendly, but never intimate. He did not seek her society, but neither did he avoid her. And never by word or gesture did he refer to anything that had been between them in the past. She even wondered sometimes if there might not possibly have been another interpretation to Olga's story. That unwonted depression of his that the child had witnessed had surely never been inspired by her.

She found the time pass quickly enough during those six weeks. The care of Olga occupied her very fully. She was always busy devising some new scheme for her amusement.

Mrs. Ratcliffe returned to Weir, and Dr. Jim determined to transfer Olga to her home as soon as she was out of quarantine. With paternal kindliness, he insisted that Muriel must accompany her. Daisy's return was still uncertain, though it could not be long delayed; and Muriel had no urgent desire to return to the lonely life on the shore.

So, to Olga's outspoken delight, she yielded to the doctor's persuasion, and on the afternoon preceding the child's emancipation from her long imprisonment she walked down to the cottage to pack her things.

It was a golden day in the middle of September and she lingered awhile on the shore when her work was done. There was not a wave in all the vast, shimmering sea. The tide was going out, and the shallow ripples were clear as glass as they ran out along the white beach. Muriel paused often in her walk. She was sorry to leave the little fishing-village, realizing that she had been very happy there. Life had passed as smoothly as a dream of late, so smoothly that she had been content to live in the present with scarcely a thought for the future.

This afternoon she had begun to realize that her peaceful time was drawing to an end. In a few weeks more, she would be in town in all the bustle of preparation. And further still ahead of her – possibly two months – there loomed the prospect of her return to India, of Lady Bassett's soft patronage, of her marriage.

She shivered a little as one after another these coming events presented themselves. There was not one of them that she would not have postponed with relief. She stood still with her face to the sunlit sea, and told herself that her summer in England had been all too short. She had an almost passionate longing for just one more year of Home.

A pebble skimming past her and leaping from ripple to ripple like a living thing caught her attention. She turned sharply, and the next moment smiled a welcome.

Nick had come up behind her unperceived. She greeted him with pleasure unfeigned. She was tired of her own morbid thoughts just then. Whatever he might be, he was at least never depressing.

'I'm saying good-bye,' she told him. 'I don't suppose I shall ever come here again.'

He came and stood beside her while he grubbed in the sand with a stick.

'Not even to see me?' he suggested.

'Are you going to live here?' she asked in surprise.

'Oh, I suppose so,' said Nick, 'when I marry.'

'Are you going to be married?' Almost in spite of her the question leapt out.

He looked up, grinning shrewdly. 'I put it to you,' he said. 'Am I the sort of man to live alone?'

She experienced a curious sense of relief. 'But you are not alone in the world,' she pointed out. 'You have relations.'

'You regard marriage as a last resource?' questioned Nick.

She coloured and turned her face to the shore.' I don't

think any man ought to marry unless – unless – he cares,' she said, striving hard to keep the personal note out of her voice.

'Exactly,' said Nick, moving beside her. 'But doesn't that remark apply to women as well?'

She did not answer him. A discussion on this topic was the last thing she desired.

He did not press the point, and she wondered a little at his forbearance. She glanced at him once or twice as they walked, but his humorous, yellow face told her nothing.

Reaching some rocks, he suddenly stopped. 'I've got to get some seaweed for Olga. Do you mind waiting?'

'I will help you,' she answered.

He shook his head. 'No, you are tired. Just sit down in the sun. I won't be long.'

She seated herself without protest, and he turned to leave her. A few paces from her he paused, and she saw that he was trying to light a cigarette. He failed twice, and impulsively she sprang up.

'Nick, why don't you ask me to help you?'

He whizzed round. 'Perhaps I don't want you to,' he said quizzically.

She took the match-box from him. 'Don't be absurd! Why shouldn't I?' She struck a match and held it out to him. But he did not take it from her. He took her wrist instead, and stooping forward lighted his cigarette deliberately.

She did not look at him. Some instinct warned her that his eyes were intently searching her face. She seemed to feel them darting over her in piercing, impenetrable scrutiny.

He released her slowly at length and stood up. 'Am I to have the pleasure of dancing at your wedding?' he asked her suddenly.

She looked up then very sharply, and against her will a burning blush rose up to her temples. He waited for her answer, and at last it came.

'If you think it worth your while.'

'I would come from the other side of the world to see you made happy,' said Nick.

She turned her face aside. 'You are very kind.'

'Think so?' There was a note of banter in his voice. 'It's the first time you ever accused me of that.'

She made no rejoinder. She had a feeling at the throat that prevented speech, even had she had any words to utter. Certainly, as he had discovered, she was very tired. It was physical weariness no doubt, but she had an almost over-mastering desire to shed childish tears.

'You trot back now,' said Nick cheerily. 'I can grub along quite well by myself.'

She turned back silently. Why was it that the world seemed so grey and cold on that golden summer afternoon? She sat down again in the sunshine, and began to trace an aimless design in the sand with the stick Nick had left behind. Away in the distance she heard his cracked voice humming. Was he really as cheerful as he seemed, she wondered? Or was he merely making the best of things?

Again her thoughts went back to Olga's pathetic little revelation. Strange that she who knew him so intimately should never have seen him in such a mood! But did she know him after all? It was a question she had asked herself many times of late. She remembered how he had lightly told her that he had a reverse side. But had she really ever seen it, save for those brief glimpses by Olga's bedside, and as it was reflected in the child's whole-souled devotion to him? She wished with all her heart that he would lift the veil just once for her and show her his inner soul.

Again her thoughts passed to her approaching marriage. She had received a letter from Blake that day, telling her at length of his plans. He and Daisy had been staying in the same house, but he was just returning to town. He was to sail in less than a fortnight and would come to say good-bye to her immediately before his departure. The letter had been courteously kind throughout, but she had not felt tempted to read it again. It contained no reference to their wedding, save such as she chose to attribute to the concluding sentence: 'We can talk everything over when we meet.' A sense of chill struck her when she recalled the words. He was very kind of course, and invariably meant well; but she had begun to realize of late that there were times when she found him a little heavy and unresponsive. Not that she had ever desired any demonstration of tenderness from him, heaven knew. But the very consciousness that she had not desired this added to the chill. She was not quite sure that she wanted to see him again before he sailed. Certainly he had never bored her; but it was not inconceivable that he might do so. She shivered ever so slightly. It was not an exciting prospect – life with Blake. He was quite sure to be kind to her. He would consider her in every way. But was that after all quite all she wanted? A great sigh welled suddenly up from the bottom of her heart. Life was ineffably dreary – when it was not revoltingly horrible.

'Shall I tell you what is the matter?' said Nick.

She started violently, and found him leaning across the flat rock on which she was seated. His eyes were remarkably bright. She had a feeling that he suppressed a laugh as his look flickered over her.

'Sorry I made you jump,' he said. 'You ought to be used to me by this time. Anyhow you needn't be frightened. My venom was extracted long ago.'

She turned to him with sudden, unconsidered impulse. 'Oh, Nick,' she said, 'I sometimes think to myself I've been a great fool.'

He nodded. Her vehemence did not seem to surprise him. 'I thought it would strike you sooner or later,' he said.

She laughed in spite of herself with her eyes full of tears. 'There's not much comfort in that.'

'I haven't any comfort to give you,' said Nick, 'not at this stage. I'll give you advice if you like which I know you won't take.'

'No, please don't! That would be even worse.' There was

a tremor in her voice. She knew that she had stepped off the beaten track; but she had an intense and almost passionate longing to go a little further, to penetrate, if only for a moment, that perpetual mask.

'Don't let us talk of my affairs,' she said. 'Tell me of your own. What are you going to do?'

Nick's eyebrows went up. 'I thought I was coming to your wedding,' he remarked. 'That's as far as I've got at present.'

She made a gesture of impatience. 'Do you never think of the future?'

'Not in your presence,' laughed Nick. 'I think of you – you – and only you. Didn't you know?'

She turned away in silence. Was he tormenting her deliberately? Or did he fail to see that she was in earnest?

There followed a pause, and then, urged by that unknown impulse that would not be repressed, she did a curious thing. She got up, and, facing him, she made a very earnest appeal.

'Nick, why do you always treat me like this? Why will you never be honest with me?'

There was more of pain than reproach in the words. Her voice was deep and very sad.

But Nick scarcely looked at her. He was pulling tufts of dried seaweed off the rock on which he leaned.

'My dear girl,' he said, 'how can you expect it?'

'Expect it!' she echoed. 'I don't understand. What do you mean?'

He drew himself slowly to a sitting posture. 'How can I be honest with you,' he said, 'when you are not honest with yourself?'

'What do you mean?' she said again.

He gave her an odd look, 'You really want me to tell you?'

'Of course I do.' She spoke sharply. The old scared feeling was awake within her, but she would not yield to it. Now or never would she read the enigma. She would know the truth, cost what it might.

'What I mean is this,' said Nick. 'You won't own it, of

course, but you are cheating, and you are afraid to stop. There isn't one woman in ten thousand who has the pluck to throw in the cards when once she has begun to cheat. She goes on – as you will go on – to the end of her life, simply because she daren't do otherwise. You are out of the straight, Muriel. That's why everything is such a hideous failure. You are going to marry the wrong man, and you know it.'

He looked up at her again for an instant as he said it. He had spoken with his usual shrewd decision, but there was no hint of excitement about him. He might have been discussing some matter of a purely impersonal nature.

Muriel stood mutely poking holes in the sand. She could find nothing to say to this matter-of-fact indictment.

'And now,' Nick proceeded, 'I will tell you why you are doing it.'

She started at that, and looked up with flaming cheeks. 'I don't think I want to hear any more, Nick. It – it's rather late in the day, isn't it?'

He shrugged his shoulders. 'I knew you would be afraid to face it. It's easier, isn't it, to go on cheating?'

Her eyes gleamed for a moment. He had flicked a tender place. 'Very well,' she said proudly. 'Say what you like. It will make no difference. But please understand that I admit none of this.'

Nick's grin leapt goblin-like across his face and was gone. 'I never expected it of you,' he told her coolly. 'You would sooner die than admit it, simply because it would be infinitely easier for you to die. You will be false to yourself, false to Grange, false to me, rather than lower that miserable little rag of pride that made you jilt me at Simla. I didn't blame you so much then. You were only a child. You didn't understand. But that excuse won't serve you now. You are a woman, and you know what Love is. You don't call it by its name, but none the less you know it.'

He paused for an instant, for Muriel had made a swift gesture of protest.

'I don't think you know what you are saying,' she said, her voice very low.

He sprang abruptly to his feet. 'Yes,' he said, speaking very rapidly. 'That's how you will trick yourself to your dying day. It's a way women have. But it doesn't help them. It won't help you. For that thing in your heart – the thing that is fighting for air – the thing you won't own – the thing that drove you to Grange for protection – will never die. That is why you are miserable. You may do what you will to it, hide it, smother it, trample it. But it will survive for all that. All your life it will be there. You will never forget it, though you will try to persuade yourself that it belongs to a dead past. All your life,' – his voice vibrated suddenly, and the ever-shifting eyes blazed into leaping flame – 'all your life, you will remember that I was once yours to take or to throw away. And – you wanted me, yet – you chose to throw me away.'

Fiercely he flung the words at her. There was nothing impersonal about him now. He was vitally, overwhelmingly in earnest. A deep glow covered the parchment face. The man was as it were electrified by passion.

And Muriel gazed at him as one gazing upon sudden disaster. What was this, what was this, that he had said to her? He had rent the veil aside for her indeed. But to what dread vision had he opened her eyes?

The old paralyzing fear was knocking at her heart. She dreaded each instant to see the devil leap out upon his face. But as the seconds passed, she realized that he was still his own master. He had flung down the gauntlet, but he would go no further, unless she took it up. And this she could not do. She knew that she was no match for him.

He was watching her narrowly, she knew, and after a few palpitating moments she nerved herself to meet his look. She felt as if it scorched her, but she would not shrink. Not for a moment must he fancy that those monstrous words of his had pierced her quivering heart. Whatever happened later, when this stunned sense of shock had left her, she must not seem to take them seriously now, with his watching eyes upon her.

And so at last she lifted her head and faced him with a little quivering laugh, brave enough in itself, but how piteous she never guessed.

'I don't think you are quite so clever as you used to be, Nick,' she told him, 'though I admit' – her lips trembled – 'that you are very amusing sometimes. Blake once told me that you had the eyes of a snakecharmer. Is it true, I wonder? Anyhow they don't charm me.'

She stopped rather breathlessly, half-frightened by his stillness. Would he understand that it was not her intention to defy him – that she was only refusing the conflict?

For a few moments her heart beat tumultuously, and then came a great throb of relief. Yes, he understood. She had nought to fear.

He put his hand sharply over his eyes, turning from her. 'I have never tried to charm you,' he said, in a voice that sounded curiously choked and unfamiliar. 'I have only – loved you.'

In the silence that followed, he began to walk away from her, moving noiselessly over the sand.

Mutely she watched him, but she dared not call him back. And very soon she was quite alone.

Chapter 37

It did not take Dr. Jim long to discover that some trouble or at the least some perplexity was weighing upon his young guest's mind. He also shrewdly remarked that it dated from the commencement of her visit at his house. No one else noticed it, but this was not surprising. There was always plenty to occupy the attention in the Ratcliffe household, and only Dr. Jim managed to keep a sharp eye upon every member thereof. Moreover, by a casual observer, there was little or nothing that was unusual to be detected in Muriel's manner. Quiet she certainly was, but she was by no means listless. Her laugh did not always ring quite true, that was all. And her eyes drooped a little wearily from time to time. There were other symptoms, very slight, wholly imperceptible to any but a trained eye, yet not one of which escaped Dr. Jim.

He made no comment, but throughout that first week of her stay he watched her unperceived, biding his time. During several motor rides on which she accompanied him he maintained this attitude while she sat all-unsuspecting by his side. She had never detected any subtlety in this staunch friend of hers, and, unlike Daisy, she felt no fear of him. His blunt sincerity had never managed to wound her.

And so it was almost inevitable that she should give him his opportunity at last.

Late one evening she entered his consulting-room where he was busy writing.

'I want to talk to you,' she said. 'Is it very inconvenient?'

The doctor leaned back in his chair. 'Sit down there,' he said, pointing to one immediately facing him.

She laughed and obeyed, faintly blushing. 'I'm not a patient, you know.'

He drew his black brows together. 'It's very late. Why don't you go to bed.'

'Because I want to talk to you.'

'You can do that to-morrow,' bluntly rejoined Dr. Jim. 'You can't afford to sacrifice your sleep to chatter.'

'I am not sacrificing any sleep,' Muriel told him rather wearily. 'I never sleep before morning.'

He laid down his pen and gave her one of his hard looks. 'Then you are a very silly girl,' he said curtly at length.

'It isn't my fault,' she protested.

He shrugged his shoulders. 'You all say that. It's the most ordinary lie I know.'

Muriel smiled. 'I know you are longing to give me something nasty. You may, if you like. I'll take it whatever it is.'

Dr. Jim was silent for a space. He continued to regard her steadily, with a scrutiny that spared her nothing. She sat quite still under it. He had never disconcerted her yet. But when he leaned suddenly forward and took her wrist between his fingers, she made a slight, instinctive effort to frustrate him.

'Be still,' he ordered. 'What makes you so absurdly nervous? Want of sleep, eh?'

Her lips trembled a little. 'Don't probe too deep doctor,' she pleaded. 'I am not very happy just now.'

'Why don't you tell me what is the matter?' he asked gruffly.

She did not answer, and he continued frowning over her pulse.

'What do you want to talk to me about?' he asked at last.

She looked up with an effort. 'Oh, nothing much. Only a letter from a Mrs. Langdale who lives in town. She is going to India in November, and says she will take charge of me if I care to go with her. She has invited me to go and stay with her beforehand.'

'Well?' said Jim, as she paused.

'I don't want to go,' she said. 'Do you think I ought? She is Lady Bassett's sister.'

'I think it would probably do you good, if that's what you mean,' he returned. 'But I don't suppose that consideration has much weight with you. Why don't you want to go?'

'I don't like strangers, and I hate Lady Bassett,' Muriel answered, with absolute simplicity. 'Then there is Daisy. I don't know what her plans are. I always thought we should go East together.'

'There's no sense in waiting for Daisy's plans to develop,' declared Jim. 'She is as changeable as the wind. Possibly Nick will be able to make up her mind for her. I fancy he means to try.'

'Nick! you don't mean he will travel with Daisy!' There was almost a tragic note in Muriel's voice. She looked up quickly into the shrewd eyes that watched her.

'Why shouldn't he?' said Jim.

'I don't know. I never thought of it.' Muriel leaned back again, a faint frown of perplexity between her eyes. 'Perhaps,' she said slowly at length, 'I had better go to Mrs. Langdale.'

'I should in your place,' said Jim. 'That handsome soldier of yours won't want to be kept waiting, eh?'

'Oh, he wouldn't mind.' The weariness was apparent again in her voice, and with it a tinge of bitterness. 'He never minds anything,' she said.

Jim grunted disapproval. 'And you? Are you equally indifferent?'

Her pale face flushed vividly. She was silent a moment; then suddenly she sat up and met his look fully.

'You'll think me contemptible, I know,' she said, a great quiver in her voice. 'I can't help it; you must, Dr. Jim, I'll tell you the truth. I don't want to go to India. I don't want to be married – at all.'

She ended with a swift rush of irrepressible tears. It was out at last, this trouble of hers that had been gradually growing behind the barrier of her reserve, and it seemed to burst over her in the telling in a great wave of adversity.

'I've done nothing but make mistakes,' she sobbed, 'ever since Daddy died.'

Dr. Jim got up quietly to lock the door. The grimness had passed from his face.

'My dear,' he said gruffly, 'we all of us make mistakes directly we begin to run alone.'

He returned and sat down again close to her, waiting for her to recover herself. She slipped out a trembling hand to him, and he took it very kindly; but he said no more until she spoke.

'It's very difficult to know what to do.'

'Is it? I should have said you were past that stage.' His tone was uncompromising, but the warm grip of his hand made up for it. His directness did not dismay her. 'If you are quite sure you don't care for the fellow, your duty is quite plain.'

Muriel raised her head slowly. 'Yes, but it isn't quite so simple as that, doctor. You see, it's not as if – as if – we either of us ever imagined we were – in love with each other.'

Jim's eyebrows went up. 'As bad as that?'

She leaned her chin on her hand. 'I am sure there must be crowds of people who marry without ever being in love.'

'Yes,' said Jim curtly. 'And kindle their own hell in doing it.'

She started a little. 'You think that?'

'I know it. I have seen it over and over again. Full half of the world's misery is due to it. But you won't do that, Muriel. I know you too well.'

Muriel glanced up at him. 'Do you know me? I don't think you would have expected me to accept him in the first place.'

'Depends what you did it for,' said Jim.

She fell suddenly silent, slowly twisting the ring on her finger. 'He knew why,' she said at last in a very low voice. 'In fact – in fact he asked me for that reason.'

'And the reason still exists?'

She bent her head. 'Yes.'

'A reason you are ashamed of?' pursued the doctor.

She did not answer, and he drew his great brows together in deep thought.

'You don't propose to take me any further into your confidence?' he asked at last.

She made a quick, impulsive movement. 'You – you – I think you know.'

'Will you let me tell you what I know?' he said.

She shrank perceptibly. 'If – if you won't make it too hard for me.'

'I can't answer for that,' he returned. 'It depends entirely upon yourself. My knowledge does not amount to anything very staggering in itself. It is only this – that I know a certain person who would cheerfully sacrifice all he has to make you happy, and that you have no more cause to fear persecution from that person than from the man in the moon.'

He paused; but Muriel did not speak. She was still absently turning her engagement ring round and round.

'To verify this,' he said, 'I will tell you something which I am sure you don't know – which in fact puzzled me too considerably for some time. He has already sacrificed more than most men would care to venture in a doubtful cause. It was no part of his plan to follow you to England. He set his face against it so strongly that he very nearly ended his mortal career for good and all in so doing. As it was, he suffered for his lunacy pretty heavily. You know what happened. He was forced to come in the end, and he paid the forfeit for his delay.'

Again he paused, for Muriel had sprung upright with such tragedy in her eyes, that he knew he had said enough. The next moment she was on her feet, quivering all over as one grievously wounded.

'Oh, do you know what you are saying?' she said, and in her voice there throbbed the cry of a woman's wrung heart. 'Surely – surely he never did that – for me!'

He did not seem to notice her agitation. 'It was a fairly big price to pay for a piece of foolish sentiment, eh?' he said. 'Let us hope he will know better next time.'

He looked up at her with a faintly cynical smile, but she was standing with her face averted. He saw only that her chin was quivering like a hurt child's.

'Come,' he said at length. 'I didn't tell you this to distress you, you know. Only to set your mind at rest, so that you might sleep easy.'

She mastered herself with an effort, and turned towards him. 'I know; yes, I know. You – you have been very kind. Good-night, doctor.'

He rose and went with her to the door. 'You are not going to lie awake over this?'

She shook her head. 'Good-night,' she said again.

He watched her down the passage, and then returned to his writing. He smiled to himself as he sat down but this time wholly without cynicism.

'No, Nick, my boy,' he said. as he drove his pen into the ink. 'She won't lie awake for you. But she'll cry herself to sleep for your sake, you gibbering, one-armed ape. And the new love will be the old love before the week is out, or I am no weather prophet.'

Chapter 38

The gale that raged along the British coasts that autumn was the wildest that had been known for years. It swelled quite suddenly out of the last breezes of a superb summer, and by the middle of September it had become a monster of destruction, devastating the shore. The crumbling cliffs of Brethaven testified to its violence. Beating rain and colossal, shattering waves united to accomplish ruin and destruction. And the little fishing-village looked on aghast.

It was on the third day of the storm that news was brought to Nick of a landslip on his own estate. He had been in town ever since his guests' departure, and had only returned on the previous evening. He did not contemplate a long stay. The place was lonely without Olga, and he was not yet sufficiently proficient in shooting with one arm to enjoy the sport, especially in solitude. He was in fact simply waiting for an opportunity which he was convinced must occur before long of keeping a certain promise made to a friend of his on a night of early summer in the Indian Plains.

It was a wild day of drifting squalls and transient gleams of sunshine. He grimaced to himself as he sauntered forth after luncheon to view the damage that had been wrought upon his property. The ground he trod was sodden with long rain, and the cedars beyond the lawn plunged heavily to and fro in melancholy unrest, flinging great drops upon him as he passed. The force of the gale was terrific, and he had to bend himself nearly double to meet it.

With difficulty he forced his way to the little summer-house that overlooked the shore. He marvelled somewhat to find it still standing, but it was sturdily built and would probably endure as long as the ground beneath it remained unshaken.

But beyond it a great gap yawned. The daisy-covered space on which they had sat that afternoon now many weeks ago had disappeared. Nothing of it remained but a crumbling desolation to which the daisies still clung here and there.

Nick stood in such shelter as the summer-house afforded, and looked forth upon the heaving waste of waters. The tide was rising. He could see the great waves swirling white around the rocks. Several landslips were visible from this post of observation. The village was out of sight, tucked away behind a great shoulder of cliff; but an old ruined cottage that had been uninhabited for some time had entirely disappeared. Stacks of seaweed had been thrown up upon the deserted shore, and lay in great masses above the breakers. The roar of the incoming tide was like the continuous roll of thunder.

It was a splendid spectacle, and for some time he stood, with his face to the driving wind, gazing out upon the empty sea. There was not a single vessel in all that wide expanse.

Slowly at last his vision narrowed. His eyes came down to the great gash at his feet where red earth and tufts of grass mingled, where the daisies had grown on that June day, where she had sat, proud and aloof, and watched him fooling with the white petals. Very vividly he recalled that summer afternoon, her scorn of him, her bitter hostility – and the horror he had surprised in her dark eyes when the hawk had struck. He laughed oddly to himself, his teeth clenched upon his lower lip. How furiously she had hated him that day!

He turned to go; but paused, arrested by some instinct that bade him cast one more look downwards along the howling

shore. In another moment he was lying full length upon the
rotten ground, staring intently down upon a group of rocks
more than two hundred feet below him.

Two figures – a man and a woman – had detached themselves from the shelter of these rocks, and were moving
slowly, very slowly, towards the path that led inwards from
the shore. They were closely linked together, so much his first
glance told him. But there was something in the man's gait
that caught the eye, and upon which Nick's whole attention
was instantly focussed. He could not see the face, but the
loose-slung, gigantic limbs were familiar to him. With all his
knowledge of the world of men, he had not seen many such.

Slowly the two approached till they stood almost immediately beneath him, and there, as upon mutual impulse, they
stopped. It was a corner protected from the driving blast by
the crumbling mass of cliff that had slipped in the night. The
rain was falling heavily again, but neither the two on the
shore nor the solitary watcher stretched on the perilous edge
of the cliff seemed aware of it. All were intent upon other
things.

Suddenly the woman raised her face, and with a movement
that was passionate reached up her arms and clasped them
about the man's bent neck. She has speaking, but no sound
or echo of words was audible in that tumult. Only her face
lifted to the beating rain, with its passion of love, its anguish
of pain, told the motionless spectator something of their
significance.

It was hidden from him almost at once by the man's
massive head; but he had seen enough, more than enough
to verify a certain suspicion which had long been quartered
at the back of his brain.

Stealthily he drew himself back from the cliff edge, and
sat up on the damp grass. Again his eyes swept the horizon;
there was something of a glare in them. He was drenched
through and through by the rain, but he did not know it.
Had Muriel seen him at that moment she might have likened

him with a shudder to an eagle that viewed its quarry from afar.

He returned to the house without further lingering, and spent the two hours that followed in prowling ceaselessly up and down his library.

At the end of that time he sat down suddenly at the writing-table, and scrawled a hasty note. His face, as he did so, was like the face of an old man, but without the tolerance of age.

Finishing, he rang for his servant. 'Take this note,' he said, 'and ask at the Brethaven Arms if a gentleman named Captain Grange is putting up there. If he is, send in the note and wait for an answer. If he is not, bring it back.'

The man departed, and Nick resumed his prowling. It seemed that he could not rest. Once he went to the window and opened it to listen to the long roar of the sea, but the fury of the blast was such that he could scarcely stand against it. He shut it out, and resumed his tramp.

The return of his messenger brought him to a stand-still.

'Captain Grange was there, sir. Here is his answer.'

Nick grabbed the note with a gesture that might have indicated either impatience or relief. He held the envelope between his teeth to slit it open, and they left a deep mark upon it.

'DEAR RATCLIFFE,' he read, 'If I can get to you through this murderous storm, I will. Expect me at eight o'clock.– Yours, B. GRANGE.'

'All right,' said Nick over his shoulder. 'Captain Grange will dine with me.'

With the words he dropped the note into the fire, and then went away to dress.

Chapter 39

By eight o'clock Nick was lounging in the hall, awaiting his guest, but it was more than a quarter of an hour later that the latter presented himself.

Nick admitted him with a cheery grin. 'Come in,' he said. 'You've had a pretty filthy walk.'

'Infernal,' said Grange gloomily.

He entered with a heavy, rather bullied air, as if he had come against his will. Shaking hands with his host, he glanced at him somewhat suspiciously.

'Glad you managed to come,' said Nick hospitably.

'What did you want to see me for?' asked Grange.

'The pleasure of your society of course.' Nick's benignity was unassailable, but there was a sharp edge to it somewhere of which Grange was uneasily aware. 'Come along and dine. We can talk afterwards.'

Grange accompanied him moodily to the dining-room. 'I thought you were away,' he remarked, as they sat down.

'I was,' said Nick. 'Came back last night. When do you sail?'

'On Friday. I came down to say good-bye.'

'Muriel is at Weir,' observed Nick.

'Yes. I shall go on there to-morrow. Daisy is only here for a night or two to pack up her things.'

'And then?' said Nick.

Grange stiffened perceptibly. 'I don't know what her plans are. She never makes up her mind till the last minute.'

Nick laughed. 'She evidently hasn't taken you into her confidence. She is going East this winter.'

Grange looked up sharply. 'I don't believe it.'

'It's true all the same,' said Nick indifferently, and forthwith forsook the subject.

He started other topics, racing, polo, politics, airily ignoring his guest's undeniable surliness, till at last Grange's uneasiness began to wear away. He gradually overcame his depression, and had even managed to capture some of his customary courtesy before the end of dinner. His attitude was quite friendly when they finally adjourned to the library to smoke.

Nick followed him into the room and stopped to shut the door.

Grange had gone straight to the fire, and he did not see him slip something into his pocket as he came forward.

But he did after several minutes of abstraction discover something not quite normal in Nick's silence, and glanced down at him to ascertain what it was.

Nick had flung himself into a deep easy-chair, and was lying quite motionless with his head back upon the cushion. His eyes were closed. He had been smoking when he entered, but he had dropped his cigar half-consumed into an ash-tray.

Grange looked at him with renewed uneasiness, and looked away again. He could not help feeling that there was some moral tension somewhere; but he had never possessed a keen perception, he could not have said wherein it lay.

He retired into his shell once more and sat down facing his host in a silence that had become dogged.

Suddenly, without moving, Nick spoke.

His words were slightly more deliberate than usual, very even, very distinct. 'To come to the point,' he said. 'I saw you on the shore this afternoon – you and Mrs. Musgrave.'

'What?' Grange gave a great start and stared across at him, gripping the arms of his chair.

Nick's face however remained quite motionless. 'I saw you,' he repeated.

With an effort Grange recovered himself. 'Did you though? I wondered how you knew I was down here. Where were you?'

There was an abrupt tremor behind Nick's eyelids, but they remained closed. 'I was on the top of the cliff, on my own ground, watching you.'

Dead silence followed his answer – a silence through

which the sound of the sea half a mile away swelled terribly, like the roar of a monster in torment.

Then at last Nick's eyes opened. He looked Grange straight in the face. 'What are you going to do?' he said.

Grange's hands dropped heavily from the chair-arms, and his whole great frame drooped slowly forward. He made no further attempt at evasion, realizing the utter futility of such a course.

'Do!' he said wearily. 'Nothing.'

'Nothing?' said Nick swiftly.

'No, nothing,' he repeated, staring with a dull intentness at the ground between his feet. 'It's an old story, and the less said about it the better. I can't discuss it with you or anyone. I think it was a pity you took the trouble to watch me this afternoon.'

He spoke with a certain dignity, albeit he refused to meet Nick's eyes. He looked unutterably tired.

Nick lay quite motionless in his chair, inscrutably still save for the restless glitter behind his colourless eyelashes. At length, 'Do you remember a conversation we had in this room a few months ago?' he asked.

Grange shook his head slightly, too engrossed with his miserable thoughts to pay much attention.

'Well, think!' Nick said insistently. 'It had to do with your engagement to Muriel Roscoe. Perhaps you have forgotten that too?'

Grange looked up then, shaking off his lethargy with a visible effort. He got slowly to his feet, and drew himself to his full giant height.

'No,' he said, 'I have not forgotten it.'

'Then,' said Nick, 'once more – what are you going to do?'

Grange's face darkened. He seemed to hesitate upon the verge of vehement speech. But he restrained himself though the hot blood mounted to his temples.

'I have never yet broken my word to a woman,' he said. 'I am not going to begin now.'

'Why not?' said Nick, with a grin that was somehow fiendish.

Grange ignored the gibe. 'There is no reason why I should not marry her,' he said.

'No reason!' Nick's eyes flashed upwards for an instant, and a curious sense of insecurity stabbed Grange.

Nevertheless he made unfaltering reply. 'No reason whatever.'

Nick sat up slowly and regarded him with minute attention. 'Are you serious?' he asked finally.

'I am absolutely serious,' Grange told him sternly. 'And I warn you, Ratcliffe, this is not a subject upon which I will bear interference.'

'Man alive!' jeered Nick. 'You must think I'm damned easily scared.'

He got up with the words, jerking his meagre body upright with slight, fierce movement, and stood in front of Grange, arrogantly daring.

'Now just listen to this,' he said. 'I don't care a damn how you take it, so you may as well take it quietly. It's no concern of mine to know how you have whitewashed this thing over and made it look clean and decent – and honourable – to your fastidious eye. What I am concerned in is to prevent Muriel Roscoe making an unworthy marriage. And that I mean to do. I told you in the summer that she should be no man's second best, and, by Heaven, she never shall. I had my doubts of you then. I know you now. And – I swear by all things sacred that I will see you dead sooner than married to her.'

He broke off for a moment as though to get a firmer grip upon himself. His face was terrible, his body tense as though controlled by tight-strung wires.

Before Grange could speak, he went on rapidly, with a resolution more deadly if less passionate than before.

'If either of you had ever cared, it might have been a different matter. But you never did. I knew that you never did. I never troubled to find out your reason for proposing to her. No doubt it was strictly honourable. But I always knew why she accepted you. Did you know that, I wonder?'

'Yes, I did.' Grange's voice was deep and savage. He glowed down upon him in rising fury. 'It was to escape you.'

Nick's eyes flamed back like the eyes of a crouching beast. He uttered a sudden, dreadful laugh. 'Yes – to escape me,' he said, 'to escape me! And it has fallen to me to deliver her from her chivalrous protector. If you look all round that, you may see something funny in it.'

'Funny!' burst forth Grange, letting himself go at last. 'It's what you have been playing for all along, you infernal mountebank! But you have over-reached yourself this time. For that very reason I will never give her up.'

He swung past Nick with the words, goaded past endurance, desperately aware that he could not trust himself within arm's length of that gibing, devilish countenance.

He reached the door and seized the handle, wrenched furiously for a few seconds, then flung violently round.

'Ratcliffe,' he exclaimed, 'for your own sake I advise you not to keep me here!'

But Nick had remained with his face to the fire. He did not so much as glance over his shoulder. He had grown suddenly intensely quiet. 'I haven't quite done with you,' he said. 'There is just one thing more I have to say.'

Grange was already striding back like an enraged bull, but something in the voice or attitude of the man who leaned against the mantelpiece without troubling to face him, brought him up short.

Against his will he halted. 'Well?' he demanded.

'It's only this,' said Nick. 'You know as well as I do that I possess the means to prevent your marriage to Muriel Roscoe, and I shall certainly use that means unless you give her up of your own accord. You see what it would involve, don't you? The sacrifice of your precious honour – and not yours only.'

He paused as if to allow full vent to Grange's anger but still he did not change his position.

'You damned cur!' said Grange, his voice hoarse with concentrated passion.

Nick took up his tale as if he had not heard. 'But on the other hand, if you will write and set her free now at once – I don't care how you do it; you can tell any likely lie that occurs to you – I on my part will swear to you that I will give her up entirely, that I will never plague her again, will never write to her or attempt in any way to influence her life, unless she on her own initiative makes it quite clear that she desires me to do so.'

He ceased, and there fell a dead silence, broken only by the lashing rain upon the windows and the long deep roar of the sea. He seemed to be listening to them with bent head, but in reality he heard nothing at all. He had made the final sacrifice for the sake of the woman he loved. To secure her happiness, her peace of mind, he had turned his face to the desert at last, and into it he would go, empty, beaten, crippled, to return no more for ever.

Across the lengthening silence Grange's voice came to him. There was a certain hesitation in it as though he were not altogether sure of his ground.

'I am to take your word for all that?'

Nick turned swiftly round. 'You can do as you choose. I have nothing else to offer you.'

Grange abandoned the point abruptly, feeling as a man who has lost his footing in a steep place and is powerless to climb back. Perhaps even he was vaguely conscious of something colossal hidden away behind that baffling, wrinkled mask.

'Very well,' he said, with that dogged dignity in which Englishmen clothe themselves in the face of defeat. 'Then you will take my word to set her free.'

'To-night?' said Nick.

'To-night.'

There was another pause. Then Nick crossed to the door and unlocked it.

'I will take your word,' he said.

A few seconds later, when Grange had gone, he softly shut and locked the door once more, and returned to his chair before the fire. Great gusts of rain were being flung against the window-panes. The wind howled near and far with a fury that seemed to set the walls vibrating. Now and then dense puffs of smoke blew out across the hearth into the room, and the atmosphere grew thick and stifling.

But Nick did not seem aware of these things. He sat on unheeding in the midst of his dust and ashes while the storm raged relentlessly above his head.

Chapter 40

With the morning there came a lull in the tempest though the great waves that spent themselves upon the shore seemed scarcely less mountainous than when they rode before the full force of the storm.

In Daisy Musgrave's cottage above the beach, a woman with a white, jaded face sat by the window writing. A foreign envelope with an Indian stamp lay on the table beside her. It had not been opened; and once, glancing up, she pushed it slightly from her with a nervous, impatient movement. Now and then she sat with her head upon her hand thinking, and each time she emerged from her reverie it was to throw a startled look towards the sea as though its ceaseless roar unnerved her.

Nevertheless at sight of a big, loosely-slung figure walking slowly up the flagged path, a quick smile flashed into her face, making it instantly beautiful. She half rose from her chair, and then dropped back again, still faintly smiling, while the light which only one man's coming can kindle upon any woman's face shone upon hers, erasing all weariness and bitterness while it lingered.

At the opening of the door she turned without rising. 'So

you have come after all! But I knew you would. Sit down a minute and wait while I finish this tiresome letter. I have just done.'

She was already scribbling last words as fast as her pen would move, and her visitor waited for her without a word.

In a few minutes she turned to him again. 'I have been writing a note to Muriel, explaining things a little. She doesn't yet know that I am here; but it would be no good for her to join me, for I am only packing. I shall leave as soon as I can get away. And she too is going almost at once to Mrs. Langdale, I believe. So we shall probably not meet again at present. You will be seeing her this afternoon. Will you give it to her?'

She held the letter out to him, but he made no move to take it. His face was very pale, more sternly miserable than she had ever seen it. 'I think you had better post it,' he said.

She rose and looked at him attentively. 'Why, what's the matter, Blake?' she said.

He did not answer, and she went on immediately, still with her eyes steadily uplifted.

'Do you know, Blake, I have been thinking all night, and I have made up my mind to have done with all this foolish sentimentality finally and for ever. From to-day forward I enter upon the prosaic, middle-aged stage. I was upset yesterday at the thought of losing you so soon. It's been a lovely summer, hasn't it?' She stifled a sigh half-uttered. 'Well, it's over. You have got to go back to India, and we must just make the best of it.'

He made a sharp movement, but said nothing. The next moment he dropped down heavily into a chair and sat bowed, his head in his hands.

Daisy stood looking down at him, and slowly her expression changed. A very tender look came into her eyes, a look that made her seem older and at the same time more womanly. Very quietly she sat down on the arm of his chair and laid her hand upon him, gently rubbing it to and fro.

'My own boy, don't fret, don't fret!' she said. 'You will be happier by and by. I am sure of it.'

He took the little hand from his shoulder, and held it against his eyes. At last after several seconds of silence he spoke.

'Daisy, I have broken my engagement.'

Daisy gave a great start. A deep glow overspread her face, but it faded very swiftly, leaving her white to the lips. 'My dear Blake, why?' she whispered.

He answered her with his head down. 'It was Nick Ratcliffe's doing. He made me.'

'Made you, Blake! What can you mean?'

Sullenly Grange made answer. 'He had got the whip-hand, and I couldn't help myself. He saw us on the shore together yesterday afternoon, made up his mind then and there that I was no suitable partner for Muriel, got me to go and dine with him, and told me so.'

'But, Blake, how absurd!' Daisy spoke with a palpable effort. 'How – how utterly unreasonable! What made you give in to him?'

Grange would not tell her. 'I shouldn't have done so,' he said moodily, 'if he hadn't given his word that he would never pester Muriel again. She's well rid of me anyhow. He was right there. She will probably see it in the same light.'

'What did you say to her?' questioned Daisy.

'Oh, it doesn't matter, does it? I didn't see her. I wrote. I didn't tell her anything that it was unnecessary for her to know. In fact I didn't give her any particular reason at all. She'll think me an infernal cad. And so I am.'

'You are not, Blake!' she declared vehemently.

He was silent, still tightly clasping her hand.

After a pause, she made a gentle movement to withdraw it; but at that he turned with sudden mastery and thrust his arms about her. 'Daisy,' he broke out passionately, 'I can't do without you! I can't! I can't! I've tried – Heaven knows how I've tried! But it can't be done. It was madness ever to attempt to separate us. We were bound to come together again. I have been drifting towards you always, always, even when I wasn't thinking of you.'

Fiercely the hot words rushed out. He was holding her fast, though had she made the smallest effort to free herself he would have let her go.

But Daisy sat quite still, neither yielding nor resisting. Only at his last words her lips quivered in a smile of tenderest ridicule. 'I know, my poor old Blake,' she said, 'like a good ship without a rudder – caught in a strong current.'

'And it has been the same with you,' he insisted. 'You have always wanted me more than – '

He did not finish, for her hand was on his lips, restraining him. 'You mustn't say it, dear. You mustn't say it. It hurts us both too much. There! Let me go! It does no good, you know. It's all so vain and futile – now.' Her voice trembled suddenly, and she ceased to speak.

He caught her hand away, looking straight up at her with that new-born mastery of his that made him so infinitely hard to resist.

'If it is quite vain,' he said, 'then tell me to go – and I will.'

She tried to meet his eyes, but found she could not. 'I – shall have to, Blake,' she said in a whisper.

'I am waiting,' he told her doggedly.

But she could not say the word. She turned her face away and sat silent.

He waited with absolute patience for minutes. Then at last very gently he took his arms away from her and stood up.

'I am going back to the inn,' he said. 'And I shall wait there till to-morrow morning for your answer. If you send me away, I shall go without seeing you again. But if – if you decide otherwise' – he lowered his voice as if he could not wholly trust it – 'then I shall apply at once for leave to resign. And – Daisy – we will go to the New World together, and make up there for all the happiness we have missed in the Old.'

He ended almost under his breath, and she seemed to hear his heart beat through the words. It was almost too much for her even then. But she held herself back, for there was that in her woman's soul that clamoured to be heard – the patter of tiny feet that had never ceased to echo there, the high chirrup of a baby's voice – the vision of a toddling child with eager arms outstretched.

And she held her peace and let him go, though the struggle within her left her physically weak and cold, and she did not dare to raise her eyes lest he should surprise the love-light in them once again.

It had come to this at last then – the final dividing of the ways, the definite choice between good and evil. And she knew in her heart what that choice would be, knew it even as the sound of the closing door reached her consciousness, knew it as she strained her ears to catch the fall of his feet upon the flagged path, knew it in every nerve and fibre of her being as she sprang to the window for a last glimpse of the man who had loved her all her life long, and now at last had won her for himself . . .

Slowly she turned round once more to the writing-table. The unopened letter caught her eye. She picked it up with a set face, looked at it closely for a few moments, and then deliberately tore it into tiny fragments.

A little later she went to her own room. From a lavender-scented drawer she took an envelope, and shook its contents into her hand. Only a tiny unmounted photograph of a laughing baby, and a ringlet of baby hair!

Her face quivered as she looked at them. They had been her dearest treasures. Passionately she pressed them to her trembling lips, but she shed no tears. And when she returned to the sitting-room there was no faltering in her step.

She poked the fire into a blaze, and, kneeling, dropped her treasures into its midst. A moment's torture showed in her eyes, and passed.

She had chosen.

Chapter 41

During the whole of that day Muriel awaited in restless expectancy the coming of her *fiancé*. She had not heard from him for nearly a week, and she had not written in the interval for the simple reason that she lacked his address. But every day she had expected him to pay his promised visit of farewell.

It was hard work waiting for him. If she could have written, she would have done so days before in such a fashion as to cause him almost certainly to abandon his intention of seeing her.

For her mind was made up at last after her long torture of indecision. Dr. Jim's vigorous speaking had done its work, and she knew that her only possible course lay in putting an end to her engagement.

She had always liked Blake Grange. She knew that she always would like him. But emphatically she did not love him, and she knew now with the sure intuition which all women develop sooner or later that he had never loved her. He had proposed to her upon a mere chivalrous impulse, and she was convinced that he would not wish to quarrel with her for releasing him.

Yet she dreaded the interview, even though she was quite sure that he would not lose his self-control and wax violent, as had Nick on that terrible night at Simla. She was almost morbidly afraid of hurting his feelings.

Of Nick she rigidly refused to think at all, though it was no easy matter to exclude him from her thoughts, for he always seemed to be clamouring for admittance. But she could not help wondering if, when Blake had gone at last and she was free, she would be very greatly afraid.

She was sitting alone in her room that afternoon, watching the scudding rain-clouds, when Olga brought her two letters.

'Both from Brethaven,' she said, 'but neither from Nick.

I wonder if he is at Redlands. I hope he will come over here if he is.'

Muriel did not echo the hope. She knew the handwriting upon both the envelopes, and she opened Daisy's first. It did not take long to read. It simply contained a brief explanation of her presence at Brethaven which was due to an engagement having fallen through, mentioned Blake as being on the point of departure, and wound up with the hope that Muriel would not in any way alter her plans for her benefit as she was only at the cottage for a few days to pack her possessions and she did not suppose that she would care to be with her while this was going on.

There was no reference to any future meeting, and Muriel gravely put the letter away in thoughtful silence. She had no clue whatever to the slackening of their friendship, but she could not fail to note with pain how far asunder they had drifted.

She turned to Grange's letter with a faint wonder as to why he should have troubled himself to write when he was so short a distance from her.

It contained but a few sentences; she read them with widening eyes.

'Fate or the devil has been too strong for me, and I am compelled to break my word to you. I have no excuse to offer, except that my hand has been forced. Perhaps in the end it will be better for you, but I would have stood by had it been possible. And even now I would not desert you if I did not positively know that you were safe – that the thing you feared has ceased to exist.

'Muriel, I have broken my oath, and I can hardly ask your forgiveness. I only beg you to believe that it was not by my own choice. I was fiendishly driven to it against my will. I came to this place to say goodbye, but I shall leave to-morrow without seeing you unless you should wish otherwise.

B. GRANGE'

She reached the end of the letter and sat quite still, staring at the open page.

She was free, that was her first thought, free by no effort of her own. The explanation she had dreaded had become unnecessary. She would not even have to face the ordeal of a meeting. She drew a long breath of relief.

And then swift as a poisoned arrow came another thought – a stabbing intolerable suspicion. Why had he thus set her free? How had his hand been forced? By what means had he been fiendishly driven?

She read the letter through again, and suddenly her heart began to throb thick and hard, so that she gasped for breath. This was Nick's doing. She was as sure of it as if those brief, bitter sentences had definitely told her so. Nick was the motive power that had compelled Grange to this action. How he had done it, she could not even vaguely surmise. But that he had in some malevolent fashion come between them she did not for an instant doubt.

And wherefore? She put her hand to her throat, feeling suffocated, as the memory of that last interview with him on the shore raced with every fiery detail through her brain. He had marked her down for himself long, long ago, and whatever Dr. Jim might say, he had never abandoned the pursuit. He meant to capture her at last. She might flee, but he was following, tireless, fleet, determined. Presently he would swoop like an eagle upon his prey, and she would be utterly at his mercy. He had beaten Grange, and there was no one left to help her.

'Oh, Muriel' – it was Olga's voice from the window – 'come here, quick, quick! I can see a hawk.'

She started as one starts from a horrible dream, and looked round with dazed eyes.

'It's hovering!' cried Olga excitedly. 'It's hovering! There! Now it has struck!'

'And something is dead,' said Muriel, in a voiceless whisper.

The child turned round, saw something unusual in her friend's face, and went impetuously to her.

'Muriel darling, you look so strange. Is anything the matter?'

Muriel put an arm around her. 'No, nothing,' she said. 'Olga, will it surprise you very much to hear that I am not going to marry Captain Grange after all?'

'No, dear,' said Olga. 'I never somehow thought you would, and I didn't want you to either.'

'Why not?' Muriel looked up in some surprise. 'I thought you liked him.'

'Oh, yes, of course I do,' said Olga. 'But he isn't half the man Nick is, even though he is a V.C. Oh, Muriel, I wish – I do wish – you would marry Nick. Perhaps you will now.'

But at that Muriel cried out sharply and sprang to her feet, almost thrusting Olga from her.

'No, never!' she exclaimed. 'Never – never – never!' Then, seeing Olga's hurt face, 'Oh, forgive me, dear! I didn't mean to be unkind. But please don't ever dream of such a thing again. It – it's impossible – quite. Ah, there is the gong for tea. Let us go down.'

They went down hand in hand. But Olga was very quiet for the rest of the evening; and she did not cling to Muriel as usual when she said good-night.

Chapter 42

It was growing late on that same evening when to Daisy, packing in her room with feverish haste, a message was brought that Captain Ratcliffe was waiting, and desired to see her.

Her first impulse was to excuse herself from the interview, for she and Nick had never stood upon ceremony; but a very brief consideration decided her to see him. Since he had come at an unusual hour, it seemed probable that he had some special object in view, and if that were so, she would find it hard to turn him from his purpose. But she resolved to make the interview as brief as possible. She had no place for Nick in her life just then.

She entered the little parlour with a certain impetuosity that was not wholly spontaneous. 'My dear Nick,' she said, as she did so, 'I can give you exactly five minutes, not one second more, for I am frightfully busy packing up my things to leave to-morrow.'

He came swiftly to meet her, so swiftly that she was for the moment deceived, and fancied that he was about to greet her with his customary bantering gallantry. But he did not lift her fingers to his lips after his usual gay fashion. He only held her proffered hand very tightly for several seconds without verbal greeting of any sort.

Suddenly he began to speak, and as he did so she seemed to see a hundred wrinkles spring into being on his yellow face. 'I have something to say to you, Mrs. Musgrave,' he said. 'And it's something so particularly beastly that I funk saying it. We have always been such pals, you and I, and that makes it all the harder.'

He broke off, his shrewd glance flashing over her, keen and elusive as a rapier. Daisy faced him quite fully and fearlessly. The possibility of a conflict in this quarter had occurred to her before. She would not shirk it, but she was determined that it should be as brief as possible.

'Being pals doesn't entitle you to go trespassing, Nick,' she said.

'I know that,' said Nick, speaking very rapidly. None better. But I am not thinking of you only, though I hate to make you angry. Mrs. Musgrave – Daisy – I want to ask you, and you can't refuse to answer. What are you doing? What are you going to do?'

'I don't know what you mean,' she said, speaking coldly. 'And anyhow I can't stop to listen to you. I haven't time. I think you had better go.'

'You must listen,' Nick said. She caught the grim note of determination in his voice, and was aware of the whole force of his personality flung suddenly against her. 'Daisy,' he said, 'you are to look upon me as Will's representative. I am the nearest friend he has. Have you thought of him at all lately stewing in those hellish Plains for your sake? He's such a faithful chap, you know. Can't you go back to him soon? Isn't it – forgive me – isn't it a bit shabby to play this sort of game when there's a fellow like that waiting for you and fretting his very heart out because you don't go?'

He stopped – his lips twitching with the vigour of his appeal. And Daisy realized that he would have to be told the simple truth. He would not be satisfied with less.

Very pale but quite calm, she braced herself to tell him. 'I am afraid you are pleading a lost cause,' she said, her words quiet and very distinct. 'I am never going back to him.'

'Never!' Nick moved sharply, drawing close to her. 'Never?' he said again, then with abrupt vehemence, 'Daisy, you don't mean that! You didn't say it!'

She drew back slightly from him, but her answer was perfectly steady, rigidly determined. 'I have said it, Nick. And I meant it. You had better go. You will do no good by staying to argue. I know all that you can possibly say, and it makes no difference to me. I have chosen.'

'What have you chosen?' he demanded.

For an instant she hesitated. There was something almost fierce in his manner, something she had never encountered before, something that in spite of her utmost effort made her feel curiously uneasy, even apprehensive. She had always known that there was a certain uncanny strength about Nick, but to feel the whole weight of it directed against her was a new experience.

'What have you chosen?' he repeated relentlessly.

And reluctantly, more than half against her will, she told him. 'I am going to the man I love.'

She was prepared for some violent outburst upon her

words, but none came. Nick heard her in silence, standing straight before her, watching her, she felt, with an almost brutal intentness, though his eyes never for an instant met her own.

'Then,' he said suddenly at length, and quick though they were, it seemed to her that the words fell with something of the awful precision of a death-sentence, 'God help you both, for you are going to destroy him and yourself too.'

Daisy made a sharp gesture; it was almost one of shrinking. And at once he turned from her and fell to pacing the little room, up and down, up and down incessantly, like an animal in a cage. It was useless to attempt to dismiss him, for she saw that he would not go. She moved quietly to a chair and sat down to wait.

Abruptly at last he stopped, halting in front of her. 'Daisy' – he began, and broke off short, seeming to battle with himself.

She looked up in surprise. It was so utterly unlike Nick to relinquish his self-command at a critical juncture. The next moment he amazed her still further. He dropped suddenly down on his knees and gripped her clasped hands fast.

'Daisy,' he said again, and this time words came, jerky and passionate, 'this is my doing. I've driven you to it. If I hadn't interfered with Grange, you would never have thought of it.'

She sat without moving, but the hasty utterance had its effect upon her. Some of the rigidity went out of her attitude. 'My dear Nick,' she said, 'what is the good of saying that?'

'Isn't it true?' he persisted.

She hesitated, unwilling to wound him.

'You know it is true,' he declared with vehemence. 'If I had left him alone, he would have married Muriel, and this thing would never have happened. God knows I did what was right, but if it doesn't turn out right, I'm done for. I never believed in eternal damnation before, but if this thing comes to pass it will be hell-fire for me for as long as I live. For I shall never believe in God again.'

He swung away from her as though in bodily torture, came in contact with the table and bowed his head upon it. For many seconds his breathing, thick and short, almost convulsed, was the only sound in the room.

As for Daisy, she sat still, staring at him dumbly, witnessing his agony till the sight of it became more than she could bear. Then she moved, reached stiffly forward, touched him.

'You are not to blame yourself, Nick,' she said.

He did not stir. 'I don't,' he answered, and again fell silent.

At last he moved, seemed to pull himself together, finally got to his feet.

'Do you think you will be happy?' he said. 'Do you think you will ever manage to forget what you have sacrificed to this fetish you call Love – how you broke the heart of one of the best fellows in the world, and trampled upon the memory of your dead child – the little chap you used to call the light of your eyes, who used to hold out his arms directly he saw you and cry when you went away?'

His voice was not very steady, and he paused but he did not look at her or seem to expect any reply.

Daisy gave a great shiver. She felt cold from head to foot. But she was not afraid of Nick. If she yielded, it would not be through fear.

A full minute crawled away before he spoke again. 'And this fellow Grange,' he said then. 'He is a man who values his honour. He has lived a clean life. He holds an unblemished record. He is in your hands. You can do what you like with him – whatever your love inspires you to do. You can pull him back into a straight course, or you can wreck him for good and all. Which is it going to be, I wonder? It's a sacrifice either way – a sacrifice to Love or a sacrifice to devils. You can make it which you will. But if it is to be the last, never talk of Love again. For Love – real Love – is the safeguard from all evil. And if you can do this thing, it has never been above your horizon, and never will be.'

Again he stopped, and again there was silence while Daisy

sat white-faced and slightly bowed, wondering when it would be over, wondering how much longer she could possibly endure.

And then suddenly he bent down over her. His hand was on her shoulder. 'Daisy,' he said, and voice and touch alike implored her, 'give him up, dear! Give him up! You can do it if you will, if your love is great enough. I know how infernally hard it is to do. I've done it myself. It means tearing your very heart out. But it will be worth it – it must be worth it – afterwards. You are bound – some time – to reap what you have sown.'

She lifted a haggard face. There was something in the utterance that compelled her. And so looking, she saw that which none other of this man's friends had ever seen. She saw his naked soul, stripped bare of all deception, of all reserve – a vital, burning flame shining in the desert. The sight moved her as had nought else.

'Oh, Nick,' she cried out desperately, 'I can't – I can't!'

He bent lower over her. He was looking straight down into her eyes. 'Daisy,' he said very urgently, 'Daisy, for God's sake – try!'

Her white lips quivered, striving again to refuse. But the words would not come. Her powers of resistance had begun to totter.

'You can do it,' he declared, his voice quick and passionate as though he pleaded with her for life itself. 'You can do it – if you will. I will help you. You shan't stand alone. Don't stop to think. Just come with me now – once – and put an end to it before you sleep. For you can't do this thing, Daisy. It isn't in you. It is all a monstrous mistake, and you can't go on with it. I know you better than you know yourself. We haven't been pals all these years for nothing. And there is that in your heart that won't let you go on. I thought it was dead a few minutes ago. But, thank God, it isn't. I can see it in your eyes.'

She uttered an inarticulate sound that was more bitter than any weeping, and covered her face.

Instantly Nick straightened himself and turned away. He went to the window and leaned his head against the sash. He had the spent look of a man who had fought to the end of his strength. The thunder of the waves upon the shore filled in the long, long silence.

Minutes crawled away, and still he stood there with his face to the darkness. At last a voice spoke behind him, and he turned. Daisy had risen.

She stood in the lamplight, quite calm and collected. There was even a smile upon her face, but it was a smile that was sadder than tears.

'It's been a desperate big fight, hasn't it, Nick?' she said. 'But – my dear – you've won. For the sake of my little baby, and for the sake of the man I love – yes, and partly for your sake too' – she held out her hand to him with the words – 'I am going back to the prison-house. No, don't speak to me. You have said enough. And, Nick, I must go alone. So I want you, please, to go away, and not to come to me again until I send for you. I shall send sooner or later. Will you do this?'

Her voice never faltered, but the misery in her eyes cut him to the heart. In that moment he realized how terribly near he had been to losing the hardest battle he had ever fought.

He gave her no second glance. Simply, without a word, he stooped and kissed the hand she had given him; then turned and went noiselessly away.

He had won indeed, but the only triumph he knew was the pain of a very human compassion.

Scarcely five minutes after his departure, Daisy let herself out into the night that lay like a pall above the moaning shore. She went with lagging feet that often stumbled in the darkness. It was only the memory of a baby's head against her breast that gave her strength.

Chapter 43

'I believe I heard a gun in the night,' remarked Mrs Ratcliffe at the breakfast-table on the following morning.

'Shouldn't be surprised,' said Dr. Jim. 'I know there was a ship in distress off Calister yesterday. They damaged the lifeboat trying to reach her. But the wind seems to have gone down a little this morning. Do you care for a ride, Muriel?'

Muriel accepted the invitation gladly. She liked accompanying Dr. Jim upon his rounds. She had arranged to leave two days later, a decision which the news of Daisy's presence at Brethaven had not affected. Daisy seemed to have dropped her for good and all, and her pride would not suffer her to inquire the reason. She had in fact begun to think that Daisy had merely tired of her, and that being so she was the more willing to go to Mrs. Langdale, whose letters of fussy kindliness seemed at least to ensure her a cordial welcome.

She had discussed her troubles no further with Dr. Jim. Grange's letter had in some fashion placed matters beyond discussion. And so she had only briefly told him that her engagement was at an end, and he had gruffly expressed his satisfaction thereat. Her one idea now was to escape from Nick's neighbourhood as speedily as possible. It possessed her even in her dreams.

She went with Dr. Jim to the surgery when breakfast was over, and sat down to wait for him alone in the consulting-room. He usually started on his rounds at ten o'clock, but it wanted a few minutes to the hour and the motor was not yet at the door. She sat listening for it, hoping that no one would appear to detain him.

The morning was bright, and the wind had fallen considerably. Through the window she watched the falling leaves as they eddied in sudden draughts along the road. She looked through a wire screen that gave rather a depressing effect to the sunshine.

Suddenly from some distance away there came to her the

sound of a horse's hoof-beats, short and hard, galloping, over the stones. It was a sound that arrested the attention, awaking in her a vague, apprehensive excitement. Almost involuntarily she drew nearer to the window, peering above the blind.

Some seconds elapsed before she caught sight of the head-long horseman, and then abruptly he dashed into sight round a curve in the road. At the same instant the gallop become a fast trot, and she saw that the rider was gripping the animal with his knees. He had no saddle.

Amazed and startled, she stood motionless, gazing at the sudden apparition, saw as the pair drew nearer what something within her had already told her loudly before her vision served her, and finally drew back with a sharp, instinctive contraction of her whole body as the horseman reined in before the surgery-door and dismounted with a monkey-like dexterity, his one arm twined in the bridle. A moment later the surgery-bell pealed loudly, and her heart stood still. She felt suddenly sick with a nameless foreboding.

Standing with bated breath, she heard Dr. Jim himself go to answer the summons, and an instant later Nick's voice came to her, gasping and uneven, but every word distinct.

'Ah, there you are! Thought I should catch you. Man, you're wanted – quick! In heaven's name – lose no time. Grange was drowned early this morning, and – I believe it's killed Daisy. For mercy's sake, come at once!

There was a momentary pause. Muriel's heart was beating in great sickening throbs. She felt stiff and powerless.

Dr. Jim's voice, brief and decided, struck through the silence. 'Come inside and have something. I shall be ready to start in three minutes. Leave your animal here: He's dead beat.'

There followed the sounds of advancing feet, a hand upon the door, and the next moment they entered together. Nick was reeling a little and holding Jim's arm. He saw Muriel with a sharp start, standing as she had turned from the window.

The doctor's brows met for an instant as he put his brother into a chair. He had forgotten Muriel.

With an effort she overcame the paralysis that bound her, and moved forward with shaking limbs.

'Did you say Blake was – dead?' she asked, her voice pitched very low.

She looked at Nick as she asked this question, and it was Nick who answered her in his quick, keen way, as though he realized the mercy of brevity.

'Yes. He and some fisher chaps went out early this morning in an ordinary boat to rescue some fellows on a wreck that had drifted on to the rocks outside the harbour. The lifeboat had been damaged and couldn't be used. They reached the wreck all right, but there were more to save than they had reckoned on – more than the boat would carry – and the wreck was being battered to pieces. It was only a matter of seconds, for the tide was rising. So they took the lot, and Grange went over the side to make it possible. He hung on to a rope for a time, but the seas were tremendous, and after a bit it parted. He was washed up two hours ago. He had been in the water since three, among the rocks. There wasn't the smallest chance of bringing him back. He was long past any help we could give.'

He ended abruptly, and helped himself with a jerk to something in a glass that Jim had placed by his side.

Muriel stood dumbly watching. She noticed with an odd, detached sense of curiosity that he was shivering violently as one with an ague. Dr. Jim was already making swift preparations for departure.

Suddenly Nick looked up at her. His eyes were glittering strangely. 'I know now,' he said, 'what you women feel like when you can only stand and look on. We have been looking on – Daisy and I – just looking on, for six mortal hours.' He banged his fist with a sort of condensed fury upon the table, and leapt to his feet. 'Jim, are you ready? I can't sit still any longer.'

'Finish that stuff, and don't be a fool!' ordered Jim curtly.

Muriel turned swiftly towards him. 'You'll take me with you!' she said very earnestly.

Nick broke in sharply upon the request. 'No, no, Muriel! You're not to go. Jim, you can't – you shan't – take her! I won't allow it!'

But Muriel was clinging to Dr. Jim's arm with quivering face upraised. 'You will take me,' she entreated.

'I was able to help Daisy before. I can help her now.'

But even before she spoke there flashed a swift glance between the two brothers that foiled her appeal almost before it was uttered. With a far greater gentleness than was customary with him, but with unmistakable decision, Dr. Jim refused her petition.

'I can't take you now, child. But if Daisy should ask for you, or if there is anything under the sun that you can do for her, I will promise to let you know.'

It was final, but she would not have it so. A sudden gust of anger caught her, anger against the man for whose sake she had one night shed so many bitter tears, whom now she so fiercely hated. She still clung to Jim. She was shaking all over.

'What does it matter what Nick says?' she urged pantingly. 'Why give in to him at every turn? I won't be left behind – just because he wishes it!'

She would have said more. Her self-control was tottering; but Dr. Jim restrained her. 'My dear, it is not for Nick's sake,' he said. 'Come, you are going to be sensible. Sit down and get your breath. There's no time for hysterics. I must go across and speak to my wife before I go.'

He looked at Nick who instantly responded. 'Yes you be off! I'll look after her. Be quick, man, be quick!'

But when Dr. Jim was gone, his impatience fell away from him. He moved round the table and stood before her. He was steady enough now, steadier far than she.

'Don't take it too hard,' he said. 'At least he died like a man.'

She did not draw away from him. There was no room for fear in her heart just then. It held only hatred – a fierce, consuming flame – that enabled her to face him as she had never faced him before.

'Why did you let him go?' she demanded of him, her voice deep and passionate, her eyes unwaveringly upon him. 'There must have been others. You were there. Why didn't you stop him?'

'I stop him!' said Nick, and a flash of something that was almost humour crossed his face. 'You seem to think I am omnipotent.'

Her eyes continued to challenge him. 'You always manage to get your own way somehow,' she said very bitterly, 'by fair means or foul. Are you going to deny that it was you who made him write that letter?'

He did not ask her what she meant. 'No,' he said with a promptitude that took her by surprise. 'I plead guilty to that. As you are aware, I never approved of your engagement.'

His effrontery stung her into what was almost a state of frenzy. Her eyes blazed their utmost scorn. She had never been less afraid of him than at that moment. She had never hated him more intensely.

'You could make him do a thing like that,' she said. 'And yet you couldn't hold him back from certain death!'

He answered her without heat, in a tone she deemed most hideously callous. 'It was not my business to hold him back. He was wanted. There would have been no rescue but for him. They needed a man to lead them, or they wouldn't have gone at all.'

His composure goaded her beyond all endurance. She scarcely waited for him to finish, nor was she wholly responsible for what she said.

'Was there only one man among you then?' she asked, with headlong contempt.

He made her a curious, jerky bow. 'One man – yes,' he said. 'The rest were mere sheep, with the exception of one – who was a cripple.'

Her heart contracted suddenly with a pain that was physical. She felt as if he had struck her, and it goaded her to a fiercer cruelty.

'You knew he would never come back!' she declared, her voice quivering uncontrollably with the passion that shook her. 'You – you never meant him to come back!'

He opened his eyes wide for a single instant, and she fancied that she had touched him. It was the first time in her memory that she had ever seen them fully. Instinctively she avoided them, as she would have avoided a flash of lightning.

And then he spoke, and she knew at once that her wild accusation had in no way hurt him. 'You think that, do you?' he said, and his tone sounded to her as though he barely repressed a laugh. 'Awfully nice of you! I wonder what exactly you take me for.'

She did not keep him in suspense on that point. If she had never had the strength to tell him before, she could tell him now.

'I take you for a fiend!' she cried hysterically. 'I take you for a fiend!'

He turned sharply from her, so sharply that she was conscious of a moment's fear overmastering her madness. But instantly, with his back to her, he spoke, and her brief misgiving was gone.

'It doesn't matter much now what you take me for,' he said, and again in the cracked notes of his voice she seemed to hear the echo of a laugh. 'You won't need to seek any more protectors so far as I am concerned. You will never see me again unless the gods ordain that you should come and find me. It isn't the way of an eagle to swoop twice – particularly an eagle with only one wing.'

The laugh was quite audible now, and she never saw how that one hand of his was clenched and pressed against his side. He had reached the door while he was speaking. Turning swiftly, he cast one flickering, inscrutable glance

towards her, and then with no gesture of farewell was gone.
She heard his receding footsteps die away while she
struggled dumbly to quell the tumult at her heart. . . .

Chapter 44

Late that evening a scribbled note reached Muriel from
Dr. Jim.

'You can do nothing whatever,' he wrote. 'Daisy is suffering from a sharp attack of brain fever, caused by the shock
of her cousin's death, and I think it advisable that no one
whom she knows should be near her. You may rest assured
that all that can be done for her will be done. And, Muriel,
I think you will be wise to go to Mrs. Langdale as you
originally intended. It will be better for you, as I think you
will probably realize. You shall be kept informed of Daisy's
condition, but I do not anticipate any immediate change.'

She was glad of those few words of advice. Her anxiety
regarding Daisy notwithstanding, she knew it would be a
relief to her to go. The strain of many days was telling upon
her. She felt herself to be on the verge of a break-down, and
she longed unspeakably to escape.

She went to her room early on her last night at Weir, but
not in order to rest the longer. She had something to do,
something from which she shrank with a strange reluctance,
yet which for her peace of mind she dared not leave
neglected.

It was thus she expressed it to herself as with trembling
fingers she opened the box that contained all her most
sacred personal treasures.

It lay beneath them all, wrapped in tissue-paper, as it had
passed from his hand to hers, and for long she strove to bring
herself to slip the tiny packet unopened into an envelope and
seal it down – yet could not.

At last – it was towards midnight – she yielded to the force that compelled. Against her will she unfolded the shielding paper and held that which it contained upon the palm of her hand. Burning rubies, red as heart's blood, ardent as flame, flashed and glinted in the lamp-light. 'OMNIA VINCIT AMOR' – how the words scorched her memory! And she had wondered once if they were true!

She knew now! She knew now! He had forced her to realize it. He had captured her, had kindled within her – by what magic she knew not – the undying flame. Against her will, in spite of her utmost resistance, he had done this thing. Above and beyond and through her fiercest hatred, he had conquered her quivering heart. He had let her go again, but not till he had blasted her happiness for ever. None other could ever dominate her as this man dominated. None other could ever kindle in her – or ever quench – the torch that this man's hand had lighted.

And this was Love – this hunger that could never be satisfied, this craving which would not be stifled or ignored – Love triumphant, invincible, immortal – the thing she had striven to slay at its birth, but which had lived on in spite of her, growing, spreading, enveloping, till she was lost, till she was suffocated, in its immensity. There could never be any escape for her again. She was fettered hand and foot. It was useless any longer to strive. She stood and faced the truth.

She did not ask herself how it was she had ever come to care. She only numbly realized that she had always cared. And she knew now that to no woman is it given to so hate as she had hated without the spur of Love goading her thereto. Ah, but Love was cruel! Love was merciless! For she had never known – nor ever could know now – the ecstasy of Love. Truly it conquered; but it left its prisoners to perish of starvation in the wilderness.

A slight sound in the midnight silence! A timid hand softly turning the door-handle! She sprang up, dropping the ring upon her table, and turned to see Olga in her nightdress, standing in the doorway.

'I was awake,' the child explained tremulously. 'And I heard you moving. And I wondered – dear Muriel if perhaps I could do anything to help you. You – you don't mind?'

Muriel opened her arms impulsively. She felt as if Olga had been sent to lighten her darkest hour.

For awhile she held her close, not speaking at all; and it was Olga who at last broke the silence.

'Darling, are you crying for Captain Grange?'

She raised her head then to meet the child's gaze of tearful sympathy.

'I am not crying, dear,' she said. 'And – it wouldn't be for him if I were. I don't want to cry for him. I just envy him, that's all.'

She leaned her head against Olga's shoulder, rocking a little to and fro with closed eyes. 'Yes,' she said at last, you can help me, Olga, if you will. That ring on the table, dear – a ring with rubies – do you see it?'

'Yes,' breathed Olga, holding her very close.

'Then just take it, dear.' Muriel's voice was unutterably weary; she seemed to speak with a great effort. It belongs to Nick. He gave it to me once long ago, in remembrance of something. I want you to give it back to him, and tell him simply that I prefer to forget.'

Olga took up the ring. Her lips were trembling. 'Aren't you – aren't you being nice to Nick any more Muriel?' she asked in a whisper.

Muriel did not answer.

'Not when you promised?' the child urged piteously.

There was silence. Muriel's face was hidden. Her black hair hung about her like a cloud, veiling her from her friend's eyes. For a long time she said nothing whatever. Then at last without moving she made reply.

'It's no use, Olga. I can't! I can't! It's not my doing. It's his. Oh, I think my heart is broken!'

Through the anguish of weeping that followed, Olga clasped her passionately close, frightened by an intensity of suffering such as she had never seen before and was powerless to alleviate.

She slept with Muriel that night, but, waking in the dawning, just when Muriel had sunk to sleep, she crept out of bed and, with Nick's ring grasped tightly in her hand, stole softly away.

Part V

Chapter 45

A gorgeous sunset lay in dusky, fading crimson upon the Plains, trailing to darkness in the east. The day had been hot and cloudless, but a faint, chill wind had sprung up with the passing of the sun, and it flitted hither and thither like a wandering spirit over the darkening earth.

Down in the native quarter a *tom-tom* throbbed persistent, exasperating as the voice of conscience. Somewhere in the distance a dog barked restlessly, at irregular intervals. And at a point between *tom-tom* and dog a couple of parrots screeched vociferously.

Over all the vast Indian night was rushing down on silent, mysterious wings. Crimson merged to grey in the telling, and through the falling dark there shone, detached and wonderful, a single star.

In the little wooden bungalow over against the waterworks a light had been kindled and gleamed out in a red streak across the Plain. Other lights were beginning to flicker also from all points of the compass, save only where a long strip of jungle lay like a blot upon the face of the earth. But the red light burned the steadiest of them all.

It came from the shaded lamp of an Englishman, and beneath it with stubborn, square-jawed determination the Englishman sat at work.

Very steadily his hand moved over the white paper, and the face that was bent above it never wearied – a face that still possessed something of the freshness of youth though the set of the lips was firm even to sternness and the line of the chin was hard. He never raised his eyes as he worked except to refer to the note-book at his elbow. The passage of time seemed of no moment to him.

Yet at the soft opening of the door, he did look up for an instant, a gleam of expectancy upon his face that died instantly.

'All right, Sammy, directly,' he said, returning without pause to his work.

Sammy, butler, bearer, and general factotum, irreproachable from his snowy turban to his white-slippered feet, did not take the hint to retire, but stood motionless just inside the room, waiting with statuesque patience till his master should deign to bestow upon him the favour of his full attention.

After a little Will Musgrave realized this, and with an abrupt sigh sat back in his chair and rubbed his hand across his forehead.

'Well?' he said then. 'You needn't trouble to tell me that the mail has passed, for I heard the fellow half an hour ago. Of course there were no letters?'

The man shook his head despondingly. 'No letters, sahib.'

'Then what do you want?' asked Will, beginning to eye his work again.

Sammy – so dubbed by Daisy long ago because his own name was too sore a tax upon her memory – sent a look of gleaming entreaty across the lamp-lit space that separated him from his master.

'The dinner grows cold, sahib,' he observed pathetically.

Will smiled a little. 'All right, my good Sammy. What does it matter? I'm sure if I don't mind, you needn't. And I'm busy just now.'

But the Indian stood his ground. 'What will my mem-sahib say to me,' he said, 'when she comes and finds that my lord has been starved?'

Will's face changed. It was a very open face, boyishly
sincere. He did not laugh at the earnest question. He only
gravely shook his head.

'The mem-sahib will come,' the man declared, with conviction. 'And what will her servant say when she asks him why
his master is so thin? She will say, "Sammy, I left him in your
care. What have you done to him?" And, sahib, what answer
can her servant give?'

Will clasped his hands at the back of his head in a careless
attitude, but his face was grim. 'I don't think you need worry
yourself, Sammy,' he said. 'I am not expecting the mem-sahib
– at present.'

Nevertheless, moved by the man's solicitude, he rose after
a moment and laid his work together. He might as well dine,
he reflected, as sit and argue about it. With a heavy step he
passed into the room where dinner awaited him, and sat
down at the table.

No, he was certainly not expecting her at present. He had
even of late begun to ask himself if he expected her at all.
It was five months now since the news of her severe illness
had almost induced him to throw everything aside and go to
her. He had only been deterred from this by a very serious
letter from Dr. Jim strongly advising him to remain where he
was, since it was highly improbable that he would be
allowed to see Daisy for weeks or even months were he at
hand and she would most certainly be in no fit state to return
with him to India. That letter had been to Will as the passing
knell of all he had ever hoped or desired. Definitely it had
told him very little, but he was not lacking in perception, and
he had read a distinct and wholly unmistakable meaning
behind the guarded, kindly sentences. And he knew when
he laid the letter down that in Dr. Jim's opinion his presence
might do incalculable harm. From that day forward he had
entertained no further idea of return, settling down again to
his work with a dogged patience that was very nearly allied
to despair.

He was undoubtedly a rising man. There were prospects of a speedy improvement in his position. It was unlikely that he would be called upon to spend another hot season in the scorching Plains. Steady perseverance and indubitable talent had made their mark. But success was dust and ashes to him now. He did not greatly care if he went or stayed.

That Daisy was well again, or on the high-road to recovery, he knew; but he had not received a single letter from her since her illness.

Jim's epistles were very few and far between, but Nick had maintained a fairly regular correspondence with him till a few weeks back when it had unaccountably relapsed. But then Nick had done unaccountable things before, and he did not set down his silence to inconstancy. He was probably making prodigious efforts on his behalf, and Will awaited every mail with an eagerness he could not quite suppress, which turned invariably however into a sick sense of disappointment.

That Daisy would ever return to him now he did not for an instant believe, but there remained the chance – the slender, infinitesimal chance – that she might ask him to go to her. More than a flying visit she would know he could not manage. His work was his living, and hers. But so much Nick's powers of persuasion might one day accomplish though he would not allow himself to contemplate the possibility, while week by week the chance dwindled.

So he sat alone and unexpectant at his dinner-table that night and made heroic efforts to pacify the vigilant Sammy, whose protest had warmed his heart a little if it had not greatly assisted his appetite.

He was glad when the meal was over and he could saunter out on to the verandah with his cigar. The night was splendid with stars; but it held no moon. The wind had died away, but it had left a certain chill behind; and somehow he was reminded of a certain evening of early summer in England long ago, when he and Daisy had strolled together in an English garden, and she had yielded impulsively to his earnest wooing and had promised to be his wife. He remembered still the little laugh, half-sweet, half-bitter, with which she had surrendered, the soft raillery of her blue eyes that yet had not wholly mocked him, the dainty charm of her submission. She had not loved him. He had known it even then. She had almost told him so. But with a boy's impetuosity he had taken the little she had to give trusting to the future to make her all his own.

Ah well! He caught himself sighing, and found that his cigar was out. With something less than his customary self-suppression he pitched it forth into the darkness. He could not even smoke with any enjoyment. He would go indoors and work.

He swung round on his heel, and started back along the verandah towards his room from which the red light streamed. Three strides he took with his eyes upon the ground. Then for no reason that he knew he glanced up towards the bar of light. The next instant he stood still as one transfixed, and all the blood rushed in tumult to his heart.

There, motionless in the full glare – watching him, waiting for him – stood his wife!

Chapter 46

She did not utter a single word or move to greet him. Even in that ruddy light she was white to the lips. Her hands were fast gripped together. She did not seem to breathe.

So for full thirty seconds they faced one another, speechless, spell-bound, while through the awful silence the cry of a jackal sounded from afar, seeking its meat from God.

Will was the first to move, feeling for his handkerchief mechanically and wiping his forehead. Also he tried to speak aloud, but his voice was gone. 'Pull yourself together, you fool!' he whispered savagely. 'She'll be gone again directly.'

She caught the words apparently, for her attitude changed.

She parted her straining hands as though by a great effort, and moved towards him.

Out of the glare of the lamplight she looked more normal. She wore a grey travelling-dress, but her hat was off. He fancied he saw the sparkle of the starlight in her hair.

She came towards him a few steps, and then she stopped. 'Will,' she said, and her voice had a piteous tremble in it, 'won't you speak to me? Don't you – don't you know me?'

Her voice awoke him, brought him down from the soaring heights of imagination as it were with a thud. He strode forward and caught her hands in his.

'Good heavens, Daisy!' he said. 'I thought I was dreaming! How on earth – '

And there he stopped dead, checked in mid career, for she was leaning back from him, leaning back with all her strength that he might not kiss her.

He stood, still holding her hands, and looked at her. There was a curious, choked sensation at his throat as if he had swallowed ashes. She had come back to him – she had come back to him indeed, but he had a feeling that she was somehow beyond his reach, further away from him in that moment of incredible re-union than she had ever been during all the weary months of their separation. This woman with the pale face and tragic eyes was a total stranger to him. Small wonder that he had thought himself to be dreaming!

With a furious effort he collected himself. He let her hands slip from his. 'Come in here,' he said forcing his dry throat to speech by sheer strength of will. 'You should have let me know.'

She went in without a word, and came to a stand before the table that was littered with his work. She was agitated, he saw. Her hand was pressed against her heart, and she seemed to breathe with difficulty.

Instinctively he came to her aid with commonplace phrases – the first that occurred to him. 'How did you come?

But no matter! Tell me presently. You must have something
to eat. You look dead beat. Sit down, won't – '

And there he stopped again, breaking off short to stare
at her. In the lighted room she had turned to face him, and
he saw that her hair was no longer golden, but silvery
white.

Seeing his look, she began to speak in hurried, uneven
sentences. 'I have been ill, you know. It – it was brain
fever, Jim said. Hair – fair hair particularly does go like that
sometimes.'

'You are well again?' he questioned.

'Oh, quite – quite.' There was something almost feverish in
the assertion; she was facing him with desperate resolution. 'I
have been well for a long time. Please don't send for
anything. I dined at the dâk-bungalow an hour ago. I – I
thought it best.'

Her agitation was increasing. She panted between each
sentence. Will turned aside, shut and bolted the window, and
drew the blind. Then he went close to her; he laid a steady
hand upon her.

'Sit down,' he said, 'and tell me what is the matter.'

She sank down mutely. Her mouth quivering; she sought
to hide it from him with her hand.

'Tell me,' he said again, and quietly though he spoke there
was in his tone a certain mastery that had never asserted itself
in the old days; 'what is it? Why have you come to me like
this?'

'I – haven't come to stay, Will,' she said, her voice so low
that it was barely audible.

His face changed. He looked suddenly dogged. 'After
twenty months!' he said.

She bent her head. 'I know. It's half a lifetime – more. You
have learnt to do without me by this. At least – I hope you
have – for your own sake.'

He made no comment on the words; perhaps he did not
hear them. After a brief silence she heard his voice above her

bowed head. 'Something is wrong. You'll tell me presently, won't you? But – really you needn't be afraid.'

Something in the words – was it a hint of tenderness? – renewed her failing strength. She commanded herself and raised her head. She scarcely recognized in the steady, square-chinned man before her the impulsive, round-faced boy she had left. There was something unfathomable about him, a hint of tenderness that affected her strangely.

'Yes,' she said. 'Something is wrong. It is what I am here for – what I have come to tell you. And when it is over, I'm going away – I'm going away – out of your life – for ever this time.'

His jaw hardened, but he said nothing whatever. He stood waiting for her to continue.

She rose slowly to her feet though she was scarcely capable of standing. She had come to the last ounce of her strength, but she spent it bravely.

'Will,' she said, and though her voice shook uncontrollably every word was clear, 'I hardly know how to say it. You have always trusted me, always been true to me. I think – once – you almost worshipped me. But you'll never worship me any more, because – because – I am unworthy of you. Do you understand? I was held back from the final wickedness, or – or I shouldn't be here now. But the sin was there in my heart. Heaven help me, it is there still. There! I have told you. It – was your right. I don't ask for mercy or forgiveness. Only punish me – punish me – and then – let me – go!'

Voice and strength failed together. Her limbs doubled under her, and she sank suddenly down at his feet, sobbing – terrible, painful, tearless sobs that seemed to rend her very being.

Without a word he stooped and lifted her. He was white to the lips, but there was no hesitancy about him. He acted instantly and decidedly as a man quite sure of himself.

He carried her to the old *charpoy* by the window and laid her down. . . .

Many minutes later, when her anguish had a little spent
itself, she realized that he was kneeling beside her, holding
her pressed against his heart. Through all the bitter chaos of
her misery and her shame there came to her the touch of his
hand upon her head.

It amazed her – it thrilled her, that touch of his; in a fashion
it awed her. She kept her face hidden from him; she could not
look up. But he did not seek to see her face. He only kept his
hand upon her throbbing temple till she grew still against his
breast.

Then at length, his voice slow and deep and very steady,
he spoke. 'Daisy, we will never speak of this again.'

She gave a great start. Pity, even a certain measure of kindness, she had almost begun to expect; but not this – not this!
She made a movement to draw herself away from him, but
he would not suffer it He only held her closer.

'Oh don't, Will, don't!' she implored him brokenly. 'For
your own sake – let me go!'

'For my own sake, Daisy,' he answered quietly, – 'and for
yours, since you have come to me, I will never let you go
again.'

'But you can't want me,' she insisted piteously. 'Don't be
generous, Will. I can't bear it. Anything but that! I would
rather you cursed me – indeed – indeed!'

His hand restrained her, silenced her. 'Hush!' he said. 'You
are my wife. I love you, and I want you.'

Tears came to her then with a rush, blinding, burning,
overwhelming, and yet their very agony was relief to her.
She made no further effort to loosen his hold. She even
feebly clung to him as one needing support.

'Ah, but I must tell you – I must tell you,' she whispered at last.
'If – if you mean to forgive me, you must know everything.'

'Tell me, if it helps you,' he answered, and he spoke with
the splendid patience that twenty weary months had
wrought in him. 'Only believe – before you begin – that I
have forgiven you. For – before God – it is the truth.'

And so presently, lying in his arms, her face hidden low in his breast, she told him all, suppressing nothing, extenuating nothing, simply pouring out the whole bitter story, sometimes halting, sometimes incoherent but never wavering in her purpose, till, like an evil growth that yet clung about her palpitating heart, her sin lay bare before him – the sin of a woman who had almost forgotten that Love is a holy thing.

He heard her to the end with scarcely a word, and when she had finished he made one comment only.

'And so you gave him up.'

She shivered with the pain of that memory. 'Yes, I gave him up – I gave him up. Nick had made me see the hopelessness of it all – the wickedness. And he – he let me go. He saw it too – at least he understood. And on that very night – oh, Will, that awful night – he went to his death.'

His arms grew closer about her. 'My poor girl!' he said.

'Ah, but you shouldn't!' she sobbed. 'You shouldn't! You ought to hate me – to despise me.'

'Hush!' he said again. And she knew that with that one word he resolutely turned his back upon the gulf that had opened between them during those twenty months – that gulf that his love had been great enough to bridge – and that he took her with him, bruised and broken and storm-tossed as she was, into a very sheltered place.

When presently he turned her face up to his own and gravely kissed her she clung to his neck like a tired child, no longer fearing to meet his look, only thankful for the comfort of his arms.

For a while longer he held her silently, then very quietly he began to question her about her journey. Had she told him that she had been putting up at the dâk-bungalow?

'Oh, only for a few hours,' she answered. 'We arrived this evening, Nick and I.'

'Nick!' he said. 'And you left him behind?'

'He is waiting to take me back,' she murmured, her face hidden against his shoulder.

Again, very tenderly, his hand pressed her forehead. 'He must come to us, eh, dear? I will send the *khit* down with a note presently. But you are tired out, and must rest. Lie here while I go and tell Sammy to make ready.'

It was when he came back to her that she began to see wherein lay the change in him that had so struck her.

From her cushions she looked up at him, piteously smiling. 'How thin you are, Will! And you are getting quite a scholarly stoop.'

'Ah, that's India,' he said.

But she knew that it was not India at all, and her face told him so, though he affected not to see it.

He bent over her. 'Now, Daisy, I am going to carry you to bed as I used – do you remember? – at Simla, after the baby came. Dear little chap! Do you remember how he used to smile in his sleep?'

His voice was hushed, as though he stood once more beside the tiny cot.

She sat up, yielding herself to his arms. 'Oh, Will,' she said, with a great sob, 'if only he had lived!'

He held her closely, and lying against his breast she felt the sigh he stifled. His lips were upon the silvered hair.

'Perhaps – some day – Daisy,' he said, under his breath.

And she, clinging to him, whispered back through her tears, 'Oh, Will – I do hope so.'

Chapter 47

It was very hot down on the buzzing race-course, almost intolerably so in the opinion of the girl who sat in Lady Bassett's elegantly-appointed carriage, and looked out with the indifference of boredom upon the sweltering crowds.

'Dear child, don't look so freezingly aloof!' she had been entreated more than once; and each time the soft injunction had reached her the wide dark eyes had taken to themselves a more utter disdain.

If she looked freezing, she was far from feeling it, for the hot weather was at its height, and Ghawalkhand, though healthy, was not the coolest spot in the Indian Empire. Sir Reginald Bassett had been appointed British Resident, to act as adviser to the young rajah thereof, and there had been no question of a flitting to Simla that year. Lady Bassett had deplored this, but Muriel had rejoiced. She never wanted to see Simla again.

Life was a horrible emptiness to her in those days. She was weary beyond expression, and had no heart for the gaieties in which she was plunged. Idle compliments had never attracted her, and flirtations were an abomination to her. She looked through and beyond them with the eyes of a sphinx. But there were very few who suspected the intolerable ache that throbbed unceasingly behind her impassivity – the loneliness of spirit that oppressed her like a crushing, physical weight.

Even Bobby Fraser, who saw most things, could scarcely have been aware of this; yet it certainly was not the vivacity of her conversation that induced him to seek her out as he generally did when he saw her sitting apart. A very cheery bachelor was Bobby Fraser, and a tremendous favourite wherever he went. He was a wonderful organizer, and he invariably had a hand in anything of an entertaining nature that was going forward.

He had just brought her tea, and was waiting beside her while she drank it. Lady Bassett had left the carriage for the paddock, and Muriel sat alone.

Had she had anything on the last race, he wanted to know? Muriel had not. He had had, and was practically ruined in consequence – a calamity which in no way seemed to affect his spirits.

'Who would have expected a rank outsider like that to walk over the course? Ought to have been disqualified for sheer cheek. Reminds me of a chap I once knew – forget his name – Nick something or other – who entered at the last minute for the Great Mogul's Cup at Sharapura. Did it for a bet, they said. It's years ago now. The horse was a perfect brute – all bone and no flesh – with a temper like the foul fiend and no points whatever – looked a regular crock at starting. But he romped home on three legs notwithstanding with his jockey clinging to him like an inspired monkey. It was the only race he ever won. Everyone put it down to black magic or personal magnetism on the part of his rider. Same thing, I believe. He was the sort of chap who always comes out on top. Rum thing I can't remember his name. I had travelled out with him on the same boat once too. Have some more tea.'

This was a specimen of most of Bobby Fraser's conversation. He was brimful of anecdotes. They flowed as easily as water from a fountain. Their source seemed inexhaustible. He never repeated himself to the same person.

Muriel declined his offer of more tea. For some reason she wanted to hear more of the man who had won the Great Mogul's Cup at Sharapura.

Bobby was more than willing to oblige. 'Oh, it was sheer cheek that carried him through of course. I always said he was the cheekiest beggar under the sun – quite a little chap he was, hideously ugly, with a face like a baked apple, and eyes that made you think of a cinematograph. You know the sort of thing. I used to think he had a future before him, but he seems to have dropped out. He was only about twenty when I had him for a stable-companion. I remember one outrageous thing he did on the voyage out. There was card-playing going on in the saloon one night, and he was looking on. One of the lady-players – well, I suppose I may as well call it by its name – one of them cheated. He detected it. Beastly position of course. Don't know what I should have done under the circumstances, but anyhow he wasn't at a loss. He simply lighted a cigarette and set fire to the lady's dress.

Muriel's exclamation of horror was ample testimony to the fact that her keenest interest was aroused.

'Yes, awfully risky, wasn't it?' said Bobby. 'We only thought at the time that he had been abominably careless. I did not hear the rights of the case till afterwards, and then not from him. There was a fine flare-up of course – card-table over-turned – ladies in hysterics – in the middle of the fray our gallant hero extinguishing the flames with his bare hands. He was profusely apologetic and rather badly scorched. The lady took very little harm, except to her nerves and her temper. She cut him dead for the rest of the voyage, but I don't think it depressed him much. He was the sort of fellow that never gets depressed. Hullo! There's Mrs. Philpot making violent signs. I suppose I had better go and see what she wants, or be dropped for evermore. Good-bye!'

He smiled upon her and departed, leaving her thoughtful, with a certain wistful wonder in her eyes.

Lady Bassett's return interrupted her reverie. 'You have had some tea, I hope, dear. Ah, I thought Mr. Bobby Fraser was making his way in this direction. So sweet of him not to forget you when he has so many other calls upon his attention. And how are you faring for to-night? Is your programme full yet? I have literally not one dance left.'

Lady Bassett had deemed it advisable to ignore the fact of Muriel's brief engagement to Captain Grange since the girl's return to India. She knew, as did her husband, that it had come to an end before Grange's death, but she withheld all comment upon it. Her one desire was to get the dear child married without delay, and she was not backward in letting her know it. Life at Ghawalkhand was one continuous round of gaiety, and she had every opportunity for forwarding her scheme. Though she deplored Muriel's unresponsiveness, she yet did not despair. It was sheer affectation on the girl's part, she would tell herself, and would soon pass. And after all, that queenly, aloof air had a charm that was all its own. It might not attract the many, but she had begun to fancy of late that Bobby Fraser had felt its influence. He was not in the least the sort of man she would have expected to do so, but there was no accounting for taste – masculine taste especially. And it would be an excellent thing for Muriel.

She was therefore being particularly gracious to her young charge just then – a state of affairs which Muriel endured rather than appreciated. She would never feel at her ease with Lady Bassett as long as she lived.

She was glad when they drove away at length, for she wanted to be alone. Those anecdotes of Bobby's had affected her strangely. She had felt so completely cut off of late from all things connected with the past. No one ever mentioned Nick to her now – not even her faithful correspondent Olga. Meteor-like, he had flashed through her sky and disappeared; leaving a burning, ineradicable trail behind him, it is true, but none the less was he gone. She had not the faintest idea where he was. She would have given all she had to know, yet could not bring herself to ask. It seemed highly improbable that he would ever cross her path again, and she knew she ought to be glad of this; yet no gladness ever warmed her heart. And now here was a man who had known him, who had told her of exploits new to her knowledge yet how strangely familiar to her understanding, who had at a touch brought before her, the weird personality that her imagination sometimes strove in vain to summon. She could have sat and listened to Bobby's reminiscences for hours. The bare mention of Nick's name had made her blood run faster.

Lady Bassett did not trouble her to converse during the drive back, ascribing to her evident desire for silence a reason which Muriel was too absent to suspect. But when the girl roused herself to throw a couple of *annas* to an old beggar who was crouched against the entrance to the Residency grounds she could not resist giving utterance to a gentle expostulation.

'I wish you would not encourage these people, dearest. They are so extremely undesirable, and there is so much unrest in the State just now that I cannot but regard them with anxiety.'

Muriel murmured an apology, with the inward reservation to bestow her alms next time when Lady Bassett was not looking on.

She found a letter lying on her table when she entered her room, and took it up listlessly, without much interest. Her mind was still running on those two anecdotes with which Bobby Fraser had so successfully enlivened her boredom. The writing on the envelope was vaguely familiar to her, but she did not associate it with anything of importance. Absently she opened it, half-reluctant to recall her wandering thoughts. It came from a Hill station in Bengal, but that told her nothing. She turned to the signature.

The next instant she had turned back again to the beginning, and was reading eagerly. Her correspondent was Will Musgrave.

'Dear Miss Roscoe,' – ran the letter, 'After long consideration I have decided to write and beg of you a favour which I fancy you will grant more readily than I venture to ask. My wife, as you probably know, joined me some months ago. She is in very indifferent health, and has expressed a most earnest wish to see you. I believe there is something which she wishes to tell you – something that weighs upon her heavily; and though I trust that all will go well with her, I cannot help feeling that she would stand a much better chance of this if only her mind could be set at rest. I know I am asking a big thing of you, for the journey is a ghastly one at this time of year, but if of your goodness you can bring yourself to face it, I will myself meet you and escort you across the Plains. Will you think the matter carefully over; and perhaps you would wire a reply.

'I have written without Daisy's knowledge, as she seems to feel that she has forfeited the right to your friendship. – Sincerely yours,

W. Musgrave.'

Muriel's reply was despatched that evening, almost before she had fully read the appeal.

'Starting to-morrow,' was all she said.

Chapter 48

Lady Bassett considered the decision deplorably headlong, and said so; but her remonstrances were of no avail. Muriel tossed aside her listlessness as resolutely as the ball-dress that had been laid out for the evening's festivity, and plunged at once into preparations for her journey. She knew full well that it was of no actual importance to Lady Bassett whether she went or stayed, and she did not pretend to think otherwise. Moreover, no power on earth would have kept her away from Daisy now that she knew herself to be wanted.

Though more than half of the three days' journey lay across the sweltering Plains, she contemplated it without anxiety, even with rejoicing. At last, the breach, over which she had secretly mourned so deeply, was to be healed.

The next morning at an early hour she was upon her way. She looked out as she drove through the gates for the old native beggar who had crouched at the entrance on the previous afternoon. He was not there, but a little way further she met him hobbling along to take up his post for the day. From the folds of his *chuddah* his unkempt beard wagged entreaty at the carriage as it passed. Impulsively, because of the gladness that was so new to her lonely heart, she leaned from the window and threw him a *rupee*.

Looking back upon the journey later, she never remembered its tedium. She was as one borne on the wings of love, and she scarcely noticed the hardships of the way.

Will Musgrave met her according to his promise at the great junction in the Plains. She found him exceedingly solicitous for her welfare, but so grave and silent that she hardly liked to question him. He thanked her very earnestly for coming, said that Daisy was about the same, and then left her almost exclusively to the society of her *ayah*.

The heat in the Plains was terrific, but Muriel's courage never wavered. She endured it with unfaltering resolution, hour after hour reckoning the dwindling miles that lay before them, passing over all personal discomfort as of no account, content only to be going forward.

But they left the Plains behind at last, and then came the welcome ascent to the Hill station through a country where pine-trees grew ever more and more abundant.

At length at the close of a splendid day they reached it, and as they were nearing their destination Will broke through his silence.

'She doesn't know even yet that you are coming,' he said. 'I thought the suspense of waiting for you might be bad for her. Miss Roscoe – in heaven's name – make her happy if you can!'

There was such a passion of entreaty in his voice that Muriel was deeply touched. She gave him her hand impulsively.

'Mr. Musgrave,' she said, 'to this day I do not know what it was that came between us, but I promise – I promise that if any effort of mine can remove it, it shall be removed to-night.'

Will Musgrave squeezed her fingers hard. 'God bless you!' he said earnestly.

And with that he left her, and went on ahead to prepare Daisy for her coming.

All her life Muriel remembered Daisy's welcome of that evening with a thrill of pain. They met at the gate of the little compound that surrounded the bungalow Will had taken for his wife, and though the light of the sinking sun smote with a certain ruddiness upon Daisy, Muriel was unspeakably shocked by her appearance.

Her white hair, her deathly pallor, the haunting misery of her eyes – above all, her silence – went straight to the girl's heart. Without a single word she gathered Daisy close in her warm young arms and so held her in a long and speechless embrace.

After all, it was Daisy who spoke first, gently drawing herself away. 'Come in, darling! You must be nearly dead after your awful journey. I can't think how Will could ask it of you at this time of the year. I couldn't myself.'

'I would have come to you from the world's end – and gladly,' Muriel answered, in her deep voice. 'You know I would.'

And that was all that passed between them, for Will was present, and Daisy had already begun to lead her guest into the house.

As the evening wore on, Muriel was more and more struck by the great change she saw in her. They had not met for ten months, but twice as many years seemed to have passed over Daisy, crushing her beneath their weight. All her old sprightliness had vanished utterly. She spoke but little, and there was in her manner to her husband a wistful humility, a submission so absolute, that Muriel, remembering her ancient spirit, could have wept.

Will looked at her as if he longed to say something when she bade him good-night, but Daisy was beside her, and he could only give her a tremendous handgrip.

They went away together, and Daisy accompanied her to her room. But the wall of reserve that had been built up between them was not to be shattered at a touch. Neither of them knew exactly how to approach it. There was no awkwardness between them, there was no lack of tenderness, but the door that had closed so long ago was hard to open. Daisy seemed to avoid it with a morbid dread, and it was not in Muriel's power to make the first move.

So for awhile they lingered together, talking commonplace, and at length parted for the night, holding each other closely, without words.

It seemed evident that Daisy could not bring herself to speak at present, and Muriel went to bed with a heavy heart.

She was far too weary to lie awake, but her tired brain would not rest. For the first time in many dreary months she dreamed of Nick.

He was jeering at her in devilish jubilation because she had changed her mind about marrying him, but lacked the courage to tell him so.

Chapter 49

The night was very far advanced when Muriel was aroused from her dreams by a sound which she drowsily fancied must have been going on for some time. It did not disturb her very seriously at first; she even subconsciously made an effort to ignore it. But at length a sudden stab of under-standing pierced her sleep-laden senses, and in a moment she started up broad awake. Someone was in the room with her. Through the dumb stillness before the dawn there came the sound of bitter weeping.

For a few seconds she sat motionless, startled, bewildered, half-afraid. The room was in nearly total darkness. Only in dimmest outline could she discern the long French window that opened upon the verandah.

The weeping continued. It was half-smothered, but it sounded agonized. A great wave of compassion swept suddenly over Muriel. All in a moment she understood.

Swiftly she leaned forward into the darkness, feeling out-wards till her groping hands touched a figure that crouched beside the bed.

'Daisy! Daisy, my darling!' she said, and there was anguish in her own voice. 'What is it?'

In a second the sobbing ceased as if some magic had silenced it. Two hands reached up out of the darkness and tightly clasped hers. A broken voice whispered her name.

'What is it?' Muriel repeated in growing distress.

'Hush, dear, hush!' the trembling voice implored. 'Don't let Will hear! It worries him so.'

'But, my darling, – ' Muriel protested.

She began to feel for some matches, but again the nervous hands caught and imprisoned hers.

'Don't – please!' Daisy begged her earnestly. 'I – I have something to tell you – something that will shock you unutterably. And I – I don't want you to see my face.'

She resisted Muriel's attempt to put her arms about her. 'No – no, dear! Hear me first. There! Let me kneel beside you. It will not take me long. It isn't just for my own sake I am going to speak, nor yet – entirely – for yours. You will see presently. Don't ask me anything – please till I have done. And then if – if there is anything you want to know, I will try to tell you.'

'Come and lie beside me,' Muriel urged.

But Daisy would not. She had sunk very low beside the bed. For a while she crouched there in silence while she summoned her strength.

Then, 'Oh, Muriel,' she suddenly said, and the words seemed to burst from her with a great sigh, 'I wonder if you ever really loved Blake.'

'No, dear, I never did.' Muriel's answer came quiet and sincere through the darkness. 'Nor did he love me. Our engagement was a mistake. I was going to tell him so – if things had been different.'

'I never thought you cared for him,' Daisy said. 'But oh, Muriel, I did. I loved him with my whole soul. No, don't start! It is over now – at least that part of it that was sinful. I only tell you of it because it is the key to everything that must have puzzled you so horribly all this time. We always loved each other from the very beginning, but our people wouldn't hear of it because we were cousins. And so we separated, and I used to think that I had put it away from me. But – last summer – it all came back. You mustn't blame him, Muriel. Blame me – blame me!' The thin hands tightened convulsively. 'It was when my baby died that I began to give way. We never meant it – either of us – but we didn't fight hard enough. And then at last – at Brethaven – Nick found it out; and it was because he knew that Blake's heart was not in his compact with you that he made him write to you and break it off. It was not for his own ends at all that he did it. It was for your sake alone. He even swore to Blake that if he would put an end to his engagement, he on his part would give up all idea of winning you and would never trouble you any more. And that was the finest thing he ever did, Muriel, for he never loved anyone but you. Surely you know it. You must know it by this time. You have never understood him, but you must have begun to realize that he has loved you well enough to set your happiness and well-being always far, far before his own.'

Daisy paused. Her weeping had wholly ceased, but she was shivering from head to foot.

Muriel sat in silence above her, watching wide-eyed, unseeing, the vague hint of light at the open window. She was beginning to understand many things – ah, many things that had been as a sealed book to her till then.

After a time Daisy went on, 'No one will ever know what Nick was to me at that time, how he showed me the wickedness of it all, how he held me back from taking the final step, making me realize even against my will – that Love – true Love – is holy, conquering all evil. And afterwards – afterwards – when Blake was gone – he stood by me and helped me to live, and brought me back at last to my husband. I could never have done it alone. I hadn't the strength. You see' – the low voice faltered suddenly – 'I never expected Will to forgive me. I never asked it of him – any more than I am asking it of you.'

'Oh, my darling, there is no need!' Muriel turned suddenly to throw impetuous arms about the huddled figure at her side. 'Daisy! Daisy! I love you. Let us forget there has ever been this thing between us. Let us be as we used to be, and never drift apart again.'

Tenderly but insistently, she lifted Daisy to the bed beside her, holding her fast. The wall between them was broken down at last. They clung together as sisters long parted.

Daisy, spent by the violence of her emotion, lay for a long time in Muriel's arms without attempting anything further. But at length with a palpable effort she began to speak of other things.

'You know, I have a feeling – perhaps it is morbid – that I am not going to live. I am sure Will thinks so too. If I die, Muriel – three months from now – you and Nick must help him all you can.'

'You are not going to die,' Muriel asserted vehemently. 'You are not to talk of dying, or think of it. Oh, Daisy, can't you look forward to the better time that is coming – when you will have something to live for? And won't you try to think more of Will? It would break his heart to lose you.'

'I do think of him.' Daisy said wearily. 'I would do anything to make him happier. But I can't look forward. I am so tired – so tired.'

'You will feel differently by and by,' Muriel whispered.

'Perhaps,' she assented. 'I don't know. I don't feel as if I shall ever hold another child in my arms. God knows I don't deserve it.'

'Do you think He looks at it in that way?' murmured Muriel, her arms tightening. 'There wouldn't be much in life for any of us if He did.'

'I don't know,' Daisy said again.

She lay quiet for a little as though pondering something. Then at length hesitatingly she spoke. 'Muriel, there is one thing that whether I live or whether I die I want with my whole heart. May I tell you what it is?'

'Of course, dear. What is it?'

Daisy turned in her arms, holding her in a clasp that was passionate. 'My darling,' she whispered very earnestly, 'I would give all I have in the world to know you happy with – with the man you love.'

Silence followed the words. Muriel had become suddenly quite still; her head was bent.

'Don't – don't bar me out of your confidence,' Daisy implored her tremulously. 'There is so little left for me to do now. Muriel – dearest – you do love him?'

Muriel moved impulsively, hiding her face in her friend's neck. But she said no word in answer.

Daisy went on softly, as though she had spoken. 'He is still waiting for you. I think he will wait all his life, though he will never come to you again unless you call him. Won't you – can't you – send him just one little word?'

'How can I?' The words broke suddenly from Muriel as though she could no longer restrain them. 'How can I possibly?'

'It could be done,' Daisy said. 'I know he is still somewhere in India though he has left the Army. We could get a message to him at any time.'

'Oh, but I couldn't – I couldn't!' Muriel had begun to tremble violently. There was a sound of tears in her deep voice. 'Besides – he wouldn't come.'

'My dear, he would,' Daisy assured her. 'He would come to you directly if he only knew that you wanted him. Muriel, surely you are not – not too proud to let him know!'

'Proud! Oh no, no!' There was almost a moan in the words. Muriel's head sank a little lower. 'Heaven knows I'm not proud,' she said. 'I am ashamed – miserably ashamed. I have trampled on his love so often – so often. How could I ask him for it – now?'

'Ah, but if he came to you,' Daisy persisted, 'if in spite of all he came to you, you wouldn't send him away?'

'Send him away!' A sudden note of passion thrilled in Muriel's voice. She lifted her head sharply. With the tears upon her cheeks she yet spoke with a certain exultation. 'I – I would follow him barefoot across the world,' she said, 'if – if he would only lift one finger to call me. But oh, Daisy,' – her confidence vanished at a breath – 'where's the use of talking? He never, never will.'

'He will if you let him know,' Daisy answered with conviction. 'Don't you think you can, dear? Give me just one word
for him – one tiny message that he will understand. Only
trust him this once – just this once! Give him his opportunity
– he has never had one before, poor boy – and I know,
I know, he will not throw it away.'

'You don't think he will – laugh?' Muriel whispered.

'My dear child, no! Nick doesn't laugh at sacred things.'

Muriel' s face was burning in the darkness. She covered it
with her hands as though it could be seen.

For a few seconds she sat very still. Then slowly but
steadily she spoke.

'Tell him then, Daisy, from me, that 'Love conquers all
things – and we must yield to Love.'

Chapter 50

Not another word passed between Daisy and Muriel upon the
subject of that night's confidences. There seemed nothing
further to be said. Moreover, there was between them a closer
understanding than words could compass.

The days that followed passed very peacefully, and Daisy
began to improve so marvellously in health and spirits that
both her husband and her guest caught at times fleeting
glimpses of the old light-hearted personality that they had
loved in earlier days.

'You have done wonders for my wife,' Will said one day
to Muriel. And though she disclaimed all credit, she could
not fail to see a very marked improvement.

She herself was feeling unaccountably happy in those
days, as though somewhere deep down in her heart a bird
had begun to sing. Again and again she told herself that
she had no cause for gladness; but again and yet again that
sweet, elusive music filled her soul.

She would gladly have stayed on with Daisy, seeing how

the latter clung to her, for an indefinite period; but this was not to be.

Daisy came out on to the verandah one morning with a letter in her hand.

'My dear,' she said, 'I regret to say that I must part with you. I have had a most touching epistle from Lady Bassett, describing at length your many wasted opportunities, and urging me to return you to the fold with all speed. It seems there is to be a State Ball at the palace – an immense affair to which the Rajah is inviting all the big guns for miles around – and Lady Bassett thinks that her dear child ought not to miss such a gorgeous occasion. She seems to think that something of importance depends upon it, and hints that I should be almost criminally selfish to deprive you of such a treat as this will be.'

Muriel lifted a flushed face from a letter of her own. 'I have heard from Sir Reginald,' she said. 'Evidently she has made him write. I can't think why, for he never wants me when I am with her. I don't see why I should go, do you? After all, I am of age and independent.'

A very tender smile touched Daisy's lips. 'I think you had better go, darling,' she said.

Muriel opened her eyes wide. 'But why – '

Daisy checked the question half-uttered. 'I think it will be better for you. I never meant to let you stay till the Rains, so it makes little more than a week's difference. It sounds as if I want to be rid of you, doesn't it? But you know it isn't that. I shall miss you horribly, but you have done what you came to do, and I shall get on all right now. So I am not going to keep you with me any longer. My reasons are not Lady Bassett's reasons, but all the same it would be selfish of me to let you stay. Later on perhaps – in the winter – you will come and make a long stay; spend Christmas with us, and we will have some real fun, shall we, Will?' turning to her husband who had just appeared.

He stared for an instant as if he thought he had not heard

aright, and there was to Muriel something infinitely pathetic in the way his brown hand touched his wife's shoulder as he passed her and made reply.

'Oh, rather!' he said. 'We'll have a regular jollification with as many old friends as we can collect. Don't forget, Miss Roscoe. You are booked first and foremost, and we shall keep you to it, Daisy and I.'

Two days later Muriel was on her way back to Ghawalkhand. She found the heat of the journey almost insupportable. The Plains lay under a burning pall of cloud, and at night the rolling thunder was incessant. But no rain fell to ease the smothering oppression of the atmosphere.

She almost fainted one evening, but Will was with her and she never forgot his kindly ministrations.

A few hours' journey from Ghawalkhand Sir Reginald himself met her, and here she parted with Will with renewed promises of a future meeting towards the end of the year.

Sir Reginald fussed over her kind-heartedly, hoped she had enjoyed herself, thought she looked very thin, and declared that his wife was looking forward with much pleasure to her return. The State was still somewhat unsettled, and there had been one or two outrages of late, nothing serious of course, but the native element was restless, and he fancied Lady Bassett was nervous.

She was away at a polo-match when they arrived, and Muriel profited by her absence and went straight to bed.

She could have slept for hours had she been permitted to do so, but Lady Bassett, returning, awoke her to receive her welcome. She was charmed to have her back, she declared, though shocked to see her looking so wan, 'so almost plain, dear child, if one may take the liberty of an old friend to tell you so.'

Neither the crooked smile that accompanied this gentle criticism nor the decidedly grim laugh with which it was received, was of a particularly friendly nature; but these facts were not extraordinary. There had never been the smallest hint of sympathy between them.

'I trust you will be looking much better than this two nights hence,' Lady Bassett proceeded in her soft accents. 'The Rajah's Ball is to be very magnificent, quite dazzlingly so from all accounts. Mr. Bobby Fraser is of course behind the scenes, and he tells me that the preparations in progress are simply gigantic. By the way, dear, it is to be hoped that your absence has not damaged your prospects in that quarter. I have been afraid lately that he was transferring his allegiance to the second Egerton girl. I hope earnestly that there is nothing in it, for you know how I have your happiness at heart, do you not? And it would be such an excellent thing for you, dear child, as I expect you realize. For you know, you look so much older than you actually are that you really ought not to throw away any more opportunities. Every girl thinks she must have her fling, but you, dear, should soberly think of getting settled soon. You would not like to get left, I feel sure.'

At this point Muriel sat up suddenly, her dark eyes very bright, and in brief tones announced that so far as she was concerned the second Egerton girl was more than welcome to Mr. Fraser, and she hoped, if she wanted him, she would manage to keep him.

It was crudely expressed, as Lady Bassett pointed out with a sigh for her waywardness; but Muriel always was crude when her deeper feeling were disturbed and physical fatigue had made her irritable.

She wished ardently that Lady Bassett would leave her, but Lady Bassett had not quite done. She lingered to ask for news of poor little Daisy Musgrave. Had she yet fully recovered from the shock of her cousin's tragic death? Could she bear to speak of him? She, Lady Bassett, had always suspected the existence of an unfortunate attachment between them.

Muriel had no information to bestow upon the subject. She

hoped and believed that Daisy was getting stronger, and had promised, all being well, to spend Christmas with her.

Lady Bassett shook her head over this declaration. The dear child was so headlong. Much might happen before Christmas. And what of Mr. Ratcliffe – this was on her way to the door – had she heard the extraordinary, the really astounding news concerning him that had just reached Lady Bassett's ears? She asked because he and Mrs. Musgrave used to be such friends, though to be sure Mr. Ratcliffe seemed to have thrown off all his old friends of late. Had Muriel actually not heard?

'Heard! Heard what?' Muriel forced out the question from between lips that were white and stiff. She was suddenly afraid – horribly, unspeakably afraid. But she kept her eyes unflinchingly upon Lady Bassett's face. She would sooner die than quail in her presence.

Lady Bassett, holding the door-handle, looked back at her, faintly smiling. 'I wonder you have not heard, dear. I thought you were in correspondence with his people. But perhaps they are also in the dark. It is a most unheard-of thing – quite irrevocable I am told. But I always thought that he was a man to do unusual things. There was always to my mind something uncanny, abnormal, something almost super-human, about him.'

'But what has happened to him?' Muriel did not know how she uttered the words; they seemed to come without her own volition. She was conscious of a choking sensation within her as though iron bands were tightening about her heart. It beat in leaps and bounds like a tortured thing striving to escape. But through it all she sat quite motionless, her eyes fixed upon Lady Bassett's face, noting its faint, wry smile, as the eyes of a prisoner on the rack might note the grim lines on the face of the torturer.

'My dear,' Lady Bassett said, 'he has gone into a Buddhist monastery in Tibet.'

Calmly the words fell through smiling lips. Only words!

Only words! But with how deadly a thrust they pierced the heart of the woman who heard them none but herself would ever know. She gave no sign of suffering. She only stared wide-eyed before her as an image devoid of expression, inanimate, sphinx-like, while that awful constriction grew straiter round her heart.

Lady Bassett was already turning to go when the deep voice arrested her.

'Who told you this?'

She looked back, holding the open door. 'I scarcely know who first mentioned it. I have heard it from so many people – in fact the news is general property – Captain Gresham of the Guides told me for one. He has just gone back to Peshawur. The news reached him I believe from there. Then there was Colonel Cathcart for another. He was talking of it only this afternoon at the Club, saying what a deplorable example it was for an Englishman to set. He and Mr. Bobby Fraser had quite a hot argument about it. Mr. Fraser has such advanced ideas, but I must admit that I rather admire the staunch way in which he defends them. There, dear child! You must not keep me gossiping any longer. You look positively haggard. I earnestly hope a good sleep will restore you, for I cannot possibly take that wan face to the Rajah's Ball.'

Lady Bassett departed with the words, shaking her head tolerantly and still smiling.

But for long after she had gone, Muriel remained with fixed eyes and tense muscles, watching, watching dumbly, immovably, despairingly, at the locked door of her paradise.

So this was the key to his silence – the reason that her message had gone unanswered. She had stretched out her hands to him too late – too late.

And ever through the barren desert of her vigil a man's voice, vital and passionate, rang and echoed in a maddening, perpetual refrain.

'All your life you will remember that I was once yours to

take or to throw away. And – you wanted me, yet – you chose to throw me away.'

It was a refrain she had heard often and often before; but it had never tortured her as it tortured her now – now when her last hope was finally quenched – now when at last she fully realized what it was that had once been hers, and that in her tragic blindness she had wantonly cast away.

Chapter 51

Muriel did not leave the Residency again until the evening of the State Ball at the palace. Scarcely did she leave her room, pleading intense fatigue as her excuse for this seclusion. But she could not, without exciting remark, absent herself from the great function for which ostensibly she had returned to Ghawalkhand.

She wore a dress of unrelieved white for the occasion, for she had but recently discarded her mourning for her father, and her face was almost as devoid of colour. Her dark hair lay in a shadowy mass above her forehead, accentuating her pallor. Her eyes looked out upon the world with tragic indifference, unexpectant, apathetic.

'My dear, you don't look well,' said Sir Reginald, as, gorgeous in his glittering uniform, he stood to hand her after his wife into the carriage.

She smiled a little. 'It is nothing. I am still rather tired, that's all.'

Driving through the gates she looked forth absently and spied the old beggar crouching in his accustomed place. He almost prostrated himself at sight of her, but she had no money with her, nor could she have bestowed any under Lady Bassett's disapproving eye. The carriage rolled on, leaving his obsequiousness unrequited.

Entering the glittering ballroom all hung with glowing colours was like entering a garden of splendid flowers.

European and Indian costumes were mingled in shining confusion. A hubbub of music and laughter seemed to engulf them like a rushing torrent.

'Ah, here you are at last!' It was Bobby Fraser's voice at Muriel's side. He looked at her with cheery approval. 'I say, you know, you're the queen of this gathering. Pity there isn't a king anywhere about. Perhaps there is, eh? Well, can you give me a dance? Afraid I haven't a waltz left. No matter! We can sit out. I know a cosy corner exactly fitted to my tastes. In fact I've booked it for the evening. And I want a talk with you badly. Number five then. Good-bye!'

He was gone, leaving Muriel with the curious impression that there really was something of importance that he wished to say to her.

She wondered what it was. That he was paying her serious attention she had never for a moment believed, nor had she given him the faintest encouragement to do so. She knew that Lady Bassett thought otherwise, but she had never rated her opinion very highly; and she had never read anything but the most casual friendliness in Bobby's attitude.

Still it disturbed her somewhat, that hint of intimacy that his words portended, and she awaited the dance he had solicited in a state of mind very nearly allied to apprehension. Lady Bassett's suggestions had done for her what no self-consciousness would ever have accomplished unaided. They had implanted within her a deep-rooted misgiving before which all ease of manner fled.

When Bobby Fraser joined her, she was so plainly nervous that he could not fail to remark it. He led her to a quiet corner above the garden that was sheltered from the throng by flowering tamarisks.

'I say,' he said, 'I hope you are not letting yourself get scared by these infernal *budmashes*. The reports have all been immensely exaggerated as usual.'

'I am not at all scared,' she told him. 'But wasn't there a Englishman murdered the other day?'

'Oh yes,' he admitted, 'but miles and miles away, right the other side of the State. There was nothing in that to alarm anyone here. It might have happened anywhere. People are such fools,' he threw in vindictively. 'Begin to look askance at the native population, and of course they are on the *qui vive* instantly. It is only to be expected. It was downright madness to send a Resident here. They resent it, you know. But the Rajah's influence is enormous. Nothing could happen here.'

'I wonder,' said Muriel.

She had scarcely given the matter a thought before, but it was a relief to find some impersonal topic for discussion.

Bobby however had no intention of pursuing it further. 'Oh, it's self-evident,' he said. 'They are loyal to the Rajah, and the Rajah is well-known to be loyal to the Crown. It's only these duffers of administrators that make the mischief.' He broke into an abrupt laugh, and changed the subject. 'Let us talk of something less exasperating. How did you get on while you were away? You must have found the journey across the Plains pretty ghastly.'

She told him a little about it, incidentally mentioning Will Musgrave.

'Oh, I know him,' he broke in. 'An engineer, isn't he? Awfully clever chap. I met him years ago at Sharapura the time Nick Ratcliffe won the Great Mogul's Cup. I told you the story, didn't I?'

Yes, he had done so. She informed him of the fact with an immovable face. It might have been a subject of total indifference to her.

'You know Nick Ratcliffe, don't you?' he pursued, evidently following his own train of thought.

She flushed at the very direct question. She had not expected it. 'It is a very long time since I last saw him,' she said, with a deliberate effort to banish all interest from her voice.

He was not looking at her. He could not have been aware of the flush. Yet he elected to push the matter further.

'A queer fish,' he said. 'A very queer fish. He has lost his left arm, poor beggar. Did you know?'

Yes, she knew; but she could hardly summon the strength to tell him so. Her fan concealed her quivering lips, but the hand that held it shook uncontrollably.

But he, still casual, continued his desultory harangue. 'Always reminds me of a jack-in-the-box – that fellow. Has a knack of popping up when you least expect him. You never know what he will do next. You can only judge him by the things he doesn't do. For instance, there's been a rumour floating about lately that he has just gone into a Tibetan monastery. Heaven knows who started it and why. But it is absolutely untrue. It is the sort of thing that couldn't be true of a man of his temperament. Don't you agree with me? Or perhaps you didn't know him very well, and don't feel qualified to judge.'

At this point he pulled out this programme and studied it frowningly. He was plainly not paying much attention to her reply. He seemed to be contemplating something that worried him.

It made it all the easier for her to answer. 'No,' she said slowly. 'I didn't know him very well. But – that rumour was told to me as absolute fact. I – of course – I believed it.'

She knew that her face was burning as she ended. She could feel the blood surging through every vein.

'If you want to know what I think,' said Bobby Fraser deliberately, 'it is that that rumour was a malicious invention of someone's.'

'Oh, do you?' she said. 'But – but why?'

He turned and looked at her. His usually merry face was stern. 'Because,' he said, 'it served someone's end to make someone else believe that Nick had dropped out for good.'

Her eyes fell under his direct look. 'I don't understand,' she murmured desperately.

'Nor do I,' he rejoined, 'for certain. I can only surmise. It doesn't do to believe things too readily. One gets let in that

way.' He rose and offered her his arm. 'Come outside for a
little. This place is too warm for comfort.'

She went with him willingly, thankful to turn her face to
the night. A dozen questions hovered on her lips, but she
could not ask him one of them. She could only walk beside
him and profess to listen to the stream of anecdotes which
he began to pour forth for her entertainment.

She did not actually hear one of them. They came to her
all jumbled and confused through such a torrent of gladness
as surely she had never known before. For the bird in her
heart had lifted its head again, and was singing its rapture to
the stars.

Chapter 52

Looking back upon the hours that followed that talk with
Bobby behind the tamarisks, Muriel could never recall in
detail how they passed. She moved in a whirl, all her pulses
racing, all her senses on the alert. None of her partners had
ever seen her gay before, but she was gay that night with a
spontaneous and wonderful gaiety that came from the very
heart of her. It was not a gaiety that manifested itself in
words, but it was none the less apparent to those about her.
For her eyes shone as though they looked into a radiant
future, and she danced as one inspired. She was like a statue
waked to splendid life.

Swiftly the hours flew by. She scarcely noted their passage,
any more than she noted the careless talk and laughter that
hummed around her. She moved in an atmosphere of her
own to a melody that none other heard.

The ball was wearing to a close when at length Lady
Bassett summoned her to return. Lady Bassett was wearing
her most gracious smile.

'You have been much admired to-night, dear child,' she
murmured to the girl, as they passed into the cloakroom.

Muriel's eyes looked disdainful for an instant, but they could not remain so. As swiftly the happiness flashed back into them.

'I have enjoyed myself,' she said simply.

She threw a gauzy scarf about her neck, and turned to go. She did not want her evening spoilt by criticisms however honeyed.

The great marble entrance was crowded with departing guests. She edged her way to one of the pillars at the head of the long flight of steps, watching party after party descend to the waiting carriages. The dancing had not yet ceased, and strains of waltz-music came to her where she stood, fitful, alluring, plaintive. They were playing 'The Blue Danube.'

She listened to it as one in a dream, and while she listened the tears gathered in her eyes. How was it she had been so slow to understand? Would she ever make it up to him? She wondered how long he meant to keep her in suspense. It was not like him to linger thus if he had indeed received her message. She hoped he would come soon. The waiting was hard to bear.

She called to mind once more the last words he had spoken to her. He had said that he would not swoop a second time, but she could not imagine him doing anything else. He would be sudden, he would be disconcerting, he would be overwhelming. He would come on winged feet in answer to her call, but he would give her no quarter. He would neither ask nor demand. He would simply take.

She caught her breath and hastened to divert her thoughts, realizing that she was on the verge of the old torturing process of self-intimidation which had so often before unnerved her.

The throng about her had lessened considerably. Glancing downwards, she discerned at the foot of the steps the old beggar who so persistently hunted the Residency gates, incurring thereby Lady Bassett's alarmed displeasure. He was crouching well to one side in the familiar attitude of supplication. There were dozens like him in Ghawalkhand, but she knew him by the peculiar, gibbering movement of the wiry beard that protruded from his *chuddah*. He was repulsive, but in a fashion fascinating. He made her think of a wizened old monkey who had wandered from his kind.

She had come to regard him almost in the light of a *protégé*, and, remembering suddenly that he had besought an alms of her in vain some hours before, she turned impulsively to a man she knew who had just come up.

'Colonel Cathcart, will you lend me a *rupee?*'

He dived in his pocket and brought out a handful of money. She found the coin she wanted, thanked him with a smile, and began to descend the steps.

The old native was not looking at her. Something else seemed to have caught his attention. For the moment he had ceased to cringe and implore.

She heard Sir Reginald's voice above her. He was standing in talk with the Rajah while he waited for his wife.

And then – she was half-way down the steps when it happened – a sudden loud cry rang fiercely up to her, arresting her where she stood – a man's voice inarticulate at first, bursting from mere sound into furious headlong denunciation.

'You infernal hound!' it cried. 'You damned assassin!'

At the same instant the old beggar at the foot of the palace steps sprang panther-like from his crouching position to hurl himself bodily at something that skulked in the shadows beyond him.

The marvellous agility of the action, the unerring precision with which he pounced upon his prey, above all, the voice that had yelled in execration, sent such a stab of amazed recognition through Muriel that she stood for a second as one petrified.

But the next instant all her senses were pricked into alertness by a revolver-shot. Another came, and yet another. They were fighting below her like tigers – two men in native dress, swaying, straining, struggling, not three yards from where she stood.

She never fully remembered afterwards how she came to realize that Nick – Nick himself – was there before her in the flesh, fighting like a demon, fighting as she had seen him fight once long ago when every nerve in her body had been strung to agonized repulsion.

She felt no repulsion now – no shrinking of any sort, only a wild anguish of fear for his sake that drove her like a mad creature down the intervening steps, that sent her flashing between him and his adversary, that inspired her to wrench away the smoking revolver from the murderous hand that gripped it.

She went through those awful moments as a woman possessed, blindly obeying the compelling force, goaded by sheer, primæval instinct to protect her own. It was but a conflict of seconds, but while it lasted she was untrammelled by any doubts or hesitations. She was sublimely sure of herself. She was superbly unafraid.

When it was over, when men crowded round and dragged her enemy back, when the pressing need was past, her courage fell from her like a mantle. She sank down upon the steps, a trembling, hysterical woman, and began to cry.

Someone bent over her, someone whispered soothing words, someone drew the revolver out of her weak grasp. Looking up she saw the old native beggar upon whom she had thought to bestow her charity.

'Oh, Nick!' she gasped. 'Nick!' And there stopped in sudden misgiving. Was this grotesque figure indeed Nick? Could it be – this man who had sat at the Residency gates for weeks, this man to whom she had so often tossed an alms?

Her brain had begun to reel, but she clung to the central idea, as one in deep waters clinging to a spar.

'Speak to me!' she entreated. 'Only speak to me!'

But before he could answer Bobby Fraser pushed

suddenly forward, bent over, lifted her. 'You are not hurt, Miss Roscoe?' he questioned anxiously, deep concern on his kindly face. 'The damned swine didn't touch you? There! Come back into the palace. You're the bravest girl I ever met.'

He began to help her up the steps, but though she was spent and near to fainting she resisted him.

'That man – ' she faltered. 'Don't – don't let him go!'

'Certainly not,' said Bobby promptly. 'Here, you old scarecrow, come and lend a hand!'

But the old scarecrow apparently had other plans for himself, for he had already vanished from the scene as swiftly and noiselessly as a shadow from a sheet.

'He is gone!' wailed Muriel. 'He is gone! Oh, why did you let him go?'

'He'll turn up again,' said Bobby consolingly. 'That sort of chap always does. I say, how ghastly you look! Take my arm! You are not going to faint, are you? Ah, here is Colonel Cathcart! Miss Roscoe isn't hurt, simply upset. Can't we get her back to the palace?'

They bore her back between them and left her to be tended by the women. She was not unconscious, but the shock had utterly unstrung her. She lay with closed eyes, listening vaguely to the buzz of excited comment about her, and wondering, wondering with an aching heart, why he had gone.

No one seemed to know exactly what had taken place, and she was too exhausted to tell. Possibly she would not have told in any case. It was known only that an attempt had been made upon the life of the British Resident, Sir Reginald Bassett, and it was surmised that Muriel had realized the murderous intention in time to frustrate it. Certainly a native had tried to help her, but since the native had disappeared, his share in the conflict was not regarded as very great. As a matter of fact the light had been too uncertain and the struggle too confused for even the eye-witnesses to know with any certainty what had taken place. Theories and speculations were many and various, but not one of them went near to the truth.

'Dear Muriel will tell us presently just how it happened,' Lady Bassett said in her soft voice.

But Muriel was as one who heard not. She would not even open her eyes till Sir Reginald came to her, pillowed her head against him, kissed her white face, and called her his brave little girl.

That moved her at last, awaking in her the old piteous hunger, never wholly stifled, for her father. She turned and clung to him convulsively with an inarticulate murmuring that ended in passionate tears.

Chapter 53

Why had he gone? That was the question that vexed Muriel's soul through the long hours that followed her return to the Residency. Lying sleepless on her bed, she racked her weary brain for an answer to the riddle, but found none. Her brief doubt regarding him had long since fled. She knew with absolute certainty that it was Nick and no other who had yelled those furious words, who had made that panther-spring, who had leaned over her and withdrawn the revolver from her hold, telling her softly not to cry. But why had he gone just then when she needed him most?

Surely by now her message had reached him! Surely he knew that she wanted him, that she had lowered what he had termed her miserable little rag of pride to tell him so! Then why was he tormenting her thus – playing with her as a cat might play with a mouse? Was he taking his revenge for all the bitter scorn she had flung at him in the past? Did he think to wring from her some more definite appeal? Ah, that was it! Like a searchlight flashing inwards, she remembered her promise to him uttered long ago against her will – his answering oath. And she knew that he meant to hold her to that promise – that he would exact the very uttermost sacrifice that it entailed; and then perchance – she shivered at the unendurable thought – he would laugh his baffling, enigmatical laugh, and go his way.

But this was unbearable, impossible. She would sooner die than suffer it. She would sooner – yes, she would almost sooner – break her promise.

And then, to save her from distraction, the other side of the picture presented itself, that reverse side which he had once tauntingly advised her to study. If he truly loved her, he would not treat her thus. It would not gratify him to see her in the dust. If he still cared, as Daisy had assured her he did, it would not be his pleasure to make her suffer. But then again – oh, torturing question! – had that been so, would he have gone at that critical moment, would he have left her, when a look, a touch, would have sufficed to establish complete understanding?

Drearily the hours dragged away. The heat was great, and just before daybreak a thunderstorm rolled up, but spent itself without a drop of rain. It put the finishing touch to Muriel's restlessness. She rose and dressed, to sit by her window with her torturing thoughts for company, and await the day.

With the passing of the storm a slight draught that was like a shudder moved the scorched leaves of the acacias in the compound, quivered a little, and ceased. Then came the dawn, revealing mass upon mass of piled cloud hanging low over the earth. The breaking of the monsoon was drawing very near. There could be no lifting of the atmosphere, no relief, until it came.

She leaned her aching head against the window-frame in a maze of weariness unutterable. Her heart was too heavy for prayer.

Minutes passed. The daylight grew and swiftly overspread all things. The leaden silence began to be pierced here and there by the barking of a dog, the crowing of a cock, the scolding of a parrot. Somewhere, either in the compound or close to it, someone began to whistle – a soft, tentative whistle like a young blackbird trying its notes.

Muriel remained motionless, scarcely heeding while it wove itself into the background of her thoughts. She was in fact hardly aware of it, till suddenly with a great thrill of astonishment that shook her from head to foot, a wild suspicion seized her, and she started up, listening intently. The fitful notes were resolving into a melody – a waltz she knew, alluring, enchanting, compelling – the waltz that had filled in the dreadful silences on that night long ago when she had fought so desperately hard for her freedom and had prevailed at last. But stay! Had she prevailed? Had she not rather been a captive in spite of it all ever since?

On and on went the haunting waltz-refrain, now near, now far, now summoning, now eluding. She stood gripping the curtain till she could bear it no longer, and then with a great sob she mustered her resolution; she stepped out upon the verandah, and passed down between shrivelled trailing roses to the garden below.

The tune ceased quite suddenly, and she found herself moving through a silence that could be felt. But she would not turn back then. She would not let herself be discouraged. She had been frightened so often when there had been no need for fear.

On she pressed to the end of the path till she stood by the high fence that bordered the road. She could see no one. The garden lay absolutely deserted. She paused, hesitating, bewildered.

At the same instant from the other side of the fence, almost as if rising from the ground at her feet, a careless voice began to hum – a cracked, tuneless, unmistakable voice, that sent the blood to her heart with a force that nearly suffocated her.

'Nick!' she said, almost in a whisper.

He did not hear her evidently. His humming continued with unabated liveliness.

'Nick!' she said again.

Still no result. There was nothing in the least dramatic in the situation. It might almost have been described as ludicrous, but the white-faced woman in the compound did not find it so.

She waited till he had come to a suitable stopping-place, and then before he could renew the melody, she rapped with nervous force upon the fence.

There fell a most unexpected silence.

She broke it with words imploring, almost agonized.

'Nick! Nick! Come and speak to me – for Heaven's sake!'

His flippant voice greeted her at once in a tone of cheerful inquiry. 'That you, Muriel?'

Her agitation began to subside of itself. Nothing could have been more casual than his question. 'Yes,' she said in reply. 'Why are you out there? Why don't you come in?'

'My dear girl – at this hour!' There was shocked reproof in the ejaculation. Nick was evidently scandalized at the suggestion.

Muriel lost her patience forthwith. Was it for this that she had spent all those miserable hours of fruitless heart-searching? His trifling was worse than ridiculous. It was insufferable.

'You are to come in at once,' she said, in a tone of authority.

'What for?' said Nick.

'Because – because – ' She hesitated, and stopped, her face burning.

'Because – ' said Nick encouragingly.

'Oh, don't be absurd!' she exclaimed in desperation. 'How can I possibly talk to you there?'

'It depends upon what you want to say,' said Nick. 'If it is something particularly private – ' he paused.

'Well?' she said.

'You can always come to me, you know,' he pointed out. 'But I shouldn't do that, if I were you. It would be neither dignified nor proper. And a girl in your position, dearest Muriel, cannot be too discreet. It is the greatest mistake in the world to act upon impulse. Let me entreat you to do nothing headlong. Take another year or so to think things over. There are so many nice men to choose from, and this absurd infatuation of yours cannot possibly last.'

'Don't, Nick!' Muriel's voice held a curious mixture of mirth and sadness. 'It – it isn't a bit funny to talk like that. It isn't even particularly kind.'

'Ye gods!' said Nick. 'Who wants to be kind?'

'Not you evidently,' she told him with a hint of bitterness. 'You only aim at being intelligent.'

'Well, you'll admit I hit the mark sometimes,' he rejoined. 'I'm like a rat, eh? Clever but loathsome.'

She uttered a quivering laugh. 'No, you are much more like an eagle, waiting to strike. Why don't you, I wonder, and – and take what you want?'

Nick's answering laugh had a mocking note in it, 'Oh, I can play Animal Grab as well as anybody – better than most,' he said modestly. 'But I don't chance to regard this as a suitable occasion for displaying my skill. Uninteresting for you of course, but then you are fond of running away when there is no one after you. It's been your favourite pastime for almost as long as I have known you.'

The sudden silence with which this airy remark was received had in it something tragic. Muriel had sunk down on a garden-bench close at hand, lacking the strength to go away. It was exactly what she had expected. He meant to take his revenge in his own peculiar fashion. She had laid herself open to this, and mercilessly, unerringly, he had availed himself of the opportunity to wound. She might have known! She might have known! Had he not done it again and again? Oh, she had been a fool – a fool – to call him back!

Through the wild hurry of her thoughts his voice pierced once more. It had an odd infection that was curiously like a note of concern.

'I say, Muriel, are you crying?'

'Crying!' She pulled herself together hastily 'No! Why should I?'

'I can tell you why you shouldn't,' he answered whimsically. 'No one ever ought to cry before breakfast. It's shocking for the appetite and may ruin the complexion for the rest of the day. Besides – you've nothing to cry for.'

'Oh, don't be absurd!' she flung back again almost fiercely. 'I'm not crying!'

'Quite sure?' said Nick.

'Absolutely certain,' she declared.

'All right then,' he rejoined. 'That being so, you had better dry your eyes carefully, for I am coming to see for myself.'

Chapter 54

She awaited him still sitting on the bench and striving vainly to quiet her thumping heart. She heard him come lightly up behind her, but she did not turn her head though she had no tears to conceal. She was possessed by an insane desire to spring up and flee. It took all her resolution to remain where she was.

And so Nick drew near unwelcomed – a lithe, alert figure in European attire, bare-headed, eager-faced. He was smiling to himself as he came, but when he reached her the smile was gone.

He bent and looked into her white, downcast face then laid his hand upon her shoulder.

'But, Muriel – ' he said.

And that was all. Yet Muriel suddenly hid her face and wept.

He did not attempt to restrain her. Perhaps he realized that tears such as those must have their way. But the touch of his hand was in some fashion soothing. It stilled the tempest within her, comforting her inexplicably.

She reached up at last, and drew it down between her own, holding it fast.

'I'm such a fool, Nick,' she whispered shakily. 'You – you must try to bear with me.'

She felt his fingers close and gradually tighten upon her own until their grip was actual pain.

'Haven't I borne with you long enough?' he said. 'Can't you come to the point?'

She shook her head slightly. Her trembling had not wholly ceased. She was not – even yet she was not – wholly sure of him.

'Afraid?' he questioned.

And she answered him meekly, with bowed head. 'Yes, Nick; afraid.'

'Don't you think you might look me in the face if you tried very hard?' he suggested.

'No, Nick.' She almost shrank at the bare thought.

'Oh, but you haven't tried,' he said.

His voice sounded very close. She knew he was bending down. She even fancied she could feel his breath upon her neck.

Her head sank a little lower. 'Don't!' she whispered, with a sob.

'What are you afraid of?' he said. 'You weren't as afraid to send me a message. You weren't afraid to save my life last night. What is it frightens you?'

She could not tell him. Only her panic was very real. It shook her from head to foot. A fierce struggle was going on within her, – the last bitter conflict between her love and her fear. It tore her in all directions. She felt as if it would drive her mad. But through it all she still clung desperately to the bony hand that grasped her own. It seemed to sustain her, to hold her up, through all her chaos of doubt, of irresolution, of miserable, overmastering dread.

'What is it frightens you?' he said again. 'Why won't you look at me? There is nothing whatever to make you afraid!'

He spoke softly, as though he were addressing a scared child. But still she was afraid, afraid of the very impulse that urged her, horribly afraid of meeting the darting scrutiny of his eyes.

He waited for a little in silence; then suddenly with a sharp sigh he straightened himself. 'You don't know your own mind yet,' he said. 'And I can't help you to know it. I had better go.'

'He would have withdrawn his hand with the words, but she held it fast.

'No, Nick, no! It isn't that,' she told him tremulously. 'I know what I want – perfectly well. But – but – I can't put it into words. I can't! can't!'

'Is that it?' said Nick. His manner changed completely. He bent down again. She heard the old note of banter in his voice, but mingled with it was a tenderness so utter that she scarcely recognized it. 'Then, my dear girl, in heaven's name, don't try! Words were not made for such an occasion as this. They are clumsy tools at the best of times. You can make me understand without words. I'm horribly intelligent, as you remarked just now.'

Her heart leapt to the rapid assurance. Was it so difficult to tell him after all? Surely she could find a way!

The tumult of her emotions swelled to sudden uproar, thunderous, all-possessing, overwhelming, so that she gasped and gasped again for breath. And then all in a moment she knew that the conflict was over. She was as a diver, hurling with headlong velocity from dizzy height into deep waters, and she rejoiced – she exulted – in that mad rush into depth.

With a quivering laugh she moved. She loosened her convulsive clasp upon his hand, turned it upwards, and stooping low, she pressed her lips closely, passionately, lingeringly, upon his open palm. She had found a way.

He started sharply at her action; he almost winced. Then, 'Muriel!' he exclaimed in a voice that broke, and threw himself on his knees beside her, holding her fast in a silence so sudden and so tense that she also was awed into a great stillness.

Yet, after a little, though his face was pressed against her so that she could not see it or even vaguely guess his mood, she found strength to speak.

'I can tell you what I want now, Nick,' she whispered. 'Shall I tell you?'

He did not answer, did not so much as breathe. But yet she knew no fear or hesitancy. Her eyes were opened, and her tongue loosed. Words came easily to her now, more easily than they had ever come before.

'I want to be married – soon, very soon,' she told him softly. 'And then I want you to take me away with you into Nepal, as you planned ever so long ago. And let us be alone together in the mountains – quite alone as we were before. Will you, Nick? Will you?'

But again he had no answer for her. He did not seem able to reply. His head still lay against her shoulder. His arm was still tense about her. She fell silent, waiting for him.

At last he drew a deep breath that seemed to burst upwards from the very heart of him, and lifted his face with a jerk.

'My God!' he said. 'Is it true?'

His voice was oddly uneven; he seemed to produce it with difficulty. But having broken the spell that bound him, he managed after a moment to continue.

'Are you quite sure you want to marry me – quite sure that to-morrow you won't be scared out of your wits at the bare idea? Have you left off being afraid of me? Do you mean me really to take you at your word?'

'If you will, Nick,' she answered humbly.

'If I will!' he echoed, with sudden passion. 'I warn you, Muriel, you are putting yourself irrevocably in my power, and you will never break away again. You may come to loathe me with your whole soul, but I shall never let you go. Have you realized that? If I take you now, I take you for all time.'

He spoke almost with violence, and, having spoken, drew back from her abruptly, as though he could not wholly trust himself.

But nothing could dismay her now. She had fought her last battle, had made the final surrender. Her fear was dead. She stretched out her hands to him with unfaltering confidence.

'Take me then, Nick,' she said.

He took the extended hands with quick decision, first one and then the other, and laid them on his shoulders.

'Now look at me,' he said.

She hesitated, though not as one afraid.

'Look at me, Muriel!' he insisted.

Then, as she kept her eyes downcast, he put his hand under her chin and compelled her.

She yielded with a little quivering murmur of protest, and so for the first time in her life she deliberately met his look, encountering eyes so wide and so piercingly blue that she had a moment's bewildered feeling of uncertainty, as though she had looked into the eyes of a stranger. Then the colourless lashes descended again and veiled them as of old. He blinked with his usual disconcerting rapidity and set her free.

'Yes,' he said. 'You've left off cheating. And if you really care to marry me – what's left of me – it's a precious poor bargain, but – I am yours.'

His voice cracked a little. She fancied he was going to laugh. And then, while she was still wondering, his arm went round her again and drew her closely to him. She was conscious of a sudden, leaping flame behind the pale lashes, felt his hold tighten while the wrinkled face drew near – and with a sob she clasped her arms about his neck and turned her lips to his.

Chapter 55

'Funny, wasn't it?' said Nick, jingling a small handful of coins in front of his *fiancée*. 'Quite a harvest in its way! I had no idea you were so charitable.'

She caught his wrist. 'You have no right to a single one of them. You obtained them under false pretences. What in the world induced you to do such a thing?'

Nick's hand closed firmly upon the spoil. 'It was a sheer, heaven-sent inspiration,' he declared. 'Care to know how it came to me? It happened one night in the Indian Ocean when I was on the way out with Daisy. I was lying on deck under the stars, thinking of you, and the whole idea came to me ready-made. I didn't attempt to shape it; it shaped itself. I was hungering for the sight of you, and I knew you would never find me out. You never would have done either if I hadn't had Daisy's message. I was just going to quit my lonely vigil when it reached me. But that altered my plans, and I decided with Fraser's assistance to face it out. You knew he was in the secret of course? He is in every secret, that chap. As soon as I heard Lady Bassett's ingenious little fiction about the Buddhist monastery, I was ready to take the war-path. But you were invisible, you know. I had to wait till you emerged. Then came last night's episode, and I had to take to my heels. I couldn't face a public exposure and it wouldn't have been particularly pleasant for you either. So now you have the whole touching story, and I think you needn't grudge me a *rupee* and a few *annas* as a reward for my devotion.'

Muriel laughed rather tremulously. 'I would have given you something better worth having – if I had known.'

'Never too late,' said Nick philosophically. 'You can begin at once if you like. Let me have your hand. Hold it steady, my dear girl. Remember my limitations. You won't refuse to wear my ring any longer?'

'I will wear it gladly,' she told him, as he fitted it back upon her finger. 'I shall never part with it again.'

Her eyes were full of tears, but she would not let them fall, and Nick was too intent upon what he was doing to notice.

'That imp Olga nearly broke her poor little heart when she gave it back to me,' he said. 'I think I shall have to send her a cable. What shall I say? OMNIA VINCIT AMOR? She is old enough to know what that means. And if I add 'From Muriel and Nick,' she will understand. A pity she can't come to our wedding! I'd sooner have seen her jolly little phiz than all Lady Bassett's wreathéd smiles. She is sure to smile you know. She always does when she sees me.' He broke off with a hideous grimace.

'Don't, Nick!' Muriel's voice trembled a little. 'Why does she hate you so?'

'Can't imagine,' grinned Nick. 'It's a way some people have. Perhaps she will end by falling in love with me. Who knows?'

'Don't be horrid, Nick! Why won't you tell me?' Muriel laid a pleading hand upon his.

He caught it to his lips. 'I can't tell you, darling, seeing she is a woman. An unpleasant adventure befell her once for which I was partially responsible. And she has hated me with most unseemly vehemence ever since.'

A light began to break upon Muriel. 'Was it something that happened on board ship?' she hazarded.

He gave her a sharp look. 'Who told you that?'

She flushed a little. 'Bobby Fraser. He didn't mention her name of course. We – we were talking about you once.'

Nick laughed aloud. 'Only once?'

Her colour deepened. 'You are positively ridiculous. Still, I wish it hadn't been Lady Bassett, Nick. I don't like to feel she hates you like that.'

'It doesn't hurt me in the least,' Nick declared. 'Her poison-fang is extracted so far as I am concerned. She could only poison me through you. I always knew I had her to thank for what happened at Simla.'

'Oh, but not her alone,' Muriel said quickly. 'You mustn't blame her only for that. I was prejudiced against you by – other things.'

'I know all about it,' said Nick. He was holding her hand in his, moving it hither and thither to catch the gleam of the rubies upon it. 'You were a poor little scared rabbit fleeing from a hideous monster of destruction. You began to run that last night at Wara when I made you drink that filthy draught, and you have hardly stopped yet. I don't suppose it ever occurred to you that I would rather have died in torment than have done it.' He broke into a sudden laugh. 'But you needn't be afraid that I shall ever do it again. I can't do much to anyone with only one arm, can I? You witnessed my futility last night. There's a grain of comfort in that, eh, darling?'

'Nick, don't, don't!' She turned to him impulsively and laid her cheek against his shoulder 'You – you don't know how you hurt me!'

'My dear girl, what's the matter?' said Nick. 'I was only trying to draw your attention to my good points – such as they are.'

'Don't!' she said again, in a choked voice. 'It's more than I can bear. You would never have lost your arm but for me.'

'Oh, rats!' said Nick, holding her closely. 'Whoever told you that – '

'It was Dr. Jim.'

'Well, Jim's an ass, and I shall tell him so. There don't fret, darling. It isn't worth it. I could wish it hadn't happened for your sake, but I don't care a rap for my own.'

'You are not to care for mine,' she whispered. 'I shall only love you the better for it.'

'Then it will be a blessing to me after all,' said Nick cheerily. 'Do you know what we are going to do as soon as we are married, sweetheart? We are going to climb the highest mountain in the world, to see the sun rise, and to thank God.'

She turned her face upwards with a quivering smile. 'Let us be married soon then, Nick.'

'At once,' said Nick promptly. 'Come along and tell Sir Reginald. He must be out of bed by this time. If he isn't I think the occasion almost justifies us in knocking him up.'

They found Sir Reginald already upon the verandah, drinking his early coffee, and to Muriel's dismay he was not alone. It was later than she had imagined, and Colonel Cathcart and Bobby Fraser had both dropped in for a gossip, and were seated with him at the table, smoking.

As she and Nick approached, Lady Bassett herself emerged through an open window behind the three men.

Nick began to chuckle. This was the sort of situation that appealed to his sense of humour. He began to chant an old-world ditty under his breath with appropriate words.

'Oh, dear, what will the Bassett say?'

Muriel uttered a short, hysterical laugh, and instantly they were discovered.

'Now what are you going to do?' said Nick.

'I don't know,' she responded hurriedly. 'Run away, I think.'

'Not you,' said Nick, grasping her hand very firmly. 'You are going to face the music with me.'

She gave in, half-laughing, half-protesting, and he led her up the steps with considerable pomp.

She need not have been so painfully embarrassed, for everyone, with the exception of Bobby Fraser, looked at Nick, and Nick only, in speechless amazement as though he had just returned from the dead.

Nick was sublimely equal to the occasion. He came to a standstill by the table, executed an elaborate bow in Lady Bassett's direction, then turned briskly to Sir Reginald.

'After two years' deliberation,' he announced, 'we have decided to settle our differences by getting married, and we are hoping, sir, that you will bestow your blessing upon our union.'

'My good fellow!' gasped Sir Reginald. 'This is a very great surprise!'

'Yes, I know,' said Nick. 'It was to me too. But – though fully sensible of my unworthiness – I shall do my best to deserve the very high honour that has been done me. And I hope we may count upon your approval and support.'

Again his bow included Lady Bassett. There was a mocking glint in the glance he threw her.

She came forward as though in answer to a challenge, her face unwontedly flushed. 'This is indeed unexpected!' she declared, extending her hand. 'How do you do, Captain Ratcliffe? You will understand our surprise when I tell you that someone was saying only the other day that you had entered a Tibetan monastery.'

'Someone must have been telling a lie, dear Lady Bassett,' said Nick. 'I am sorry if it caused you any uneasiness on my account. I should certainly never have taken such a serious step without letting you know. I trust that my projected marriage will have a less disturbing effect.'

Lady Bassett smiled her crooked smile, and raised one eyebrow. 'Oh, I shall not be anxious on your account,' she assured him playfully.

'Quite right, Lady Bassett,' broke in Colonel Cathcart. 'He'll hold his own, wherever he is. I always said so when he was in the Service.'

'And a little over probably,' put in Bobby Fraser. 'Miss Roscoe, if you ever find him hard to manage, you send for me.'

Muriel, from the shelter of Sir Reginald's arm, looked across at the speaker with a smile of unwonted confidence.

'Thank you all the same,' she responded, 'but I don't expect any difficulties in that respect.'

She is far more likely to fight my battles for me,' remarked Nick complacently, 'seeing my own fighting days are over.'

'And what have you been doing with yourself all this time?' demanded Sir Reginald suddenly. 'You have been singularly unobstrusive. What have you been doing?'

Nick's answering grin was one of sheer exuberance of spirit. 'I've just been marking time, sir, that's all,' he replied enigmatically. 'A monotonous business for everyone concerned, but it seems to have served its purpose.'

Sir Reginald grunted a little, and looked uncomfortably at his wife's twisted smile. 'And now you want to get married, do you?' he said.

'At once,' said Nick.

'Well, well,' said Sir Reginald, beginning to smile himself. 'All's well that ends well, and Muriel is old enough to please herself. Mind you are good to her, that's all. And I wish you both every happiness.'

'So do I,' said Bobby Fraser heartily. 'And look here, you jack-in-the-box, if you're wanting a best man to push you through, I'll undertake the job. It's a capacity in which I have often made myself useful.'

Right O!' laughed Nick. 'But you won't find I want much pushing, old chap. I'm on my way to the top crag of Everest already.'

'Ah, Captain Ratcliffe, be careful!' murmured Lady Bassett. 'Do not soar too high!'

He bowed to her a third time, still with his baffling smile 'Thanks, dear Lady Bassett!' he said lightly. 'But you need have no misgivings. Forewarned is forearmed, they say. And on this occasion at least I am wise – in time.'

'And dear Muriel too, I wonder?' smiled Lady Bassett.

'And dear Muriel too,' smiled Nick.

Chapter 56

Night and a running stream – a soft gurgle of sound that was like a lullaby. Within the tent the quiet breathing of a man asleep; standing in the entrance – a woman.

There was a faint quiver in the air as of something coming from afar, a hushed expectancy of something great. A chill breath came off the snows, hovering secretly above the ice-cold water. The stars glittered like loose-hung jewels upon a sable robe.

Ah, that flash as of a sword across the sky! A meteor had fallen among the mountains. It was almost like a signal in the heavens – herald of the coming wonder of the dawn.

Softly the watcher turned inwards, and at once a gay, cracked voice spoke out of the darkness.

'Hullo, darling! Up and watching already! Ye gods! What a sky! Why didn't you wake me sooner? Have I time for a plunge?'

'Perhaps – if you will let me help you dress after it. Certainly not otherwise.' The deep voice had in it a tremulous note that was like a caress. The speaker was looking into the shadows. The glory without no longer held her.

'All right then, you shall – just for a treat. Perhaps you would like to shave me as well?'

'Shave you!' There was scorn this time in the answering voice. 'You couldn't grow a single hair if you tried!'

'True, O Queen! I couldn't. And the few I was born with are invisible. Hence my failure to distinguish myself in the Army. It is to be hoped the deficiency will not blight my Parliamentary career also – always supposing I get there.'

'Ah, but you did distinguish yourself. I heard – once' – the words came with slight hesitation – 'that you ought to have had the V.C. after the Wara expedition – only you refused it.'

'I wonder what gas-bag let that out,' commented Nick. 'You shouldn't believe all you hear, you know. Now, darling, I'm ready for the plunge, and I must look sharp about it too. Do you mind rummaging out a towel?'

'But, Nick, was it true?'

'What? The V.C. episode? Oh, I suppose so, more or less. I didn't want to be decorated for running away, you see. It didn't seem exactly suitable. Besides, I didn't do it for that.'

'Nick, do you know you make me feel more contemptible

every day?' There was an unmistakable quiver of distress in the words.

'My own girl, don't be a goose!' came the light response. 'You don't exactly suppose I could ever regret anything now, do you? Why, it's a lost faculty.'

He stepped from the tent, clad loosely in a bathsheet, and bestowed a kiss upon his wife's downcast face in passing. 'Look here, sweetheart, if you cry while I'm in the water, I'll beat you directly I come out. That's a promise, not a threat. And by the way, I've got something good to tell you presently; so keep your heart up.'

He laughed at her and went his way, humming tunelessly after his own peculiarly volatile fashion. She listened to his singing, as he splashed in the stream below, as though it were the sweetest music on earth; and she knew that he had spoken the truth. Whatever sacrifices he had made in the past, regret was a thing impossible to him now.

By the time he joined her again, she had driven away her own. The sky was changing mysteriously. The purple depth was lightening, the stars receding.

'We must hurry,' said Nick. 'The gods won't wait for us.'

But they were ready first of all, and the morning found them high up the mountain-side with their faces to the east.

Sudden and splendid, the sun flashed up over the edge of the world, and the snow of the mountain-crests shone in rose-lit glory for a few magic seconds, then shimmered to gold – glittering as the peaks of Paradise.

They did not speak at all, for the ground beneath their feet was holy, and all things that called for speech were left behind. Only as dawn became day – as the sun-god mounted triumphant above the waiting earth – the man's arm tightened about the woman, and his flickering eyes grew steadfast and reverent as the eyes of one who sees a vision . . .

'"Prophet and priestess we came – back from the dawning,"' quoted Nick, under his breath.

Muriel uttered a long, long sigh, and turned her face against her husband's shoulder.

His lips were on her forehead for a moment; the next he was peering into her face with his usual cheery grin.

'Care to hear my piece of news?' he questioned.

She looked at him eagerly. 'Oh, Nick, not the mail.'

He nodded. 'Runner came in late last night. You were asleep and dreaming of me. I hadn't the heart to wake you.'

She laughed and blushed. 'As if I should! Do you really imagine that I never think of anyone else. But go on. What news?'

He pulled out two letters. 'One from Olga, full of adoration, bless her funny heart, and containing also a rude message from Jim to the effect that Redlands is going to rack and ruin for want of a tenant while we are philandering on the outside edge of civilization doing no good to anybody. No good indeed! I'll punch his head for that some day. But I suppose we really ought to be thinking of Home before long, eh, sweetheart?'

She assented with a smile and a sigh. 'I am sure we ought. Dr. Jim is quite right. We must come back to earth again, my eagle and I.'

Nick kissed her hair. 'It's been a gorgeous flight, hasn't it? We'll do it again – heaps of times – before we die.'

'If nothing happens to prevent,' said Muriel.

He frowned. 'What do you say that for? Are you trying to be like Lady Bassett? Because it's a vain aspiration, so you may as well give it up at the outset.'

'Nick, how absurd you are!' There was a slight break in the words. 'I – I had almost forgotten there was such a person. No, I said it because – because – well, anything might happen, you know.'

'Such as?' said Nick.

'Anything,' she repeated almost inaudibly.

Nick pondered this for a moment. 'Is it a riddle?' he asked.

She did not answer him. Her face was hidden.

He waited a little. Then, 'I shall begin to guess directly,' he said.

She uttered a muffled laugh, and clung to him with a sudden passionate closeness. 'Nick, you – you humbug! You know!'

Nick tossed his letters on the ground and held her fast. 'My precious girl, you gave the show away not ten seconds ago by that blush of yours. There! Don't be so absurdly shy! You can't be shy with me. Look at me, sweet. Look up and tell me it's true!'

She turned her face upwards, quivering all over, yet laughing tremulously. 'Yes, Nick, really, really!' she told him. 'Oh, my darling, are you glad?'

'Am I glad?' said Nick, and laughed at her softly. 'I'm the happiest man on earth. I shall go Home now without a pang, and so will you. We have got to feather the nest, you know. That'll be fun, eh, sweetheart?'

Her eyes answered him more convincingly than any words. They seemed to have caught some of the sunshine that made the world around them so glorious.

Some time elapsed before she remembered the neglected correspondence. Time was of no account up there among the mountains.

'The other letter, Nick, you didn't tell me about it. I fancied you might have heard from Will Musgrave.'

'So I have,' said Nick. 'You had better read it. There's a line for you inside. It's all right. Daisy has got a little girl, both doing splendidly; Daisy very happy, Will nearly off his head with joy.'

Muriel was already deep in Will's ecstatic letter. She read it with smiling lips and tearful eyes. At the end in pencil she found the line that was for her.

'Tell Muriel that all's well with me, and I want you both for Christmas. – Daisy.'

Muriel looked up. 'I promised to spend Christmas with them, Nick.'

Nick smiled upon her quizzically. 'By a strange coincidence, darling, so did I. I should think under the circumstances we might go together, shouldn't you?'

She drew his hand to her cheek. 'We will go to them for Christmas then. And after that straight Home. Tell Dr. Jim when you write. But – Nick – I think we should like to feather the nest all ourselves, don't you?'

'Why, rather' said Nick. 'We'll do it together – just you and I.'

'Just you and I,' she repeated softly.

Later, hand in hand, they looked across the valley to the shining crags that glistened spear-like in the sun.

A great silence lay around them – a peace unspeakable – that those silver crests lifted into the splendour of Infinity.

They stood alone together – above the world – with their faces to the mountains.

And thus standing with the woman he loved, Nick spoke, briefly – it seemed lightly – yet with a certain tremor in his voice.

'Horses,' he said – 'and chariots – of fire!'

And Muriel looked at him with memory and understanding in her eyes.

VIRAGO MODERN CLASSICS
&
CLASSIC NON-FICTION

The first Virago Modern Classic, *Frost in May* by Antonia White, was published in 1978. It launched a list dedicated to the celebration of women writers and to the rediscovery and reprinting of their works. Its aim was, and is, to demonstrate the existence of a female tradition in fiction, and to broaden the sometimes narrow definition of a 'classic' which has often led to the neglect of interesting novels and short stories. Published with new introductions by some of today's best writers, the books are chosen for many reasons: they may be great works of fiction; they may be wonderful period pieces; they may reveal particular aspects of women's lives; they may be classics of comedy or storytelling.

The companion series, Virago Classic Non-Fiction, includes diaries, letters, literary criticism, and biographies – often by and about authors published in the Virago Modern Classics series.

'Good news for everyone writing and reading today' – *Hilary Mantel*

'A continuingly magnificent imprint' – *Joanna Trollope*

'The Virago Modern Classics have reshaped literary history and enriched the reading of us all. No library is complete without them' – *Margaret Drabble*

VIRAGO MODERN CLASSICS
&
CLASSIC NON-FICTION

Some of the authors included in these two series –

izabeth von Arnim, Dorothy Baker, Pat Barker, Nina Bawden,
Nicola Beauman, Sybille Bedford, Jane Bowles, Kay Boyle,
ra Brittain, Leonora Carrington, Angela Carter, Willa Cather,
olette, Ivy Compton-Burnett, E.M. Delafield, Maureen Duffy,
Elaine Dundy, Nell Dunn, Emily Eden, George Egerton,
George Eliot, Miles Franklin, Mrs Gaskell,
Charlotte Perkins Gilman, George Gissing,
Victoria Glendinning, Radclyffe Hall, Shirley Hazzard,
Dorothy Hewett, Mary Hocking, Alice Hoffman,
inifred Holtby, Janette Turner Hospital, Zora Neale Hurston,
Elizabeth Jenkins, F. Tennyson Jesse, Molly Keane,
Margaret Laurence, Maura Laverty, Rosamond Lehmann,
se Macaulay, Shena Mackay, Olivia Manning, Paule Marshall,
F.M. Mayor, Anaïs Nin, Kate O'Brien, Olivia, Grace Paley,
Mollie Panter-Downes, Dawn Powell, Dorothy Richardson,
E. Arnot Robertson, Jacqueline Rose, Vita Sackville-West,
laine Showalter, May Sinclair, Agnes Smedley, Dodie Smith,
vie Smith, Nancy Spain, Christina Stead, Carolyn Steedman,
Gertrude Stein, Jan Struther, Han Suyin, Elizabeth Taylor,
Sylvia Townsend Warner, Mary Webb, Eudora Welty,
Mae West, Rebecca West, Edith Wharton, Antonia White,
Christa Wolf, Virginia Woolf, E.H. Young.

I CAPTURE THE CASTLE

DODIE SMITH

New Introduction by Valerie Grove

It's a great day for the impoverished Mortmain family when they move into the picturesque but ruinous castle. Father is a famous but irascible author suffering from prolonged writers' block. His second wife, Topaz, is a gentle bohemian beauty, while his children – lovely Rose, adolescent Cassandra (whose diary tells the story) and schoolboy Thomas – don't really see why everyone else regards them as profoundly eccentric. And then the American heirs to the castle turn up, energetic mother and two eligible sons . . . The stage is set for a truly original romantic comedy.

THE SHEIK

E M HULL

New Introduction by Kate Saunders

'He was looking at her with fierce burning eyes that swept her until she felt that the boyish clothes that covered her slender limbs were stripped from her.' Wilful Diana Mayo is kidnapped and subjugated by the cruel but strangely compelling Sheik Ahmed – later portrayed by Rudolph Valentino in his greatest screen role. In an astonishing and touchingly artless expression of female sexual masochism, Diana finally surrenders to the desert lover who is not all he seems. Edith Maude Hull was a farmer's wife who, between 1921 and 1939 wrote eight novels and a travel book, and lived very quietly.

THREE WEEKS

ELINOR GLYN

New Introduction by Sally Beauman

Scandalously successful, this 1907 novel is one of Virago's trio of old-fashioned erotic bestsellers. Young aristocratic Paul Verdayne is bewitched by the mysterious beauty staying at his Swiss hotel. And, in various exotic settings, 'the Lady' initiates him into the arts of love, bestowing an intoxicating three weeks of passion. Only when she has left him does he learn her august and tragic secret. Elinor Glyn (1864–1948) liked 'to sin on a tiger skin', living and writing at an impressive pace.

Books by post

Virago Books are available through mail order or from your local bookshop. Other books which might be of interest include:–

☐ Curious If True	Mrs Gaskell	£6.99
☐ I Capture the Castle	Dodie Smith	£6.99
☐ Palladian	Elizabeth Taylor	£6.99
☐ She Done Him Wrong	Mae West	£6.99
☐ The Sheik	E M Hull	£6.99
☐ Three Weeks	Elinor Glyn	£6.99

Please send Cheque/Eurocheque/Postal Order (sterling only), Access, Visa or Mastercard:

☐ ☐ ☐ ☐ ☐ ☐ ☐ ☐ ☐ ☐ ☐ ☐ ☐ ☐ ☐ ☐

Expiry Date: _____ *Signature:* _____

Please allow 75 pence per book for post and packing in U.K.
Overseas customers please allow £1.00 per copy for post and packing.

All orders to:
Virago Press, Book Service by Post, P.O. Box 29, Douglas,
Isle of Man, IM99 1BQ.   Tel: 01624 675137.   Fax: 01624 670923.

Name: _____

Address: _____

_____

Please allow 20 days for delivery.
Please tick box if you would like to receive a free stock list ☐
Please tick box if you do not wish to receive any additional information ☐

Prices and availability subject to change without notice.